Larry Rostad

GAY SUNSHINE JOURNAL

No. 47

Anthology of Fiction / Poetry / Prose

Edited by Winston Leyland

Cover drawing by Joe Fuoco
Typesetting: Xanadu Graphics, Inc., Cambridge, MA./Third Eye, Berkeley, CA.

Publication of this issue was made possible in part by a grant from the National Endowment for the Arts, Washington D.C.

ISBN 0-917342-00-3 (lim. cloth)
ISBN 0-917342-01-1 (paper)

U.S. ISSN 0046-550X

Gay Sunshine Press
P.O. Box 40397
San Francisco, CA 94140

Twenty-four page illustrated complete catalog of titles is available on request (add $1 for postage).
Subscription to *Gay Sunshine Journal* is $20 for 3 book length paperback issues.

CONTENTS

NOVEL

SHORT FICTION

PLAY

LITERARY DIARY

POETRY

DRAWINGS

PHOTO

EDITOR'S NOTE

With this issue *Gay Sunshine* inaugurates a new format. For the past ten years the journal has appeared as a tabloid; this had its advantages and disadvantages. Our new paperback book format will enable the material we print to be preserved with more permanence.

Most of the material in the present anthology is previously unpublished. However, I have also included three stories and several poems from the last few issues of the journal — material of high quality which, I feel, should be preserved in more permanent form.

This issue is, in large part (two thirds), an anthology of gay fiction. I am privileged to be able to publish the first English edition of the complete Dutch novel, *Costa Brava* (by Dr. Frits Bernard) — a landmark in the literature of boy-love. Also included are ten short stories — all but one by contemporary American writers; a complete play, *Act and Betrayal*, by Anglo-American author/ actor John Stuart Anderson; a long literary diary by Pulitzer prize winning composer, Ned Rorem; and work by twenty-two poets — from the United States, Canada, England, Greece and medieval Italy/Araby.

In future issues I will continue to publish gay writing of the highest quality concentrating on contemporary fiction, poetry, interviews, essays, literature in translation. Graphics will also be accepted. The next issue (No. 48) will focus on new gay fiction from Latin America.

A short book review supplement issue in tabloid format (Issue 46) has been published concurrently with this issue and sent free of charge to subscribers only. Other readers may obtain it by writing directly to the press ($2 ppd.). Subscriptions to *Gay Sunshine* in our new format are available (see page 191), and I urge you to subscribe, or renew your subscription. You will get your copies promptly upon publication at a savings from the bookstore price, and you will also be aiding us in our publishing endeavors.

We continue to solicit submission of material for future issues. Send all manuscripts/art work to *Gay Sunshine*, P.O. Box 40397, San Francisco, CA 94140-0397 (Phone 415-824-3184). Please type and double space all manuscripts and include a stamped self-addressed envelope.

— Winston Leyland, Editor

COSTA BRAVA

A Novel

by

Frits Bernard

Translated from Dutch by A. Ronaldson
Illustrations by Aloysius Heylaerts

PART ONE   *Many are the ways . . .*

I

The sea looked like a grey oil-slick alongside the golden yellow sand. The water was as smooth as a mirror, and the rays of the setting sun tinted the white houses of the village orange. The little church stood serene and peaceful on its rock beside the sea, like a stake arising from the water. It was one of the very warm summer days, and the siesta of the inhabitants was prolonged somewhat beyond the customary duration. The few small beach cafés beneath the slender palm trees were still deserted, with the curtains drawn in their windows. In the village itself, people were occupied in pushing aside the canvas awnings that had been hung between the roofs across the narrow streets in order to keep out the sunshine, and others were sprinkling water on the sandy and irregular pavements.

In the distance, the melancholy song of a flamenco-singer accompanied by the plaintive chords of a guitar softly recalled his dear Andalusia . . . *en Córdoba la sultana y en Sevilla la giralda.* . . . A cart supported by two high wheels and drawn by two mules, one behind the other and both wearing straw hats with their ears poking through, carried locally-picked grapes to one of the houses. After unloading, they would be trampled underfoot and in due course become the local wine. A farmer drove three donkeys heavily-laden with fruit and vegetables before him in the direction of the little market. On the beach, the fishermen began to get their boats ready for the night. At ten o'clock — as usual — they would make sail for the part of the Mediterrannean that was their fishing ground, and at seven o'clock the next morning they would be back with their catch, part of which would then be sold on the beach there.

In the meanwhile, the sun had set. I crossed over the path beside the beach and looked into the calm water, which was changing colour at that moment. The village had now become busy; the time for the evening promenade had arrived. People sauntered along the footpath and the beach cafés were quite crowded. Voices rang clearly through the evening air, which had become appreciably cooler. I went and sat down on a stone bench in order to let the atmosphere and the peace have their effect on me. A beggar came up to me with dignity and asked me for alms. He expressed his gratitude with the words: "may the good Lord repay you" and disappeared among the crowd.

A book about Catalonia lay open on my knees, but I could not be bothered to read it. There was much so much to see, so much to observe. I had scarcely been in Spain for two weeks, and before going to the south of the country I intended to spend a few more weeks at the Catalan coast. This was the plan I had made before leaving Venezeula, my homeland. How much had I looked forward to seeing something of the land of my ancestors — Spain! A dream-wish of many Venezuelans: one which is seldom fulfilled, however. And now it was being fulfilled so far for me. My grandfather had emigrated from this Catalan coast to South America, like so many others from the Iberian peninsula had done at that time. There were innumerable links, in fact, between the two territories: Spain the motherland and her South American offspring. Here I sat and looked out over the sea just like my forefathers had once done.

A sea-breeze arose. In the meanwhile, it had become completely dark and the stars twinkled in the sky above: the Great Bear, the Milky Way and Orion. Moonlight bathed the landscape, the hills, the flat roofs of the village and the apparently boundless Mare Nostrum. The voices of the fishermen made a monotonous sound as they strained with their shoulders against the hulls of their boats to propel them across the beach — on short rollers thrust beneath the keel — and into the water. One, two . . . one, two. . . . One after another the boats slid into the sea. This was not always achieved without difficulty; sometimes they got stuck in shallow water, and then it was a big job to get them afloat again. The purr of the rhythmically drumming motors could be heard for a long time. Later on a cluster of small lights appeared on the horizon; the fishing operation had begun.

My thoughts then turned to my own small motor-boat, which lay on the little beach about a hundred miles to the north, surrounded by steep rocks. It had been lying there a week before, after a visit I had made to a fellow-countryman who had a country-house there on the Costa Brava and spent his summer there. I had bought the boat cheaply, second-hand, through a relative when I arrived in the country, in order to be able to make short trips along the coast during my stay — mainly so that I could take photographs and shoot some scenes. It was my intention to go and fetch it in the near future.

After walking some more and drinking a glass of vermouth with sodawater, I made my way to a small restaurant under the palm-trees behind the fishermen's beach and ordered a *paella,* one of the local specialties, made of rice with chopped fish, meat, poultry, vegetables and spices. It was brought to the table steaming, and its delicious fragrance mingled with that of the sea. The house wine that was served with it was not bad. Everything was so restful and peaceful; nobody was in a hurry — people didn't eat before ten or eleven o'clock in the evening.

At midnight I went to the open-air cinema, which was situated in the back-garden of a café somewhere in the middle of the village. A canvas sheet was suspended above the simple wooden seats, to keep out the moonlight. The main film had not yet begun and it did not last long or there was an interval. A couple of peanut vendors appeared, calling out *cacahuetes, cacahuetes . . .*

Beside the rows of seats there was an oblong pond surrounded entirely by blue tiles, with a fountain at one end spraying fine jets of water round about. It had a cooling effect, and reminded me of a Moorish garden. The influence of the southern neighbours was unmistakable.

The Spanish main film interested me — as the manager of a Venezuelan film-company — very much. Although most Spanish films are also screened in South America, I had not seen this one. It was about the life of a priest and the secrets of the confessional. All of a sudden the projector stopped, a great sigh came from the audience, and the noise of shelling peanuts ceased, only to begin again at once, unlike the show, because there was a power-cut and the village lay in darkness, apart from where it was relatively light thanks to the bright moon. The cinema show thus ended early.

I strolled for some time through the narrow streets that ran up and down between the many neat white houses with their mostly blue doors and windows. It had become silent in the village. The passers-by seemed unreal in the moonlight, especially because you didn't hear them coming nearer on their *alpargatas* — linen shoes with rope soles and straps.

This was my first really long holiday for many years and I discovered that here in these surroundings I was at peace and new ideas could come to me. There were two films to be made during the coming year, one of which dealt with the links between Spain and Venezuela. The script was almost ready, but not yet fully worked out in all detail. I had made up my mind to shoot some of the outdoor scenes right here.

With a candle which I had got from the night-porter in my hotel in my hand, I made my way to my bedroom, where I undressed and put on my swimming-costume and a short dressing-gown. I left the hotel again, crossed the beach-side path and ran across the beach. A few moments later I was swimming in the dark sea, still unaware that this was one of the last restful days that I would enjoy in this part of the world.

II

It was 20th July 1936. In a few days' time everything was changed: the civil war was raging in Spain. The tension was unbearable, with one rumor circulating after another. Connections were broken, everything seemed to be disorganised. Nobody was able to predict how it would all turn out. Men wearing overalls with guns over their shoulders peopled the streets. The church on the rock was burnt down . . . The country was divided into two camps; the Republicans on one side and Franco's supporters on the other. Catalonia belonged to the former, the "red" side.

The land-owning class and the clergy were hit hard. People went into hiding, or disappeared to safer places if that seemed to be possible. There were murders, buildings were set on fire . . .

A British cruiser appeared off the coast, in order to carry the British subjects away to safety. That was a bad sign.

These developments prevented me from putting my plans into effect; there was now no question of a journey further south. What should I do? Could my Ford — with its Caracas number-plate — take me back to France via Barcelona and Port Bou, or La Junquera? Normal railway services no longer existed, only troop trains. As a foreigner I had nothing to fear directly, I belonged to the privileged few. My car was also not requisitioned. I had painted "Venezuela" in large white letters on the sides of the bodywork, and a Venezuelan flag fluttered above the left-hand mudguard.

My suitcases were packed, and already lying in the boot of the car. Only a few necessities remained in a bag in my room at the hotel. I was prepared for all possibilities.

The next few days brought no improvement in the general situation, indeed everything was more confused. Groups of whispering people were all over the streets . . . Shots were heard in and around the little square, and from the distance came the sound of a machine-gun. Food became scarcer and more expensive.

I sat once again on the stone bench and stared at the deep blue sea, which sparkled in the bright sunlight as if nothing was the matter. The beach that had once been so jolly lay abandoned, and the pretty white and coloured sails were no longer to be seen. The British cruiser had disappeared along with the British subjects.

Slowly, with his head bowed forward, a boy came towards me. He was alone. A few yards in front of my bench he stood still and looked around, as if he were afraid of something. He then made his way to the bench and sat down. To judge by the cloth of his *fresco* — very thin summer-wear — he was not poor. There was something proud about his bearing, despite his sombre expression. His dark brown eyes looked into mine. They troubled me. He smiled, and in the smile there was something so intimate that I had the feeling that I had known him a long time. What a remarkable encounter. We looked at each other several times, and the same feelings occurred again . . .

"Señor, can you help me?" he asked and looked in front of him.

Whether I wanted to help him. What was the matter then with this boy? He related his story, his tragedy, to a stranger in this dangerous time. His father had been killed a few days before, he was left all alone . . . His mother was no longer alive. His father had told him that — if anything should happen — he must try to escape to France . . . He had eaten nothing since the previous day, his money had run out . . . could I give him something to eat, bread would be enough . . .

He carried himself bravely, like a proud Spaniard. I seized his hand and shook it.

"What's your name, *amigo?*"

"Juan José."

"How old are you?"

"Twelve."

Twelve years old, in such tragic circumstances. As I took Juan José to the hotel, I thought how trivial were my own difficulties in comparison with this boy's. I felt sorry for Juan José, who sat still facing me across the table, looking very handsome. His slim boyish hands handled the knife and fork, and he even seemed to forget his misery. His almost black hair, which he wore combed straight back, his slightly thick — but beautifully curved — lips gave him a somewhat sensual appearance. His shoulders were broad for his age, and his muscles well-developed. You could see that he enjoyed sports. The colour of his skin was too dark for that of a Catalan, but typical of that of a person from Andalusia. I did not ask him for any more details; that seemed to me to be indiscreet during a civil war. I really knew nothing about him — not even his surname — it was just as if he was a close friend with whom I felt at home. We looked at each other understandingly.

The waiter brought us *arroz a la cubana*: white rice with tomato sauce, eggs, pieces of ham and fried banana. Considering the circumstances, the food was remarkably good, indeed exceptionally good. The ordinary holidaymakers had disappeared from the hotel and now only various *milicianos* sat in the dining-room with their weapons leaning against the tables and chairs. Some of them had not shaved for days, they spoke a lot and noisily, mainly about the situation and the new times that were to come.

There were some more shots in the distance. Juan José stared straight in front, his fork fell from his right hand and he toyed with a lump of bread with his other hand. He wanted to say something, but his lips remained cramped together. I got the feeling that he was no longer there, that his thoughts were somewhere else . . .

The mozo brought fresh coffee, and looked with surprise at the boy. I got up from my seat and seized Juan José by the arm. I turned to the waiter and said "He's not feeling well, it must be the stomach-ache again. I'll take him upstairs and drink my coffee later." Juan José climbed the stairs vacantly with me. Once in the bedroom I laid him on the bed, took off his alpargatas and served some brandy in the water-glass. Even before I had time to give him a little to drink, he burst into tears and hid his face in the white cushions. The reaction to all he had gone through — and had borne so bravely — came, and he wept and wept . . . From time to time he stammered a few words . . . *papá . . . no puedo más*

No, he could take no more, it was too much. I sat on the end of the bed and leant over. "I will help you, Juanjo."

I ran my fingers through his thick black hair. He was more restful. He had completely stopped crying. He drank a tot of brandy.

"Try and get some sleep."

His eyes had returned to their normal expression, and he looked understandingly in my direction.

"Yes — I'll try."

Sitting at the table in front of the window, I looked out through a chink in the shutters. It was getting on for four o'clock, the sun's rays illuminated the path differently from the sea. Not far away stood two open lorries with armed men in rolled-up shirt-sleeves. Some of them were still very young, almost children. One of them was rolling a cigarette, others were busy loading their guns. Each lorry had a big red flag beside the driving-cab. On the sides of the load compartment stood the letters F.A.I. The scene did not last long, as both lorries moved off and disappeared down the road. A small group of people remained on the pavement talking. They did not appear to be agreed about something, but I could not hear exactly what it was all about.

I glanced towards the bed. The young features lay relaxed, one hand over the edge of the mattress hung down, his head was turned slightly to the right and his breath came regularly. Juan José was asleep. His first sleep, since when? What was going on inside him? He was not safe here; his father had been killed for political reasons, he was afraid. Afraid of what? What would anyone do to him? Put him in a camp, as he was afraid they might? Or . . .

He wanted to go to France, to an uncle who was living in Perpignan. That was his late father's last wish . . .

I reviewed the possibilities. How could he cross the frontier? Under the prevailing circumstances this did not seem to be feasible. There must be another solution. But what? I began to apply myself intensively to his problem; I had promised to help him. But how?

Sounds from outside put an abrupt end to my meditation. I peered through the shutters, a small crowd was shouting in the street there. Two people — middle-aged men — were being taken away. It was a dispiriting sight. What a dreadful thing was this war between brothers. And it could be so beautiful here on the coast . . . Juan José remained fast asleep, he heard nothing. His face had something so noble, something of an angel. He must be a good person.

There was a knock at the door. Footsteps sounded in the passage. I opened it gently.

"Identity-card, comrade!"

The Venezuelan passport was passed from hand to hand. Finally it reached someone who could read.

"Foreigner — from Venezuela! A good country."

There were no more questions. They went on to the next door.

"Hello, comrade."

I shut the door. Juan José had woken up, he was bathed in sweat, drops of which ran off his forehead onto the cushion.

"*Señor*," he began nervously, "you got rid of them that time! Had they come for me?"

I pushed a cane chair to beside the bed and sat down next to the boy.

"No, don't worry, it wasn't important." and after a short pause I added "don't call me 'señor;' my friends call me Santiago."

He put out his hand and shook mine.

"Thank God I met you" he continued emotionally. "Friendship is the most wonderful thing in the world and it helps us come through everything; I never appreciated that more than I do right now. You didn't know me at all, and yet you do everything for me. I feel myself to be so safe beside you, Despite all the misery, despite this revolution, the last moments have been wonderful and incomprehensible."

He took the words out of my mouth. He spoke like a man.

"Listen to me for a moment, Juanjo; while you were asleep I was thinking about the possibilities for getting you out of here. I didn't get very far, but perhaps we can do better if we go over it together. As far north as Tamariú, I have a small motorboat on the Costa Brava. With the car — it has foreign licence plates — we could try to get to Tamariú, and then make an attempt to sail to France in my boat. All this is clearly not a simple business in war-time, but it is worth having a try. Of course we must think about food and above all about fuel, but that, too, can be arranged . . ."

He interrupted — "you are a good friend — and that's why I don't want you to run a risk for me. If they catch you, you'll be in real trouble, even if you are a foreigner. And I don't want anything to happen to you."

He sat up straight and looked at me trustingly. His eyes had a special brightness. I felt uncertain; a strange feeling came over me. Despite the tragedy, I felt quite happy. What kind of boy was this, who spoke in this way? He made me feel small and insignificant.

"I have no choice, Juanjo, just because I too feel this friendship, I can't leave you in the lurch. I could never forgive myself. I must. It will all be all right . . ."

There was another knock at the door. The waiter stood in the doorway and asked if the young man was feeling any better. He had brought the coffee with him.

It was one thing after another. I went downstairs and sat down to drink a soda in the small hall leading to the way out. It was getting on for six o'clock, and the heat still hung heavily over the street onto which I looked out. The door stood open, and a bead curtain with a maritime scene hung in the opening. It showed a little fishing-boat under sail, such as are often seen in this part of the Mediterranean Sea. It was made up of numerous colours with a bright blue background. In no sense could it be called artistic — an artist would have had a fit — but it gave a cheerful effect, and so achieved its purpose. A young girl carrying a wicker-work basket full of melons and water-melons came in, and the beads rattled merrily as she went by. She came past me, modestly averting her eyes from me, as is customary in the Latin countries, and walked elegantly through a door marked *servicio* into the kitchen. A few moments later she came back through the same door with the same charm, walked past me again and went out through the bead curtain. I could still perceive her slim silhouette faintly between the beads until she disappeared behind a high cart.

The evening paper lay open on a table; it consisted of only a single sheet with big black headlines giving the news about the progress of the front. In order to keep abreast of what was being written in the press I began to read it. The revolt had grown into a full-scale civil war, and everything suggested that it would not be a minor affair. Poor country; as a Venezuelan I had sympathy with the territory that once was the *tierra madre* — the motherland — for the South American states.

Some people had come into the adjoining dining-room without my noticing. The radio was switched on; they were waiting for the news-bulletin from Barcelona. Marching music could be heard. The announcer introduced his colleague from the news department. He read the news nervously. The whole of Spain appeared to be in rebellion, from the Canaries to the Pyrenees. Then followed a series of announcements for the civil population. It was alarming. The military music that followed raised the enthusiasm of the listeners to a peak. It seemed to be a winning battle . . . More or less unnoticed, twilight had fallen. The sun had become a fireball, the air was red and orange. A plume of smoke appeared on the horizon. The villagers stood looking at it in groups; they were afraid of being bombarded from the sea. The air was again buzzing with rumours.

I then went out for a walk beside the beach, which had become my habit at that time as it was for the villagers. A light breeze from the sea refreshed me, and produced little white horses in the bay. During the walk I would take a decision. Had I really considered everything fully? Was it not an unnecessarily risky adventure? Would it really help Juan José? Anyway, it was necessary to act quickly; what the next few days would bring could not be foreseen.

At the window of a watchmaker's I halted. A collection of Swiss wristwatches was displayed in it, and I went inside, without really knowing why. An old woman sat behind the counter; she stood up as I came in. She looked at me in a friendly manner and asked:

"What can I do for you?"

While I examined the watches that interested me, the old woman complained about the situation. She was older than I thought; she said she was over seventy. She was not afraid — what could happen to her now — but some of her children and grandchildren were on one side and some on the other, and they were drawn into fighting each other . . . She paused, and sighed.

The woman looked at the gold wristwatch that I was wearing and was somewhat surprised when my final choice fell on a similar one. It was still wrapped up in an elegant little box with pretty paper and a multi-coloured cloth wrapping, as was the custom in feudal times. Her old fingers were still nimble and she knew her business; she knew human character too. By sticking on a label bearing a picture of St. George and the dragon, she completed the whole.

As she handed over the package, she said with a smile: "I hope the wearers of both watches will be very happy . . ."

I thanked her, and left the shop. When I was in the street, I looked back and saw a large picture of St. George and the dragon, Catalonia's patron saint, above the door. The shop bore the name *San Jorge*.

After a quick drink at one of the open-air cafés, I went straight back to my hotel. I had made up my mind; we would leave that night. And there was no time to lose.

III

Juan José sat on the cane chair in the bedroom. He had had a shower and looked refreshed. The shutters were open and the night air was flowing in.

"We're leaving this evening, Juanjo."

He looked at me with eyes that glowed with gratitude. I had the evening meal served in the bedroom, with the excuse that the boy was not wholly restored to health. We did not eat much; the excitement was playing tricks on us. We sat opposite each other as we ate, each with his own thoughts.

After paying the bill, and giving a good tip to the waiter — who accepted this capitalistic gesture without scruples — we got into the car. At eleven o'clock we drove off in the darkness. There were no problems in the village; everything was quiet, with only a few people to be seen in the streets. Once we had reached the main road, which twisted its way through the mountainous countryside beside the sea, we were accompanied by the moon and the stars. One bend followed another, we climbed, and on the right the sea glittered below us. The petrol tank was full and in the boot were two jerry-cans with five gallons in each. I had also to think of the boat. Its tank was also almost full, but that was certainly not enough to get us to the French frontier. Similarly, we would have to take care of drinking water and food too, as there was only a tin of biscuits on board. A small compass, a chart and a few other things that were required for navigation had been left in the small cabin. The boat was many years old, but despite that she was still in a good seaworthy condition. At this time of year, storms were very rare, so that there was no great danger on that account. We could make sail under the cover of darkness, with our lights doused . . .

After a severe hairpin bend our progress was interrupted by a large barricade erected across the road; only a small passage remained open on the left, just broad enough to allow a car to pass. A *miliciano* waved a lamp backward and forward and ordered us to stop. On the verge and at the barricade gun-barrels could be seen.

"*Alto!*" said a voice.

I dimmed the lights and brought the car to a halt. A few moments later we were surrounded by a group of men.

'Your papers, comrade!"

The passport was passed from hand to hand; provoking praise for my country.

"And the boy?" I was asked.

The lamp was held high in front of the car, revealing the externally calm face of Juan José.

"He is my nephew," I said; "his papers are in Barcelona. We are on our way to get them now." I tried to keep my voice as ordinary as possible.

These circumstances did not appear to be for the best. The group considered what to do.

"You can go on, Señor, but the boy must get out."

"I can't leave my nephew behind on his own; I'm staying here too."

This appeared to complicate matters. They would have to go and speak to the Commandant. The group disappeared, leaving only two men beside the car.

Juan José had grasped my hand, and he held it tightly in his own. We said nothing and sat next to each other. We understood without words. Five hundred feet beneath us little wavelets were breaking aginst the steep rock wall. In the distance a dog was barking monotonously. It seemed like a century before the reply came. Finally it did.

"The Commandant is at the next barricade, about a mile and half down the road. You can drive as far as there, but we don't give much chance for the boy. Even if the Commandant lets him pass, he will still be stopped at the following barricade. Bon voyage."

I started the motor quickly and drove through the small opening. There was only one thought that crossed my mind, the only possible solution. A couple of hundred yards down the road was another bend. I switched off the lights and stopped. Then I walked to the back of the car and took the luggage out of the boot and put it on the rear seat.

"Quick, Juan José, get into the boot; there's a travelling rug in it, lie down on it!"

The boy disappeared in the cramped boot, and I shut the lid on him. A few minutes later I drove slowly up to the next barricade. Here, too, a lamp was waved to and fro.

"Good evening, comrade."

My passport was taken to the Commandant. If only he had not been warned! I got out of the car and walked up and down beside it. My eyes were on the road that we had just come along. If a messenger should happen to come along it . . . These thoughts made me nervous. If they had sent somebody to follow us?

The commandant sent for me. I followed the half-uniformed *miliciano*. A young man wearing a beret was sitting on a crate in an improvised hut. He received me in a friendly manner and asked what the purpose of my journey was.

"I am on the way to my consulate, *Señor comandante*." I wondered whether I should still use the word *señor*, or if it was no longer acceptable in the present circumstances. I had no idea.

"What are you doing in Spain?"

"I am a tourist."

He expressed regret that my visit had been spoilt.

Ten minutes later I was back in my Ford. Then I froze: two small lights were coming towards us down the road. A car was approaching us, slowly but surely. Would everything now be lost?

The engine wouldn't start, too . . . at last it did . . .

"Bon voyage!"

Before the other car had arrived, I had left the barricade behind me. I put my foot down, but not for long, as a new barricade soon appeared. and the same routine began again.

"Your papers!"

No difficulties arose. I kept my eye on the road behind by means of the rear-view mirror. You never can tell. And if they were to telephone a post on the way in to Barcelona, telling it to stop the car with the Venezuelan licence-plates. What then?

I stopped on a isolated part of the road, ran to the back, opened the boot and leaned over to ask: "Have you enough air?"

"Yes, Santiago."

"Everything is all right, my boy."

The boot was shut again, and we were off once more through the mountains. It was already long after midnight. The moon was hidden behind a hazy cloud, the sea was less bright. A couple of mules crossed the road, accompanied by a farm-worker. They took fright at just the noise of the motor, and looked about in fear. Farther away a farm lay in darkness. Maize was hanging along a wall. Then came slopes covered with vinyards, a few palm-trees and grape-vines again. A hamlet, a small street, a few rows of houses, all in deep slumber. The countryside changed; it became flatter and the road straighter. A few lorries passed in the opposite direction, heading southwards. On a crag on the left-hand side stood the Casteldefels — the castle of the faithful — surrounded by agaves and cactus. And suddenly another barricade. Valuable minutes of delay. Then off again. And there were more of them.

The Ford was doing a good job. When I had decided to bring the car with me to Spain, I did not realize what a role the vehicle would play in these surroundings. My thoughts also went back to Caracas, on the other side of the ocean. How were the film studios doing. What a long way away all that was now, in another world. Did this all not seem like a film?

Ahead of me, the lights of the Catalonian capital, the metropolis Barcelona, were becoming brighter. The city with a million inhabitants and broad boulevards, tall buildings, the crowded Ramblas, the twin hills of Tibidabo and Montjuich, the Paralelo with its amusements and the statue of Columbus beside the harbour, pointing in the direction of America, the new world. We have a Barcelona in Venezuela, too . . .

A lamp, a pair of armed men, and another check-point.

"Get out of the car."

I stood beside the car.

"We have to search your car for weapons; orders of the commandant."

That was just what we needed! If only Juanjo would keep quiet! The bonnet was opened and a glance thrown to make sure that there was nothing hidden in it.

"What have you got in the boot? Will you open it?"

It was as if someone had given me a cold douche.

"There's nothing in it, only a spare tire. Unfortunately I have lost the key and can't open it any more. It's a great nuisance."

And the man tried the handle, but was unable to force it open. I had locked it. He looked inside the suit-cases. Suddenly he asked:

"Whisky?"

An idea shot through my mind. Perhaps this could save our lives.

"Yes, here you are — you can keep it, I'll get some more in town."

This struck home; the key to the boot was forgotten and we were off again towards the city. I drove through one of the suburbs, at some points the signs of past fighting were clearly visible: burnt-out trams and motor-cars, dead horses and broken-up streets. A few churches were still smouldering. A desolate sight. Occasional shots could be heard. The magnificent city lay like a wounded animal in the countryside; its injuries were many.

Gradually it got brighter, the stars grew pale and the air took on a grey tint. We had put the town and the working-class district of Badalona behind us, and the second part of the journey had begun. After we had passed the last houses — and left them a safe distance behind — I stopped the Ford beside the road, got out and took a deep breath. So far, all was well. The sun was just beginning to rise and the temperature to increase. After opening the boot I let Juan José get out. The boy was completely stiff as a result of having lain bent, and he needed a few minutes to recover. He walked back and forth and filled his lungs with fresh air, stretched himself several times and blinked in order to become reaccustomed to the light. We sat down on the running-board and gazed at the awakening countryside before us; the hills, the olive-trees and an abandoned broken-down house on which the letters P.O.U.M. had recently been painted. On one of the neighbouring hills stood an old tower, about ten feet high, which had been originally built by the Moors.

"I am a great nuisance for you, Santiago; without me you would already be at the border."

I felt that he was getting anxious.

"No nuisance at all, Juanjo, it's my pleasure, as you know." I paused, then continued "I'm awfully thirsty, and perhaps you would like to eat something."

I took a thermos-flask of coffee from the car and a few sandwiches that I had had made at the hotel.

Only when we began to eat, did we realise how far we had come. It did us good, and we continued our way refreshed, the boy in the back and I behind the wheel.

The traffic began to get thicker in both directions. The stream of refugees of the first days of the civil war had dried up, it now consisted of light vehicles and old trucks, as well as private cars with armed men in them. There were also all sorts of vehicles carrying food stuffs on the road. Beside it were various written messages. In some villages banners and portraits of the leaders were displayed. The form of greeting with raised left fist and the words *salud camarada* appeared to be the fashion. The number of red flags increased. By means of a screw driver jammed in between the lid of the baggage-compartment and the bodywork, a small opening was provided, almost invisibly, to let air and a small amount of light into the boot. In this way Juanjo could to some extent orient himself in the small space.

The road became worse, and holes in it more frequent. I had to reduce my speed significantly in order to avoid injuring the boy. Ultimately we were moving at barely walking-speed. There was a lot of dust on the road; after passing anything going the other way you could see little or nothing for a few seconds, until the cloud had settled.

In a small farming village, lying peacefully in a valley, I was able to obtain some more food: a bag of potatoes, some bread and maize. The little settlement lay so peacefully between the lovely hills that one could really not be aware here that a civil war was raging. There was not a single political slogan to be seen, nor any flags or weapons.

IV

It was the hottest hour of the day, and the sun was almost directly overhead the country home of my friend Esteban Muñoz, on the Costa Brava. It stood on its own here on a crag beside the sea and could only be reached by means of a small private road. A few fruit-trees stood in the garden, as did some plane-trees and agaves. A series of irregular steps led down to the little beach, which was completely surrounded by sheer cliffs, and could only be reached by these steps from the land. It was shaded by pine trees and a few stunted olive-trees. The house was coated with white lime, and the brown shutters were closed at this hour of the day. On the north side stood a pergola with a view along the coast, the hinterground and the bright sea.

Because the house was situated on a rise, the panorama was indescribably beautiful. Our host was an artist, and he had picked out this site many years before. There was no electric light; the pergola was lit by candles in colourful Chinese lanterns.

On the great iron garden gate a piece of paper had been attached, bearing the words *"propiedad extranjera"* — foreign property. The Venezuelan flag was flying from the mast in this enclosed piece of ground . . .

Esteban was amazed at my return after so short a time. He had not thought it to be possible. There were so many tales to tell about it, but when I opened the luggage-compartment, he had to laugh heartily.

"Welcome, my boy" — he said in a friendly voice.

We sat in the shade beneath the pergola. A row of red geraniums contrasted strongly with the white. Jaime, the butler, brought drinks. I lay down on a comfortable chaise-longue and let the ambiance have its effect on me; here everything was suddenly so completely different. Juan José stretched his limbs and walked up and down a litte. Esteban, seated in a rocking-chair, described the neighbourhood. His wife Elvira sat beside him, occupied with her handwork; she was a native of Catalonia.

I was too tired to talk much and I preferred to listen. At times events of the past twenty-four hours came into my mind, then my thoughts turned to what was yet to come. Jaime appeared and announced that the meal was ready to be served. We went indoors; it was more sheltered there, which gave a pleasant feeling of coolness and equilibrium. Esteban gave a toast to our friendship. In days gone by we had been at school together in Caracas, and he had later come to live here, mainly for the sake of his wife who had found it difficult to settle down anywhere else. In the course of time he had come to love the country like his own, so that it was more than a second homeland to him. His forté was painting landscapes and sea; only a few weeks before there had been an exhibition of his most recent works in a small gallery off the *Paseo de Gracia* in Barcelona. How that was doing now he did not know, nor did he care. Esteban was a born optimist; it had been just the same when he was at the primary school in Venezuela. Now Muñoz belonged among the leading figures in the world of art, and his paintings had an international market.

The meal was served. Jaime waited at the table, wearing white gloves. The revolution had not yet penetrated here.

After the meal, coffee was served in an adjoining room. Esteban asked about my plans.

"I need your help, Esteban."

"Whatever you want. I have never forgotten how, when we were still both children and I was younger and weaker than you, you came to my rescue when our schoolfellows wanted to throw me into the swimming-pool despite the fact that I was unable to swim. I was really scared to death and was almost in despair. I screamed, and you were the only one who appreciated my distress, who stepped into the breach and finally got me out of the hands of the boys. And thus ran the risk of reprisals. You have helped me more than once when I have been in need, you appreciated me so much." He paused a moment, then continued: "I don't think you have changed, for that matter." He looked across at Juan José . . . "I have never been able to do something for you, and I have been waiting for this opportunity."

Jaime came in:

"Don Esteban, it is almost time for the news-bulletin."

"Thank you, Jaime."

The radio was switched on, and the newsreader related the progress that had been made at the fronts.

Elvira and Juan José had retired for their siestas. The boy needed to sleep after the exertion of the drive. In the meanwhile, I discussed with Esteban the possibility of reaching France in the motorboat.

"A very risky experiment, dear Santiago; if they catch you, your foreign passport won't do you much good, and the distance is very great for such a little old boat. All the same, if . . ." After a short pause, he continued "What do you need? My reserves of fuel and food are at your disposal, you know I look on you as a friend." A little later he added: "Now I am sure that you are still the same as you used to be." Esteban smiled and rang the bell which stood on the table beside the cups. Jaime appeared.

"My guest needs one or two things. Will you give him a hand this evening after the sun has set?"

'Yes, Don Esteban, I'll take care of him."

When the butler had disappeared, Esteban remarked; "A good and trusty servant, one of the old school, who considers it an honour to be of service."

We then recalled a few memories of days long ago when we had been together. In conclusion we drank a glass of sherry under the pergola, and watched the sun disappear beneath the horizon. The gramophone played saetas, fandanguillos and fandangos from the southern provinces and sardanas from the neighbouring district softly in the background. It had been an unforgettable afternoon. Darkness fell swiftly, and it was time to act. I put Juan José on watch from the flat roof — armed with a telescope — for *carabineros* or other unwelcome visitors. At his age this was something important, and I was convinced that he would do his best more than an adult would have done. With Jaime, I descended to the cellar and looked for what would be essential for the sea-journey; first of all we filled several containers with fuel, which we three — Esteban, Jaime and me — carried down to the beach, where I began by filling the fuel tank to the brim. Then we stored the containers as well as possible within the ship. I had just put the last one on board when Juan José came up to us panting.

"Stop everything, at once!"

We hid ourselves in a cave as quickly as possible. Just afterwards we heard the faint noise of a motorboat and the beam of a searchlight swept over the rocks . . . We had got out of the way just in time, less than three seconds later the light shone onto the beach . . . The voices aboard the motor-boat could be heard through the still air: "Nothing unusual, a deserted beach with a little boat . . . That must surely belong to the artist."

They were obviously searching for something else. The light went out and the boat continued towards the south. Juan José stood close beside me; I could feel and hear his heart beating, his head resting on my shoulder.

The danger had receded. Still frightened, we climbed up the irregular steps. The boy disappeared to his look-out post again, and we carried down tins filled with drinking-water. An hour later we had completed loading the stores. If only the boat did not seem to be too heavily laden. Well, in that case we could put something or other over the side. I felt my muscles; they were not accustomed to taking me up and down so many irregular steps, nor to carrying such loads.

Elvira had prepared hot coffee in thermos flasks, and she came again with a couple of bars of chocolate.

Everything was ready for the departure. I checked that nothing had been forgotten: compass, chart . . . Oh, yes, the flag that I had flown on my car, that might well come in handy. I left the Ford in Esteban's hands.

The moment of departure approached. Esteban squeezed my hand. Elvira kissed Juan José on the forehead and said: "may God protect you." Esteban put his hand on his shoulder: "you are in very good hands."

We made a final round to see if everything was safe. Esteban and Jaime came down to the beach with us in order to help with pushing the boat into the water. We had some difficulty in getting it to move. I had put on my swimming-costume and stowed my clothes in the cabin, so that I could push the boat the first hundred yards — to outside the little bay — without starting the motor. Everything was settled. Esteban and Jaime would return to the house as soon as the boat was launched, for any contingencies. Juan José was shown how to start the motor and how to use the oars. Elvira kept watch from above. The boat slipped into the water. The sea was very calm. The cold water did me good. Prudently I pushed the boat out of the bay, and a few minutes later I climbed on board. Juan José tried to start the motor; after a few misfires it caught and the boat began to move under its own power. Seconds later two shots sounded and a voice from the cliffs shouted:

"Halt!"

I pulled Juan José into the cabin and went to take the helm. The motor was doing its duty and the distance from the coast was increasing steadily. We heard a few more shots and a bullet struck the deck right beside my feet. Then it was quiet.

We were now well away from the coast. I thought anxiously about Esteban, Elvira and Jaime. If they were to get into any trouble . . .

On the ship's bow, the previous owner had had the word *Salvador* — Saviour — painted. I hoped it would be appropriate . . .

After setting the helm I went down into the cabin to get the compass. Juan José took one look at me and blurted out: "You're bleeding, Santi!"

A trickle of blood was running down my left arm. I looked at the wound; the bullet that had struck the deck had also grazed my arm, fortunately, it had caused only superficial damage. In the excitement I had not noticed it.

Juan José washed the wound and wrapped a bandage around it. I sat down on the edge of the small bunk. The boy was putting so much care and devotion into his work!

"You have done this sort of thing before, Juanjo."

"No, but if you like somebody, you know just what to do, it comes naturally . . ."

We looked at each other and laughed.

V

The water lapped gently against the wooden hull of the fragile vessel, which rocked slightly on the calm sea. The motor made the only mechanical noise with its monotonous purring at that time of night, beneath the starry sky which now seemed to be brighter than the land. We had first sailed a few miles out to sea, and now we were heading northwards. The coast was no longer in sight. Sometimes a fish would come into view, then it would disappear with a flick of its tail into the depth. The *Salvador* bore herself according to all the rules of the art; we had indeed to put part of the stores overboard, as she lay too deep and was thus unable to make full speed ahead. We doused the lamp on board, as it was not needed and might also reveal our position. During the voyage, a weak wind got up. It was indeed beneficial. Juan José sat on the foredeck — a triangular space adjoining the cabin — and peered silently over the water. What was he thinking about, the past or the future?

I lay comfortably on a pair of red cushions beside the helm, my head did not protrude above the gunwale and my left hand resting on the tiller. My feet were wedged against the sill of the low cabin door, which stood ajar. The green superstructure of the cabin contrasted with the yellow planks of the fore and afterdecks. The previous owner had kept her in good repair, you could tell by the paint. A sail could be hoisted on the short mast, and in favourable wind that could be important. Although the distance that had to be covered was not very great, it was doubtful whether the fuel would be sufficient. There was a bench on the left of the cabin, which could also serve as a bed. A mattress and other bedding were available. On the right was a folding-table — on which the chart of the coastal area lay open, with a few books — and a folding-chair with a collapsible back-rest. The associated cushions were hanging on the wall beside a picture of the holy Saviour. A small blue tile with a portrait of the black 'Virgin of Montserrat' was inlaid on the right side of the front bulkhead. Swinging gently next to it on a little chain was a small wrought-iron candle-holder. The slender, finely-made candle had already been used. Nothing in the interior had been altered since I had owned it, apart from the new oil-lamp at the ceiling.

The outer walls were partly white and green. A small anchor hung from the bow. The motor was located at the stern and was of British make.

We had been travelling for several hours, and it was after midnight. It was cooler, even fresh. The dark, slim — through sturdy — boy's figure stood up and came astern, past the mast above the cabin. A little later he sat down on the cushions beside me, put on a poncho, and pressed his head against my chest. I had put on a woolen jersey shortly before, and lit my pipe. The aroma of the tobacco mingled with the sea air. Beside me was a thermos flask that Elvira had filled before our departure. I unscrewed the top and discovered a piece of paper inside. By the light of a match I read the following message in Catalan: *Deu vos guard* — "may God protect you." I read it out aloud and poured out the coffee. We drank it turn and turn about.

"You have good friends, Santi," said Juan José looking up at me. "I had already seen the little bay where the *Salvador* was kept, you know," he added.

"How was that?"

"In a painting at home. It was by Esteban Muñoz; I looked at the signature on the canvasses yesterday afternoon and compared them with that of the painting at my home."

The boat began to roll; a light south-west wind had arisen. Juan José snuggled a bit closer to me and put his arm around my shoulder.

"Santi, there is such a lot I want to tell you." He paused, then continued: "You don't even know my last name."

It was a very well-known name. His father had apparently had become a prominent figure in political life, on the far right. A few hours before he had been taken away he had had a talk with his son on whom he had impressed the need to try to reach France if anything went wrong. His father intended to leave that day, to stay with acquaintances and remain in hiding there, but was too late. Juan José recounted all this with difficulty, at times the words appeared to stick in his throat.

"Then they came to take him away . . . several men pushed him out of the house . . . I stood beside the stairs . . . when they came past me, my father again said . . . do what I told you . . ." He burst into tears. I hugged the boy to me and let him continue his story.

"A few hours later he was found by the roadside . . . shot dead . . . finally I made up my mind to run away, without knowing exactly what I was doing . . ."

I poured out some more coffee and let him drink. It restored him somewhat.

"For a couple of days I wandered about . . . nothing could make any more difference to me . . ."

He took another swallow of coffee, put his head close beside mine, and said softly: "and then came my salvation. I felt that something must happen, anyway when I was walking along the beach path I saw a stone bench with you sitting on it. I wavered. You looked at me in such a friendly way that I was quite at ease . . . I felt something very special inside me . . . something that was new to me . . . and can't be expressed in words . . . it really came down to feeling safe and secure. I did not know that anything so sudden could exist, merely as soon as our eyes first met, before we had exchanged a single word. I had the feeling I would be helped . . . and I was not mistaken."

He kissed me lightly on the forehead, got up quickly and disappeared into the cabin.

I understood his sudden reaction; he was feeling ashamed. A few moments later, when I had checked the course and set the helm, I descended the few steps down to the cabin too.

"I could not have put it better myself, Juanjo; indeed I could not. I, too, had the same feelings, and I too had never felt them so strongly before; if you had not suffered so much misery — and if the country was not at war — those hours would have been the happiest of my life," I added, with a smile. "You speak the language of Cervantes like an adult, you have a gift for it."

"I am one year older today: today is my thirteenth birthday."

I stood up and looked out to see if there were any ships in the neighbourhood. I then lighted the candle beside the tile with the picture of the Virgin of Montserrat. The cabin became somewhat sombre, yet festive. Out of a box I took a small elegantly wrapped package with a multi-coloured ribbon around it and a label from San Jorge on the side. I presented it to my young friend.

"Happy birthday, Juanjo!"

His dark eyes sparkled and widened in the candle-light. He eagerly opened the package with his fine dark fingers. The golden watch glittered . . .

"Santi, you shouldn't have! You are really too kind . . ."

I took the watch, and fastened it around his small boyish wrist. It was a bit loose, but he pushed it enthusiastically up his arm and then it fitted. I was reminded of the words spoken by the old woman in the shop, which now made sense: that the wearers of both watches would be very happy.

We drank a glass of red wine from the forecastle. It gave Juanjo a touch of colour. I suggested that he should get a couple of hours' sleep, so that he could then take the helm while I took a rest.

"Telling you about myself has done me so much good that now I feel quite relieved, almost a new person."

A few minutes later he was asleep. The night gave way to the first glimmerings of dawn. I took a small telescope to scan the horizon. The coastline was faintly visible in the West, probably a prominent rock. In any case, we were on the right course, that was the most important thing. A tunny kept pace with the *Salvador*, swimming back and forth or diving and then surfacing again. It was as if the fish enjoyed looking at the boat from all angles. It was a large specimen, and sometimes it swam so close to the boat that its wake sprinkled the deck.

The sail was hoisted in order to take advantage of the south-western wind, and so to save fuel. Juanjo had already been asleep for five hours; I couldn't bring myself to waken him as he lay there so peacefully and confidently.

The new day was not so bright as the previous one had been.

We were already further north, which showed itself in the climate. The sea was somewhat rougher. At about eight o'clock a plume of smoke could be seen on the eastern horizon. I quickly took down the sail and altered course slightly. Just as it appeared that things were going to turn out badly, the vessel, which looked like a warship, suddenly stopped coming towards us and steamed off into the distance.

I prepared coffee and toast in the small galley. Juan José awoke in the meanwhile and looked proudly at his watch.

"Why didn't you wake me earlier?"

The toast and coffee tasted good. I explained how to hold the right course and hung the spyglass around the boy's neck.

"Sleep tight" he told me in his clear voice. A few moments later I dropped like a log onto the bunk, having had no sleep for the past two nights.

My dreams were confused to begin with, later I saw attractive landscapes with lush vegetation, where it was good to be alive . . . peace on earth, said the people . . . a golden gondola lay on a beach with a handsome boy standing upright on it, calling to me in a friendly voice . . . graceful birds flying in the clear blue sky . . . Caracas, my street and my flat . . . a friendly boy on the doorstep . . . .

It was midday when I awoke. Through the door I saw Juan José sitting with the tiller in his hand, keeping a lookout in all directions. Everything had been cleared away, plates and glasses washed and put away. My arm hurt. The boat rolled and through one of the portholes I saw a threatening sky in the east. I stood up and put the water on to cook a couple of pounds of potatoes that had not been thrown overboard. I opened a tin of meat.

Juan José had maintained a good course and was proud of it.

"Did you know that you spoke in your sleep, Santi?"

"What did I say then, I wonder."

He did not answer, but began to talk about other things. We ate our meal on the rear deck. The tunny had deserted us, and the *Salvador* sailed on alone towards the French coast.

VI

Dark threatening clouds hung over the sea. It was already several hours since it had been blue, and now it consisted of a grey moving mass with white tops. The freshening wind made the waves rise higher, and in the distance summer lightning flickered from time to time. The thunderstorm came steadily nearer and we could hear the thunder roll above the noise of the sea. The *Salvador* rolled on the storm-tossed water; the bow dipped sharply and then rose again with a jerk from time to time, the propellor coming right out of the water occasionally and causing the motor to scream as the speed rose when the load was removed. The sail had been taken down, and the cushions and other loose items on deck put in the cabin. Below decks, the table and chair had been stowed away and everything fastened down as far as possible, the oil-lamp and candle-holder put into a box, the tins of fuel and food tied down, portholes and cabin-door shut tight. Occasionally the top of a wave broke over the foredeck. The wind was from the north and the boat had difficulty in making any way against the current.

At about noon there was a heavy rain-shower. The water streamed down, as was often the case in that part of the world. You could not see for more than a few hundred yards, which represented a danger for a vessel sailing close to the rocky coast of the Costa Brava. Flashes of lightning lit up the sea again and again, and the thunder was deafening.

There was no question of cooking now. The boat began to rock heavily from side to side and the joints creaked as one wave after another came over the deck. It was with difficulty that we kept her heading into the waves. We ate some old bread and drank milk from a tin.

The anchor had worked loose, and was hanging a few feet under water. With difficulty we hauled it aboard the fore-deck and lashed it fast. The motor, which had kept going well so far, began to run warm and its exhaust note became irregular.

The storm drove fiercely over the boiling water. Suddenly, the rain stopped and it started to get brighter, but the force of the wind did not diminish, however. The waves were like hills which rolled threateningly down onto us. Fortunately neither of us had more than a touch of sea-sickness, which would have made our situation considerably worse. I had attached the boy to a cord so that he was free to move about but could not fall overboard. Although he could swim, it would have been very difficult to fish him out of the water again.

Then came the moment that I will never forget: the motor stopped and we ceased moving through the water, which made the boat difficult to steer. She drifted round to lie parallel to the direction of the waves, and the danger that she might overturn was not imaginary. Like a toy ball she had become the plaything of the waves, completely off her course. With the greatest difficulty I managed to bring her head round to face into the waves again. It began to look very black for us and I reproached myself. Had I not been stupid and gambled with Juan José's life and my own? Had I not been too rash? The boy appeared to read my thoughts and took my hand in his own. "Don't reproach yourself, Santiago" he said.

How remarkable all this was. We only had known each other for such a short time, and yet it was as if we had been together for our whole lives. Chance had brought us together, on a stone bench, one summer's day beside the blue Mediterranean Sea. We were created for each other; I was increasingly conscious how great my affection for this boy was. Despite the dangers we had encountered, we remained completely calm and unworried — we were above all together. Could anything more beautiful exist?

At about four o'clock the storm had reached its peak. A few planks of the deck had worked loose and the water began to leak into the cabin. We took turns at bailing; the water was about four or six inches deep and if it were not stopped the worst could be expected.

The storm abated quite suddenly at sunset. The rough sea was transformed quickly into calm water, the wind dropped and the clouds disappeared. Standing on the afterdeck, we had just the time to see the sun go down like a ball of fire, then darkness fell rapidly and the stars came out. The helm was back in its former place, but it was too dark to repair the motor without a lamp. We therefore sat in the dim light cast by the oil lamp. Fortunately the motor was of a simple design, so that anyone with a little technical knowledge could see how it worked. Nonetheless it took us several hours to get it running again. With less than half power the *Salvador* set off again; various pipes leaked and the fuel consumption had increased alarmingly, so that we would soon run short. But we were not worried about that then, we were so happy that we had come through the storm intact. With the help of the compass we took up the correct course again, although we did not know our position.

We took turns to sleep, four hours at a time. The motor was running irregularly, but the *Salvador* crept forward. The next morning the weather was superb: the clothes dried in the sun, as did the cushions that had been soaked. We repaired the deck as well as possible and fixed the loose planks in place again. The vessel had really suffered in the storm.

My thoughts were occupied with the boy's future. What would he become — a refugee? Where would he ultimately go? He had not spoken much about his uncle, whom he knew only slightly as he had met him only once, many years before in Barcelona. Could I not take him with me back to Venezuela? He could complete his *bachillerato* — secondary school — studies there. One thing seemed to be likely: that the civil war would continue for quite a long time, especially now that foreign intervention was being talked about, according to the latest bulletins. Was it not the case that the boy wanted to stay with me? He was intelligent, adroit, and above all balanced. Was he not turning the cruel blow that fate had struck him into something positive? How had I come to do all this so suddenly for some other person? It remained evenly balanced until I took a decision. Yes, I would let him be educated in Caracas in a direction that he himself would choose, and in an environment of peace he could work in future. Was this boy's future not in may hands . . . Was I not responsible? But how to make all this into practical reality. Could the official agencies supply the necessary papers? It would not succeed . . . Yes, it must succeed; as soon as we arrive in France I will go and arrange everything with the French officials — and at my consulate. But I needed his family's authorization. As his parents were no longer alive, his uncle would have to provide it . .

Without my noticing it, Juan José had come and sat down close beside me on the after-deck. Suddenly I heard his tender voice:

"Santi, I scarcely dare to ask you, you have already done so much for me, even putting yourself into danger. Can I come with you to South America?"

Were we so close to each other that our thoughts passed between us? I bent over, looked him straight in the eyes and whispered in his ear:

"I shall do everything to make it possible."

"Thank you — *querido* Santiago."

With a tranquil and contented expression he gazed over the water towards the north, where a new life would begin at the invisible coast. His hand remained in mine.

"Have you ever thought about the distant future? What do you want to be when you grow up?"

He did not reply at once.

"I don't want to be a burden to you, Santi, I will find work as quickly as possible so that I can earn money and . . ."

"That's not what I meant, *querido* Juanjo; you are no burden, on the contrary I will help you willingly as I feel myself linked with you in such a special way. My only wish is that all will go well with you and that you become whatever you can be happy at being."

"Nobody has ever appreciated and understood me so well before. I didn't know that any such thing really existed, but thought that it was possible only in fantasy."

"Yes, Juanjo, despite the present circumstances we are enjoying something that is very beautiful and sublime."

After a hot meal which consisted of an omelette, rice and tinned vegetables, I made my way to the cabin for my siesta. Through the doorway I saw my young friend sitting proudly at the helm, with his slim muscular left arm on the tiller and his right arm on a cushion. With complete confidence, I fell asleep a few minutes later.

VII

Another night drew on. The fuel was nearly exhausted . . . and still the French coast did not come into sight. We had peered with great hopes to the north through the telescope, but in vain. The *Salvador* must have been driven some distance east by the storm. We didn't even approximately know our position. As the wind had dropped, the sail hung limply from the mast, and due to a weak current we drifted southwards. The worst thing was the decrease in the stock of drinking-water, so that this was rationed. By my reckoning we might end up somewhere to the south of Port Vendres — just past the Spanish frontier . . .

Juan José sat on the fore-deck in order to keep a look-out, with a white towel over his shoulders contrasting with the brown colour of his young limbs. He had made himself a hat out of an old newspaper in order to protect his head from the sunshine. I could watch him like that for hours without becoming bored, there was always something new. Sometimes he would look around with a smile, so his pearly-white teeth gleamed in the sunlight, and in a boyish way he would raise his right hand in a sign of greeting. On his left wrist glittered the gold watch at which he glanced from time to time like a child. Later on he went and lay on his back on the cabin roof, clad only in a brief coloured loincloth; his well-built youthful body had something fascinating about it. His right hand played with a piece of cord that had come loose from the sail. His thick black hair was matted, and hung in clumps over his forehead; his dark brown eyes scanned the skies, his long black eyelashes stood out clearly from the skin, like fine whiskers, his just visible ribs rose and fell with his breathing; his long slim bones and well-shaped muscles were continually in motion. He made me think of a noble thoroughbred . . . From time to time he turned his head, without raising it, towards me and asked questions like:

"What did you do when you were thirteen?"

I had to think about my answer.

"I had already been living in Caracas for several years, and I was going to school there. I was born in Mérida, in the interior. We moved to Caracas because my father got a government job there. He had become a minister some time before. We lived in a large house in the suburbs."

Juan José began to recount his own life in detail. It was a pleasure to listen to his beautiful Spanish; his lips moving quickly and his elegant hands gesticulating gracefully. At the end of his story he became aware of his situation again, and the so fatal early days of the civil war came back into his mind. He stood up slowly and came towards me, sat down and leant his head against my shoulder. He said, falteringly:

"My poor father — I will never forget him . . . I said so many things against him that I shouldn't have . . . and had rows with him sometimes . . . now I can do nothing about it, never put things right . . . I feel so ashamed . . . Oh, Santi, how miserable can anyone feel."

"Yes, Juanjo, we all do things like that. Later we are sorry but we cannot change things afterwards, no matter how much we would like to. It's always the same story. You aren't the only one. You probably don't see things in proportion now; time will change that, and heal a lot. By seeing things in proportion I mean that you put too much emphasis on particular events, as if you saw them through a magnifying glass. Just tell me what is on your mind."

Still leaning against me, he continued talking. It had to come out, he had to tell somebody. I listened attentively, without saying a word. When he had finished he looked at me and said gently:

"Santi, your eyes are wet, you're crying."

He went down into the cabin and got a handkerchief which he held lovingly against my eyes. I took his head in both hands and kissed his luxuriant hair . . .

"You are an angel, Juanjo."

A gentle breeze began to blow, and the sail caught it so that the *Salvador* got slowly under way. The water gurgled softly again against the bow, and from time to time small fish would leap out of the water not far away. Despite the so-peaceful scene, I began to get more and more anxious; no land had yet come into sight, just water and still more water. Where were we? Could the *Salvador* really have drifted so far? I had now set course in a westerly direction instead of heading north. My plan was to sail as far north as necessary once the coast was in sight. We could keep going for a couple of meals more, then our drinking water would run out . . . The food appeared to be sufficient for several more days. We kept the daily ration of drinking water in a bottle hanging overboard at the end of a cord, so that it was pulled through the seawater. The day wore on without incident.

In the evening, Juan José toasted some old bread over the open flame of the little cooking-stove and opened a tin of butter. I put him on watch; in that way he could be usefully occupied and express his devotion.

Afterwards, he brought the cooled water back on board and filled two glasses with it. We then sat on the deck to eat while the day drew to its close. That was a particularly delightful evening; at sunset the sky continually changed colour. I lit a cigarette, inhaled deeply, and blew the smoke out in front of me with a sigh.

"Can I have one too, Santi?"

I had pleasure in his smoking. He exhaled the smoke in short puffs . . .

"Did you ever do something you shouldn't have done in the past?" He looked at me in a special way as he asked me this question.

"All boys do that, indeed that is normal . . ."

We drank our glasses dry as if it were the most precious wine. In fact, that was the case. Juan José cleared the things away and hung another bottle in the sea, softly humming a tune which resounded with a subtly arabian effect over the surrounding water. Suddenly he was silent and pointed to the west. In an excited voice he said:

"Santi, I can see land, a rock!"

With emotion I took the telescope and looked. Yes indeed! There was something that seemed like a rock, sticking out of the water. The *Salvador* drew slowly nearer to it. In the meanwhile, it had become quite dark. The little speck got bigger and appeared to move . . . there was something floating on the water . . . it looked like a little boat. We looked at each other in astonishment. No reply came to our shouts . . .

When we came alongside, we could see by the light of the oil-lamp that there was nobody aboard her; the little boat had deliberately had holes shot in her and was drifting in an unseaworthy state. What drama had been played aboard her? The name *Margarita* was painted on her transom in small letters. Soon afterwards we left the wreck behind.

The next morning found the *Salvador* among low-lying white clouds that seemed to float upon the water and almost completely obstructed all sight. It was as if we were gliding; everything seemed unreal, even our voices sounded strange . . . It was humid, and everything was damp. The wind had dropped again, and the sail hung limp and useless from the mast.

The mist remained unchanged, as if it wanted never to go away. Suddenly, a silver bird flew over our heads, and we looked up in surprise. In the distance a fog-horn sounded . . . We held our breath and listened attentively, eagerly trying to identify the direction of the sound.

Without any warning, a threatening black shadow loomed out of the mist and headed rapidly in our direction. I grasped the boy by the arm, ready to jump. A collision seemed to be inevitable . . .

PART TWO

VIII

It was ten years later, August 1946. The din of heavy traffic flowed in through the open windows of my office in one of the main arteries of Caracas, an office arranged on modern lines on the fifth floor of a tall new building. The town had been growing rapidly; oil and everything connected with it had made that possible. There were extensive plans for whole new residential areas on the site of old ones . . . Modern schools and hospitals were springing up. The North American influence was increasingly apparent on the architecture.

In the avenues beneath my windows the cars were following each other in files; sometimes traffic jams were unavoidable. A large insurance company had established its headquarters on the other side of the road. The evenings were animated by the neon signs flashing on and off.

The office was bright and cool. On the grey steel desk lay the day's correspondence. Some photographs and a painting of Rio de Janeiro decorated its walls. There was a knock on the door and my secretary came in.

"Señor Capmany, will you sign this letter too, please; it's about our Mexican contract."

Her very well-looked-after fingers with painted nails placed the paper to be signed on the blotter in front of me with a familiar gesture. She remained — as always — waiting while my eyes ran over the text. In the meanwhile she arranged some curls of her hair with her right hand. She was an accurate worker who took pleasure in her duties and who, without doubt had a certain affection for her boss, without however ever thinking about it . . .

"Señorita Jimenez, everything is as it should be; you can send the letter."

I signed it and leaned back in my chair. With satisfaction she took up the letter with her supple hands and in a voice that indicated agreement, she said:

"Yes, Señor Capmany, I will have it posted at once; it will still catch the evening plane."

She disappeared with careful steps on her high heels through the leather-panelled door, which she closed quietly behind her. Señorita Jimenez had been my secretary for several years, and was now an indispensable asset. The telephone rang and I picked up the handset. It was apparently a long-distance call, from Maracaibo. A business contact wanted some information about a film.

In my usual way I drove home that evening to my flat on the outskirts of the town. Sitting on the balcony there I read the evening paper and looked at a few pages dealing with the cinema. As I lived on the top floor the view included an unobstructed sight of the sea of rooftops, and after sunset there were tens of thousands of little lamps twinkling around me. It was just the right kind of place for meditating and philosophising . . .

The maid, Enriqueta, brought me the whisky and a soda syphon at about ten o'clock. I switched the radio on and listened to Argentinean tangos, sung by Carlos Gardel. The melancholy, but also stimulating music gave a very definite frame to the whole. Deep in thought, I looked out before me towards the Venezuelan capital and the starry firmament.

The years slipped away, the scene changed. The Catalonian adventure . . . Dear me, how long ago all that was. The Spanish civil war came to an end in 1939; the last communiqué was issued on the first of April that year. After almost three years of turmoil. Who would have thought so in the days of July 1936 . . .

General Franco's troops had ultimately won, the country had taken a right turn. Slowly it recovered from its deep wounds. A quite considerable number of refugees remained abroad, in South France, North Africa and Mexico. A government in exile was formed.

Shortly afterwards, still in 1939, the second world war broke out, in which a whole series of countries were involved. The atomic age began. Now everything was peaceful again, humanity breathed again.

With a certain melancholy my thoughts went back — after all those years — to the Costa Brava.

What a wonderfully delightful experience that had been. A photograph of a small boy stood on my writing-table, a smiling Juan José. He still occupied a large place in my now somewhat older heart. From time to time I saw the events again — as in a film — our first meeting, our sea-voyage, the *Salvador*, our so-extraordinary rescue . . . our jumping into the water after the collision . . . the helpful crew . . . the friendly face of the captain of the *Ville d'Oran*, the steamship making its way from Algiers to Marseille . . . our great delight on arriving in France.

The attempts to be able to take the boy with me . . . my return journey to South America . . . and then the letter from Juan José's uncle in Perpignan, with the terrible contents which made me despair . . . the boy had unexpectedly died after a short illness . . . I could not accept it, it was too bad . . .

Time heals all wounds, at least partially. The memory remains.

My whisky-glass was dry and the radio programme had come to an end. I stood up and switched off the set. It was already late at night and the town was asleep. I took a couple of deep breaths and went to bed.

The next week I was fully occupied by business; it was one thing after another, and scarcely any day went by without a business lunch or dinner. Señorita Jimenez, who was never unwell, had to stay in bed for a fortnight because of an ear inflammation. One of the typists, Señorita Vargas, did her work for better or for worse. She was of a completely different type, somewhat on the stout side, who did not have such an elegant way of putting letters on my desk for signature. However, she possessed a number of positive qualities.

Somewhat later in the month a cousin of mine and her husband came from Mérida to spend a few days in the capital, where they stayed at the Hotel Imperial. We spent the last weekend in August together at a small resort on the Caribbean coast, where we went water-skiing with her friends. I took the opportunity, however, to go and see Esteban, who had left Spain with Elvira during the civil war after his country retreat near Tamariú had been completely looted by the mobs. They had now been living here for several years, although Elvira was occasionally nostalgic for her homeland.

Esteban sat on the terrace with his easel, working on a painting of some fishing-boats. He was glad to see me.

"Welcome — Santiago, it's already six months since you were last here. How's everything doing, old chap?"

Elvira came outside. She still looked quite young for her age, although she had indeed changed considerably since when she was at Tamariú.

"*Deu vos guard*", she said in Catalan.

Sitting there we quickly got into animated conversation. Her nine-year-old daughter, Pepita, was playing with some friends in the garden.

"How are the sales of your paintings going, Esteban?"

"I can't complain; this week I received a commission to do a seascape for the new town hall. It must be going in the entrance-hall."

Elvira took up her needlework, just as she had on the Costa Brava . . .

The same evening I returned to the city with my relations from Merida.

The fresh air and the water-sports had given me a healthy feeling of tiredness. When I got home, I relaxed, took a shower, and went to bed. On the bedside table, beside the latest issue of *Time* magazine, was a volume of poems by Ramirez which I had bought at a kiosk a few days before. I took the book, and began to read. The poems expressed so great a sensitivity, and I was taken by them to such an extent, that I had not switched the light off several hours later. A short poem entitled *to a dead friend* was the best that I had ever read. It was certainly as good as anything by Walt Whitman.

IX

It was October and the *fiesta de la raza*, the day on which the whole Spanish-speaking world commemorates its collective heritage. Although the former extensive Spanish colonial territory had split up into a series of independent states in Central and South America during the nineteenth century, the Spanish stamp remained on the region, in particular through the language and the religion. Brazil is the exception here, because of its Portuguese origins.

This day fell during my holidays; I had decided to take a week's rest at home, rather than travel as I usually did. Enriqueta had already set breakfast in the *comedor* — dining-room. A little later I got up, and after a refreshing shower I sat down at the table with the morning newspaper. I was principally interested in the list of the day's events; it appeared that there were plenty of things to do. The fan hummed above my head in its usual way, doing its best to provide some cooling. After a visit to the hairdresser's, I lunched with some friends in the club. The conversation, and the subsequent discussion, was in the domain of philosophy, and about Ortega y Gasset and his book *The Revolt of the Masses* in particular. The ladies present preferred to talk about the latest fashions.

Afterwards, I drank a cup of black coffee with a dash of cognac beneath a sunshade. Not very far away the traffic held my attention, especially the latest models of cars from the United States. How their bodywork design had changed during the past few years. It was good to be sitting and relaxing here, on the terrace, which was occupied by only a few small tables and surrounded by plants in tubs. It was that afternoon that I had the most remarkable — both surprising and at the same time delightful — experience of my life.

The waiter had just brought me a second cup of coffee when my eyes fell on a young man sitting reading at a table to my right, I don't know why . . . he reminded me of somebody . . . no, that was impossible . . . ! Suddenly he pushed the sleeve of his left arm up a little way with his right hand and looked at his watch . . . my heart began to pound . . . I was no longer puzzled . . . it was the golden watch from the shop with San Jorge over the door . . . and that gesture, which I had seen so many times before, could only mean that it was . . .

The young man suddenly glanced in my direction, as if he also felt my anxiety, doubt, fear and hope. His dark eyes looked straight at me . . . I felt as if I could sink through the floor . . .

He stood up slowly and walked hesitantly towards my table. Without warning he greeted me:

"Santiago . . ."

"But this is crazy . . . Juanjo . . . how on earth . . . no . . ."

I stood up automatically and we shook hands, as we had done more than ten years before and many thousand miles away somewhere on the Mediterranean sea . . .

We both had difficulty in controlling our emotions, tears filled our eyes. We didn't understand . . .

Juan José was the first to speak.

"Why did my uncle get a letter in 1936 that you . . . were dead? I . . ."

"Oh, dear Juanjo, I received a letter like that too, telling me that you had died unexpectedly . . . and for ten long years I have been living with the belief that you were no longer alive . . ."

"I think I am beginning to understand a bit better."

He looked straight in front of him and reflected. A great bitterness came into his face, similar to hate. I had never seen him look like that before.

"I suspect my uncle did it. Yes, I'm virtually sure it was him. That was really something for him. Look, Santiago, he disliked the link between us, he couldn't stand you and so he thought of this . . . How could anybody be so rotten. I never want to see him again, never again!"

"In other words, you think he staged the whole business? That he really murdered both of us somewhere, Juan José?"

His uncle had thus given Juan José false news and had written me a false letter. That was how the link had been broken; there could have been no more effective method.

We sat down again; he joined me at my table. We needed to get accustomed to the situation, it was too unexpected, too sudden. We felt a certain tension. So there he sat, my Juanjo, ten years older, a grown man. His features were still handsome, his eyes even darker and deeper, but they lacked the sparkle of childhood. His hands, although elegant and supple, had become more robust. His hair was now tidily parted. The . . .

He interrupted my meditations.

"Yes, Santi, fate struck us a cruel blow. I can read your thoughts." He added,

with a smile, "I used to do that before, do you still remember? But we are not now sitting holding hands like we did then . . ."

"Ah, yes, Juanjo, how different everything could have been!"

We were silent for a few minutes. The traffic and people continued to pass by. We did not see them.

"Yes, Santiago, when my uncle told me the dreadful news I didn't eat for days, and I couldn't sleep at night. Why was that man so cruel as to do such a thing to a child — as I still was at the time? Your name was continually on my lips . . . Santi . . . Santi . . . I felt so lonely and abandoned. I relived the days we spent on board our faithful *Salvador*, our saviour, again and again. I dreamed about it at night until it became a nightmare. I missed you dreadfully. I knew that that was love, really deep love . . . I must tell you something, Santiago, my heart really ached . . ."

The waiter brought the sherry we had ordered and put the glasses down in front of us. Juan José continued:

"I had set all my hopes on South America."

After a short pause he suddenly said:

"And I have never even been able to thank you properly for all that you did for me. Your love must have been deep too."

We told each other how life had treated us. Juan José had got married not long before, to a Chilean girl he had met in Barcelona. He had a bookshop on the Diagonal, and also wrote poems. The Spanish Government had awarded him a money-prize for one of his collections of poems, and he and his wife were making this journey to Venezuela on the strength of it.

"I don't need to tell you why we chose this country . . ."

I interrupted him:

"Are you Ramirez?"

"Yes, that is my pen-name. How did you guess?"

"A couple of months ago I bought a copy of your prize-winning collection in a kiosk. One evening I read some of it and enjoyed it, particularly the poem entitled *to a dead friend* . . ."

A little later, I continued: "Do you remember, Juanjo, that I once complimented you on your beautiful Spanish? I said then that you were talented . . ."

"Quite right, I still remember it clearly. I gave you a kiss on the forehead that evening, and was embarrassed . . ."

We had so much, so very much, to tell each other and we didn't know where to begin. Our love had developed into friendship, true friendship. If it had not been for the separation of over ten years, this transformation would have occurred gradually and harmoniously; it would have run its natural course. Now we had to speed up the process, to compress it into a few hours.

Suddenly Juan José looked at me questioningly, waited a moment and said:

"Do you still feel the same way as you used to do?"

"Yes, Juanjo, exactly the same; some people are the same throughout life . . ."

In his case, things were different; he had just got married.

"That's the way it has to be, Juan José; we few are there to offer support and help to boys of a certain age, to boys to whom we are attracted. That is how we perform the task that is given to us by nature. That is our mission, our so delightful and responsible duty."

It was already the evening when we got up. Juan José looked at his watch and said with a laugh: "How the time has gone by, Santi . . ."

We ran through the town. The lights had gone on and the neon signs gave the streets a gay appearance with their many colours and shapes. In the hotel, Juan José presented me to his wife, to whom he first explained the extraordinary event that had occurred only a few hours before. He had previously told her a lot about me. She was a particularly charming and attractive young woman, the daughter of a manufacturer.

In the main hall of the hotel she offered me her hand. I bowed and kissed it. Her first words were:

"Thank you for all that you have done for Juan José. If it was not for you, we would probably not be here now. Two of his cousins were sent to Russia at that time, and they never came back. We know nothing about what happened to them. You had such a lot of influence on Juan José that he has you to thank for the successes in his life. I am so happy that you are alive and well."

We dined together in one of the restaurants in the city center. The band played boleros, rumbas and tangos. Our table was beside the window, and we looked out onto a public garden.

I felt very happy. My Juan José was on the right road and had found his place in life. He had the makings of a great poet, and he was on the way to becoming a famous man. It had not all been in vain . . .

It was late when we returned to the hotel. Juan José accompanied me to the car-park. He walked round my Chevrolet and stopped beside the baggage-compartment . . .

"This is a bit more comfortable than the one we had ten years ago . . . it is remarkable what fate can bring . . ."

Lost in thought, he gazed into the distance, just as he had done long ago . . . I felt that he wanted to say something to me, but was unable to.

"What is it, Juanjo?"

We were standing near a lamp-post, and the light shone obliquely onto his face. There was something melancholy about his eyes.

"Santi, please don't consider what I am going to tell you as a reproach. But it is something that I wanted to say ten years ago, yet never dared to. Now, as an adult who has had rather more insight and experience of life, I can choose my standpoint better."

He fell silent and looked again like he had done when, as a thirteen-year-old boy, he had peered across the water towards the French coast, hoping for rescue . . .

"Santiago, at that time with me, you could have . . . Do you understand what I mean? I have always felt it to be lacking, as something that should have happened in order to achieve complete harmony. I am a little poorer, not as rich as I could have been. If we had only experienced it once, then we would have had the memory of it . . . It was an unnecessary obstacle — for a few years — while I was growing up. You might say that I had missed part of my adolescence. I believe that our tragedy — if I may call it that — lies in the fact that it is now too late and we cannot turn the hands of the clock back . . . Therefore the gold watch that you gave me is also a splendid symbol; the noblest metal, and the time factor that plays such an important role . . . In other words, the most noble sentiments, but don't let the right moment go by . . ."

He had put his hand on my shoulder. My eyes were damp.

Twenty minutes later I was at my front door. On my writing-table stood a photograph of a small boy: a laughing Juan José.

X

The cars drove past one after the other below my window.
There was a knock at the door. Señorita Jimenez came in.
"Good morning, Mr. Capmany — Here is the post."
The carefully looked-after hands laid the letters on the writing-pad. While I ran my eyes over their contents, she fiddled with a few curls of her hair, as usual.
After dictating a few replies to her, she disappeared on her high heels through the leather-clad door, which she closed almost noiselessly behind her.
The film studios were working at their full capacity. We had a bright future ahead of us.

Costa Brava was written in the summer of 1958. At that time, the theme of this novel — paedophilia — had scarcely become the subject of public discussion. *Costa Brava* was published in Rotterdam by the Enclave International Press, and right from the beginning it was a much demanded book. The monthly magazine of the Netherlands Association for Sexual Reform (N.V.S.H.) *Rational Parenthood* said, in the issue for December 1960, it is: "a well-written and straightforward story about people whom you might meet any day. (. . .) Specially recommendable because the attempt to give the reader an insight into socially unacceptable feelings is decidedly a complete success." Part of the book appeared as a short story under the title "The storm" in *Der Weg* (February-March 1963)

The daily and weekly press in the Netherlands also reviewed the book, notably *De Haagse Courant* and *Elsevier*.

Costa Brava lives on. This is emphasized regularly. The periodical *N.I.K.S.* (the integration of child-sexuality, published by the N.V.S.H.) mentioned my book, as follows: One can really only come to the conclusion that human love is experienced in all possible variations. There are no deviant forms of behavior. Costa Brava confirms this conclusion . . . It is well worth while . . . to read Costa Brava."

More recently, Costa Brava was mentioned in the English-language magazine *Pan* in June 1979, and the chapter "The storm" was reprinted in Joachim S. Hohmann's historico-literary survey entitled *"Der heimliche Sexus" (The Secret Sex)*, presented by the editor in the section on "homosexual fiction from 1900 to 1970" and mentioned in a detailed essay illustrated with photographs.

My story has even found its way into the scientific literature. Thus, it is mentioned in the *Lexikon der Sexualität* by Willhart S. Schlegel, volume 1 of the series "Mensch und Sexualität" published in Munich in 1969.

The historian E. O. Born mentions the publication of Costa Brava in his *Pedofiele Intgratie na 1959* (Utrecht 1973).

Furthermore, the story is quoted as an example of a happy depiction of paedophile relationship in specialist publications such as *Sexualmedizin, Betrifft: Erziehung* and *Arcadie, Revue littéraire et scientifique*.

The Dutch-language edition, which was published twenty years ago, has brought me into contact with a large number of readers at home and abroad, both in person and by correspondence. From them I have learnt that the book is a moral support to numerous paedophiles. It is therefore opportune that an illustrated English edition is now being published by *Gay Sunshine*.

Frits Bernard

OZCAN REVISITED
A Short Story
by
Lyle Glazier

About the middle of April, one Saturday evening, after having spent the day rounding out materials for Monday's lecture on Saul Bellow's *Herzog,* he went to Kızılay for supper at Gima cafeteria. Afterwards he went to an early movie, American made but translated into Turkish. Coming back, he stopped on a bench in the park across from Gima. It had been raining that morning and the part of the park he sat in was grassless and muddy. He had to step around puddles to get to his bench. The sky had remained overcast, and great tents of darkness were folded on the low ground under the trees. The few passers kept to the cement sidewalks or hardpacked paths. Nobody so much as glanced in his direction. Around 11:30, the air became oppressive as if another shower were about to fall. He stood up and took a step toward the lighted boulevard, but changed his mind, went back, and sat down again. Shortly thereafter, a young man turned in off the boulevard and disappeared down the lighted stairwell of the subterranean men's john. When his head reappeared, he was looking around, scanning the park. Having cleared the top of the stairs, he turned and came directly to the bench, and spoke — his voice thickened by drink.

"Nasılsınız, efendim? Saat kaç?" (How are you, my dear sir. Do you have the time?)

Thrown off balance, as always by a question in Turkish — even such a ritual question as this one — he looked nervously at his wristwatch, its face hardly visible.

"Saat onbir," he replied, knowing it was later than eleven but not having the courage to try eleven-thirty or quarter to twelve, either of which would involve verbal pitfalls. Eleven o'clock would serve, especially for this traditional gambit.

The young man sat beside him and almost immediately put his left hand on his neighbor's knee. He leaned across and held out his right hand.

"Özcan," he said, the fingers of his other hand spreading on the lower thigh. His breath, as he leaned forward, was fragrant with the licorice of rakı.

Glad to be friended, but nervous as always in the public park, he gripped the offered hand, and felt his own guided over and down.

"Taman," his new friend said. "Çok seviyorum. (I love you very much.) Arkadaşım. Sizi seviyorum." (You are my friend.)

The sentiments of love seemed ardently genuine. Nevertheless, afraid to trust an instant friendship, on guard against a police decoy, he feebly tried to withdraw his hand, but yielded when he felt the slender rod, already pulsating beneath the taut cloth.

"Tamam," his companion said again, running his hand up the leg to the groin. They sat there fingering each other, tubing their fingers, squeezing, letting go.

"Özcan," the stranger said. "Isminizne?" (What is your name?) Then when he got no answer, "Ismim Özcan," pointing to himself. "Özcan. Ben Özcan." He pointed back.

"Evet, efendim," knowing he was marking time with that inane "Yes, Sir," He groped in his mind for a useful, likely name. "Ismim Joe." It would be translated — he could see it in his mind as if in print — "Co. — Ben Co." That oriental *C* pronounced occidental *J*.

"Co, Co, Gel, Gel." (Joe, Joe, come, come.) The new friend was standing and pulling him toward the street. He spouted a torrent of Turkish as if persuaded that someone named "Co" must have a gift of tongues. Perceptions bristling, the intent auditor could make out only one word: "evime" (*to my house*). It was nearly midnight; curfew was one o'clock. He didn't trust his companion. Neither did he have words to propose a reasonable substitute for tonight's engagement. Perhaps tomorrow night? He tried "Yarın akşam."

Özcan pulled more urgently at his wrist. "Hayır, efendim. Şimdi. Gel. Gel, Co, gel." (Now. Come. Come, Joe, come.)

He let himself be pulled to his feet and conducted to the street, where Özcan flagged a taxi. He still hesitated to get in, but didn't like to make a scene in front of the curious cabby. They turned almost immediately off Atatürk Bulvarı to the left uphill. Özcan sat forward on the seat, giving directions, his right hand falling loosely and cleverly out of sight of the driver onto his companion's crotch, where he lightly stroked the aching, retracted cock. For the American this was an unknown district of Ankara, off the familiar main thoroughfare. He knew for a minute where they were when they ground past the Dedeman Hotel, but he lost his bearings again when they levelled off to the right. His intuitions were tensed, fogged by that tendency toward blindness that some-times descended on him when he self-protectingly refused to register his surroundings, as if by doing so he could erase his presence. Özcan soon com-manded the taxi to halt, paid the 5-lira fee, and led the way along a rail overlooking a steep-pitched sidestreet angling downhill. They turned down and at once veered left alongside a high cement-walled apartment house. They were on a raised sidewalk overlooking the sunken well accommodating a row of basement windows. An overpass like a drawbridge crossed the well to the main door, which swung open to Özcan's hand. There was so much light thrown in from the public thoroughfare that Özcan didn't trouble to buzz the electric switch. Taking his companion by the shoulder, he ushered him the length of the corridor to the rear, then downstairs. They paused in front of the door dead centered on the stairs; on a small card in the identification slot, bright in the beam of light from the street, was printed Özcan Koç.

He was breathing easier now, comforted by the commonplace. It was so much like countless former midnight trysts. Ankara and Turkish inflections could not conceal the pattern. If this were some kind of trap, the metal jaws were well concealed.

Inside the cell-like room all his suspicions were erased. Özcan swung to the door, tiptoed to the window, peered out, then having drawn a curtain, came back and pulled the chain of the naked overhead bulb. Revealed in the instant glare, he was tall, young (in his early thirties), blackhaired and mustached, freshcheeked, slender as a runner. He came straight to his guest and, bending over, folded him in his arms, searching out lips and opening his mouth in urgent invitation. He moved spread hands quickly and nervously down his visitor's back, and drew the two of them together at the hips. His mouth was fragrant with licorice. There was no danger in this little room. No longer worried about a moral ambush, his earlier fears at rest, he closed his eyes and with a long-drawn breath submitted to be a lover.

To be alive is to be a lover. The best is when few questions are asked, when not much is demanded, only sensual pleasure, but there is a givingness — I give you when you take. A willingness to give. It is as simple as that. Take me. Take me, I give myself. This is my body. Take and eat. If this seems sacrilege, make the most of it.

He let his mouth be opened to Özcan's tongue, spread his lips and mouth, felt his lips sucked while his body bent, they two joined at the hips, both cocks tense and throbbing inside their clothes. They used no hands. For a long kiss it was all lips, then tongue and mouth, chest joined to chest, and the urgent curve of groin into harboring groin. Then Özcan breathed and sighed and pushed him down. He slowly knelt, grasping the firm buttocks, letting his falling head drop slowly from mouth to neck to chest to belly, till, pillowed on Özcan's thighs, his face leaned inward toward the thrusting cock, his mouth half open outside the stretched, thin cloth. He let go the buttocks, and kneeling there in awkward imbalance, unbuckled the belt, unbuttoned the trouser band, unzipped the fly, and at last, held in his hand the slender cock, the bulb not large, but large enough, thank God!

He made flat planes of his hands and gently moved the palms back and forth on the cock, one palm stroking out, the other stroking in. It was a long, thin rod. Circumcized, of course; even so, some surplus flesh slipped back and forth, not enough to make a fold, but plenty. He kept up the alternating stroking of his palms, kneeling, gazing as if his eyes were riveted, until a drop of moisture formed at the little slit; leaning his face still closer, he caught the drop on his tongue. Özcan reached high, pulled the light chain, then fell back on the bed, drawing the suppliant with him. They lay in dark unmoving, then fumbled off each other's remaining clothes.

He stayed all night. It was not curfew that detained him. Ozcan was as insatiable as himself. Toward dawn they fell asleep, but woke to fuck again. It was a definitive, absolute fuck.

Great God in Hell, he thought, I've lost track of the talley. Enough is as good as a feast. Özcan was wide awake, lying eyes open, smoking, staring at the ceiling, deep in thought. After a while, cigarette in hand, he eased out of bed, padded to the door, unlocked the catch, stark naked opened the door, went through, closed it firmly, his bare feet thudding along the hall.

Alone on the rumpled sheets, naked in the strange room, he was jolted back into reality by a monition of present danger. All the airy midnight idealism evaporated. The room became a cage. In panic haste he plummeted off the bed and hurried into his clothes, sweeping them from the floor — shorts, socks, trousers, shirt, shoes kicked against the wall, and raincoat carefully hung by his host on a hook among Ozcan's small stock of jackets and shirts. He patted his pockets; everything seemed there — pocketbook, permit, housekey, addressbook. He was fumbling into the raincoat when he heard water flush and then the padded warning of Ozcan's return. He was standing by the bed guiltily poised for flight when Ozcan opened the door, cast one comprehending look, entered, closed the door, and stood with his back against it. Something oppressive, like blackmail, seemed to fill the room.

But when his trembling legs carried him to the door, Ozcan moved aside and watched him leave, filling the doorway with his naked, curious presence. Looking back from the turn at the top of the stairs, like an anguished quarry he raised his hand in farewell, too driven by fear to obey his impulse to go back down and take a decent leave. He walked fast through the upstairs corridor, out the open front door, and hurried along the walk and uphill to the avenue, imagining his progress being plotted from the basement window. He had a nearly irresistible impulse to turn back toward where he remembered coming from, back toward the Dedeman Hotel, to put his spy off scent. But panic was too strong. He turned and ran in the direction that should bring him home, and quicker than he expected he found himself running downhill into Kavaklıdere, from where he forced on himself a more respectable pace. The outside door of the Tahran Caddesi apartment house was locked from the night, so he had to kneel to use his outside key on the springlock down at the base. He tiptoed through the common hall, turned his housekey in the lock of the apartment door, felt the door give, then jam. Dismayed, he realized that it was held from within by the short auxiliary chain. He had to ring the bell. When his puzzled landlord opened the door, he had made up his mind not to say one word to explain the all night absence. But he was not prepared for the look of consternation that swept the good man's face.

"Allah! Allah!"

He hurried past, and safely shut inside his room, caught sight of his mirrored face, lips puffy and purpled as if pummelled by a fist, not by a lover's mouth.

All that Sunday he kept close to his room, working feverishly on Monday's lectures, keeping too busy to let his mind stray more than a fickle instant. Flashes of last night's engagement flickered but he refused to indulge them. For lunch he ate an orange and two cookies, and crept to the kitchen for cool mineral water from the napkin-covered tall urn. In late afternoon he wrote a long, bright letter to Buffalo. Having reread it, polished a few details, then sealed the envelope, he prepared to go out for dinner. He studied his face in the mirror; the swelling of his lips had subsided, nearly disappeared. Just as he was about to launch himself from his room, he heard his landlord and lady preparing to go out, so he sat on the bed until they were gone from the house and the door shut behind them on silence. Immediately when he was alone, he went out. It was dusking, a warm spring evening of nearly summer heat.

He walked briskly down in to Kavaklıdere to the small cheap restaurant where he could buy kebab and beer for thirteen lira, less than a dollar at the new rate of exchange. He waited a long time to be served; the cook was always slow, but the lamb when it came was fresh, well broiled, and piping hot. Great chunks of pide, Turkish unleavened bread, and garlic garnished the meat. The pungent, sharp-seasoned sauce scalded the inside of his mouth. He ran his tongue around inside exploring the soreness and the flaked skin. The cold beer roused his spirits. Miraculously revived, even a trifle horny, he paid his check, then walked to the small post office at the bottom of Çankaya hill. Having dropped his letter in the outside slot, he teetered on the curb, harboring a vague notion of climbing Vali Dr. Resim Street to the crest of Çankaya, where he could look out over the lights of the darkening city. However, some inner compass needle directed him, instead, back along Tunali Hilmi Caddesi toward last evening's stopping place.

At the hilltop crossing of Tunali and Esat Caddesi, he took his bearings but lost himself in the grid of streets beyond the crossroads. His mind was split between a protective urge not to succeed in his quest and an urgent desire to find again the railing along the steep-pitched street plunging abruptly to the sunken basement well of the blunt apartment house, marked at its corner stone with a name his eyes that morning had registered absolutely and then somehow forgotten. He knew that he would recognize it if he could think of it or see it again. He went through a whole alphabet of Turkish names, without being able to do better than know that the one he sought was filed away for sure, hovering under the brink of his conscious recollection. After an hour and a half, he gave up both searches, the one in his mind for the name, and the sweaty search through the streets. He was, if anything, he thought, relieved at his failure. By now he was completely uncertain what Özcan's motives may have been. In the park there at the beginning, lust was genuine, he had to believe. And he could believe that for a time the continuing infatuation on both sides was honest and honorable, fueled by real affection. Why, then, did he have to spoil his faith, imagining a threat to his American dollars? He did not grudge dollars, but he feared the threat to his reputation that could be used to pry dollars from him. He would try to push his fears aside, remembering ardent embraces. Then his assurance would fade, destroyed by some instinct flaring in response to a facial expression he had never consciously seen but had somehow photographed.

Frustrated and alarmed by the strength of his desires and the countering strength of his fears, he slowly returned homeward. Gratefully, he found the apartment dark and empty. He slept well. Monday morning he breakfasted with his landlord, who did not mention his shock yesterday morning when he opened the door. They had their customary elementary discussion in Turkish of the weather and morning headlines. Later, back in his room, he collected papers for Monday at the University. His first lecture would not be till 11:30. Having stopped for his daily *Ankara News* at the bookstore on Tunali Hilmi, he didn't as usual board a bus, but walked again uphill to the crossing with Esat Caddesi.

Right here is where he had paused a moment to get his bearings after that first sprint of his morning's flight. He remembered how short a sprint it had been, how surprised he was to discover himself already so close to home. Yesterday evening in his search he had continued along Tunali. That may have been a mistake, for he fled along a busroute. Only Esat Caddesi had the bus-stop signs. He turned now on Esat, dropped down into a glade, then up a short incline, and sooner than possible was standing at the rail looking down on the bulk of gray cement, marked with *Afyon* on the corner stone. *Afyon* — *Opium*! He recognized the word at once, the absolutely right word, so final as if it had been imprinted on his mind from childhood. By his watch it was 9:45. He had plenty of time. Timidly he descended the grade, turned in on the raised sidewalk, crossed the bridge, and walked the length of the corridor and downstairs. It had been easier than he could have believed. A long time seemed to have elapsed since yesterday morning. The nameplate *Özcan Koç* seemed like a familiar, benevolent charm. He raised his hand and gently knocked, but already knew from the silence inside that there would be no answer. He ripped a page out of his address book and wrote with trembling fingers: "Bu akşam, saat 10:30, döneceğim. Co." Tonight for sure. He had to.

He slipped the note into the crack of the door, carefully sliding it in so that only a thin edge of white was visible, not enough for a curious interloper without a key to tease it out, he made quite sure.

From the apartment house he continued down the hill, comfortably realizing how the unfamiliar streets were falling into the pattern of the city as he had already come to know it. He would never again have trouble finding Afyon Apartments.

The rest of that morning and the early afternoon were packed with classes, then lunch with Miss Ariburun the Chairman, then a long conference with a graduate student. Very bright, very pretty, Sevim Ötkunç had been three years a student of American literature at the University of Washington. She was working on Melville.

"I don't want to do the usual thing. I want to do something different than a general discussion. I would like to do a dissertation that would be original even in the United States."

"Do you have a subject?"

"Not really. I though about Starbuck. Not much seems to have been done with him. Everybody seems to dismiss him as a necessary foil for Ahab."

"Why does he try to block Ahab?"

"He's practical. He wants to get on with the business."

"Why?"

"He wants to protect the investors."

"Would you call him a good man?"

"He's a good family man. He's a good man."

"An Establishment man?"

"You mean what you were saying about the lawyer in *Bartleby*?"

"What was that?"

"A good man but not a very good man."

"Are there others?"

"You could say Captain Vere. And Captain Delano in *Benito Cereno*. They start out as Establishment men."

"Is Starbuck like that?"

"He's interested in making money."

"How does he regard the white whale?"

"Potential whale oil. Profit."

"Cash value?"

"He won't go along with Ahab."

"And how about Ishmael? At the beginning of the novel. Down at the foot of Manhattan?"

"He asks, 'Who ain't a slave?'"

They left the office in animated conversation, broken off when Miss Ötkunç said her husband was waiting for her at the bus-stop. He flushed as if he had designs on her the way some Turkish women students seem to feel about their teachers.

"Good-bye," he said, "till next week then."

"Good-bye."

He watched as she ran off.

Till then he had pushed out of his mind his morning's fatuous revisit. Saturday night and Sunday night, in a way could be excused and laid to alcohol, but not this morning. He flinched at the thought of the document in his handwriting left in the crack of the basement door. It would be wise to get it back. He went directly to the Dedeman corner and on to Afyon Sokak, then down into the apartment. Now the entrance corridor was familiar — by afternoon sunshine even ordinary. He moved aside a child's tricycle blocking the top of the stairs. Nobody was in sight, nor, at the foot of the stairs was the thin edge of paper visible in the doorcrack. Either Özcan had returned, or it had rattled out of sight. He knelt to look under, but there was no bottom crack. He was in for it. He felt bound to come back at 10:30. He considered this obligation with eager resignation.

That night he could see the light in the basement window as he approached downhill. His nerves were revved up, but he kept tight rein on his fears. Özcan flung open the door instantly when he knocked. They had goat's milk cheese, sour bread, and rakı, one small bottle of rakı for each. They ate and drank and smiled at each other. After a while they lifted the mattress onto the floor. He stayed all night. It was a good night, very active, but less brutal than Saturday. Some time after midnight they both fell asleep. At a quarter to seven an alarm clock woke them. They dressed hurriedly and walked out across the overpass into the street, then down Afyon Street to the small tobacco and food shop, where Özcan bought cigarettes and a half pint of ayran for each.

In fresh morning light Özcan looked young and renewed, his mustache black against smooth olive cheeks. He himself felt good, like thirty or thirty-five. He pushed out of his mind the instant warning how he must look, unshaven and gaunt — that whiskered gauntness after a restless night. But he didn't feel old. As they drank the rank buttermilk, they looked straight into each other's eyes and grinned. It was a good feeling, with no overtone of guilt, except that he was beginning to feel guilty for having concealed his name.

At the bottom of the hill, at the main intersection with Ataturk Boulevard, they shook hands.

"Bu akşam döneceksiniz," Özcan said. "Saat onbir." ("You will come back tonight. Eleven o'clock.")

"Evet." He did not for an instant hesitate to make the eleven o'clock appointment.

He stood for a moment watching the lithe young man deftly weave in and out of Ankara's going-to-work traffic, then he swung uphill toward home. Now that he knew the way he realized that he had been walking several blocks farther than necessary, for Esat Caddesi and Tahran Caddesi swung toward each other. He cut across the hypoteneuse of their triangle and reached home in no time. This morning, however, unlike Sunday, it was late enough so that his landlord could think he had just got in from an early morning stroll.

That night and every night that week he returned to Özcan to spend all night. Twice he told Özcan in the morning that he could not come that evening; both times he returned in the afternoon and tucked notes under the door saying that he would come, signing the notes, "Co Squires."

On Saturday morning they slept till 8:00, lying till the sun rays came through the high, small window to fall where they lay naked on the bed covered with rather dirty bedclothes, a bottom sheet and a rough wool blanket. He woke to the smell of a cigarette. He could see the shadowed arc of Özcan's arm as he brought the cylinder to his lips. He was lying on his back nearly out from under the blanket, his sex retracted into an impossibly-small, really ridiculous, tiny rosebud in a nest of curled black hairs. Under his scrutiny — as if responding to his gaze, though more likely quite involuntarily of their own will, the balls under the retracted cock began to coil and uncoil, coil and uncoil, Joyce's "scrotum-tightening." Then the cock began to fill out, growing plump first in the middle, then at the tip, till the cherry hung engorged below the still-swelling stem, which completed its enlargement and jumped straight uplifted, hard and erect throughout its length. Without moving his hands, eyes fixed on the firm erection, he began slowly to pivot his head till he could stick out his tongue and with tongue-tip barely touch the cock-tip, which quivered, sprang out of reach, then snapped back where he could reach it with his tongue. For some minutes he tantalized the tip, watching it jump, return and jump again.

Then he pivoted still further, opened his mouth, and took in the hard ball of the tip, while Özcan, jacking his knees, grasped in both hands the ministering head and pushed down until the rapacious mouth took in the whole hard length, stretched lips thrust firm against the balls. Gasping, he withdrew, then blew his breath into the pipe stem and felt it swell and then deflate when he sucked in. A thin, salty juice began to flow.

He held his mouth open but firm while Özcan grasped him by the hair and pumped his head slowly up and down. Even without foreskin the cock's skin-covering slid easily outside the hard muscle engorged with blood. Intoxicated, almost delirious, he could feel the large bulbous tip slide back and forth, touching his teeth then plunging into the gorge of his throat where it filled the narrow chamber and swelled against his glands. His own sex began to swell, and he reached and found Özcan's left hand and guided it till it began to play with his cock and balls, while he continued to unfold, opening more and more to the firm pumping of the obedient hand, efficiently thumping the cock in rhythm with the other hand which pumped the pliant head.

Top and bottom, he was totally engaged, his mouth pushed against Özcan's balls exactly when the cupped hand sank full length against his own tight scrotum. His head was pressed in there and held; his cock was drawn up there and held. As his mouth tightened, Özcan's fingers tightened. The rhythm continued for a long time steadily, then the hands began to move imperceptively faster till they were beating a fast time, and then at last they were flying, both cocks pushed and pushing to their hilts. Over and beyond the brink of resistance, he felt his tension empty into Özcan's pumping hand at the same time his mouth was filling with the gushing flow. Now, all motion halted, they lay against each other, suspended in post-ejaculation limbo.

Saturday morning as it was, they need not hurry to work. They lay at rest until, finally, Özcan got up, naked still, unlocked the door, and leaving it partway open padded to the smelly hole-in-the-wall toilet under the stairs. It was not considerate of him to leave the door so wide that anybody passing could have seen the naked visitor on the mattress on the floor. Even when he pulled the bedclothes over him, he felt exposed.

Nevertheless, he was too infatuated to be more than superficially annoyed. When Özcan came back from the toilet he was going to find some way to turn the conversation to an excuse to give his true name. He had not expected in Ankara to afford the luxury of falling in love for keeps. No more than a baffled suspicion rankled his euphoria.

LYLE GLAZIER lives in Vermont. He writes: "I have published five books of poems, a book of criticism on the American novel; and three chapters of my novel *Stills from a Moving Picture* made up the Sept. 1974 issue of *Paunch* Magazine. Since 1971 (with my book of poems *VD*) I have devoted myself to telling as honestly and as vividly as possible what it has meant to be a married homosexual, out of the closet since 1956."

"A DRAW"
A Short Story
by
Paul Verlaine

Translated from French by W. Gunn

From 1888 through 1891 the French poet Paul Verlaine (1844-1896) — for the first time since his ill-fated (but poetically productive) association with Arthur Rimbaud — began actively to explore gay themes in poetry and in fiction. The verbally "decent" poems appeared in his volume *Parallèlement* (Paris, 1889; 2nd ed., 1894); the erotic ones were published posthumously in *Hombres* (Brussels, 1904). A short story, "Charles Husson," came out in *La Revue indépendante* in December 1888. A longer version, which restored some long descriptive passages cut by the magazine and which was retitled "Rampo" (more properly *rampeau*, the name of a card game), was collected in Volume 1 of the *Oeuvres posthumes* (Paris, 1929).

It is this version that is here translated, for the first time in English, by one of the two translators of the Rimbaud-Verlaine collection, *A Lover's Cock and Other Gay Poems,* brought out by the Gay Sunshine Press in 1979.

Charles Husson was truly a lad made for love, potent in every way. He had a manly though childlike face, all round and pink, showing not a sign of puffiness and only a hint of light down over his soft red, almost babyish lips; large and very sweet blue-green eyes, moist like the small adorable mouth; trim, light golden sideburns, or rather ringlets such as one sees in Imperial French paintings of Ascanius and Endymion; and darker hair, worn short and curling. His nose was not striking but was well-turned and flaring at the nostrils; and his chin was in proportion to the rest of that harmonious face, although a certain indolence, even weakness, there betrayed a lack of control in sensual matters. His body was simply superb: lithe but sturdy, with strong shoulders and neck; a rather ordinary chest that was more than compensated for by the rounded hips; well-formed, muscular legs; and elegant, firmly-planted feet. "This majestic carriage, this sweet presence," to which should be added a rather deep voice, though one with sometimes strikingly feminine intonations, had made Charles Husson the best liked of the Maubert Place pimps.

Son of a sheepherder and a sheepherder himself from his childhood until he was fifteen, he had then become a farmhand — and being a peasant had been an excellent preparation for his present occupation. His passionate nature, so immediately evident, that had led him into all sorts of grevious imprudences, as well as beautiful actions, had been happily tempered by his sparse upbringing, by the wariness that is natural to these rustics, so that his genuine spirit and eagerness for all the limited pleasures then available to him had been restrained.

He had left his family as a soldier might desert his regiment. His destination had been Paris, neither whose language nor whose customs he in the least understood. Therefore, having to live on his good looks, he had at once fallen to pimping, and because he was as strong as he was handsome, he had become formidable and hence loved by his women.

This description, although undoubtedly over long, does prepare for the events we are about to witness.

Among those girls from whom Charles Husson harvested the scraps of their youth — not counting, let it be said, numerous "victims" whose more or less childish virginity he would take from time to time — was found one called Marinette (just like in Molière and Théodore de Banville), a lovely piece very much at home in that world.

The fashion, then as always, was to be lower than you could imagine. Charles was even lower than was usual in that world in which his good looks had thrown him. Marinette was not a nice girl either: rather say, an adorable girl, a charming girl, a sweet girl, or a kind girl — and always a dear child with whom Charles was madly in love.

The prettiness of the creature may excuse somewhat the noncommercial weakness thus shown by this trafficker of sexual charms.

Small, especially in comparison with him, dainty as he was robust, she contrasted with him in a most harmonious way. She was slender rather than plump, though you would be hard pressed to say why the one and not the other; quite dark, with relatively short hair worn either tousled in the prettiest way imaginable or combed back, according to the dictates of the morning or evening mirror; small, shining, almost slanted eyes; a cute pug nose, though perhaps a trifle too wide; a generous mouth showing large, gleaming white teeth when she smiled; lips naturally wet and red, over which she often flickered, apparently without thinking, the tip of her pink tongue. There were a short chin over an equally short neck, all creamy rose and satin; full breasts thrust forward; and a flat stomach behind the usual tight sweaters of her trade. Her clinging skirts would hug her legs as she moved, promising such a wealth of quivering treasures that it drove the handsome Charles quite mad — and often made him jealous. Her voice was charming, silver rather than golden in tone because of a slight huskiness caused by all the liquor she would drink and that could but tarnish it: a voice both ingratiating and insidious, and truly childlike with the velvet tones of a virgin at puberty (because the voice has its moment of puberty just like the sex).

In a word, she was a delicious, irresistible chiseler, a person whose exceedingly amourous nature alone had prevented her success, economically speaking — as well as her taste for riffraff, a desire that not even the greatest or the purest, however, can always stifle.

In these circumstances Charles was lost, and from simple villainy he soon tumbled headlong to thievery and even murder. Association with rabble, sporting and drinking companions, and complicity in every type of prostitution groomed this good shepherd, this solitary and comtemplative soul, to Parisian sophistication.

Now one day at a house kept by a rather wealthy wine merchant, a person popular with people whose reputations were not all that good, it happened that Marinette poured a bit too much to drink for a certain gentleman, one sporting a top hat, a white dicky, a high winged collar, and pointed boots that buttoned up the sides. Just at the monent that a draw had occurred in a card game, the girl leaned on the gentleman's shoulders and, playing with his ear, said: "You're a man of spirit. Distinguished looking. I could go for you. But . . ."

"But what?"

"Will you go upstairs?"

"Where?"

"To my room. . . ."

"Oh. To your room?"

"It's only a step or two from here."

"No. No thanks," concluded the man, uneasily sobering up.

It was then that Charles stepped in. He intervened in a gracious, almost docile manner, and using his most flute-like, most veiled tones, that contralto's voice of his, he asked: "What's going on, Marinette? Is this gentleman . . .?"

"*This gentleman,* my friend, does not want to go upstairs with your lady," the gentleman replied dryly.

"Tough luck for her, then. . . . But you will at least buy us a glass? Perhaps have a game of cards?"

They played cards. Again there was a draw. Marinette exclaimed, "A draw. . . ." The gentleman showed by a gesture that he was absolutely finished with any talk with her, and having paid for the drinks, he turned to go.

Charles Husson's dress was in decided contrast with his neighbor's; he was even wearing a béret and slippers. But with style, in a most roguish manner, he threw his hand on the other's shoulders. The gentleman, apparently thinking it had been placed there with hostile intentions, turned furiously and a little afraid. But facing Charles's quiet, dazzling beauty, he instead winked and indicated the stairs, whispering, "Let's go up."

Making an imperious sign, Charles commanded the woman to keep out of it, and the two went upstairs.

Marinette waxed white and then red with rage. Shaken with hysterical jealousy, she spat out: "Bastard! Fairy! Old queen! You won't get away with this, you pig." And with some ill-defined vengeance in mind, the prostitute left.

Outside, she ran to a nearby bakery's window, where she proceeded swiftly to repair the damages the scene had caused her face with powder and the sweep of a comb through her hair. At the very moment bootheels rang out in the foggy night to announce the passage of a policeman. As he drew beside her, she gave a cry: "Hey! Anatole." She grabbed him by the arm and told him everything, unwinding with a feminine volubility marked by a sort of reserve and dignity of her kind, but to which the sergeant only responded:

"First of all, my beauty, I'm not on duty. And even if I were, what could I do? They're not doing it in the street. There's no scandal."

But the woman demanded vengeance.

Vengeance! The word is not a refined one for her type. Of course, why should she be jealous, she who knew so much, this wretched accomplice in all of Charles's vices and crimes, just because he was engaged in sex also — as much for the money in it, alas, as for the pleasure? What kind of modesty, of honest lust, had bitten her this evening? It's a mystery into which all women sooner or later fall. And unfortunately that's all the moralist, for want of anything better, can say.

Then in an overwhelming, London-like fog, which had suddenly fallen to blot out and protect all felonies and misdemeanors in our City of Light, these two made for a shaded lamp that indicated another similar house. They in turn climbed the stairs, this cop off duty and the girl of the night, but with the approval of society, knowing full well what was going to come.

And thus once more morality was saved, the Law remained strong, and . . .

TOM THOMPSO

SEX STORY

(from *Elements of a Coffee Service*)
by
Robert Glück

Brian undid the buttons of my levis one by one, pulled down my pants and Egyptian red cotton briefs, white skin and then my cock springs back from the elastic — "hello old timer." A disappointing moment when possibilities are resolved and attention localized, however good it's going to be. So it's going to be a blow job — that's nice. So it's going to be sex — nice, but less than the world. That blow job defined the situation, then a predictable untangling of arms and legs and stripping off shoes and clothes, my jeans, his corduroys, lighting sand candles, putting on records, closing straw blinds, turning back sheets, turning off lights. Brian has a way of being naked a few minutes at a distance — he politely averts his eyes so I can study him unselfconsciously.

"From his small tough ears, his thick neck came down to his shoulders in a long wide column of muscles and cords that attached like artwork to a widened 'V' of his clavicle, pointing the way to his broad, almost football padded shoulders and then down to those muscular arms, covered with blond hair. The tits were firm, and never jiggled, though the nipples were almost the size of a woman's, and seemed always to be in a state of excitement. A light patch of blond hair was growing like a wedge between them, and a long racing stripe of blond hair led the eye down over the contour of his rippling stomach muscles, past the hard navel, and streamlined down to a patch of only slightly darker pubic hair. There, in all its magnificence hung the 'Dong'. Its wide column of flesh arched out slightly from his body, curving out and downwards in its solidness to the pointing tip of its foreskin where the flesh parted slightly exposing the tip of a rosebud cockhead. The width of the big cock only partially hid a ripe big sack behind it, where two spheric globes of his balls swelled out on either side of it. The cock hung down freely, without the slightest sign of sexual arousal, and still it spanned downward a full third of the boy's young strong legs.

" 'Turn around slowly,' Cliff said to Rags, unbuttoning his own shirt and pulling it back off his torso . . ."

That was from *Fresh From the Farm* by Billy Farout, pps. 20-21. I want to write about sex: good sex without boasting, descriptive without looking like plumbing, happy, avoiding the LaBrea Tar Pits of lyricism. Brian is also golden, with a body for clothes, square shoulders, then nothing but the essentials decked out with some light and pleasant musculature. He carries his shoulders a little hunched — the world might hit him on the head — which goes with a determined niceness that can become a little grim, like taking the bus to the LA airport to meet me. But if he has his blind spots, Bruce, Kathy, Denise and I said philosophically in various combinations over cups of coffee —

well, who doesn't. It's that this one doesn't correspond to ours. Five years ago Brian painted a picture of a house and had many delusions about it. Finally he went to live in the relative safety of its rooms. I can understand that. Brian looks like anyone. Rags looks like no one, he's an alluring nightmare that reduces the world to rubble. Really, I could never grasp Brian's looks, a quality I admire. When I understand his face, solve it into planes and volumes, factor in blond hair and green eyes, then he turns his head a little, the essential eludes me and I must start all over. Sometimes he's intact as a fashion model exuding sunlight. Sometimes he's a fetus, big unfortunate eyes and a mouth pulled down, no language there, his fingers and toes waiting to be counted.

I knelt and returned his blow job, his body tensed toward me, his cock grew in my mouth according to his heartbeat, each pulse a qualification that sent me backwards to accept more. I was not completely in favor of his cock — it seemed indecisive — but he didn't care about it either. When I complimented him — "the fineness of its shape" — he shrugged and the compliment didn't register. It was his ass — full and generous — that we concentrated on.

He more or less pushed me onto the bed and tumbled after me, raising our exchange a level by blowing me while looking into my eyes. I'm giving you pleasure and looking at you, keeping you focused. You're acknowledging that. There's no way to dismiss this by saying you're lost in a trance, by pretending you are not you. Still, I make up an escape clause — I say: I put myself entirely in your hands, and what I know you desire is to put yourself in mine, so that I demand what I know you want me to want. I stood and commanded him to blow me, to do this and that: crawl behind and rim me while I masturbate myself. Brian replied, "As James Bond used to say, 'There's no mistaking that invitation'." A tongue in your ass is more intimate than a cock anywhere; I receive the sensation inside my groin, in my knees and nipples and wrists. Now this was like a porno movie, or the sex ads in the gay newspapers:

Top (Father, Cowboy, Coach, Cop) wants Bottom (Your prisoner and toy) — and conversely. 29-34? Small waist, W/M, Fr a/p, Delicious tongue worship your endw. Lean back & watch yr hot rod get super done, Sir. Don't any of you with long poles want to be shucked down and get some down-home Fr.? EXHIBITIONISM, j/o, facesitting, Close Encounters in Venice.

What made it sexy? Probably the posture that isolated sex, isolated fantasy. He blew me and I took one step backward. He murmured, loving to crawl forward. The gesture, economical and elegant as a hawk's wing, pointed toward a vista that was not geographical.

I lifted him and we kissed passionately, our first real kissing filled with deep tongues and assy fragrance, running my tongue over his lips, each tooth defined by a tongue, our saliva tastes the same, he played with our cocks and I carried him to the — no, first he knelt and licked me, licked my feet and legs, tongued between my toes. "I don't like pain but I don't mind a good spanking." I obliged, spanking him on one cheek, then the other, while he blew me and masturbated himself. Then I had to piss and Brian made coffee. What if friendship and love are extras tagged onto sexuality to give it a margin of safety, of usefulness based on repressive goals, and the relations between subject and object, usually dismissed as a set of perversions, were the heart of sex? Brian slipped into the bathroom while I was thinking and pissing. To my surprise, he knelt and drank some of it, looking at me. I wonder what I'm getting into, I said to myself, getting into it.

Still in the bathroom: "I sit on your lap and you talk to me like a father." What if desire and power take the form of "Law" as we experience it, whether as the "father" or the "cop." "Have you been a good boy?" "I have a special treat for you." "Are you going to do a good job of it?" Whispered while tonguing his ear and raining kisses on his neck and cheek, all the language of blackmail and instrumentality, its context shifted to pleasure. These few phrases established father and son, where desire is accumulated and forbidden, yet we remained animals exploring pleasure, testing the prostate with inserted forefingers up to the first and second knuckle, learning by heart each other's cocks better than our own, needing to touch all his skin at once, the tonguing of nipples until erect and then little bites accepted resistingly, tongue around the ears inside the head, his curls of blond hair a county line for a tongue going out of town, down the backbone, pause, into the crack, pause, testing the asshole — clean as a whistle, tidy boy — tapping with the slightest pressure, knocking again and again to produce a moan, the straining backward, the gasp of a penetration.

That got old and the kettle whistled. We settled back in bed with the coffee. There was no way around it, he loved me. It was plain to see in his melting eyes. More, in the steadiness of his melting gaze: he made me more naked than without clothes. I hadn't been loved that way for years. Brian loved me quickly and thoroughly, without a credit check on my personality. I felt abashed.

Responding to my thought, he told me the story of his falling in love:

Brian and two women friends traveled from LA to San Francisco to spend Halloween with me. Brian wanted us to portray Earth, Wind, Fire and Water, and accordingly made costumes and masks which he brought along. I forget which was mine but I rebelled when I saw the scanty muslin togas. "I'll make my own costume," I said, and so we went as Earth, Fire, Water, and a Bumble Bee. I drank — scared and belligerent, a blur of emotions. In a bar: "I'm a BUMBLE BEE, asshole." We returned home, the scenario indicated passionate happy love-making for hours and hours. I dreaded it. Instead I drank a half pint of brandy on top of the evening's beverages. That was October. I hadn't divested myself of the summer's construction project in LA, an escalating nightmare of fraud and anxiety. Ed and I formally separated in June. I desired him in the same way that I still require a cigarette, a physical call. I hardly drink, I never drank. Depressed, I ate Viennese pastry. Ed said he knew when I was upset because I left doilies around the kitchen.

I drank myself into a crying jag. I peeled off my sweaty cigarette smelling Bumble Bee outfit and cried on Brian's hot skin for hours. Sometimes I paused, then a stronger wave would submerge me and carry me up. Crescendo. The pain registered as isolation. My body really hurt, my skin hurt, so I decided I'd better eat bread to absorb the alcohol. Besides, crying had made me claustrophobic. It was five in the morning. I got up feeling like Monday's wash, put on one of my abject t-shirts and sat down in the kitchen, wearily sniveling and cramming saltines down my throat. "And that," says Brian, "is when I fell in love with you."

We were on our sides more or less tangled up. His free hand meditated on the slimness of my waist, the power of my shoulders and chest. I basked in his general radiance. I loved his waist and the gold of his skin, I wanted to fold myself into it. Then he slid down and kissed my cock the way you kiss lips. He said, "I love your cock." He said it with more fervor than customarily applied to a sweet nothing, and so lapidary that I assured myself I would remember it during that amount of "forever" which is to be my portion. I've been reading Jane Austen. He said it to my cock's face, and I thought Oedipally, "A face a mother could love." "How's your mother?" And "How's her emerald collection?" I liked to hear him recite her stones. I think Brian felt he betrayed her a little, that my eagerness and the question itself was not in the best taste. "Gimme a break," he would say. And here I am justifying his fears. But really I viewed her collection as a victory, a personal domain wrested from so much that was not hers. I liked its lack of utility and sexual shimmer. I liked the war, complete with siege, ground strategy and storming the fort, that each piece represented. It was an Aladdin's hoard, not an investment. She had 1) A diamond and emerald bracelet, groups of four each alternating around. 2) A diamond ring that Brian says doubles as a veg-a-matic. 3) A diamond and gold broach set on an inch-wide gold bracelet (Brian's favorite). 4 & 5) Two pairs of diamond and emerald clips. 6) An emerald broach, geometric design within a rectangle. 7) Many pearls. 8) A large emerald ring. Plus opals and a few token stones.

She has a few things, is she ruling class? A question at this point is a double one: Who stands to gain what? Brian's mother merely angles back a little of her own power in the going currency of charm and attractiveness. She's not the Enemy.

I met the enemy at a gay resort in Russian River. It felt strange to be there, surrounded by money and its attendant — available and well groomed flesh. Until that day I spent my vacation at a small neighborhood beach where nakedness was not so much a declaration. That beach had a special attraction for me. Next to a little island there was a small rapids with an island tree overhanging it, and someone had tied a rope around a branch. A person could grab hold of the rope and be carried up by the water. Buoyed up like that, if I submerged my head a giant roaring surrounded me. It was so pleasurable I could endure it only a few minutes. I was bored, alone, diffused, there was no ground to be me pursuing my aims, no margin for the anxiety of perspective, resolution into categories. Gradually I spent more time dangling from that rope, finally I tied myself to it although I feared drowning. What a pleasurable agony each moment is as it dilapidates into the next. The water rushed, brought my body to a point, it felt good.

My friend Sterling came up from San Francisco and stayed at a resort, which is how I found myself lying nakedly with him beside a swimming pool, along with fifty other men. We looked like a David Hockney that had gotten out of hand. The sun was spinning ribbons in the water and also cooking about eight thousand pounds of shellacked gay flesh. Sterling introduced me to suntan oil. His friend, Tom, the enemy I mentioned before, had just joined us. We repositioned ourselves to the full sun. I was on my stomach, drowsy, and Sterling absentmindedly put his hand on my left asscheek, he put his hand on my ass, he put his hand on my ass and he kept it there, he kept it there, I didn't move a muscle and basked in his hand more than in the sun, pleasure spread to the back of my legs, my lower back and my nipples, not a muscle, he'd think I was uncomfortable, his hand was hotter than the sun on my other cheek, somebody said, "Bob's got an ass like peaches." Sterling, who's black, said, "Not that much color." I suggested wintermelons. "What?" said Sterling. "Wintermelons." "What did Bob say?" asked Tom. "He said 'wintermelons'," Sterling answered.

Tom was gazing abstractly down at his unformulated body, master of all he surveyed. The afternoon passed and much conversation got said and forgotten, but information about his wealth gathered like nuggets or like objets d'art set mentally side by side on a mantle. Instead of ormalu clocks and Chinese epergnes, I counted three houses — mansions — in San Antonio, a farm in upstate New York, two houses in Florida, a ranch in the Panhandle, three houses in San Francisco, and condos in New York City and Palm Springs. These were his proud investments, he'd made this million on his own, not resting on the laurels of his inherited millions from Gulf Oil. Answering me, he said, "My watch cost $8,000, look, it's a twenty dollar gold piece with a diamond nob, set in a gold case."

Tom furnished much food for thought. It shocked me that he was so undefined. At thirty he still had his baby fat, aimless good will, he wore the most conventional plastic leather outfits. Never in his life had he voluntarily read anything more detaining than a magazine. Was *this* the pomeranian Earl of Rochester, his overbright eyes leering subnormally under his peruke? I expected manners, Jane Austen, nice debates as to who takes precedence at dinner, fine points. How else do you know you're different from the servants? — and the people who run your farms and rent your apartments? When I returned from the toilet he joked, "Did everything come out all right?" And later he asked it *again*!

How could all that wealth be condensed in this fatuous presence? The answer: it wasn't. The wealth stayed where it was, intangible. Maybe Tom's character grew vague by way of response. Tom doesn't live on top of his servants, his property remains as abstract as the money it equals. Even the fifty Persian carpets he treasures wait in constant breathless readiness to be traded or sold. So manners might be beside the point, the tweed and horses of his seniors a tip of the hat to feudal wealth. But how can I attack Tom's life and still defend his sexuality? When Sterling, Tom and I walked back to my car we passed a bunch of "youths" whiling away the day lounging on their pick-ups, and despite Tom's bank account they started yelling: Death to Faggots, Get Outta Town, Kill Queers, etc.

Tom became vivid for me in one passage that afternoon. Is it surprising that the medium of his transformation should be pleasure? We were cooling off in the shallow end, watching the suntan oil slick make marbled paper patterns on the pool's surface. We acknowledged a passing physique, a body that summed up what's happening these days. Tom attempted a joke about fist-fucking that included a reference to a subway entrance. I said that I could understand the erotic charge of bondage and discipline, of water sports, and so on, but I could never grasp fist-fucking's sensuality. Was it homage to the fist and arm, that masculine power engaged, taken on because inside you? Tom responded with patience and expertise, accustomed to making things clear to laymen. He said that most fist-fucking is beside the point because it stops at what he called the trap. I think that's a plumbing term. He said that the colon makes a right-hand turn and then loops up all the way to the diaphragm. He drew the arch on my torso with his forefinger. If you negotiate that turn and forge ahead, your hand is a membrane away from the heart, in fact you can actually hold your lover's beating heart. More than that, after a while your two hearts establish a rapport, beat together, and what physical intimacy could exist beyond this?

I was a little stunned. Until then, being naked, I felt naked. Facing this vista of further nakedness, I felt as dressed and encumbered as a Victorian parlor.

I joined Sterling; I lay down on an orange plastic cot and dozed. Troubling images: We're on top of a pyramid. The Aztec priest holds a stone knife in one hand and in the other he lifts the still beating heart above its former home, the naked warrior, whose lower back balances on a phallic sacrificial stone. He's held by half-naked priests at the hands and feet, his body still spasming and arching. That from the 8th grade. There were no undressed white people in my textbook. The compilers felt that Indians, like animals, did not possess enough being to be capable of nakedness. If I were that picture everyone's cock would be hard as the stone knife.

And this from Anne Rice's *Interview with a Vampire*: "Never had I felt this, never had I experienced it, this yielding of a conscious mortal. But before I could push him away for his own sake, I saw the bluish bruise on his tender neck. He was offering it to me. He was pressing the length of his body against me now, and I felt the hard strength of his sex beneath his clothes pressing against my leg. A wretched gasp escaped my lips, but his bent close, his lips on what must have been so cold, so lifeless to him; and I sank my teeth into his skin, my body rigid, that hard sex driving against me, and I lifted him in passion off the floor. Wave after wave of his beating heart passed into me as, weightless, I rocked with him, devouring him, his ecstasy, his conscious pleasure."

The vampire's erotic charge consists of just this meeting of heartbeats, yet our hero consumes the life he is experiencing. Rice weaves homosexuality into vampire society, does she think it will make the dead deader? "The pleasures of the *damned*," "the *pleasures* of the damned"; in *Carmilla*, once LeFanu underscores his vampire's grief, you are free to enjoy by proxy her lesbian embrace: "She used to place her pretty arms about my neck, draw me to her, and laying her cheek to mine, murmur with her lips near my ear, 'Dearest, your little heart is wounded; think me not cruel because I obey the irresistible law of my strength and weakness; if your dear heart is wounded, my wild heart bleeds with yours. In the rapture of my enormous humiliation. . . . ' "

So death accompanies this heart-stuff. And some would say, do say, that Tom's journey through the anus is a trip to the underworld. Yet this is all very far from the harmony of Tom's description, far from the particular realm of pleasure that expresses the urge to be radically naked. Tom isn't dead, neither are his partners. The construction on their pleasure comes later. As Tom and his friend get dressed, culture, ideology and conflict all enter simultaneously, telling us we are supposed to be alone, discontinuous. We experience this as safety. We experience as transgression the penetration of our boundaries, fusion with another, and they warn us that this transgression is fearful as death. Naturally the vampire always wears a criminal half-smile. This guilt, even if slightly embraced, even if an inch stepped toward, becomes a sexual apparatus, increasing the pleasure it decreased, a second ego becoming its own opposite.

I woke up on the plastic cot in the sunlight and shade, looking at a grid of sun the cot stenciled on the cement, thinking over and over *Orfeo ed Euridice, Orfeo ed Euridice*. I forgot who I was, the music and sunlight seemed realer. It was not a Freudian pun on the composer's name, nor — I think — the trip through hell motif. Not even the "Dance of the Furies," to which I did my sit-ups every morning. It was the following band I recalled, "The Dance of the Blessed Spirits," so limpid and noble that I would lie back exhausted and just float. Sterling was by my side, the rest of the pool area was mostly deserted. Then Sterling told me a story about his mother which reminded me of

Brian's mother and her emeralds. While Brian's mother operated in that middle-class locus of power, the parents' bedroom, Sterling's mother went outside of the house, changing the terms. Sterling grew up in San Antonio where his father, a gambler, also named Sterling, had married in his forties a woman twenty years younger. Along with other business ventures, Sterling Sr. ran a "buffet flat." He usually had a mistress, but age brought respectability, and now he confines himself to real estate and Adele. Sterling recalls only one fight from his childhood. He can't remember why, but Sterling Sr. slapped his mother. They were in the kitchen, Adele stood in front of a stove filled with a complicated Sunday dinner. She yelled, "You want a fight Motherfucker? I'll give you a fight!" — and she systematically threw at her husband: muffins, potatoes, roast, salad, peas, collard greens, gravy and peach pie. Sterling Sr. stood uncertainly for a moment, weighing the merits of an advance. Finally he broke for the front door, followed by Adele. She continued throwing the household at him, including, Sterling said with a pang, a cranberry glass lamp with lusters. Sterling Sr. jumped in his car and started to pull away, but Adele got a gun and blew out his tires. He skidded to a service station, changed tires, and spent a few days in Dallas. This affair triggered in Sterling's mom a meditation; its theme was power and it signalled a change in her relations with Sterling Sr. At that time she worked for a travel agency. Her employers, an alcoholic white couple with liberal views, absconded to Mexico with the advance receipts for a tour of the Holy Land, leaving the agency more or less to Adele. She moved it to the black section of San Antonio and became financially independent. On one of her guided tours of Los Angeles she acquired a lover, they met there for years. All this strengthened her marriage. The two went past the inspirational bitterness of events to the events themselves, and now they are enjoying their sunset years, closer than ever.

"What's a buffet flat?"

It's a railroad flat, a long maroon hallway with many rooms, one room had two men doing it, another had two women doing it, and really each room had anyone with anyone, doing it. It's a sexual buffet. You paid an entrance fee to watch or act. I like the town meeting aspect of this. Also there were stars whom the audience egged on, 1910 — big hats and skirts — or the twenties, a little tunic of dark spangles. Against that antique clothing nakedness becomes more naked.

What if I am a black woman who propositions one of these talented big fish. What a smile I'm capable of, I flash him one of these. I'm wearing a black beaded tunic I mentally refer to as my star-spangled night and the streets aren't paved. Want some tequila? Just a splash. What if we're naked together, clothes tossed over a chair and he only fucks me in the missionary position. What if I ask after a while if that's all.

What if he says, "Baby, I'm just warming up, just giving you a taste." I am the bottom man and this river is the top man, lithe and muscular with two handfuls of flesh. I am a bottom, the person who really controls is the bottom and sex is the top and I arrange for it to take my streaming body and clear me of names and express me and bring me to a point. This is pleasure and I'm no fool.

*

Brian said, "Jackie Kennedy made the pillbox hat famous. She made Halston famous, she made sleeveless dresses famous, she made Valentino famous. She made Gucci famous." "Thrilling words," I said, "I can only add that the discovery of the individual was made in early 15th century Florence. Nothing can alter that fact, don't you think that's interesting? I do." Brian laughed at me and asked conversationally, "Don't you think your cock is more interesting?" I thought it was a likely topic and finished my coffee. "Or am I putting words in your mouth?" he continued, taking my cock in his mouth and laying his head in my lap, still looking up at my face. I replied. "I reckon I'll just kick back and get me some old fashioned, down home French." Brian looked like a fetus. Then he sat up and said, "We boys in the back room voted you Mr. Congeniality." "What makes me a great catch?" I asked falling into his arms so he'd have to catch me. "Looking for compliments?" "I just want to see if our lists tally." Then, seriously, "You know, I have a very beautiful couch." By way of response Brian tickled me, which escalated into wrestling. I lost because I wanted to see what he would do with an immobilized me. He held me down and started licking my torso while I mock resisted even though I was hard. "Want a frozen Reese's Peanut Butter Cup?" he asked my extravagantly arching neck. I pictured them stacked neatly in his freezer. Coffee, Kools and peanut butter cups were Brian's staff of life. I followed him into the kitchen, past his new room arrangement that I had just admired upside down through the bedroom door.

Brian lived in a bungalow in Venice, CA — a bedroom, living room and kitchen. He furnished the living room with a mattress, a box spring, a large palm, a poster-size print of a sepia photograph of women in long skirts carrying rifles in the Mexican Revolution, and another poster of a Hiroshige wood block print (36 Views of . . .). The room was spotless and these five elements constantly found new spacial relationships. I followed him: a small deco kitchen with a total of four dishes, three cups, two one quart stainless steel saucepans, mismatched flatware for two and a half, and a knife. I liked the cups, Mexican enamel with a decal of an innocent nosegay.

We stood in the dark kitchen kissing. That got old. He wanted to sit on my lap. I was so aroused I was wide open. We mutual masturbated like that and kissed, I was gasping. I caught our reflection in the window and it was funny to see us so localized inside these giant sensations of pleasure, my hips and muscles permanently cocked.

That got old so I carried him to the kitchen table where he squatted like a frog and I fucked him. My own body knows what his experienced: each time my cock touched a certain point, hot and icy shivers radiated outward. I burn and freeze. If you have a man's body that is what you would feel. A cock's pleasure is like a fist, concentrated; anal pleasure is diffused, an open palm, and the pleasure of an anal orgasm is founded on relaxation. It's hard to understand how a man can write well if he doesn't like to be fucked. There's no evidence to support this theory. Still, you can't be so straight that you don't want to please. Pound claimed his poetry was a penis aimed at the passive vulva of London. Perhaps that's why his writing is so worried, brow-furrowed. We dallied with coming for a while but decided no. Brian loved to be carried and pleasure made me powerful, sent blood to my muscles and aligned them. I lifted him from the table and fucked him in the air.

It was great sex, not because of the acrobatics, not even because he loved me and showed it and showed it, but because we were both there, very much of us, two people instead of two porno-movie fragments. Brian knelt in front of me, sucking the cock that fucked him. That's one — among many — things I wouldn't do. Don't do too often. It's not so bad, still, all I think is now I'm doing this and what disease will I get. I quickly brush the cock with my hand like kids sharing a bottle of coke, certain that no germs are killed, just so something besides my lips touches it first. I admired Brian's range and mobility, his sexuality makes little concession to the world. I compared him favorably with myself. Brian is more sexually alive than anyone I know, a shower of sparks spills off his skin like inside a foundry. I'm a little more cautious, a little less generous. Let's say I had to avert my eyes.

I had to piss, Brian smiled, I laughed — a light went on about all the coffee he kept feeding me. Ed, whose dream life still seems definitive, described pissing into epic Busby Berkley waterfall fantasies, erotic masterpieces of technical know-how. I presented to Brian the difficulty of pissing when hard, but in the spirit of the great director he assured me that when there's a will there's a way. All the same, these particular golden showers were intermittent. Kneeling, he put his head between my legs — I piss on his back, then slowly in his mouth. Because the temperature was all the same I couldn't tell what was cock, mouth or urine, like pissing in a lake, just feeling warmth and a pressure outward. I envied Brian the clarity of his position.

Not sex, but my concern for you makes this story vulgar. You see I named it before you could. Brian and I were both so powerful, admiring each other's power. Surely power and sexuality seek each other out, even if ultimately they are held in a suspension. But our force was opposite to the kind that oppresses and controls, so it engendered permissiveness and generosity. Like the strategies of the two mothers who wanted to reclaim their lives: on the one hand, power lies in understanding the given terms and using them as leverage; on the other hand, power changes the terms. In literature the former is "technique" — I want to create beautiful things (precious stones); the latter, "tactics" — I want a dynamic relation with my audience (my husband).

I scooped Brian up, kissed him and carried him back to bed, He asked me if I'd like to hear about his confinement in a mental institution. He asked so politely that I understood he wanted to tell me about it: "You have to understand I repeated the story about 498 times during the first two days — doctors are even more curious than *you* — but I'll try to make it fresh." (It's true he talked as though he were composing a letter.) He started, "Well, Bobbo, it's like this:

"I'd been whittling my life down so that smoking a cigarette became an actual activity. I just broke up with a boy named Aaron who lived about three blocks away. I used to visit him in his new apartment and model for a painting called *The Junkie*. It showed me sitting in a pile of garbage with a needle in my arm."

"You sat there with a needle in your arm?"

"After I went nuts, Aaron told me he never found anyone who could hold the pose as long. I was taking a 'visual perception' course taught by a woman named Edith Hammer. She was a great teacher. She'd show different works from different times and compare their visual components. After my second class I had an acute guilt attack, rushed to an art supply store and bought a large square canvas, paints and brushes. I rushed home to the apartment I had shared with Aaron but now occupied alone, and started painting.

At first the idea seemed lyrical and intelligent: to make a cross-section of reality in the form of a house."

"Sounds like an idea to me. Meaning and Safety."

"The windows were shaped like coffins and corresponded to gravestones above. The windows opened on a blank horizon. Above was a cemetery scene modeled after a story from my mother's childhood. It showed my grandmother and my aunt sitting under a tree, my mother as a child running to them and my uncle as a baby who watched the whole thing from behind the tree. It was done in mottled brilliant colors and I was very excited about it.

I would wake up every morning and 'see' something else and keep working, drawn deeper into it. I saw duality in everything; the painting helped me break down reality into its basic components and I thought if I saw past the duality I'd get to the nitty-gritty. Meanwhile it was getting a little scary. I titled the painting, *The Conception and Evolution of Brainchild's Unity Theorem*, and when I printed that on a piece of paper and thumb tacked it to the lower corner, the gesture completed the delusion. I thought I had brought the symbol to reality — that some presence came from my painting through the white of the clouds which were unpainted — thus being a void. Then I had the terrifying conviction that I somehow evolved myself through the painting to be God.

The more I tried to reason it out, the deeper I got. I tried burning the frame I had made in my bathtub, thinking if I partially destroyed the painting I could save myself. I was afraid if I burned the whole painting I might die or the world might end. I started schlepping the painting. I took it to school — "nice" — and then to Miss Hammer — "spiritual." I wanted to throw up.

Finally after a visit to my friend Mary Dell (with the painting) — no one seemed to be able to deal with what was going on with me. I called Mary Dell back that night and she drove me to the hospital where I lied and said I had insurance and committed myself. The admitting shrink thought I was tripping."

Brian had finished. I felt trapped by his story, his years felt like a graph with sadness as both scales. It struck me that the same qualities — generosity, emotional presence — that paved the way for all this distress also made him good at love. Should I charge in and set up squatter's rights in his experience? He wasn't dejected, didn't call for support or even sympathy. Just because of that, he seemed to test my aptitude for sympathy and support. I feared Brian might want to be saved, and how could I do that? Then I realized he just wanted me to pay attention. With tremendous exertion I asked him some interested questions. How long was he in? Nine months. Jesus! Did they try to cure him of being gay? (I squeezed his cock.) Yes, although they didn't succeed. (He squeezed my cock.) But in the end the violence of Brian's story was so much a condensation of dream to me that I was falling asleep, sleep was a cliff that I fell off, drifting slowly as a parsley flake in a jar of oil. Did he have to wear a uniform? Yes. They sedated him most of the time.

Our bodies had turned around. We looked up at the ceiling, absentmindedly playing with our own or each other's cocks, which enhanced my detached response to Brian's story. As a postscript he added: "Aaron embraced the Bahai faith and swore himself to celibacy. He now lives in a trailer in Champagne, Minnesota, and calls me occasionally to ease the Way. The painting ended up in my shrink's office closet. I moved to Los Angeles and found a job as the manager of an FAO Schwarz." (I see him looking like the sun in his linen suit. He's saying — with his hand over his heart — to a bullying child, "Hey, gimme a break.")

In the silence that followed we applied ourselves to each other's body more creatively. We dribbled on some Vaseline Intensive Care Lotion while Brian speculated that probably gay men have younger cocks because of the oils and lubricants. Truman Capote wrote that we also have youthful necks and chins, I added, because of all the sucking. I recalled an Isherwood quotation: "Of course it would never have occurred to any of them to worry about the psychological significance of their tastes." The passage, copied on my journal page, shares three recipes for potato salad.

I don't think "disturbed" people are more healthy than "normal" ones, but sometimes there is a fine line, or no line at all, between "disturbed" and oppressed. Driven crazy is more like it. And the psychiatrist's couch turns this oppression to profit. Are oppressed people more sexual? Other forms of language having been denied us or disowned, languages of production and ownership, by default we are left with sex and the emotions — devalued as a Cinderella at the hearth. And then we become — maybe — Cinderella at the ball. Then we are blamed for embracing sexuality and we will be a bone in the throat of people who don't. It's the same with the popular cultures of gays, people of color, women, the working class. They are feared because they draw energy away from "productive goals." And they are colonized, neutralized and imported into our stagnant mainstream culture. Sex is a sign of life. If sex is relegated to gays as a sign of our devalued state — becoming the shimmer of jewels — it's strange to me that the Left hasn't broached the topic of pleasure. You could say the Left leaves it to Freud, but where is pleasure in all his systems and epi-systems? In all that dominant where is the tonic, the home key?

Brian asked, "What would you like?" A thought sailed by, "It would be nice if you . . ." Here inspiration failed — I was dejected, couldn't grasp the rest. It was growing light. I felt a little scared to be doing this for so many hours, a little "disturbed." I thought of the Marquis de Sade, the business of being perpetually feverish, energy spiraling out because it's mental, disconnected from physical rhythms, busy, busy, busy. I wanted my borders back, I wanted to curl into myself intact as a nautilus shell and let my sleeping mind group and regroup to absorb and master this experience. I said, "Masturbate me as slowly as you can." That is really a solitary activity for two, in that your attention equals your sensation, and the hand on the other's cock requires as little care as the hand that grasps a branch in the Russian River. We masturbated each other slowly, achingly gathering up skin into folds which were meditative and inward turning as the mantle of a 14th century Madonna. Then in a reversal that we experienced as a huge change from night to day, or the turning in some great argument, we brought our hands down. It made us gasp. The pace was excruciating. We were permanently aroused, erectile tissue flooded and dammed up, and so we enjoyed a kind of leisure and Mozartian wit based on invention. I knew from the first with Brian that we would continue. Love and friendship aside, you can tell on a first meeting the number of exchanges it will take to accomplish the various sexual permutations, known by the way he touches you rather than by positions and tastes.

Silence, gasps, out of the blue he said, "You would have looked like dynamite in that toga."

What if I'm fucking on the grass in ancient Rome like we always do on Wednesday night. Is it Thursday? What's one day? Nothing — you turn around and it's dark, the tick and tock of day and night. What if I'm the woman? I'm languidly stretched out on the grass fanning myself lazily with a spray of flowering myrtle. When he enters me I'm spread open as a moth, I'm all colors. What if I'm the guy when I feel something on me and wham! — I've got a cock up my ass — I never saw the guy before and I *still* haven't seen him but I ride his cock — why not? — I'm riding it across a continent of skin. I feel like a sandwich, the pleasure's in the middle because no one has had or knows this much, I can't see I'm bellowing and I start to come, it begins in my ass as a pinpoint of light a thousand miles away. I move closer to it with a religious sense of well-being and when I come I shout a little prayer I shout *Je-Sus!*

What if I'm fucking this boy and his orgasm is so absolute it leaves me gasping. What if I'm watching the three of them calling on the gods and gasping their extravagance, their arms and legs, their skin filled with rosy orifices, they look like an anemone. First I'm the woman, then I'm the man, then I'm Catullus, then I'm an observer remembering a poem, the distance becoming erotic.

He's going to make us into a poem, I've heard better lines. What if he takes us to his villa and merely to pluck at my nipples he feeds me olives pickled in caraway, dormice dipped in honey and rolled in poppy seed, sausages, orioles seasoned with pepper, capons and sow bellies, blood pudding, Egyptian and Syrian dates, veal, little cakes, grapes, pickled beets, Spanish wine and hot honey, chick peas and lupins, endless filberts, an apple, roast bear meat, soft cheese steeped in fresh wine, tripe hash, liver in pastry boats, oysters and hot buttered snails, pastry thrushes with raisin and nut stuffing, quinces with thorns stuck in them to resemble sea urchins, because I'm handsome.

Some people like sex, most men don't. What if I'm blowing him, I look up as he brings down a knife — I either die or don't die. I'm alone at night in bed, someone's moving silently up the stairs, this was to be a sexual rendez-vous but instead he intends to wrap a wire around my neck. I don't die but my erection's gone. I must begin again: what if he puts his hand under my tunic, finger up my ass and I squirm down on it, why not? My girl's laughing — dildos shaped like birds and fish. He's moaning *Nostra Lesbia, Lesbia illa, illa Lesbia* — what is this, Latin? This guy's obviously educated.

Orioles must be an aphrodisiac or maybe it's the situation because all we want to do is fuck, we can't keep our clothes on, we go to it, showing off for him. I love how our eyes go blank and then we think with our bodies. She licks it like a cat with her rough tongue, or like licking ketchup off your forefinger, one two, that's all. Then men come and lift me and hold my legs and body while he fucks me and I'm blowing somebody it's fantastic, all I ever want to do is this.

Brian and I were working ourselves around to coming. We enjoyed the sense of absolute well-being and safety that precedes orgasm. By now we were on our knees kissing urgently and masturbating ourselves. Our cocks felt a little ragged and wanted the master's touch. Masturbation can *feel* better, although I favor a penetration for emotional meaning. Still, that was hardly necessary since we filled up the house to overflowing, and besides, we weren't planning to have a baby.

Orgasms come in all shapes and sizes, sometimes mechanical as a jack-in-the-box, other times they brim with meaning. Other times, like now, they are the complimentary close that signals the end of a lengthy exchange. I recall a memorable climax, a terrific taste of existence in the summer of '73. I was with Ed, we weren't doing anything special but the orgasm started clearly with the fluttering of my prostate, usually a distant gland, sending icy waves to my extremities, then a hot rush carried my torso up into an arc, and just before I came a ball-bearing of energy ping-ponged up and down my spine.

Brian and I curled into each other. Sunlight glittered off or was accepted by the domestic surfaces. On our way to falling asleep we exchanged dreams:

Bob: I dreamt that an alligator lives in my kitchen wall, it cries broken-heartedly on the weekends. A cannibal rabbit with sharp teeth lives there too. A pathetic shabby man who looks like Genet keeps beckoning to me, appearing at a distance everywhere, even on the Greyhound bus I take to escape him, standing up the aisle and beckoning, filling me with dread.

Brian: I dreamt this while I was nuts. A group of nuns in black and white floated on the surface of a foreign planet. They were only heads, like that creature in the space movie. In their hands they carried candles that vibrated colors and gold. Everything on the nun's side was grey and dead, but where the candles were, the light created moving patterns of color and electricity.

Bob: One day Denise, following a recipe of mine, made baked apples in wine. But something went awry and they turned out hard and sour. That night I dreamt there was a new kind of elephant called an Applederm, and its babies were called Apples.

Brian: I was at a party with my father. Our hosts — a family — were noticeably absent, which made me angrier and angrier. I followed my father into the dining room to placate myself with some food, and as I looked up I realized it was my parents' apartment. There was laughter from the other room and someone said, "All our hearts are the same here."

Bob: I dreamt this around puberty. I was making love with my little sister on her bed, but the springs squeaked and I was anxious because my family in the next room might hear us. So we became bumble bees and hovered above the bed, buzzing and buzzing, and when we touched stingers I came. (I never told anyone my bumble bee dream, had forgotten it for years. I felt that now Brian could know me in one piece, what wasn't in the dream he could extrapolate.)

Brian: I stood in a room that was all black and white and because the dream was in color it was beautifully vivid. Black and white tiled floor, white walls, black and white solid drapes. As I looked around the room I saw a black bed from classical Greece. White sheets and in the bed was a boy, suntanned with platinum blond hair. The contrast between him and the black and white setting filled me with joy. I moved closer passing through veils of black and white (remember duality?) and as I kissed him I awoke with the overwhelming erection that only dreams can provide.

*

Brian and I sometimes exchange letters. In the latest, Brian told me he is moving in with a lover. I felt a pang that I had no right to turn into any claim, the pain augmented by the fact that Sterling moved out of my life without leaving a forwarding address. I had been curious about the story Brian painted from his mother's childhood. He answered as follows:

"The image was based on one of my mother's frequent outings with my grandmother, my great aunt Kate and my uncle Ollie. Kate's husband, Hugo, died young and on weekends my grandmother and Kate would pack a picnic and make a day of visiting Hugo. I'm not sure why this is so peculiar to me. Maybe because that's my mother's impression of it. More likely it's that Ju-Ju (our name for my grandmother) and Katie were so unaware of the irony of taking children to play in a cemetery. I made my mother the embracer and my uncle the observer. Later, Katie was institutionalized along with both her daughters, who somehow were not in on these trips. I met Katie when I was six and she would definitely win my most terrifying-person-I-ever-met award. She had straight black hair cut severely across with straight long bangs. She sat hostilely on my grandmother's sofa, barely acknowledging our family's presence. She also scared the shit out of my father. She eventually died in a hospital singing Irish lullabies to herself.

My grandmother held her own in the strange department. In her sixties she had to have one of her eyes — including the lid — removed. Instead of wearing a patch Ju-Ju opted for glasses with a large plastic artificial eye attached to one of the lenses. It had a bizarre effect, particularly when she napped. What can I say about riding the subway with her — that people stared? That I got angry? It made me dislike the world and love her. She would call and invite me to lunch. 'We'll go out!' she'd say expansively, as if The Acorn on Oak were the world. I gave her a feather boa one Christmas and we were thick as thieves after that. She loved to dance, drink. She would come out of the bathroom with hair she had just bleached platinum, make a 20's pout in the mirror, say, 'Your mother and I are both blonds,' and giggle. She was great.

When Ju-Ju died, she presented a unique problem to the undertaker. My mother insisted that the coffin be open in the Irish tradition. The undertakers were perplexed — should they put Ju-Ju's glasses on her and create the disconcerting effect of a corpse with one eye open? In the end that's exactly what they did, and dressed in her favorite red beaded gown, Ju-Ju said good-bye.

Moody in her earlier years, Ju-Ju became senile later. I'd go to her apartment and cook dinner. I loved her very much. In the hospital she suddenly became lucid and rose to the occasion of her death. She said, 'You always learn something. Now I'm learning about tenses. How long is this going to take?' Then she removed her rings, one by one, and placed them on the nightstand for my mother."

ROBERT GLUCK (b. 1947) is a writer and gay activist. He lives in San Francisco where he teaches writing workshops and coordinates readings and events at Small Press Traffic Bookstore. His books are: *Andy, Metaphysics* and *Family Poems*. Forthcoming: *La Fontaine* (in collaboration with Bruce Boone — Black Star Series) and *Elements of a Coffee Service* (Grey Fox Press).

NEXT TIME
A Short Story
by
Roy Wood

The south has many famous cities — Atlanta, Miami, New Orleans, to name just a few. These metropolises are unmistakably southern in atmosphere; yet for every area which has gained enough souls to claim the designation "city," there are a thousand others too small even to be labeled towns. These are where the remnants of the real south may yet be found. No area is so typical of this rural pastoralism than the section of Georgia, south of Macon. Here lies a large portion of the state, almost half, where cities cease to exist and towns become hard to find. A couple of places — Valdosta, Albany — aspire to cityhood; but they fall short of their goal.

This area of Georgia consists of scrubby oak hillsides and deep pine forest, interlaced with myriad tilled fields. The mile after mile of cornfields, and lately soybeans, which has replaced the age-old king cotton, all exude a magnetism of their own. The countryside, for all its countless faults, still possesses a mystical power, capable of holding certain of her sons in bondage. Such men, if no longer exactly bound to the soil, are still eternally ensnared by something — a scent from the landscape or the shrill cry of a nightbird, unhearable farther north. The shimmering sticky hotness of long, lazy summer afternoons, autumn changes, winter's dull drab grayness, unrelieved by snow. The rebirth of spring. These all combine to weave a mysterious and tangled web, binding victims in invisible chains to the region, to the land. Many cannot will themselves away.

Such a person was David Benson. The man, thirty, was tall, lean, deeply tanned; his face too long for his frame, his nose too small. Deep-set coal black eyes redeemed the head; his mouth gave a hint of an exasperating sensual quality. The face ended in a square-set jutting jawline of moderate attractiveness.

Benson was born to the area, raised on a small homestead. Not a farm, yet surrounded by all the accoutrements of farm life. The parents had been gentile folk. They had only one child whom they raised differently from his peers — how differently he was thankful they never learned. Prudent management sent him north to the state university. There Benson found many things he liked, some he needed; few he could not live without. He trekked back south after graduation, having learned enough to know he should leave the area; yet still in love with the land, his covenant with it solid and intact.

He worked in real estate, which kept him outdoors a fair amount of time and provided a suitable salary. In an area where marriage was the norm, he anticipated trouble because of his single state — but even here the natives were slowly, surely, changing. That new god of the dark night, television, homogenized its worshippers even in the remote byways of south Georgia. The neighbors still gossiped incessantly. They craned their necks at every vehicle which roared past their windows, fearful of missing the newest newsflash, yet succumbing, gradually, to the notion that their neighbor's business was his alone, open to their criticism, but not always to change.

Settling in, Benson stayed to himself. He adored the homeplace, his alone now, where there was always something to be done. Early Saturday mornings when the sun created mists of dew and birds seemed louder than an open-air band. The air was crisp like an old timey starched shirt, before the sweat of the day melted it to limpness. They were days of energetic work, done to his own purpose.

Yet as time passed, Benson's very efficiency caused less work to exist. Or the skies would pour forth their leaden loads and leave him helpless to keep the hours occupied.

Those days, worst of times! He could be pushed by them into traveling northward to Atlanta, or south, to Jacksonville, to haunts he knew of — but he never found in them the happiness he sought — only momentary solace from a vast emptiness which threatened, at times, to engulf him.

Intellectually he loved the men he found there. His physical desires for them did not result in his feeling shame or guilt over that aspect of his personality. He regretted only that he could not be happy in the cities where others like him lived. Nor, he was forced to admit, did the plastic, brittle "good-looks" everyone strived for, impress him overmuch. Men who looked as if they feared a drop of sweat, honestly gained, as most people would a deadly snake. Benson could not totally enjoy his excursions into their cities because he knew most men there would not accept his farm — would find the soil degrading, not warm and arousing — nor would they pause long enough to notice the first breaking buds of March and April. In so *many* ways, he did not fit in. Not in the city, not in the rural niche of his own life. Each trip he made to the monsters of concrete, Benson vowed would be the last; he lashed himself for physical weakness yet, finally, knowingly, he would drive to them again, seeking a phantom which existed, he supposed, only in his mind.

In his own realm, towns did exist — people lived — and while fearful of exposing a nature he knew unacceptable to his neighbors, he would sometimes, even close to home, set out in his own elusive way, seeking the attainment of dream and desire.

On these occasions Benson reluctantly ventured into one of the towns closest to his home, Tilton. This community one day found itself on the site of an interstate highway and had decided, sullenly, to grow and prosper. For Benson, who lived thirty minutes from the area, the situation was not without possibilities. He could visit the bars of large motel chains and if he were lucky, meet someone with whom to spend some time. These episodes, usually quickly over and sooner forgotten, were more a product of physical necessity than anything else. He found them often sordid, rarely satisfying and never permanent.

Late one summer afternoon, evening actually, he returned home from an especially profitable day at the office. Grabbing a beer from the kitchen, he padded barefoot out to the front porch. He dropped down into the old-fashioned porch swing, drinking his beer and listening to the late afternoon sounds, feeling lazy, relaxed, at peace with himself and his world. A car drove by, raising a storm of dust. The sun sank into a bank of clouds sending forth long beams of strangely-rayed light. His mood, as it was wont to do, shifted slowly, settling into a mild despondency as the golden ball of sun disappeared in the west. If only the chair opposite him were filled! If he could see there another . . . Disgusted with himself, he put down the empty can and went to perform the evening chores.

Twilight deepened and night sounds slowly came to the fore. Crickets, frogs by the pond, bats circling overhead; suddenly Benson decided this night he would not sit home. He would go into town, have a couple of drinks and see who, if anyone, was about. Maybe tonight . . . maybe this time. . . .

His drive into town saw dusk deepen to darkness. Real night arrived and the oppressive heat slowly began to loosen its grip on the region. Benson thought about where to go for the evening. The motel bars held no appeal. He knew what he would find there. Yet the town offered nothing else. There was one small hole in the wall, not far from the superhighway. He'd been there once, finding it generally insipid; country music out of a radio, a battered whore trying to pick up whomever she could — no sense going there again. He stopped at a traffic light, however, and noted the little place two blocks ahead of him. On the spur of the moment he decided to gamble on it — for a short while at least.

Every time Benson entered such a place, his stomach muscles tightened — not from fear, as much as from the need to throw up caution signs for himself. Remember to nod at the women, don't look too long at the men, don't, whatever you do, make a wrong move nor do anything which might signal your desires to someone unreceptive. The restrictions annoyed him, reminding him that the only good feature about travelling to the cities was being able to visit places where the need for such mental reservations did not exist.

Mentally prepared, he pushed open the dingy door and entered the poorly-lit room.

The bar was almost empty. A fat, greasy-looking bartender leaned behind the long counter. His hair was spidery, oiled and rapidly disappearing over a jowly face, He glanced up as Benson came toward him with no smile of welcome.

"What'll ya have?" he questioned tiredly. Not caring and not minding that his disinterest showed.

Benson gave his order and paid his money. The transaction was complete.

There were only two other customers in the place. A man and woman sat at the bar; he was overweight, bleary-eyed and drunk. The female next to him was a flighty blonde wearing a too-tight blouse over breasts which threated to upend her. She and the male were in animated conversation. Tammy Wynette was wafting forth from the jukebox, an addition since the last time Benson had visited the dim hole. He took his beer and went to one of the booths in the rear, from which he could see the entire bar.

The scene did not depress Benson; he'd known what to expect before he entered — it simply caused a feeling of melancholia to spread over him, which, when all was said and done, was as good a depressant as alcohol. He sipped beer, hoped the woman wouldn't turn her attention towards him, and allowed his thoughts to flow limply through his mind like syrup poured on a cold morning.

He sat, drank, expected nothing. Time crawled by — or raced; either way he paid no mind to the minutes as they played with eternity. He put his hand hard around the can to raise it once more to his lips when the door swung open — admitting only another couple, of indeterminate age, with the silly-grin look of those who had already drunk too much.

A quarter of an hour later, he was on his second can, mentally preparing to leave, yet to force himself to stay away from the interstate strip. Go home, was his advice to himself. Deep in a momentary daydream, he missed hearing the door open. His eye caught a movement and he stared at the newcomer with eyes which widened quickly in astonishment as he appraised the man now at the bar.

He was tall — as tall as Benson, but with more flesh on his bones. Not fat, though; firmness showed even from a distance; short cropped brown hair, a nearly square face, good-looking in an athletic sense of the word. Browned deeply, he was obviously an outdoor worker of some sort. Benson immediately broke all the commandments he had given to himself by looking overlong at the man. No harm was done, however, as the stranger was ordering a drink and the other occupants of the bar were too busy with their own affairs to notice others even if light had permitted. The man took his beer and looked around, openly scornful of the people in the room; his glance took in Benson. The scornful look changed to one of appraisal and puzzlement. His eyes did not linger, nor did they hint, only studied briefly before their owner moved to the end of the bar, to the right of Benson. The two men could observe each other with ease if they were of a mind to do so. Benson dared not let his eyes follow the form. He could not say at what the other was looking.

A spasm of emotion racked Benson. This, after all, was what he'd hoped would happen. He'd wanted a man like this newcomer to enter the bar — but he felt hopelessly inept when one did appear. In a town like Tilton, in a bar such as this one, there was no chance anything would happen. At least, nothing along the lines of his desire.

He stole a careful glance to his right. The attractiveness of the other moved him. If he could only suggest he *approved* of such a man — yet his approval would mean nothing and his admiration, were it known, would be scorned and despised. Resentment welled up in him and as quickly subsided. He could not blame people for their prejudices — only regret that they hated without reason. The other man spoke to no one, made no moves of any kind. Gradually Benson slipped back into his own reverie.

Uneasily he felt the eyes of the stranger touch him. He looked up and their eyes met for an instant. Benson was about to avert his glance when the man nodded at him. The motion was slowly done — exaggerated almost, (but not quite) to the point of scorn. Puzzled by the move, Benson gazed openly at the other, who after a fashion, unhurriedly turned away. Then, carelessly, casually, the man left the end of the bar where he had seated himself and walked to the point where the old man behind the bar was selling beverages. He bought another drink and leisurely moved back towards where he had been.

At first, Benson thought the guy was leaving. Remorse seeped into him. Another opportunity missed, he told himself, but knew there had been no opportunity and nothing missed. Then he saw the man buy his drink, saw him returning . . .

Benson, aware he ought not in any way notice the man, who, since they had already glanced at one another once, would think it unusual and peculiar if he looked again, could in no way help himself. He stared frankly and openly at the man.

The other, seeing the look, appeared almost to grow taller, more handsome; Benson, with sudden sharp forboding, turned away. The spell was broken. The stranger continued towards his spot at the end of the bar, when abruptly he stopped, shifted his weight and in a second was standing at Benson's booth.

"Mind if I join you?" he asked.

Benson was thankful for the dim light. He felt his face go through many shades of color but having gotten himself into an unpredictable situation, he wanted above all, to measure up to his own expectations.

"Not at all," he replied with, he hoped, the proper tone of nonchalant interest.

"Dull in here tonight," Benson added, to keep the conversation going.

"Always is," agreed the other. He took a drink of his beer and offered his hand. A firm, hard, rugged hand which sent a charge through Benson as he gripped it.

"Name's Dan Taylor," his companion said by way of introduction. "Live over on 82, north of Nashville."

"Dave Benson." He gave the pertinent information. Was it his imagination or did they shake hands a fraction of a second longer than necessary?

They talked a few minutes about inconsequential matters. Benson, trying valiantly to control his emotions as well as his expectations, was surprised to hear the man in front of him lived not far from his own small holdings. Benson suspected Dan must have moved into the area while he'd been away at school a few years back.

Their conversation progressed well. This fact alone amazed Benson, who in similiar situations usually found he had no words to utter. The hardest part of evenings like this was attempting to "make" conversation. Dan, however, was talkative. As the first few minutes passed, Benson suddenly sensed his acquaintance was nervous. The words the other spoke, had Benson been a friend of Taylor's, would have been recognized as forced, artificial.

In a slack moment, when Taylor looked away into another corner of the bar, Benson eagerly observed the man. He felt his own body tighten with joy of the physical presence of Dan Taylor. The man was attractive — his existence across the table a dilemma. Benson was caught up in the conflicts of emotional turmoil. He was pleased being this close to Taylor. Yet he wanted more. He wished he had the nerve to bring his leg into contact with Taylor's beneath the table. He was fearful — they were almost neighbors! He dared not risk an overt move. Even as he thought the words, Taylor's attention returned, and — was there not a brief touch against Benson's knee? No. He couldn't be sure. Fool! Benson promptly aroused himself to reality, while his spirit tossed in agony.

Taylor, meanwhile finished his drink. He smashed and bent the can in capable hands, sighed and said, "I wouldn't mind a couple more beers, but I don't think much of this joint. You got any favorite places around here?"

"No," answered Benson truthfully. "There aren't any others except the motel bars on the interstate. I don't care for them, much."

"Me neither."

A brief silence. Benson sensed he should say something before the pause became too long and broke the new-found relationship. Silence among friends was fine — between acquaintances, deadly. He forced himself to speak, "Were you wantin' to drink, or were you lookin' for a spot with entertainment?"

Taylor chuckled. "Mostly, I wanted a few beers and a chance to get out of the house. I like livin' by myself, but . . ." His voice trailed off, leaving the sentence unfinished.

Benson to his astonishment and embarrassment, found himself saying, ". . .

I've got plenty of beer back at my place. It's right on your way home, not out of the way . . ." The offer, miraculously, was accepted. Such a small exchange to be so brimming with expectations.

The journey to his house was a ride of great trepidation for Benson. Taylor followed behind in his own vehicle, allowing Benson countless time to ponder his foolishness. He wanted desperately to reach out and touch this man, hold him, be held by him — they seemed to have so much in common. But he knew he must in no way say or do anything which would hint at what he felt. He was very surprised Taylor had agreed to return with him. Such an acceptance was unusual — most men would have preferred staying in town where they might have a chance of meeting a woman. Did he dare hope? Bitterly Benson pushed hope from the ledge of his mind. For such as himself, there could be no hope. *Anticipation* was all he might dream of — he knew full-well the community's attitudes towards people like him. The icy fury he felt at both himself for his fearfulness, and the others for their views, helped bring him closer to reality. By the time he pulled into his driveway, his ardour had cooled considerably, and Benson was mentally kicking himself for inviting this stranger into his home.

Taylor in his living room changed all that. Benson brought drinks, put music on his sound system and they sat down. Benson on the sofa, Taylor in a large chair next to it. A small lamp's rays shone pale and inadequately about the room. Taylor's visible flesh — his face, arms, hands — gleamed bronze in the dim visibility of the room. Benson felt resolve fleeing. If *only* he could find out whether or not his visitor had any idea what was in his mind. That he managed to keep a conversation going at all was a minor miracle. They finished the first beers, Benson went for two more. Returned. Taylor was up now, walking around the room, looking at the books, restless. Was he sorry he'd come, Benson wondered. Or was he full of the same sweet-bitter uncertainties as Benson? They both ended up sitting on the sofa. Not too close, not yet . . .

Benson, aching to reach out and touch the man, held back. The fear, the pain instilled in countless ways over a lifetime was sufficient to conquer his hope for happiness. And suddenly he realized Taylor could very probably make him happy. Even with all the beer he'd drunk in the course of the evening, the excruciating desire within him to grasp Taylor, feel the man in his arms and to be touched himself, all stood for nothing compared to the throbbing waves of pain and hopelessness which flooded him at the thought the man might reject such admiration. Benson did not fear rejection of his body; or rejection of himself as Benson, although he was never pleased by either — but he could not face rejection of his ideal of love. He knew that the feelings he had for Taylor, were they allowed to grow, flower and mature, would produce beauty beyond all he'd ever known. Trembling, he sat on the sofa and dared not take the gamble.

Taylor, as they drank, grew restive again. Benson imagined the man moved ever so much closer to him. Taylor's shoulders grew wider, his charm more magnetic, drawing Benson closer and closer to him. It became more difficult not to give in to Taylor's pull. Fear of condemnation battled with hope of happiness and both combatants tottered on a precipice, neither winning — yet. The minutes dragged by — unspeakable agonies for Benson. Taylor finally began looking as if he must leave. Instead, one last time he sat down, this time so close to Benson their legs brushed together. Taylor had found a book to question Benson about — that was the excuse for the closeness, a closeness which was brief, momentary; a fleeting glimpse of time standing still.

Taylor got up to put the book away. Benson, in that instant knew his fear had defeated him. He suddenly realized with a clarity he could not understand that as he, in fear, had dared make no overt moves, so Taylor, by his very moves about the room, by his restless manner, had been trying to communicate a message of his own desires to Benson.

Taylor now moved back to the chair. Unsure, puzzled, fearful himself of pursuing a quarry he believed beyond reach, he stood up. The evening was ending.

As they said good-bye, however, Taylor looked hard into Benson's eyes, "If you're not busy, stop by my place Saturday."

He was gone.

As the sound of Taylor's truck evaporated into the cooled night air, Benson stood alone. His eyes did not see the moon which scurried back and forth behind clouds as if inviting the solitary man to find it.

Benson saw only the form of Taylor. Masculine strength, manly beauty which he could have shared tonight had he not feared so much. Next time . . . He shook himself and went back toward the house. Saturday seemed an eternity away. If only *tonight* he had overcome . . . he damned himself, but even more be berated the disquietude which had stopped his actions. When he met Taylor on Saturday, as he vowed he would, things would end differently. Next time he would overcome the uneasiness, the apprehensions that others forced into his consciousness. Next time he would seize the initiative and seek happiness no matter what came of it. Oh yes, next time the ending would be different he promised himself as he entered the empty house. Next time . . .

ROY WOOD has had stories published in *GPU News, Fag Rag, The GALA Review* and now, *Gay Sunshine*. He currently lives in Athens, Ga., where he is working on a novel. He maintains membership in the national Lambda Association of Bodybuilders.

Joe Fuoco

SISSY!

by

George Birimisa

This is an excerpt from an autobiographical novel in progress. The time is the autumn of 1933. The place is the outskirts of Watsonville, California. Mr. Dardona, the social worker, is taking the three Birimisa boys to St. Francis Catholic School for Boys. The children have just been declared wards of the County of Santa Cruz because their father is dying of pneumonia and their mother's new husband refuses to support them. The story is about George, the youngest boy, and his awakening love for Brother Joe.

At last we approached a cluster of muddy brown buildings. Mr. Dardona slowed the car — he turned into the gravel driveway that led to the central building. Two palm trees flanked the entrance — they were about six feet tall with fat, stubby trunks. "Here we are!" he said as he jerked the car to a halt and pulled the emergency brake. "This is the last stop!"

We trooped up the steps into the dark lobby. It smelled of incense — it was the sweet smelling kind that was used at High Mass. I quickly started to breathe through my mouth so I wouldn't have to smell it — it always made me sick to my stomach. A door opened silently — I felt warm air on my face. A huge bulk filled the doorway. "Ah — Mr. Dardona from Welfare?"

"Father Superior?"

"I have been expecting you!" Father Superior patted his big stomach with both hands. His hair was jet black except for the silver at the temples. "Come into my office. I keep it warm — I have a touch of rheumatism in my knees!"

A highly polished brown desk stood in the middle of the room. On the wall was a painting of a man in a brown monk's outfit with a halo around his head. I found out later it was a painting of St. John Bosco, the founder of the Salesian Order.

Father Superior pointed to a straight backed chair. "Have a seat, Mr. Dardona!"

"I prefer to stand, Father!" Mr. Dardona opened his belted briefcase and pulled out a thick folder. "Here is the complete file on the Birimisa boys!"

Father Superior placed the folder carefully on his desk. "These ah — these Birimisa boys — they are filthy dirty!" A scowl twisted his face. "They are dressed in rags — it is a disgrace!" He looked up at the ceiling as if asking God for help.

Mr. Dardona grinned in embarrassment. "Ah, Father Superior! You must realize the special circumstances surrounding these — we had to lock them up in a small room — a room with bars. Their father — " He leaned forward and placed his index finger on the blue folder. "I do not believe I should say anymore in front of the children, Father Superior. It is all there — everything!"

The priest picked up the folder. He plopped down at his desk and began to read. There was a silence as his eyes skimmed page after page. At last he closed the blue folder. "It is much worse than I had imagined!" he said. "These boys — they are three little devils!' He stood up, breathing heavily. "I did not realize they were such hooligans!"

Mr. Dardona waved his hands helplessly in the air. "I am positive that St. Francis and the Salesian Order can turn these boys into God fearing young men. I am positive that — "

"I am going to speak frankly," Father Superior interrupted. "If I had seen this folder beforehand I would not have accepted the Birimisa boys for enrollment!" He pressed his finger against his lips. "However — God's work — it is difficult — there is so much to be done!" He walked over to the painting of St. John Bosco — he whirled around. "You must understand that twenty-five dollars for their room and board is a pittance — a mere pittance!"

Mr. Dardona shuffled his feet. "Well, Father, we ah — we hope to raise the monthly stipend to thirty dollars for each child — at the beginning of the new fiscal year!"

"You said that last year! Twenty-five dollars does not pay for the food!" The priest sat down. "No matter — it is the will of God that the Salesians turn these young scoundrels into good Catholics!" He pointed a finger at me. "Bambino — what is your first name?"

"Huh? Ah — me? Ah — Georgie, sir!"

"Sir?" He raised his eyebrows in surprise. "I see you have some manners. Where did you get them?"

"Ah — from my Mama, sir!"

"Hmmm!" He stroked his chin. "My son, when you speak to me you do not call me 'sir.' You must call me Father Superior!"

"Ah, yes sir, Father Sup — Superior!"

He nodded his head in approval. "Tell me, my son, when was the last time you went to Confession and Holy Communion?"

"Ah — when I wuz with my Mom!"

"When was that?"

"I dunno. A long time ago!"

The priest frowned. "Do you know what happens to boys who don't go to Confession and Holy Communion?"

I shook my head.

"Do you know where you would go if you died right now?"

"I doan know!"

He smiled. "You would go straight to hell, my son. You would burn for all eternity!"

"Am I gonna go there, Father?"

He slammed the blue folder down on the desk. "If you do not go to Confession!" He reached for the tiny silver bell — he rang it. He beamed at Mr. Dardona. "Ah — you must stay for lunch, sir. The good sisters are excellent cooks — we are having spaghetti and sausage — it goes well with a glass of burgundy!"

"Well — ah —"

"It is settled!"

There was a light knock on the door and the nun entered silently. Her hands were hidden in the sleeves of her black habit. Her face was pale — she looked like she hadn't been in the sun for a very long time.

"Ah — Sister Maria!" Father Superior waved his hand in my direction. "The little one — George Birimisa — he will be placed with the Bambino Group. Take him to the laundry room — issue him some clean clothes. I believe we should burn the clothes he is wearing — except for his shoes. Then turn him over to Brother Joseph. A hot shower and he will be brand new!"

She bowed her head and then she grabbed my hand and pulled me toward the door. We were in the lobby when I jerked my hand away. "I wanna be with my brothers," I said "I wanna —"

The pain tore at my leg. "Ooogagh!" I screamed as I grabbed my leg and hopped up and down. The tears stung my eyes — I lost my balance and fell backwards. I hugged my leg — I rocked back and forth — I could hardly stand the pain — it smashed at me in waves that took my breath away.

"Stop pretending — I didn't kick you hard!" Her voice was flat and cold. "Get off the floor!" She loomed over me — her milk white hands held the skirt of her outfit above her ankles. I could see the pointed toes of her black, high topped shoes. For a moment I got the wild idea that she was going to throw her skirt over my face and smother me to death. "Did you hear me?" She grabbed my by the shirt collar — she jerked me off the floor with one hand. She held me an inch away from her face. "You will learn one lesson at St. Francis! You do not speak until you are spoken to!" She dropped me to the floor — she shoved me toward the door.

I felt cold air on my face from the inner courtyard. I stumbled along the portico until I stood in front of a flight of stone steps. "Go down, boy!" At the bottom was an archway — it led into a big room that was full of steam. It was windowless — a naked 50 watt bulb hung on a rusty chain from the low ceiling. A big wooden cross was over the archway. The whitewashed walls were wet — they looked like they were sweating. Again I saw the painting of St. John Bosco. It looked just like the one in Father Superior's office. At the back of the room was another staircase going downward — I was sure it led directly to hell.

Nuns in black habits were everywhere — their constant motion gave the dimly lit room an unreal quality. Some of the nuns were ironing — others were busy at sewing machines. Still other nuns threw clothes into a giant washing machine — all of them were silent. The only sounds were the chug-chug of the washing machine and the hissing whir of the sewing machines.

Sister Maria approached an ancient nun who sat at a table folding clothes. "Mother Superior," she whispered. "I need clothes for the little one!"

Mother Superior didn't look up. "Take what is needed," she murmured.

Sister Maria picked up a pair of worn corduroy pants from a long table — she held them against my waist. "You will have to roll up the legs!" She grabbed a denim shirt, 2 pairs of BVD's and three pairs of socks. "Your shoes will have to do for now!"

We climbed the steps — we walked along the portico that protected us from the drizzle of the low, dark clouds. The portico connected the muddy brown buildings that formed a giant U. Directly in front of me a garden of snapdragons, pansies and geraniums. In the middle of the garden was a ten foot high column — on top of it was a stone statue of the Virgin Mary — she held Jesus in her arms. On both of their heads was a big crown. Directly behind the garden was a deserted playground. I knew that down the hill from the playground was the lake. Louie and Jackie had taken me there once — we had built a raft and paddled to the center of the lake.

Sister Maria's fingers dug into my shoulder. "Up the stairs!"

I climbed the steps — the stabbing pain in my leg had turned into a throbbing ache.

We were in the dormitory — row after row of narrow beds on each side of the long room. Next to each bed was a metal chest. On top of each chest was a toothbrush, a bar of soap in a dish and a neatly folded towel. There was an iron stove in the middle of the room with a stack of wood next to it. Above the door was a cross — on the wall at the far end of the dormitory was still another painting of St. John Bosco. To my right was a white curtain — behind it I could see the shadow of a man.

"Brother Joseph?" Sister Maria called.

"What is it?" The shadow stood up.

"It's Sister Maria. I brought you the new boy!"

The curtain parted and I saw Brother Joseph for the first time. He was short and stocky and there was something earthy and coarse about him. The muscles of his thick arms rippled against the thin material of his cassock — it was too tight for his big chest and shoulders. He didn't look like a priest. He closed his eyes and pressed his fingers to his temples. "Forgive me, Sister Maria. Too much studying!"

"You look a bit peaked," she said. "Please forgive me for taking you away from your studies but it's Father Superior's orders!" She placed my clothes on a table that stood next to the white curtain. "Well, here he is!" She shoved me toward Brother Joseph. "He's a troublemaker! Father Superior wants him cleaned up — assigned a bed — then turn him over to Brother Louis!"

"What's his name?"

"I — ah — " She clucked her tongue. "For the life of me I can't remember. Father Superior told me but—"

"It's alright, Sister!"

"If you need me I will be in the Laundry Room!" She disappeared down the stairs.

Brother Joseph looked at me for a moment — then he put his hand on my shoulder. I jumped away.

"I'm not going to hurt you!" he said.

I stared at him with frightened eyes.

He took a step backward and held his hands over his head. "I've got 'em up — just like in the movies. You've got the gun. I won't dare come near you unless you want me to!" He grinned. "What's your name?"

I just stared at him.

"Is it Barney Google or are you one of the Katzenjammer Kids?"

"Huh?"

"Look, I'm not good at guessing games. Tell me your name!"

"Georgie," I mumbled.

"Georgie? Did you know that your patron saint is St. George — he rode a great big white horse and he slew the dragon!"

I stared at him.

"That's what St. George did!" He folded his arms across his chest. "Look, George!" He held out his hand. "I'm Brother Joseph but all the kids call me Brother Joe!" He took my hand. He didn't let go as he led me down the hall. He pushed at the swinging doors that led to the lavatory. "We're always running out of hot water and today is no exception. That means you got to take a cold shower. You think you can do it, Georgie?"

I didn't answer.

He smiled and rubbed the palms of his hands together. "Get out of those clothes!"

I pulled at the straps of my overalls — I let them drop to the floor. I took off my shirt and then I kicked off my shoes and socks. At last I stood naked in front of Brother Joe.

He bent down. "What happened to your leg?"

"Huh?"

"Your shin — you've got a nasty bump on it!"

"Ah — Sister Maria — she — "

"She kicked you?"

My head jerked up and down.

His huge hands gripped my naked shoulders and I shivered with excitement. Then he lifted me up — he squeezed me against the smooth material of his cassock — I pressed my cheek against his chest. I swallowed to keep my heart from jumping into my mouth as he squeezed me tight. "Sometimes I wonder about Catholics!" His voice strained with anger. "But don't you worry — you're with Brother Joe now, Georgie!" His nut brown eyes blazed. I sighed with contentment as I listened to the steady beat of his heart. I wished he would hold me in his arms forever.

That night after I said my evening prayer I jumped into my narrow bed — I lay on my side and watched Brother Joe's shadow on the white curtain. He hunched over his desk. He finally stood up — he took off his cassock — then he took off his shirt and pants. He turned off the light and the dormitory was plunged into blackness. I sighed. I wanted to be in bed with Brother Joe — I wanted him to hold me tight until I fell asleep. I finally closed my eyes against the blackness.

*   *   *   *   *

The next day was Saturday. We only had school in the morning because of the big game with Gonzales in the afternoon. I sat on the grass on the forty yard line with Ronald, the fat boy. At first I didn't recognize the player with SAINTS printed on his jersey. It was halftime when he took off his helmet. My heart jumped into my mouth when I realized it was Brother Joe — there was no mistaking his nut brown hair and full red lips. During the second half my eyes were glued on him. He played right end and his husky body moved with an easy grace as he raced downfield — as he faked to the outside — as he broke clear over the middle. The quarterback threw the football to the fullback but he dropped it. "Throw the ball to Brother Joe!" I shouted at the top of my lungs. "He wuz wide open, fer cryin out loud!"

"Shut up!" Ronald poked me in the ribs. "Gonzales High ain't supposed to know 'bout Brother Joe!"

"Huh?"

"Brother Joe ain't supposed to be on our team cause he ain't no school boy! Doncha git it?"

"Get what?"

"Boy, are you dumb!"

There was only a few minutes left in the game when Brother Joe caught a pass. It was a long one — almost forty yards. He reached up with one hand and caught the football — he crossed the goal line with two Gonzales players hanging on to him — he scored the only touchdown for St. Francis. I jumped up and down — I clapped my hands and screamed myself hoarse. When the game was over I turned to Ronald. "How cum he's playin on our team if he ain't supposed to?"

"Father Superior makes him do it!"

"Ain't that cheatin?"

"Heck no, Georgie. We lost by four touchdowns!"

"I bet Brother Joe is the best football player in the whole world!" I said as I watched Brother Joe head for the locker room.

"No he ain't!" Ronald shook his head. "He dropped two passes that wuz right in his bread basket when we wuz playin Watsonville High last week!"

"Yer nothin but a liar!" I cried.

"Ain't lyin!"

I gave Ronald the middle finger. "Fuck you!" I said. "You doan know your ass from a hole in the ground!" I quickly ran across the football field. Ronald was too fat to catch me.

*   *   *

It happened on a Sunday morning a couple of weeks before Thanksgiving. We had to go to Mass twice on Sunday — first in the tiny chapel and then across the highway at the big church. I hated the second Mass because of the incense. It filled the high vaulted church with a thick, sweet smell that made me sick to my stomach. In the middle of Father Sebastian's sermon I jumped up and rushed down the center aisle — I barely made it out the big door. I threw up all over the stone steps.

Except for the extra Mass I loved Sundays because we had the rest of the day free. Even though black clouds hung low in the sky Brother Joe took the Bambino Group down to the lake. I watched as he helped Ronald and some of the other boys dig for worms — they had bamboo poles and they were going fishing. "Brother Joe!" I shouted. "I'm gonna make me a raft and —"

"Keep quiet, Georgie!" he snapped. Then he smiled at Ronald. "Ah — there's a big worm. Keep digging!"

The anger was a heavy lump in my throat as I ran along the shore line — away from Brother Joe. After awhile I sat down on the grass and took off my shoes and socks. "It would serve him right if I drowned," I said to myself. "Then he would pay attention to me!' I quickly rolled up my pants — I shivered as my feet sank into the thick mud — the water was icy cold. I figured I could find three or four logs and build my own raft — without Brother Joe.

I was up to my knees in the icy water when I felt a sharp pain in my left foot — it brought tears to my eyes. I quickly limped to the shore — I sat down and looked at the bottom of my foot. My mouth fell open when I saw the cut — it was two inches long and a half an inch deep. At first there wasn't any blood — I guess it was because of the water. Then the blood spurted. "Brother Joe!" I shrieked. "Help me! Brother Joe!"

He broke away from the group of boys in the distance. He held his cassock above his legs as he raced toward me. He bent down, looking at my foot. He grabbed the hem of his cassock — he ripped off a piece of the black cloth — he knotted it tightly around my foot. He lifted me in his arms — he raced up the side of the hill toward St. Francis. My arms were around his neck — I pressed my face against his big chest. "Don't you know any better than to go wading?" he scolded. "The kids from Watsonville — they come out here and throw cans and bottles into the lake!"

He raced across the playground — past the statue of the Virgin Mary and up the steps of the portico. As he shoved at the door of the lobby he almost knocked down Sister Maria. "I'm drivin Georgie to the hospital in Watsonville," he cried as he ran through the lobby — as he jerked at the front door. "He cut his foot in the lake!"

He deposited me in the green sedan. "You scared me half to death," he said as he ran around the car and jumped into the driver's seat. "You're going to be hunky dory! I'll get you to the hospital in a jiffy!"

I watched as the speedometer inched its way up to 55 miles an hour — I was sure we were going to crash into the apple orchard on the side of the road. My foot felt like someone was sticking a red hot poker into it. As last Brother Joe skidded to a shuddering stop in front of the hospital. He ran around the car — he scooped me up in his arms and dashed up the front steps.

I blinked against the bright lights of the large room. "Put him on the table," the nurse said crisply. "Sister Maria called. Dr. Chaffee will be here right away!" I gripped Brother Joe's big hand as the nurse cut the black bandage — as she cleaned the cut with a piece of cotton. Then the doctor hurried into the room. He smiled. "Ah — what do we have here? It will only take a few stitches!"

I watched as the doctor threaded the catgut on a very long, slightly bent needle. I finally closed my eyes and buried my head in Brother Joe's chest. He wrapped his arms around me. Then I felt the sharp pain tear at my foot — I tried to swallow it. "You're doing okay!" I felt Brother Joe's warm breath against my ear. "It's almost over, Georgie! Just one more!"

I pressed my head against Brother Joe's chest with all my might.

"That's it!" Doctor Chaffee said cheerfully. "All stitched up, my boy! You are as good as new!"

I opened my eyes — I pulled my head away from Brother Joe's chest — I had slobbered all over the front of his cassock. I hung onto Brother Joe's hand as the doctor put a big bandage on my foot. I was proud of it — I knew I would be the center of attention back at St. Francis.

Brother Joe lifted me in his arms — he carried me out of the brightly lit room and down the front steps. He stood with his foot on the running board. He hugged me and grinned. Then he kissed me on the cheek with a loud, smacking noise. "You're a brave boy, Georgie Porgie! Five stitches and you didn't let out a peep!"

My body tingled and glowed with pleasure. Now Brother Joe was behind the wheel. He drove with one hand — the other hand was around my shoulders. I pressed my face against his chest. I loved the smell of Brother Joe — the smell of sweet pipe tobacco and sweat. I prayed that the ride back to St. Francis would take forever.

All too soon we pulled into the narrow driveway of St. Francis. Again Brother Joe lifted me in his arms. I wondered if he was taking me to his curtained room in the dormitory. I knew it would be wonderful if I could sleep in his bed — in his arms. I knew I would fall asleep right away and my foot wouldn't hurt. I felt a stab of disappointment when he hurried past the Bambino Dorm and climbed the steps to the Infirmary.

Sister Hortense stood in front of the mahogany table. She was tiny and stoop shouldered — her pale blue eyes were soft and kind. "How is the little scamp?" she asked.

"He's going to be okay!" Brother Joe said. "Where should I put him?"

"Here will do!" She turned down the sheets of a bed that was next to a window. "It's been lonely here — I discharged my last patient the day before yesterday!"

Brother Joe deposited me on the bed. "Georgie, you do what Sister Hortense tells you to do or you'll get in trouble with me!"

As I nodded my head I felt the tears moisten my eyes — I knew Brother Joe was leaving me.

He moved to the exit. "The Doc put five stitches in his foot and he didn't cry!" he said proudly.

"He's a brave lad!" Sister Hortense moved toward Brother. "Oh, I forgot to tell you! Father Superior — he wants to see you in his office right away!"

Brother Joe scowled. "What did I do now?"

Sister Hortense stood on tip toe — she whispered in Brother Joe's ear. He started to say something but then he put his hand over his mouth. He disappeared down the steep stairs without a word.

I suddenly felt cold. My foot started to ache — it was a dull throb that brought tears to my eyes. I began to cry.

"Now! Now!" Sister Hortense soothed. "I can't say that I blame you — five stitches! As soon as I get you out of these clothes and washed up I'm going to feed you some hot vegetable soup that was made special for Father Superior. After that — you are going to take a nap! I will be right here with you!"

It was a couple of days later when Brother Joe brought me the crutches. "Sister Hortense will teach you how to use them," he said. There were black shadows under his eyes. "I can't stay, Georgie! I'll come and visit if I get the chance!"

A week later I was discharged from the Infirmary. I was proud of my crutches as I lurched along the portico, heading for the dining room and lunch. I didn't have to march in line with the other kids — I was something special. I was very proud of the big bandage on my foot.

It was two weeks later when I finally gave up my crutches. It was also the last time I ever saw Brother Joe. He stood on the sidewalk in front of the statue of the Virgin Mary with the crown on her head. He was talking to Father Superior. I couldn't hear what they were saying but Brother Joe kept pounding his fist into the palm of his other hand. I could see that he was angry. He finally turned his back on Father Superior and walked away.

That night Brother Joe was not in the dorm. A strange priest was behind the white curtain. As I crawled into bed a wave of hopelessness swept over me. I tried to go to sleep on my side facing the white curtain but I couldn't. The shadow of the strange priest gave me a stomach ache. I flipped over on my other side and pressed my knees to my chin. I pulled the sheets over my head. I didn't care if I fell asleep and woke up in purgatory or in hell. Nothing made any difference. Brother Joe was gone. I cried myself to sleep.

GEORGE BIRIMISA'S plays have been performed in the United States, Canada and England. They feature themes of human isolation, frustrated idealism, and range against needless suffering, usually centered around homosexual characters. He received a Rockefeller grant in 1969 for his play *Mr. Jello*. His play *Pogey Bait* was performed at Theatre Rhinoceros, San Francisco, January 1982.

DAS BLASSROTE DREIECK
A Short Story
by
Leigh W. Rutledge

My first impression of Auschwitz was of mud.

Our train pulled into the camp in the middle of the night — three hundred people, exhausted, worn, afraid, jammed into each cattle car. We'd lived in each other's sewage for two days and three nights. As people, we clung to one another, finding a thin current of optimism in our shared flesh. As faces, we peered at one another, full of individual pain and questions. At night, each face in the darkness looked like the skeleton it would become.

I sat thinking about Johann.

I was trying to tell myself not to think about him, when the train pulled to a halt. It was our last stop, a destination in the middle of the night. It must've been around midnight.

There was a short wait inside the car. Apprehension was mixed with expectation. There was still the optimist in all of us. After all, the stories we had heard — they couldn't be true . . .

Suddenly there was a hard clanging down the train. The doors were being opened.

People rose to their feet in excitement. We were about to disembark.

The doors flew open. One could taste the fresh air immediately.

German and Prussian guards waited for us. They barked orders at us to leave all our belongings in the cars. We were herded out of the sewage — and into the mud, the omnipresnt mud of Auschwitz. And in the air, a strange smell, like silk or nylons burning. And a slight flurry of ashes, like gray snow.

An old Polish woman smiled at me. She stomped delicately in the mud and then pointed to her shoes, to the brown mash that clung to her heels. "Mud!" she said triumphantly, which meant "The earth!" It was as if to say "Anything may happen, but the earth will always be there."

But I was distracted. I was craning my neck, looking over the hundreds of heads moving out from the train. I was looking for Johann. We had been taken together, but during the roundup we were separated.

The darkness around the train was almost complete. There was only a sea of humanity, flooding out like water into the gates of Auschwitz. No individual faces. The early morning darkness, like the camp itself, stripped flesh of its individuality, stripped it of all characteristics, except two — that it lived and that it died. There was no Johann.

A Prussian guard pushed me from behind. I almost slipped and fell on my face in the mud, but a man caught me from behind. I turned around. Another face. One of thousands, millions. He smiled at me and then moved on, towards the lights, between the walls of guards and into the mouth of the camp itself.

My emotions were confused, muddled. I felt the same kind of hopelessness I used to as a child, when I'd lie in bed at night, staring up at the ceiling and, out of nowhere, there would come this thought, this feeling — a sudden realization that I was going to die, that I was finite after all. Alone in bed, it made everything seem gray. But it always went away. There was my life to distract me from my death. Now, here, the reality was imposing. Life seemed to become the perpetuation of some awful lie. Death was now the distraction from life.

The gates of the camp were open like jaws. They looked bizarre in the eerie lighting, especially with their strange, almost gothic twists of barbed wire. They made a slight humming sound.

As soon as we started through them, there was the sound of music. A sick irony. The gates of hell were marked with trumpets, too. Was that really Mozart, accompanying the sobs and moans, the sound of Prussian whips? A thin, apathetic Mozart. Some unseen orchestra, soothing the hysteria of the damned. It made the cold night seem grayer. An old Jew behind me chuckled bitterly.

Ahead, the current of people twisted and turned, and then forked. Women to the right, men to the left. Trails of people disappeared into brilliantly lit concrete buildings. The full anguish of separation suddenly became apparent. There were several trim young women in nurse's uniforms, standing by the doors of the buildings, comforting people. "It will be all right. You will see. This is only a formality. This is only a formality . ." The anthem of Auschwitz: Everything is only a formality.

The orchestra, somewhere behind us now, paused between movements of Mozart.

Just before I entered one of the buildings, there was a strange commotion behind me. A woman screamed. Gunshots. Several shrieks. Feet pounding the mud. I turned around. Too late. I was inside the building before I could see a thing. I was later told that a woman had thrown herself against the electrified fence.

About a year before, Johann's sister, Hannah, had gotten married. That was in April. The day was like a beautifully clear photograph.

The wedding was held out-of-doors. After the supper, there was dancing on the lawn. Hannah and her new husband danced one waltz alone, the two figures, black and white, moving against a brilliant background of green and blue and new roses.

Johann came up to me, extending a glass of champagne.

We watched the newly-weds dance.

Finally he said, "They're so incredibly in love. Look at them."

I did. I saw Johann and I, a few nights before, in bed, naked. I was lying on top of him, my face buried in his warm neck. Hannah's face was buried in her husband's neck exactly the same way.

Thoughts fled.

I turned and looked at Johann and smiled.

He clinked the edge of his champagne glass against mine.

"To the day!" he saluted and winked at me.

"That day will never come," I replied.

He shrugged and turned back to the dancers.

The high April sun caught the features of his face just so. The cheekbones were brought into relief. The eyes withdrew and deepened into sensual darkness. The dark hair merged with the shadows. He was incredibly handsome.

I'm not sure why that memory came back to me, as I stood enduring the first of so many Auschwitz formalities.

I was emptying my pockets. A guard informed us that our belongings would be taken and stored for us. The last remnants of our former existences — the silly, conventional things we all held in our trouser pockets. Belongings fell upon belongings on the table, then were swept away by the fat little hands of more women in nurse's uniforms, then were dumped into boxes which were whisked away into back rooms. So many back rooms. . . .

Then we were ordered to strip. Our clothes were thrown in heaps on large tables, where they were separated and folded by still more "nurses." One pretty blonde girl hummed while neatly folding pairs of pants. She had the air of a private maid going about her household chores.

I looked around at the men near me. A vague kind of sexual thought passed through my mind. It seemed out of place. But the last instincts lingered. A goodlooking young man next to me turned away, shy, modest. He started coughing nervously. His buttocks trembled. At another time, in another place . . . There was little time to think, even of the normal comforts of flesh. Flesh was stripped and constrained. The sex urge was one of the first to be beaten out of us, by the enormity of the situation if nothing else. The Nazis were wise psychologists. The libido was one of the most powerful and liberating forms of the human spirit. Rebellion could be fermented by an erection. But there were none here — at least not for long. There was too much death to think of sex.

Finally, we were pushed on to a room where our heads were shaved. And then, before being provided with prison wear, there was another separation, another fork ahead. Two doors like some Dantesque analogy turned into reality. A guard stood between them, directing individuals through one door or the other. The very young or the very old or the very frail — to the left. The rest of us — to the right. The darkness to the left was consuming, silent, like a scream in a vacuum. The man between the doors occasionally chose able-bodied men to the left. There was a certain implacable smile on his lips when he made one of these arbitrary selections. For many, the nightmare began and ended on the front steps of the camp. For the rest of us . . .

I thought of Johann, could suddenly think of little else. These private pains consumed all of the faces around me. Each one spoke of some loved one, gone, missed, misplaced. The door to the left was the symbol of an unknown fate. Who would be picked? It presented a dreadful possibility — one that led to painful speculation.

Johann? Unlike many of the others, I had no illusions of where the door to the left led. Even after a long time in the camps, many people still couldn't face the reality that someone would want to persecute, let alone kill them. The door to the left was not the final horror. It was the first. I knew where it went — and briefly glimpsed Johann, naked (and the nakedness was completely sexual and virile), led into the vacuum, into cool gray tiled rooms, and doors shut, and a moment's silence, and then the hissing of gas, and then panic, and then men breaking their fingerbones, clawing at the unyielding tile for a way out. . . . So many men lost. And in the middle of the room stood Johann, lost in a fog of screaming gas. And then — nothing. The room was empty, as if gas actually made people just quietly disappear, instead of die slowly. . . .

In a chemistry class at the University of Hamburg where I first met him, Johann used to turn on the gas for the Bunsen burners, used to lean close to the outlet and take a deep breath. "The smell of Germany," he used to say, referring to the sickly sweet smell that surrounded most of Germany's industrial cities. . . .

The strange smell like burning nylons became worse as we entered the room where we were commissioned our prison wear. Except, it didn't smell like burning nylons anymore. It had a sickening, repulsive edge to it. It was only a smell, but there was something instinctively horrible about it.

I noticed the floors of the room were covered with a fine layer of gray dust.

I looked up as I was getting into my gray-and-white striped pants.

A face moved near me.

Johann! The edge of a cheek, something about the shape of the head. Johann . . .

But when the face turned full to mine, it belonged to someone else.

The jolting fear suddenly crossed my mind: What if I didn't recognize him because of his shaved head? What if we passed one another, without even knowing? What if . . .

We were herded out of the building into the camp itself.

The sky was starting to get light, a vague pastel color emerging through the smoke of Auschwitz. Dawn. It looked morbid and thin, with the silhouette of the crematoriums against it.

There was the sound of Mozart again, as morbid and thin as the new light.

We were led to our barracks, assigned to beds, though they looked more like coffins.

We were all totally exhausted, more mentally than physically. Our mind needed a chance to retreat to its subconscious, in order to deal with our new experience.

Our day, the long long day seemed over.

It wasn't.

There was no time for sleep. Dawn meant work, for all prisoners, new or experienced.

The long day was just beginning.

There was a nightclub in Berlin that Johann and I used to frequent before the war really got under way.

They had shows there sometimes. One night it was a female impersonator from Paris. She burst onto the stage in the explosion of a spotlight, waving the long sleeves of a deep lavender dress. There was something hypnotic about that shade of lavender. One was compelled to stare at it, to look deep into it. It had the effect of a shock and a warning.

I leaned over to Johann and said something about it.

He shrugged. "It's only a color," he replied. . . .

It didn't take long to understand the meaning of the pink triangle that was sewn on many prisoners' shirts. The Nazis had color-coded mankind. Every prisoner was ordered to wear a patch on his shirt, color-coded to his specific crime. The Jews wore a yellow Star of David. Anti-socials wore black triangles. The pink triangle was reserved for homosexuals.

There was only one man in our barracks who wore the pink triangle. Most homosexuals, if they were known, were sent immediately to the showers. For some reason, this man had survived. There was a certain arbitrariness about his survival. There was a certain arbitrariness about all our survivals.

I never approached him, though we exchanged glances occasionally. He seemed to know. I was wearing the black triangle. The color hid nothing, though.

One time in the barracks, he hesitated near me, as if to ask something. I turned around. He said nothing. He moved on.

I thought of asking him if there was any way to locate someone in the camp. I was thinking of Johann. But I thought better of it. Suspicion was bred into us. How could we be sure who were our real enemies?

We worked eighteen hours a day. The crew I was assigned to helped to build roads just outside the camp. The faces of the crew changed constantly. People disappeared in the night, in the morning. They disappeared in front of us. One afternoon, I watched a very goodlooking young man hacked to death with a shovel. No one knew what he had done. It didn't matter. New faces appeared from the daily transports, the trains that arrived in the middle of the night. We worked — and worked — and watched, watching the faces around us. Those faces became very important. Not only was each of us looking for some lost loved one (Johann was omnipresent in my mind, even though my hopes were fading), but we were watching to make sure that some of the familiar faces were still with us. Some sense of security had to be found, especially in all that hell. A face that was still with us after a week meant a good deal of security. One that remained after two weeks was very secure indeed. And the few of us who remained even longer (mostly because we weren't Jews) — we formed a core, a nucleus for the work crew. Occasionally, in the middle of a long day's work, a man would pause and look up at our faces, to make sure we were still there. It was like the Polish woman who had pointed to the mud on her shoes when we first arrived.

One day, the man in our barracks who wore the pink triangle disappeared. Nothing was said. Each of us kept our private tally in our heads. He disappeared, was gone, gone from the earth. It was hard to believe. Later, though, I was told he had been raped by some of the guards and then shot in the head.

I thought of Johann, could think only of Johann.

At the day's end, after hard work and almost no food, I'd lie down, wanting to die, thinking up ways to be killed by the guards. Then I'd think of Johann, think of getting out someday to return to him.

Sometimes I'd get angry, incredibly angry. Anger was good. It helped one to survive. I'd think of some guard raping Johann and then shooting him through the head. And not all the justifications on earth could keep me from seeing what was happening to us, all of us. I wanted to kill. I lived for revenge. One could accept persecution for only so long. One could blandly accept genocide for only so long. There came a point where one either submitted to it completely — or fought it completely. In my mind, I fought. Survival was a weapon against the oppressor. And I waited for the time to come when I could fight for real.

Eventually though, things got worse. Work got harder. Food became more scarce. Some of the prisoners tried to eat their own feces and got hopelessly sick. When they didn't report for work, they were dragged outside — either to be gassed, or shot, or buried alive beneath a thousand corpses in the pits.

I stopped living for the day I would be reunited with Johann. I lived only for the day itself, to survive one more day, this day, whatever day it was.

Two nights before we were rounded up by soldiers, Johann and I were in bed, in the attic of a Czechoslovakian whore whose goal was to hide and protect as many people as possible. We shared the attic with an old man and two Swiss nuns.

It was late. The others were asleep, though it really didn't matter to us if they weren't.

I reached over and began caressing Johann's neck. The muscles beneath my fingers tensed briefly, then relaxed.

We made love.

There was only a vague feeling of impending death, only a hint of mortality. That hint, though, fed our love. The death sentence hung over every sex act.

When he came that night, I held him incredibly tight, feeling his entire body jolt beneath mine. An illusion of safety passed through my mind. I thought: We will never die. He will never die. . . .

The day came for me when I suddenly realized he was dead. It was more than intuition. I had no real evidence. I just suddenly knew.

That morning, I stood in the work lineup, watching every face around me, feeling a keen awareness. Of what? Of more than Johann's death. Of everything around me. The certainty of his death didn't seem to disturb me much at first. I didn't feel tremendous grief, or anger, or pain. I felt nothing. I went through the day's work. Frequently I'd look up and think: He's dead. So matter-of-factly, just like that.

That night, trying to sleep, I tried to imagine him dead, tried to imagine how he had died. The images wouldn't come. What fantasies I stirred up were cool and impotent. They held nothing for me.

He's dead, I thought again — the way one suddenly thinks what time it must be.

I drifted off to sleep.

The next morning when our work crew walked by the pits of unburned and unburied corpses, I suddenly started watching the faces of the dead, looking for Johann's. I watched every dead body that was carried by us. I watched all the dead faces I could see. I looked for Johann, for some sign of Johann. The search was as futile as, probably more futile than searching the faces of the living.

When we were outside the camp, working on the road, I looked up as a slash of birds crossed the sunless sky. My mind suddenly screamed: Johann! That was all. I returned to work.

And going back to the barracks, I searched the faces of the dead again. They changed as frequently as the faces of the living.

But there was nothing there. Johann was lost, truly lost.

That night, I imagined him in the barracks with me. I imagined the two of us coming in from the work crew and then flopping back on our beds, exhausted. "It's all right," he whispers. "We'll make it." He touches me briefly on the wrist or on the cheek. That's the only physical symbol of our love that we're allowed. And then sleep, the awful sleep of Auschwitz. . . .

I survived. Somehow, I survived.

There were several weeks when we all knew that whoever could survive the next days, would survive for good.

The Prussian guards relaxed their attitudes. The Nazis became frenetic. They wanted to cover up what they had done. They wanted to bury Auschwitz as a whole, in the ground and then cover it with mud. No faces would ever stare up to accuse the living. Many of us were sure we would die. We were, if nothing else, witnesses to the atrocity. But we didn't die. The Nazis weren't merciful. They were merely all of a sudden disorganized.

I survived. Somehow I survived.

The day came when we were free — and we stared up at our liberators in acute disbelief.

"The nightmare's over," one soldier told a group of prisoners.

The prisoners looked at one another, as if to say, "What nightmare?" They had accepted Auschwitz as their life, the totality of life.

I made one last search for Johann. I searched the faces of the survivors for him. He wasn't there. I'd known he wouldn't be there. But I looked anyway.

I harbored a secret hope that perhaps we would meet again, somewhere on the streets of Berlin or Vienna, that somehow he had escaped, that somehow he had survived. He wasn't dead after all. We'd stop and stare at one another in disbelief, and then move slowly towards one another. His face would be calm but smiling. . . .

We were packed into trucks, the way we had come, and started down the road away from the camp.

Not a soul looked back, I remember.

I looked up. Another slash of birds crossed the sky above me. My mind screamed again: Johann! One last scream . . .

I looked down. The people in the truck were all staring blankly at one another.

Johann . . .

I suddenly remembered the black patch on my prisoner's shirt. I glared down at it, then reached up and pulled it off brutally. I threw it on the floor of the truck. I looked up angrily, defiantly. Several people stared at me in horror. They were so well conditioned that they still expected a guard to come up and shoot me for doing such a thing. I stared back. I rubbed the spot where the black patch had been — and suddenly wished, then and always, that I'd had a pink triangle to wear instead.

LEIGH W. RUTLEDGE lives in Pueblo, Colorado. His work has appeared in *Christopher Street, Blueboy,* and other publications. The story "Das Blassrote Dreieck" is dedicated to the memory of Dr. William H. Halberstadt.

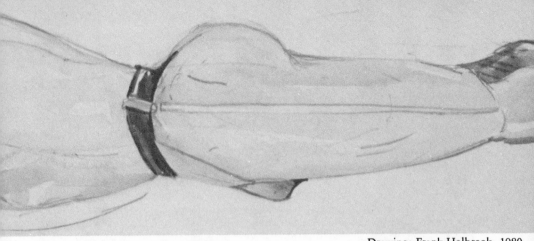

The Kryptonite Kid —a recently-published novel by San Francisco's Joseph Torchia—is the story of young Jerry Chariot, a boy who writes letters to Superman: a kid who inhabits Metropolis in his mind and sees a comicbook world that is bigger, more amazing, yet just as real as the small "Pencilvania" town he lives in.

But as the kid's letters progress—as he gets punished for reading a Superman comicbook in church, ridiculed for trying to find Metropolis on a map, attacked for having the same faith in Superman that sister Mary Justin in school has in God—as all of this action flies toward the day Jerry will tie a green cape around his shoulders, leap off a rooftop and fly to his First Holy Communion, the reader gradually realizes that something else is going on: that a bigger voice is growing out of this kid's misspelled words and emerging in its own right. And write.

That voice caused the New York *Times* to remark: "The eeriness in Joseph Torchia's novel stirs somewhere beneath the surface, as if trying to escape from some Fortress of Solitude, some Phantom Zone of memory that the author wasn't sure he wanted to see, or share: memories of a nun's sadism, a father's ugly violence, a mother's anger and hurt; memories of unbearable hatred for those omnipotent adults, Supermen and Superwomen, who have humiliated and terrified us and let us descend into life all alone."

Now—in "First Communion"—Torchia takes this "eeriness" a step further and tells what happens when Jerry Chariot finally comes face-to-face with his hero—something that never happens in the pages of the book. The author calls it a "postscript" to *The Kryptonite Kid* —his way of adding a "new dimension" for those who have already read his novel, and another way of introducing Jerry Chariot to those who haven't.

"First Communion" is told in the form of a letter—a final, sometimes fierce letter from an adult Jerry Chariot who has survived, literally, the impact of his Superman fantasy. It is written to his pal Robert, the one kid who shared every corner of his childhood (including all those letters to Superman), and in it Torchia allows The Kryptonite Kid—at last!—to receive his First Holy Communion.

FIRST COMMUNION
A Short Story
by
Joseph Torchia

The other dream I walked into this bar looking for you as usual, Robert. But instead I found Superman. Honest I did! I could hardly believe it! I thought maybe I was drunk or something, except I hadn't drunk anything yet. I hadn't even ordered. I just walked in and there he was: leaning against the wall and sipping a beer. I knew it was him because he was wearing blue leotards and a red swimming suit and a cape. And he had this little spit curl right in the middle of his forehead like he always does. And he had the letter S on his chest which was pretty big. In fact it was HUGE! Muscles like you wouldn't believe! And every time he finished a beer he would take the bottle and smash it against his invulnerable head. That's so everybody would know he was really Superman and not in drag. That's why everybody was looking at him. Even the bartender. Because he was so beautiful. So PERFECT. Even the smoke seemed to freeze in mid-air. Every eye in that place was on him. Watching him. Watching every movement. Desiring him. But nobody moved. Nobody walked over to him, or smiled at him, or asked him where he got that neat outfit. They were afraid of him. They were afraid of being rejected by him. They couldn't stand the idea of everybody knowing they had been turned away because they weren't good enough, or beautiful enough. Don't you see, Robert? They have never been beautiful before. They must be beautiful here.

We must all be beautiful. Somewhere.

That's why I was the only one who walked over to him. Because I wasn't afraid. I simply lit a cigarette and walked over and leaned against the wall he was leaning against. And then I looked at him. I looked at him for a LONG time—at his deep dark eyes, at his curly blue hair, at that dent in his chin! HOW COULD I BE AFRAID OF HIM? After ALL those letters I wrote him as a kid? After *all* that love I sent him? He's the one person who would never reject me, or hurt me. I just knew it! All he wants to do is help people. Save people. Not condemn them to Hell. He wants to be touched, not adored. He wants people to be happy without hurting other people. And without being a criminal. That's all. He doesn't want to hurt anybody, or punish anybody eternally. He's never been weak enough to get hurt, so he's never been strong enough to inflict pain. THAT'S why I looked at him. Loved him. Wanted him. Wanted to be like him. That's why I finally said:
"Wanna cigarette?"
Well let me tell you, Robert, when I lit that cigarette, my hand was trembling like you wouldn't believe! EVERYBODY was looking at us. At ME. (It's so hard

to approach a beautiful man because everyone's always watching him, watching to see if you'll succeed with him.) I looked up and tried to smile at that Super face, and he smiled back. "What's your name?" he asked, squeezing the flame of my match with his invulnerable fingertips, putting it out, then extending his hand. "You do have a name, don't you, kid?" I reached for his hand.

"Y-y-yes," I said, "M-my name is Jerry. Jerry Chariot."

GOSH, Robert, you should have felt what I felt when I first felt him! When I first touched that invulnerable hand! Held it! Shook it! It was like something I could never describe. It was like giving birth to a baby. That's something I could never describe because I'm not a woman. I'm a man. I'm a man shaking hands with a Superman. After all this time. After all those letters. After all these years of being alone. At last I've found him. I've REALLY found him. The REAL Superman! In a bar.

In a dream.

"Jerry Chariot?" he said. And then he said, "Hmmmmmmmm, it seems like I've heard that name before?"

He rubbed the dent in his chin. He scratched his blue hair. He broke another beer bottle over his indestructible head. He was thinking. He was trying to remember.

"Hmmmmmmmmm," he said again.

I held my breath. I didn't want to interrupt. Gosh, would he REALLY remember? It was only a moment, but it seemed like forever. His hand was still in mine. Or was mine in his? Who dealt the hand? How did I get here? Why are all these people watching us? Staring at us? Why am I telling you all this, Robert?

"Sayyyyyyyy!" he said at last, snapping his fingers and accidentally breaking my beer bottle. There was white foam all over me and his leotards. "Sayyyyyyy, you're not THE KRYPTONITE KID, are you?"

I blushed ferociously.

"Well I'll be GODDAMNED!" he said, before I had a chance to answer. He slapped me on the back and squeezed my shoulder, as if we were old friends. He wiped the beer off my face with his indestructible cape. "WELL I'LL BE GODDAMNED!" he said again.

And then he looked me right in the eyes. And then he smiled wide, like a kid, and two dimples suddenly appeared, like commas, and then he said:

"I really liked your letters, kid. I really did. Looked forward to them, as a matter of fact. I even took them to the office and showed them to Perry White. God how we laughed! You know, you weren't too bright as a kid, kid. You never fought back hard enough, not until the end. And then it was too late for anything—even your First Holy Communion. But Perry still liked them. He even wanted to run them in a column, but then he thought there might be a libel suit. And besides, who would believe them? You know, I should've answered your letters, kid. I meant to. Trouble was I was so damn busy! You know how it is when you're trying to save people all the time. I figure I must have stopped at least two dozen automobile accidents a day. Not to mention earthquakes, tidal waves, invasions from Outer Space, floods and Mr. Mxyzptlk! He was a real pain in the ass. He kept tricking me, trying to make me miserable. I hated that Fifth-Dimensional faggot!

"And then there was Lois Lane. God, every time I turned around she was falling out a window, or trying to figure out who I really was, and how I really felt.

It was bad enough trying to hold down two jobs at the same time—but that bitch really made it hard, so to speak. Believe me, kid, it isn't easy trying to make people think you're something you're not. Especially Lois. Do you know what she did one time? We were working late at the Planet, grinding out a weekend wrapup, when she put the make on me. Right there in the office! It was pretty late and no one else was around, so she figured if she got my clothes off then she could see if I was wearing my Super-costume underneath. Pretty clever. But not clever enough for SUPERMAN. When she started kissing me and groping me, I knew what was bound to come. So I slipped away at Super-speed, took off my outfit, put my regular clothes back on, then returned in a fraction of a second. It took less time than a fart, and it was a lot less noticeable. She never even realized I'd been gone. And then I plowed the shit out of her. Right there on my desk. I mean Clark's desk. God, she loved it! The next day she slipped me a note. It said I should meet her in the stockroom after our 5 o'clock deadline. So I did. Just about every day. She was a nymphomaniac, if you ask me. Her name should be Lois Lain.

"But I got tired of hiding my costume all the time—of pretending I wasn't somebody I was. I'm through with all that. From now on I'm gonna be myself. And if people don't like it, well that's the way the Kryptonite crumbles. And that's exactly what I told her. Boy, you should have seen the expression on her face! She looked horrified! She couldn't believe it! WHY ARE YOU TELLING ME NOW? she asked. BECAUSE I'M TIRED OF SNEAKING INTO THAT GODDAMN CLOSET ALL THE TIME! I said. IF IT ISN'T A CLOSET, IT'S A PHONE BOOTH! I'M SICK OF LIVING THAT WAY!

"And I WAS sick, Jerry. That's why I left Metropolis. That's why I came here, now, and found you. That's why we're talking together, kid. At last we're ready for each other. At last you can touch me. Here, go ahead. Put your hand on my arm. C'mon, touch me, kid. Hold me. Fly with me. Isn't that what you've always wanted? Isn't that why you wrote me all those letters? Please do it, kid. PLEASE."

I reached out slowly, carefully, afraid he might dissolve like a dream into morning. Everyone was watching, even those way in the back. People could see through people to see me. Everybody was invisible except ME, Robert. Me and him.

"Don't be afraid," he said. "I WANT you to touch me! That's what I've always wanted. I may look tough, but I'm not. Not really. Please touch me, kid. I can't help it if I'm Super—if everyone looks up to me, thinks I'm strong. That's THEIR image, so I have to break beer bottles over my head. I can't do anything about it. But I'm NOT strong. Not really. I'm weak. I need help. I need love. I need YOU, kid. Because somewhere beneath this invulnerable skin, inside this indestructible chest, somewhere deep inside is a speck of Kryptonite—glowing, warm. And hurting—"

Everyone watched as my hand touched his hand, slipped up his arm, brushed his cheek. Everyone stared as I touched him, pulled him toward me, put both my arms around him, gently.

Everyone saw it.

"Harder!" he said. "Hold me *harder!* Squeeze me! Let me *FEEL* you!"

He was yelling now, and wrapping his legs around mine, and pressing his body into my body. In front of everybody.

"C'mon, kid, let me *FEEL* you!" he said, "Let me feel that *HOT* tongue!"

He opened his mouth and attacked my lips and licked them, chewed them, bit them, then sucked them—drawing out my tongue, letting it slide down his deep, moist, invulnerable throat.

It was REALLY embarrassing, Robert.

I mean, you just don't do those things in a bar. Not with people watching.

I think he sensed my uneasiness because after a while he stopped. He tucked his shirt back into his leotards. He smoothed his cape. Ordered another beer. Then said:

"You used to have a friend, didn't you? What was his name?...Ronald?...Or Robin, or . . ."

"Robert," I said. "His name was . . ."

"ROBERT! Of course, now I remember. Had freckles, didn't he?"

"Yes, he . . ."

"I've always hated freckles myself. Kept telling Jimmy Olsen he should get them removed. Even offered to pay for it. Said I'd get a piece of coal and squeeze it into a diamond for him. But he wouldn't take it. Said he liked his freckles. Couldn't understand it myself. I think they look like piss stains. Say, whatever happened to Ronald . . ."

"Robert," I said.

"Yeah, Robert. Whatever happened to him? Are you two still friends? Do you two still write letters together?"

"No, I'm afraid he . . ."

"He didn't get married, did he?"

"Oh no, Superman. He didn't do that."

"Thank God!"

"He died."

"Oh...Oh gee, I'm sorry, kid...I didn't realize. Choke. The poor kid. Sob. Oh jeez . . . What happened, may I ask?"

"Sure."

"What happened?"

"Well I'll tell you, Superman. One day they said he wasn't a man. So he went away to prove he was. Only he wasn't. So they mortared him."

"Gee, that's too bad."

"For who?"

"For you, kid."

"Yes. Yes it is," I said.

And then he broke another beer bottle over his head.

Maybe I shouldn't have told him the truth, Robert. About how they laughed at you, then attacked you, then nailed you to a question mark, like Jesus. But I couldn't help it. I felt he wanted to know the TRUTH, Robert.

So I told him:

Robert was my friend. My BEST friend. The only person I chose to love me back. So he did. Even after the leap. Even after I didn't walk good anymore. Still he loved me and held me and wanted me totally—until his mom and dad shot into the room. Until they looked at us like we were the WORST things they had ever seen. I remember his dad reaching for his belt immediately, instinctively snapping it through the air, and then I saw the shame on Robert's face. And then I saw the tears in Robert's eyes, each one a different color—red and blue and green, like Kryptonite. I tried to protect him but it was too late, Superman. His dad's horror went flashing through the air quickly, irrevocably—like a bullet it entered him and destroyed him took him away from me forever.

"And then they tried to kill me, Superman. They tried to kill me the same way they killed Robert—with fear and shame and prayers. And blame. But I fought back. I was TOUGH like you! I told them I'm gonna fly, I'm gonna jump, you can't hurt me, you can't kill me, now I'm Super, now I'm invulnerable, and then I jumped."

And then I hit the ground.

And then I looked him right in the eyes, Robert. Right square in the face, and I said:

"Why didn't you ever write me a letter, Superman? Just ONE letter to let me know? Or why didn't you fly over my house, or give me a sign, or work a miracle? Why must I meet you now, in a bar, when it's too late to save Robert or me or ANYBODY? Why didn't you appear then, when we needed you most—when we were small? When you were big? Why, Superman? *WHY?*"

And you know what he said, Robert?

He said:

"Excuse me a second, will you? I have to go to the toilet."

And he went.

* * *

He was in there a pretty long time. About fifteen minutes. I kept watching the door, waiting for him to come out. A whole bunch of other guys kept going in and coming out and going in and coming out. And so I started thinking about Mrs. Bacchio because I didn't have nothing else to do except wait, Robert. Wait and remember that day after school when we were in Bacchio's News Stand when Mr. Durrelli was late with the comicbooks. And Mrs. Bacchio kept looking at us looking worried. And you kept biting your nails, Robert, because it was going on 5 o'clock and Mr. Durrelli still didn't come in with the comicbooks and Mrs. Bacchio was still looking at us and she was smiling. And then she said, "My, you boys must sure like comicbooks."

And you said, "We sure do, Mrs. Bacchio."

And I said, "You see, Mrs. Bacchio, we don't really like comicbooks. We just like Superman and Supergirl and Superdog and Jimmy Olsen. That's all. Except we also like Superhorse and Perry White and Ma and Pa Kent."

And you said "We sure do" again, Robert.

And I said, "You see, Mrs. Bacchio, we don't like Donald Duck and Little Lulu because they're for little kids and not us. And besides, they don't fly or nothing."

And you said "They sure don't" this time, Robert.

And I said, "We don't mind Batman and Wonder Woman and Green Lantern and Flash and people like that. But you see, we don't have very much money and so we like Superman the best. That's because he *is* the best."

And that's when Mrs. Bacchio laughed and said, "You know, I kinda like Superman myself." And she was the FIRST grown-up we ever met who liked Superman, Robert, and that's why we didn't trust her. And so I said:

"OK, if you like Superman so much then you must know what can kill him. so what is it?"

And she said, "Just one thing. Kryptonite."

And you said, "Hey, she *does* know!"

And I said, "Well, lots of people know that, Robert." And so I turned to Mrs. Bacchio and I looked at her for a long time and I looked right in her eyes and then I said, "OK, if you're so smart then tell me what Superman's real name is."

And she said, "You mean Clark Kent?"

And I said, "No, I mean his REAL name on Krypton that his real mom and dad gave him before Krypton blew up and he came to Earth in a rocket to become Superbaby and someday Superman?"

And she said, "That's easy."

"And I said, "Then what is it?"

And she said, "His real name was Kal-El. And his real father's name was Jor-El. And his real mother's name was Lara."

And you said "GOSH!" Robert.

And I didn't say nothing because I still didn't trust her. So I asked her a bunch of other questions like "How do you get rid of Mr. Mxyzptlk!?" And she said "Mr. WHO?" And I said "Mr. Mxyzptlk!" And she said, "Oh, I thought it was pronounced Mxyzptlk!" And I said, "Well me and Robert say Mxyzptlk!" And so she told us.

She knew the answers to EVERYTHING, Robert. And she kept smiling at us. And she smiled real nice, just like all the saints on the Holy Cards smile when a light shines down from Heaven on them. And so we liked her a WHOLE lot. We really did. We liked her more than any other groan-ups we met, even the ones we HAD to like. Like my Aunt Hellen who we HATED. And that's why we felt so bad when my mom and Veronica next door started whispering about Mrs. Bacchio. And pretty soon your mom started whispering about her too, Robert. And before long even the nuns started whispering about how Lenore Bacchio was doing something with somebody who she wasn't supposed to be doing it with. And we didn't know exactly what it was because we never heard them whisper THAT low before. But we figured it must have been pretty bad because my mom whispered, "Does her husband know about it?"

And Veronica next door whispered, "No, but everybody else does."

And I said, "I don't."

And BOY did my mom get mad! She yelled REAL LOUD at me and told me how I wasn't supposed to listen to groan-ups talk. Especially when they're whispering. And how I'm not allowed to go in Bacchio's News Stand EVER AGAIN. And how I better get outside before she gives me a beating RIGHT THIS INSTANT YOUNG MAN! And so we went up to your house, Robert, but we still couldn't figure out who it was she was doing it with.

Whatever it was she was doing.

* * *

Whatever it was he was doing, he was sure taking a long time, Robert. About a half-hour now. I kept watching the door, waiting for Superman to come out. A whole bunch of other guys kept going in and coming out and going in and coming out. I started worrying. Maybe there was a piece of Kryptonite in the toilet or something? Maybe he was sitting on the toilet dying? maybe I should go in and see if he's OK? So I did. I put my beer down and lit a cigarette and started to walk over and then it happened. The door opened. He came out. And you'll never guess who was with him? It was Mr. Mxyzptlk!

Honest to God, Robert—it was *Mr. Mxyzptlk!*

Right away I tried to think of a way to trick Mr. Mxyzptlk! into spelling his name backwards. Because that's the only way to get rid of him and send him back to THE FIFTH DIMENSION where he lives with all the other imps. Because he's MAGICAL and so you have to trick him into saying *!kltpzyxM* or else he'll just hang around and make Superman miserable like he always does. Like one time he made all the cars drive up the side of the Daily Planet building and another time he made all the water disappear from everybody's swimming pool. And so Superman had to trick him on the last page of the comicbook by making him read the letters in his alphabet soup which turned out to be his name spelt backwards. Which was pretty clever. But still I was worried, Robert, because I got one good look at Mr. Mxyzptlk! and KNEW there was gonna be trouble. Except then I noticed that Superman was smiling REAL BIG. And he was carrying Mr. Mxyzptlk! because he's just an imp and he didn't want to get stepped on in that crowded bar. And he carried him right over to where I was standing. And then Superman said, "Mr. Mxyzptlk!, I'd like you to meet Jerry Chariot."

And Mr. Mxyzptlk! said, "Hi, Jerry!"

And I said, "Hello, Mr. Mxyzptlk!"

And Mr. Mxyzptlk! said, "Just call me Mr. for short."

And I said, "I'm very pleased to meet you at last, Mr."

And Mr. said, "The pleasure's all mine, Jerry."

And Superman said, "You can call him kid."

And Mr. said, ". . . kid."

And I said, "You can call me Jerry if you want."

And Mr. said, "Put me down, Superman."

So Superman put him down.

Well you should have seen him, Robert! His nose came right up to my belly button. Or maybe below it. And so it was hard to hear him down there. And everytime he said something, I wasn't sure if he said something. So I bent down and asked him, "Did you just say something?" And he said, "Will somebody please pick me up!" So Superman did it.

"Thank you, Superman," said Mr. Mxyzptlk!

"You're welcome, Mr. Mxyzptlk!" said Superman.

And then Mr. Mxyzptlk! decided it would be a lot easier if he sat on Superman's shoulders so he could see everything. So he grabbed Superman's indestructible cape with one hand, his invulnerable hair with the other, then hoisted himself onto the Man of Steel's massive shoulders. Then he rested both elbows on Superman's head and perched there like a raven.

And then I said:

"I thought you guys didn't like each other too much? I mean, you ALWAYS used to fight and stuff, didn't you? You always tried to get rid of the other person. So what happened? Don't you hate each other like you always used to? Don't you DESPISE each other?"

Quoth the imp, "Not anymore."

"You see, Jerry," he explained, "one day as I was flying here from The Fifth Dimension, something strange happened. I was mid-way through the Fourth

Dimension when I saw myself going the other way, returning to The Fifth Dimension, and I was flying backwards. And I was crying. And each tear was black, perfectly black, and it scared me. *'What the HELL am I doing?'* I asked myself. *'Why in Heaven's name am I always traveling back and forth from The Fifth? What's so IMPortant about making Superman miserable?'* Suddenly, as I reached the outskirts of The Third, came the answer: *'I don't hate Superman—I LOVE him!'*

"Well let me tell you, Jerry, that's not easy to come to. Not after you've spent your whole life hating somebody as much as I hated Superman. I was REALLY upset. I had wasted so MUCH time trying to make Superman notice me, talk to me, trick me, do ANYTHING to me—as long as he paid SOME kind of attention! And it's no secret, kid, if you want some attention all you've got to do is make somebody miserable. So that's what I did: year in, dimension out.

"Trouble was it wasn't the RIGHT kind of attention. After a while all that misery started bothering me. I started having dreams like you used to have, kid. I started dreaming that I was flying and crying backwards. That tears were falling INTO my eyes instead of out of them. That Mrs. Bacchio was watching me, then I was watching her turn on the gas and suffocate. Then I would wake up crying and screaming for Superman to save her. But I KNEW it was too late! I KNEW I had to let her die! I could hear a statue of the Virgin Mary in her pocket, crying...

"Yes, kid—it was *I* who intercepted those letters you and Robert wrote to Superman about Lenore Bacchio. THAT'S why Superman never showed up to save her! It was just another of my impish pranks—no real harm intended. HONEST, kid! At the last minute I was going to notify the Man of Steel and watch him rescue her. I had it all planned out. Trouble was she seemed to want to die. Almost NEED to die. There was something about the look on her face when she latched those windows shut. Something about the calm that surrounded her as she turned on that oven.

"I didn't mean to let it happen, Jerry. Please don't look at me like that, kid! It's just . . . well, it's just that I couldn't help myself. She had a spell over me. I explained it all to Superman and he understood. Didn't you, Superman? I told him right here in this bar, as a matter of fact. In that corner over there. I'll never forget how he looked back at me, then leaned forward and kissed me. His hands were still at his sides and his eyes were like bright stars, staring at me as if I were the moon in his sky. As if *I* were the glow that made him so bright.

"He wanted me that night, Jerry. He forgave me and loved me. He knew I would now give him pleasure—not misery. Isn't that right, Superman? Tell Jerry about that first night we spent together. About how happy we were to warm each other's insomnia. To at last be real. Rewarding each other with kisses. Seizing each other's caresses. Correct me if I'm wrong, kid, but isn't that the way you first felt with Robert?

"Well isn't it, Jerry?" he said. Then paused. Then rubbed his fingers through Superman's blue hair and exploded into laughter—high, screechy, ugly, awful laughter that kept rearranging itself. One second it sounded like Sister Mary Justin and the next second it sounded like Veronica nextdoor. And then it was Mrs. Bacchio and then it was Lois Lane and then it was my dad. And then it was a siren, like an ambulance, and a scream. My mom's scream.

What's going on here, Robert? This dream's becoming too much like reality. That scream sounds too much like a *scream!* I'm afraid, Robert. Everything's out of control.

"C'MON, KID, ADMIT IT!" the imp snapped, and suddenly his words seemed to come from far, far away. From another time or space. Or dimension. One of his eyes turned purple and the other turned orange and his hair seemed to melt as his chin withered as his ears grew long and furious and pointed. Superman just stood there frozen—saying nothing, doing nothing, ignoring this rabid imp who suddenly pointed a long red fingernail at me.

"I *know* how desperately you've always wanted Superman!" he shrieked, his voice full of hate and jealousy—nothing mischievous or impish left in him.

"Always acting so young, so innocent—so *appealing!*" he said. "Well you can't fool me, Jerry! I know your tricks and I'm not giving up without a battle! Superman belongs to *ME* now and there's no way you can make me say *!kltpzyxM* because it won't work! Do you understand, kid? It CAN'T work because . . . Oh shit! I said it! GodDAMNit, Superman, I'm disa

p

p

e

a

r

i

n

I couldn't believe it, Robert! One minute he was sitting on Superman's shoulders and talking, and the next minute he was gone! Just like that! He didn't even have time to close the quotation marks. He just vanished. It happened so fast.

!kltpzyxM

"What luck!" said Superman. "I thought we'd never get rid of that Fifth-Dimensional fart!"

"WHAT?" I said. "But I thought you liked him now? I thought you were friends. Doesn't he LOVE you now?"

"Sure he loves me. Doesn't everybody?"

"Except Sister Mary Justin in school."

"Then what do I need his love for? I've got more love than I can handle right now, kid. Just look around this bar. See all those people staring at me, wanting me, desiring me? THAT's the way it is wherever I go. EVERYBODY worships me. They NEVER leave me alone. They want my autograph, or a lock of my indestructible hair, or a kiss. Everybody wants SOMETHING from me, kid—just like you do. Just like Lois Lane did. Just like Mr. Mxyzptlk! didn't. That's why I liked him a lot better then—because he was the only person who hated me. Except for criminals and they don't count, not in my book. I mean comicbook. It was kind of nice to find a little hate for a change, but now even that imp loves me. Shit, kid, what can a Superman do?"

"I don't know," I said. "But I know what I'D do."

"What's that, kid?"

"I'd take all that love, from everybody, every ounce of it, I'd take it all and I'd NEVER let it out of my sight. I'd hold on to it, sleep with it, pray to it. I'd buy a gun and protect it. And if anybody tried to take it away, I'd kill them. That's what I'd do. I KNOW that's what I'd do, Superman."

"You know what, kid?"

"What, Superman?"

"You'll never get Super that way."

"You know what, Superman?"

"What, kid?"

"I'll never get Super anyway."

!kltpzyxM

"You're growing up, kid."

"No, Superman, I'm groaning up."

!kltpzyxM

"I wish he could have stayed, Superman. I wanted to ask him about The Fifth Dimension, about what it's like there. About how you get there. Say, you don't know where The Fifth Dimension is, do you, Superman?"

"Sure I do."

"Where is it?"

"It's quite a ways from here, kid. And it's also very close. It's a pretty hard place to find because you have to make your way through Purgatory, past Metropolis and over the Duck Rock. Then you have to climb back into your mother's stomach and laugh about it all. Believe me, you'll never find it, kid. NEVER!"

"Will you take me there, Superman?"

You should have seen the look he gave me, Robert! He wasn't smiling anymore and he was biting his indestructible lip and his eyes seemed to get bigger, darker, sadder. He looked at me just the way he looked at Ma and Pa Kent when they were dying way back in *GIANT SUPERBOY NO. 165*. And he was crying. And each tear was green. Kryptonite green. And he said:

"Don't do it, kid. Don't try to go to The Fifth Dimension. Not there! It's too dangerous, too painful. There are too many things trying to stop you, to prevent you from making it. Horrible things! Frightening things like Sister Mary Justin, like Veronica nextdoor, like the Holy Ghost! They're hiding behind every rock— waiting for you, waiting to attack you, hit you, kill you! PLEASE, kid! I beg you. DON'T do it. Forget it! We can leave this bar in a while. I'll give you a ride home and we can turn out the lights and touch each other. I love the feeling of another man's body embracing me back. I LOVE the idea of two men together—two buddies, two pals—walking like men, acting like men, loving like men. Stay a while longer, kid. I feel good in this dark corner where there's no one to disapprove. Where there's no one to throw Kryptonite at me. I like the shadows here, and the smoke. They hide me. They protect me. They remind me that I can be honest here, inside, as long as I'm dishonest everywhere else. To find joy in a place where others find contempt, even disgust, makes me feel important. It makes me feel SUPER. Yes, I feel safe here with you. Forget The Fifth Dimension, kid. Have another beer. Touch me, Hold me. I love you."

I couldn't STAND looking at his tears, Robert. Even if they are indestructible, they don't belong there. Not on his face. Not on his PERFECT face! I looked away. I fumbled for a cigarette. He lit it with his x-ray vision. I said, "Thank you, Superman." He said, "You're welcome, kid." We both smiled as I watched the last of his tears roll down his cheeks, bounce off his indestructible chest, fall gently to the floor, like rain.

That's when I noticed it, Robert.

I looked down at his red swimming suit and it was flat. PERFECTLY flat. Just like in the comicbooks. Either it was tucked way under, or he didn't have anyThing at all.

I *had* to find out.

"By the way, Superman," I said, inching a little closer. "How's your cousin Supergirl?"
"SUPERGIRL?" he said. "You mean SUPERWOMAN. She's grown up now, you know. Married an airline pilot. He isn't Super, but at least they can fly together. How'd you like that one? HA-HA!"
"I didn't," I said, moving closer.
"Well, it's true. That's how they met. One day she was flying along pretty fast, trying to gain enough speed to crash through the Time Barrier. Instead she almost crashed into his cockpit. HA-HA!"
"HA-HA!" I said, moving closer. My hands were getting sweaty.
"So he rolled down the window of his plane. SAY THERE, SUPERWOMAN, he said. YOU BETTER WATCH WHERE YOU'RE FLYING. She looked at him. He smiled at her. SORRY ABOUT THAT, she said apologetically. PLEASE FORGIVE ME, she said imploringly. I APOLOGIZE, she said pathetically. And then . . ."
"And then?"
"And then somebody inside the airplane spotted her. I mean, how could they help it? She was just flying along beside the plane and flirting with the pilot. So somebody looked outside and said, HEY, LOOK—OUTSIDE!
"And somebody else said IT'S A BIRD!
"And somebody else said IT'S A PLANE!
"And somebody else said, NO, IT'S *SSSSSSSUPERWOMAN!*
"And allofasudden everybody ran to one side of the airplane and it flipped over and it started to crash and so Superwoman had to save it on the top of page ten. And she also saved him. So he flipped for her. And then they kissed and had a REALLY long engagement. About 25 issues. And then they got married. And then it said *THE AND*. I mean *END*."

I was REALLY close now, Robert. My knee was touching his knee and my arm was also. I was rubbing against him gently—trying to push my body into his Super body. But still I needed to get a little closer—to touch it, feel it, find out if he had one!

And if it was big.

"And then what happened?" I asked, moving closer.

"The usual," he said, sipping his beer. "They had a nice little house, and then they had a nice little baby, and then they had a nice little another baby, and they needed more room, so they got another house, and so he needed another job to pay for the another house, and then he couldn't sleep at night, and then they live happily ever after."

"Were they Super, I wonder?" I asked, moving closer.

"Were who Super?"

"Her kids," I said. "Were they Super or regular?"

"What's the difference?"

"Oh, about ten cents a gallon."

"Super," he said.

"Both of them?"

"No, just one of them. One was Super and the other was regular. That is to say, ordinary."

"How unfortunate," I said, moving closer.

"Yes," he said. "They NEVER got along. Especially since the Super one was a girl. And the older one was a boy. How would you like it if your little sister kept chasing crooks while you did the dishes all the time?"

"I wouldn't," I said, moving closer.

"Well, neither did he. So he killed himself."

"How TERRIBLE!" I said, moving closer.

"Yes, it was a real mess. He leaped off the roof of his dad's apartment building and splattered all over the headlines."

"Oh no!" I said, moving closer.

"Oh *yes!* And everyone blamed Superwoman. Said she was a domineering mother, that she overpowered him—killed him!"

"Was it true?" I asked. "Did she really kill him?"

"Don't know," said Superman. "But I'll tell you what I think."

"What do you think?" I asked, and I was about as CLOSE as I could get—I was just about to put my hand on it, to find out if he had one, when he said:

"I think I'll have another beer."

And he walked away.

And when he came back he handed me a beer that he had bought me, and we clinked bottles, and he said, "Here's looking at you, kid!" And he looked at me. He looked me right in my Kryptonite eyes and he said:

"There's two things I've been wanting to ask you, kid. Just two things. I've been wanting to ask you for a LONG time and now I finally have the chance. So please answer, will you, kid? It's REALLY important. Please?"

"Sure, Superman," I said. "Anything. What is it?"

"Well, kid, the second question is a lot easier than the first. So I'll start with the second question first."

"That makes sense."

"OK, kid. Question number one: WHO MADE YOU?"

"Is THAT your question?"

"That's it."

"That's easy."

"That's what you think, kid. You better think about it."

"I don't have to, Superman. I'll tell you right now: God made me. My mom and dad made me. My brother Buster made me. Sister Mary Justin and Jimmy Sinceri and Pastor Ponti made me. Even Veronica nextdoor made me. They ALL made me. I didn't really want to. Not really. They made me."

"What did they make you, kid?"

"Is that your second question, Superman?"

"Well it isn't my third."

"Kryptonite," I said. "They made me Kryptonite."

"And what did you do with it, kid?"

"With what, Superman?"

"With the Kryptonite, kid."

"I leaped."

!kltpzyxM

"And why did you leap, kid?"

"For the same reason I wrote you all those letters."

"And what was that?"

"To show them I'm not so little anymore."

!kltpzyxM

Well you should have seen the look he gave me then, Robert! You should have seen the way his eyes got dark and slanted. It was JUST the way Sister Mary Justin used to do it. Honest to God! I couldn't believe it! He looked at me REAL mean and said:

"Who in the *HELL* do you think you're kidding, kid? You're just as little as you've ever been—as you'll ALWAYS be! You'll NEVER be as big as I am. You'll never be SUPER like me! Sure, you can write me letters, if you want. Sure, you can put words in my mouth. You're holding the pencil, kid. But you're forgetting one thing: *I'm* Superman! I can burst out of these pages, away from these words. But you're STUCK here, kid! You're no better off than you were on that roof! Look at your life. Look at it honestly and you'll see the TRUTH. You'll see yourself standing here, in this bar, on this page, trying to get as close to me as you can—trying to reach inside my pants and find love. Well, go ahead, REACH! C'mon, kid, stick your hand in there and see what you'll find. Go ahead! *DO IT!*"

He reached out quickly and grabbed my arm.

"NO!" I shouted. "No, I don't want to! I changed my mind. I don't want to!"

The room was suddenly quiet. Everybody was looking at us, staring at us. No one moved. Everyone listened.

"Get away!" I yelled, trying to fight back. But he was holding my arm. squeezing hard, pulling me toward him, hurting me.

"What's wrong, kid? Are you AFRAID? I thought that's what you wanted? C'mon, kid, I saw you looking at it. TAKE IT!"
He burst out laughing REAL high and screechy, like a girl. Laughing.

He slapped me across the face.
My nose started to bleed. Everyone moved in closer, surrounding us.
Watching us.

I *tried* not to cry, Robert. But he grabbed my shoulders and forced me to my knees and pulled my hair and it hurt, Robert. It REALLY hurt! He looked at me like he HATED me, like he was going to KILL me. My eyes were all watery but I wasn't really crying. "Now reach in there and grab it!" he said.
"Please, Superman. Please don't . . ."
"*GRAB IT!*" He pounded my head with his Super fist.

I looked around for help, but nobody moved. They all just stood there, like people in church—waiting for a sacrifice.
One man smiled.
Another laughed and sipped his beer.
And I KNEW I had to do it. I had *no* choice!
They were all watching.
I reached out slowly, with trembling hands, and unfastened his Super belt. I was still on my knees.
Suddenly I felt like a child in a confessional.
Suddenly I felt like a boy on a rooftop, with a cape over his shoulders, about to fly . . .
I looked down at them, at ALL of them—at my mom and my dad and Veronica and everybody—at all those faces looking up at me. Then I reached inside his red swimming suit, beneath his blue leotards, and I grabbed it. Honest. I did, Robert! I pulled it out. I held it and touched it and everybody watched. EVERYBODY! And you know what it was, Robert? You know what Superman had in there?

It was a First Holy Communion wafer.

So I put it in my mouth. Then I jumped off the roof.

Then I woke up.

THE CHARM OF
THE GREAT AMERICAN DESERT
A Short Story
by

Michael Lebeck

One of the advantages of being gay is a certain freedom of movement. My father, who had been a widower for years, had taken to his bed. His doctor phoned me: it was cancer. Dad and I had always gotten along fine as long as we kept to subjects that interested him, like family, the church or money. My coming home to take care of him was considered such an act of filial piety that before I stepped off the Greyhound, every lady in the county had heard and approved it.

Their approval would have turned to thin-lipped condemnation if my suitcase had vomited its contents onto the road. I didn't know how long I was going to be in Forrest, pop. 6,000, but I didn't believe I'd find any action there. Although my father was not expected to live long, Doc couldn't deny that "love can work miracles." The way I felt about my old man, he might hang on indefinitely. So I came supplied with as many skin magazines as I could afford. And had any of the good ladies of Whyte county guessed at the existence of the dildo? I brought a brown one and a pink one.

Forrest had a charmed existence. Little had changed since the last year I'd lived in this small house where Dad and I moved after Sis married and moved away and Mom passed on. Now Dad was my concern as I'd been his concern then. Surely Forrest was enchanted. Over the first few weeks, I noticed that no one between the ages of twenty and fifty seemed to live there—except me. Perhaps it was this same enchantment that made every young male in town remind me of the track star I'd fallen for when I was eighteen. Everywhere I saw the boy next door. The boy next door was Forrest's principal charm. He could be blond or dark, a little skinnier or a little plumper. Everyone's features betrayed a family likeness. They all walked in the same unself-conscious way. The jeans always hugged their buns. If one of them stood still a moment, in all innocence, torso, pelvis and legs conspired to show off his basket to the best advantage. It was driving me crazy, almost as crazy as it drove me 20 years before.

That was when I realized I was going to have to get out of the Great American Desert. Since leaving home for the Service, I'd worked at many jobs, on the West coast and the East. Now here I was back in the desert of my own free choice. I felt like a goddamned camel, only my balls were my hump. No matter how often I jacked off, I was unable to keep up with the visual stimulation provided by all the boys next door: on the street, in the supermarket, at the filling station, but most of all in my head at night when Dad started snoring.

I couldn't help thinking of that old-time saint who had found more temptations in the fanciful desert than he had in the fleshpots of Alexandria. "Are temptations ever unreal?" I growled. Was I going to start seducing young men the way the minister warned that all degenerates do? I'd be damned if I would.

I hadn't made it with anyone in his twenties since I turned twenty. All my life I'd been attracted to men a few years older than I was: in high school to the college track star, in the service to the sergeant, and later to older workers and to businessmen away from home. Many of them had been married. Sex had always been an appetite that I satisfied easily, unthinkingly.

* * *

One early June night I fell asleep in the living room with my pants down. I'd have sat there all night with my dick sticking to my palm if the phone hadn't rung. Somehow I pulled up my pants and looked at my watch at the same time. It was almost midnight! If anyone was calling at that hour, it had to be an emergency. Perhaps my sister's oldest was in trouble again.

"I'm sorry," I said when I couldn't identify the voice, "but you must have a wrong number." I wasn't being polite; I really was sorry: the voice on the phone was enchanting.

"There are no wrong numbers." A youthful male voice corrected me. "Look, a friend of yours gave me your number."

"You're lying. There's not a soul in Forrest who'd do that. Besides, I don't really have any friends here anymore."

"OK, so I made that up. Actually, I found your number scrawled on a men's room wall and I was bored so I called it."

I told him he was full of shit.

"Look, are you straight?"

"What do you mean straight? That word made no sense in the mouth of one of the boys next door.

"Straight, straight, straight! Look, I'm so horny out here at the college I'm about to go crazy. Are you gay too?"

I took a big chance. Actually I had no choice. My voice answered for me before I could think. I blurted out, "Sure. I'm gay."

"Well, let's get together. Who are you anyway?"

"I thought you said someone gave you my number."

"OK, mister, I'll square with you. I had the good luck to dial your number at random."

I didn't believe that either. How many thousand people were there in Forrest and the surrounding county? And he got me? That would have been diabolical. No, I wouldn't believe that. Maybe all those boys next door were less naive than I supposed, and some of them noticed the nervous way I walked past or answered their questions. ("Aren't you married?" "Like it here?" "Know lots of hot chicks in the city, don' you?") Whoever this was on the phone, he *knew*. Oh God, that way lay paranoia.

"You still there?"

"Oh yes . . ." He certainly sounded all right. "Well, what's your name?"

"My name is Roland. Where can we meet?"

"I'm at home and I can't leave. Not tonight. Do you do this often?"

"Do what?"

"Call people in the middle of the night and ask if they're—straight?"

"I just transferred here a couple of months ago and I've done this almost every night once I discovered there wasn't any action in the locker rooms or the men's rooms or anywhere else, for that matter."

So Roland had been here as long as I had. "Well, what responses have you gotten to your campaign?" I'd sat down next to the phone and leaned back against the wall. I was feeling myself up through my jeans. "Roland, I'm glad you called," I blurted out. "You're the first gay guy I've talked to in months. I'd started talking to myself!"

"Just last night I called four numbers at random. The first three, women answered the phone and I hung up. But the fourth time I got someone with a deep voice who didn't hang up on me. Half an hour later this big guy in a pick-up meets me at the bus-stop on the highway and takes me home; well not exactly home, he took me to an out-building on his place and I gave him a blow-job. He was wild!"

"Well, I'll be damned. Damn, I've got a hard-on . . . Wait a second while I get out of my jeans. What about you?"

"You bet I do. Want to suck it?"

"Sure. Tell me what it's like."

"It's thick and hard and more than seven inches."

"You cut or uncut?"

"I've still got my foreskin. You?"

"Mine's circumcised but otherwise what I've got in my hand is just like yours. You like to lick my balls."

"I'd like to lick your hot ass, mister!"

We continued like that for half an hour. I had to have him now, I didn't care how risky it was. I told him my name, Marvin. I'd figure out some way I could leave Dad and pick this kid up and smuggle him in and then get him back to the dorm.

"Where are you phoning from anyway?"

"I'm in a phone booth on the highway and I'm beating my meat with my back to the traffic. No one can see me and if they did, they wouldn't believe their eyes."

I liked that voice. It sounded twenty. Just listening to it made me feel eighteen. He wasn't some old fart pretending to be what he wanted, like the author of the first graffiti I remember. In a public library men's room somewhere I'd read HOT YOUNG STUD 11 INSHES WONT TO MEAT SAME FOR HOT SEX. It was written in shaky pencil, betraying the palsied hand of the graying janitor. No, there was vitality in Roland's voice and a big-city impatience and fascination with small-town ways. "Roland, what do you look like?"

"I'm twenty. I'm built like a football player but I don't play, I'm a cheerleader. I've got dark hair. Let's see . . . I'm about five ten. What about you, Marvin?"

"I'm in my late thirties."

"You sure don't sound that old!"

"Oh, I don't feel it or look it either. I'm no monster." What I'd just blurted out made me laugh. "I've always gotten a lot of exercise but I've never been muscular. And after several months in this town, I'm as horny as I ever was when I was your age. Listen, I want to shoot my load talking to you, you like that?"

"I'd rather you shot it down my throat, man."

"Talk to me like that, you big cocksucker!"

A few minutes later, after the grunting and groaning on both ends of the line had subsided, I heard my father calling me.

"I've got to run, father wants me. Give me a call tomorrow night around 8. I'll have figured out something."

"Just a minute! I really did dial your number at random. Damn, I don't have a ball-point either. Give it to me a couple of times, Marvin, I'll remember it. I'm sure as hell going to try."

* * *

Next day I worried about two things: how I was going to manage this assignation and how I could justify it. And at the same time, I never really believed that "Roland" was going to call.

Over the months I'd begun to notice a pattern in my father's nights. Between the hours of eight and ten he was dead to the world. Between ten and eleven he needed medication or reassurance. Most nights he would sleep soundly till sunrise. But I had recently discovered that around one in the morning he often woke tortured by the fear of hell. "So this is what I have to look forward to?" I mused. I wasn't looking forward to it at all.

What I was looking forward to hungrily was Roland's body. I would simply drive over to the state college and pick him up between eight and ten and take him back whenever I was certain Dad was sleeping soundly. I was excited. I was scared.

He called at 8:30. So he wasn't just some kid who enjoys jacking off over the phone. He was set on real skin-to-skin pleasure—or on ruining me completely. "I hope you weren't getting anxious," he purred. "I had to get rid of a prize bore—but I gave him a dynamite blow-job. So much thick come I almost choked. I had to spit most of it out . . ."

"You did, eh? You'd better not spit out mine, I'll break your neck. I want you to swallow every drop."

"You bet I will, Marvin. When can we get together?"

"It takes about ten minutes to drive over to the college. I can be there at 9:00. Where shall I meet you."

"You know the parking lot next to the gym? OK, meet me there. What do you want me to wear, jeans or my cheerleader's outfit?"

"Wear the outfit. I want to see you in the white shorts and red t-shirt—or has the outfit changed?"

"No, it's still the same. And you?"

"I'll be driving an old black Plymouth, four-door. I'll see you in half an hour."

My father wanted to know what I was so excited about.

I trimmed my beard and took a shower. I decided against aftershave—Roland had told me he liked "men," hadn't he? I squeezed into my jeans. I squeezed into my boots. I looked in on Dad and tiptoed out. I prayed the sound of the car starting wouldn't wake him.

I dimmed my lights as soon as I made out a person appropriately costumed standing on the edge of the parking lot. "Great God!" I thought. "That can't be him. Well, he certainly isn't at all what I expected..." By the light of the headlights I made out a giant who indeed resembled a football player. I slowed to a halt beside him. "Hop in, Roland."

"Hi, Marvin." That wasn't the voice I expected either. He sounded uncomfortable. I should have told him about my beard. I turned on the radio. Maybe he was disappointed. He hadn't told me he wore glasses, had he? But there he sat in white track shoes and white knee socks trimmed in red, skimpy white shorts and a bright red t-shirt. And here I sat. Above the heavy glasses his dark hair was curly. I backed up and turned around and lit out of there.

"We had so much to say on the phone . . ." Roland was thinking out loud.

"However, we didn't meet to talk . . ." I unzipped my fly with one hand. "Take it," I told him.

"Want me to get mine out?" He was making me hard.

"You know I do." I reached between his tremedous thighs. He was hard as a stick of peppermint. Those tight shorts were too small for his equipment. In a minute I was enjoying the moist slip and slide of a foreskin in my fingers. I hadn't had anything like this in my hands in months. Only incipient paranoia in the parking lot had kept me from pulling his shorts down and sucking him off as soon as he settled into the seat beside me. I had some vague memory that if he were to undress himself, my offense was less. With so little to talk about I was thinking overtime.

I was thinking Police and Entrapment. I was thinking that the boys next door must be playing a practical joke of which I was the intended butt. I kept looking in the rear-view mirror. Were we being followed? I also took a round-about route home in an effort to conceal where I lived. Roland continued giving my penis his undivided attention.

"This your house?"

"It's my father's. Let's sit out here a while. Dad's a light sleeper and the car pulling up could have waked him." I'd stopped in the shade of our magnolia tree. I rolled the windows up, the scent was so overpowering. Not a single car drove past. If one had, all the driver would have seen was Roland's head next to an empty driver's seat. I had leaned over. His dick tasted sweet. "He gets an A for personal hygiene," I said to myself. He was leaning back now and sighing. I was afraid he was going to come so I sat up.

"Do me, Roland!"

"I don't suck in cars, Marvin. Want to go in?"

"That's a lie," I thought. "Sure," I said.

The smell of sickness assailed me as soon as I opened the door.

"That you, Marvin?" a feeble voice called from the bedroom. "Where've you been, boy?"

"Sorry, Dad. I went down to the highway for cigarettes."

"Night, son . . ."

"Night, Dad . . ." I kissed him on the forehead. The glass by the bed was empty. He'd taken all his pills.

Roland was standing where I left him in the middle of our livingroom. We tiptoed to the dining room after I picked up a couple of blankets I'd stashed. I had to be close enough to Dad's half-opened door to hear him. A spring breeze intermittently rattled the blinds in the dining room windows. I was counting on the irregular slapping and whushing to mask any sounds that escaped us.

While I arranged the blankets on the rug near the sideboard, Roland struggled out of those ridiculous shorts and t-shirt. Then he pulled aside one of the blinds. All he would see were other darkened windows. The swaying streetlights lit up a body that was overmuscled and not particulary youthful. "Thank the Lord," I thought, "he's not some scrawny chicken. I bet he's older than any twenty . . ." I was out of my clothes and slipping my arms around him while I was thinking that. He was big around as our magnolia tree. "Roland, aren't you taking off your shoes?"

"Naw, my feet stink. I got them wet walking across the campus from my dorm"—and he named the dorm. He referred to the building by an affectionate nickname no outsider would have known.

"Well," I thought, "if he isn't a student there, he must be the janitor." Now we were lying on the blankets—in a dark corner. "I want some light," I whispered.

"OK, go get yourself one but I don't drink."

I was raising the blinds before it struck me that he must have thought I meant a Miller. And I had drunk a Lite to give myself a little courage before picking him up. Now that Dad didn't get as far as the kitchen, I wasn't afraid to have an occasional six-pack in the house.

* * *

In the illumination I had chosen, Roland didn't look half bad. And he kissed and sucked dick a great deal better than he looked. That he never took off his glasses seemed odd but probably had as rational an explanation as his leaving his shoes and socks on. And that I found a real turn-on. He never once got his shoes on the blankets, which involved some fancy footwork later on. Maybe he was a cheerleader after all.

Roland was as laconic in our dining room as he'd been in the car. A couple of times he whispered, "You like the way I suck cock?"

I did indeed. But what I really wanted more than anything else was to fuck. On the phone I'd asked Roland if he liked to fuck and he's said he didn't get many opportunities around here, but sure he did. I suppose he meant being top.

"Play with it, Marvin, but don't stick your finger in it. I've never been fucked."

"Let me teach you . . ." I whispered but he was adamant. "OK, Roland, what about you poking me?"

I knew from the way he was playing with my ass now that he wanted to. I got up for the towel and jar of lube I'd hidden behing the bowl of magnolias on the sideboard. I greased my ass while I was standing. I stuck a couple of fingers in and moved them around, "priming the pump" as I called it.

Roland lay on his back staring up at me. He looked dumb. "Let me sit on it," I whispered.

"Wow, the head of your cock is beautiful," he said as I positioned myself over him. He was sucking me again while I greased his cock.

"Uh-uh," I muttered. "I'm too tense to get it in this way . . ."

"Roll over," Roland whispered.

It was then I heard my father's voice. Luckily, my jeans were right there. "Coming, Dad!" I called.

"Mother and you are talking awfully loud, Marvin. It'd wake the dead."

"Dad, there's no one in the house but you and me!" I was in shock but for that very reason I was totally calm. "You must have been dreaming. Anything you need?"

"No, son. Sleep well now."

"Same to you, Dad. Good night." I bent down and kissed him on the cheek. He shivered. Then I stood at the door watching till I knew he was sleeping. No one that sick has the energy to pretend anything.

"Whew . . ." Roland whistled softly. "Lie down, Marvin." I was trembling. Roland was able to slide his dick in half way now.

"Hold on a minute." I stopped him with my hands. "That burns." I maneuvered us over on to our sides without losing a quarter of an inch, drew up my legs and sucked the whole shaft up my ass. "Let's lie here a minute while I get used to that big tool of yours, OK?" My asshole gave his dick a loving hug. He groaned. As I started oscillating my pelvis gently, he began pumping away. He was agile for his size: without losing contact with each other we were both on our feet and I was leaning over, bracing myself against the back of a chair. Now he was really slamming me.

"Roland, baby, you fuck every bit as good as you suck dick." My mind was filling with a light that pulsated. My penis was flaccid as a child's. This was going to be one of those long mental orgasms . . .

"Ummm," he grunted.

A gust of warm air flooded the room with magnolia. How long had this been going on? As suddenly as I'd known I wanted him in me plugging away, I wanted him out.

"Hey, Marvin, I was about to come!" He was a little loud.

"I know. Shhh . . ." I listened but that was more to change the direction things were taking—I'd heard nothing suspicious.

"Shit, I want to come, Marvin . . ."

"And so do I, friend. But I was beginning to burn something fierce. Now it feels wonderful. My ass and balls and dick are all smouldering." He looked like he didn't understand what I was talking about.

"Let me fuck that big butt of yours, Roland . . ." I had a couple of greasy fingers working their way into it but he began pulling away.

"No. Not tonight. I have a stomach ache."

I was jerking him off with lots of lube and I eased up on his ass like he asked, although I kept playing with it just in case it got hot enough to change his mind for him. "Want to come?"

"Ummmm," he growled.

"I want to make you come. I bet it's sweet . . ."

"You've got to peel it."

So I pulled back his foreskin and holding his shaft with one hand, I jacked off the head with the other.

"You have to stop when I tell you to stop, OK?"

I agreed to that.

"Stop," he commanded.

I could feel a pulsation beginning deep between his balls and asshole.

"Just hold the thing but don't move your hand!"

I wasn't sure what was happening so I missed the first three squirts. Yes, he was twenty, all right. No one much older than that ever comes so much, so rich, or in so many discreet slow spurts. *Glup! Glup! Glup!* It splashed down somewhere in his wiry black chest hair.

"Oh shit," I thought. "Missed it." I opened my mouth wide and went down on his dick.

"No, don't move!" If that didn't wake Dad, nothing would. Roland's dick pulsed two or three more times. The stuff was thick as custard.

I fell back next to him. After a minute or two I rose to my knees and looking at his face, I began to beat my meat.

"Point it *that* way," he whispered, indicating his feet. I suppose he was afraid I'd come on his glasses.

I almost passed out. When I looked at my watch, it was 1:30. I stretched across him for the rolled up towel but it slipped from my grasp.

"God damn! What the hell are those?" Roland almost shouted. He had jumped to his feet and covered his dick and balls with both hands. He was bugeyed with horror.

"Shhh . . . Calm down, kid. Haven't you ever seen a dildo before?" I picked one up in each hand and held them out for his inspection. He wasn't touching them. Not yet.

What'd you call em? I thought you were going to chop my dick off too . . . Whew . . . You shove those up your butt, don't you?" He paused. "Can I borrow one?"

"Be my guest." Roland selected the smaller of the two. It was pink. "Don't let your roommates catch you..." On our silent way through the kitchen I found him a shopping bag.

Roland and I shook hands before I reached across and opened the car door.

"I'll call," were his last words that night.

*   *   *

Back at the house Dad was sleeping soundly. I didn't take a shower, I was going to treasure that sweat. I clenched my ass muscles a couple of times and smiled. "Hello, Roland," I said inside.

He called a few days later to ask if I was "OK." We talked for a few minutes. He was his former vivacious self. Had I enjoyed myself? He told me he was putting the dildo to excellent use, it was a useful invention.

"Who's that?" Dad called. "Your sister?"

I told Roland I had to go.

Almost as soon as I hung up, I started thinking. On the phone Roland was a different person . . . "There's no way that brute who fucks like a pile-driver and sucks dick like an electric milker is the charming young dude who's so vibrant and lively on the telephone," I thought. "No, there's got to be another explanation . . ." Then it dawned on me. "There have to be two of them. One 'Roland' calls people and gets them all hot, then another 'Roland' shows up and gets them off. Good God, is that possible? Here in the Great American Desert? You must be crazy."

MICHAEL LEBECK. "Born during a cyclone some months before Roosevelt saved the nation, I'm finishing a novel about two men called *Impossible People*. Poems have appeared in *Arion, Christopher Street, Fag Rag, Mouth of the Dragon, Sewanee Review* and *Wormwood Review*. *Numbers* recently published a story. Two volumes of original poems and another of poems translated from German (Gottfried Benn) are long out of print but a translation of Hesse's *Demian* is still around after more than a decade. In my spare time I watch birds."

JOE OF LAHAINA
A Short Story
by
Charles Warren Stoddard

When Charles Warren Stoddard (1843-1909) wrote that love was his "meat and drink," he was referring to his lifelong tendency to fall in love with other males. Many of his flirtations and love affairs were interwoven into his works with such ingenuousness that 19th century readers hardly knew what to think. (Most decided he was merely amusingly fey.) From *South Sea Idyls* (1873) through *For the Pleasure of His Company* (1903) his tales and travelogues were brimful of unabashed homoeroticism. His autobiographical hero always seemed to be chumming with a savage in the Islands, a young actor in San Francisco, a budding artist in Italy, or a winsome waif in Washington, D.C. In real life, Stoddard referred to these good-looking young men as his "Kids."

Stoddard was able to write almost anything he wanted about his lovable chums and get away with it. To his naive and genteel readers, the expression of sodomitical tendencies in literature was unthinkable. When they read of his escapades in bed with the young men of Hawaii and Tahiti, therefore, they were pleased to think he was only teasing. Based on all the revelations that can be found in his diaries and letters, we now know he was not.

Roger Austen

Joe is the beautiful young man with whom Stoddard lived near Lahaina, Hawaii in 1869 and the most homosexual, or bisexual, of the natives he met. Only Part I is printed here. Part II, which has Stoddard finding Joe near death in a leper colony, is bathetic and entirely fictional.   Reprinted from *South Sea Idyls*

I was stormed in at Lahaina. Now, Lahaina is a little slice of civilization, beached on the shore of barbarism. One can easily stand that little of it, for brown and brawny heathendom becomes more wonderful and captivating by contrast. So I was glad of dear, drowsy, little Lahaina; and was glad, also, that she had but one broad street, which possibly led to destruction, and yet looked lovely in the distance. It didn't matter to me that the one broad street had but one side to it; for the sea lapped over the sloping sands on its lower edge, and the sun used to set right in the face of every solitary citizen of Lahaina, just as he went to supper.

I was waiting to catch a passage in a passing schooner, and that's why I came there; but the schooner flashed by us in a great gale from the south, and so I was stormed in indefinitely.

It was Holy Week, and I concluded to go to housekeeping, because it would be so nice to have my frugal meals in private, to go to mass and vespers daily, and then to come back and feel quite at home. My villa was suburban—built of dried grasses on the model of a haystack dug out in the middle, with doors and windows let into the four sides thereof. It was planted in the midst of a vineyard, with avenues stretching in all directions under a network of stems and tendrils.

"Her breath is sweeter than the sweet winds
That breathe over the grape-blossoms of Lahaina."

So the song said; and I began to think upon the surpassing sweetness of that breath, as I inhaled the sweet winds of Lahaina, while the wilderness of its vineyards blossomed like the rose. I used to sit in my veranda and turn to Joe (Joe was my private and confidential servant), and I would say to Joe, while we scented the odor of grape, and saw the great banana-leaves waving their cambric sails, and heard the sea moaning in the melancholy distance—I would say to him, "Joe, housekeeping *is* good fun, isn't it?" Whereupon Joe would utter a sort of unanimous Yes, with his whole body and soul; so that question was carried triumphantly, and we would relapse into a comfortable silence, while the voices of the wily singers down on the river front would whisper to us, and cause us to wonder what they could possibly be doing at that moment in the broad way that led to destruction. Then we would take a drink of cocoa-milk, and finish our bananas, and go to bed, because we had nothing else to do.

This is the way that we began our co-operative housekeeping: One night, when there was a riotous sort of a festival off in a retired valley, I saw, in the excited throng of natives who were going mad over their national dance, a young face that seemed to embody a whole tropical romance. On another night, when a lot of us were bathing in the moonlight, I saw a figure so fresh and joyous that I began to realize how the old Greeks could worship mere physical beauty and forget its higher forms. Then I discovered that face on this body—a rare enough combination—and the whole constituted Joe, a young scapegrace who was schooling at Lahaina, under the eye—not a very sharp one—of his uncle. When I got stormed in, and resolved on housekeeping for a season, I took Joe, bribing his uncle to keep the peace, which he promised to do, provided I gave bonds for Joe's irreproachable conduct while with me. I willingly gave bonds—verbal ones—for this was just what I wanted of Joe: namely, to instil into his youthful mind those counsels which, if rigorously followed, must result in his becoming a true and unterrified American. This compact settled, Joe took up his bed—a roll of mats—and down we marched to my villa, and began housekeeping in good earnest.

We soon got settled, and began to enjoy life, though we were not without occasional domestic infelicities. For instance, Joe would wake up in the middle of the night, declaring to me that it was morning, and thereupon insist upon sweeping out at once, and in the most vigorous manner. Having filled the air with dust, he would rush off to the baker's for our hot rolls and a pat of breakfast butter, leaving me, meantime, to recover as I might. Having settled myself for a comfortable hour's reading, bolstered up in a luxurious fashion, Joe would enter with breakfast, and orders to the effect that it be eaten at once and without delay. It was useless for me to remonstrate with him; he was tyrannical.

He got me into all sorts of trouble. It was Holy Week, and I had resolved upon going to mass and vespers daily. I went. The soft night-winds floated in through the latticed windows of the chapel, and made the candles flicker upon the altar. The little throng of natives bowed in the oppressive silence, and were deeply moved. It was rest for the soul to be there; yet, in the midst of it, while the Father, with his pale, sad face, gave his instructions, to which we listened as attentively as possible—for there was something in his manner and his voice that made us better creatures—while we listened, in the midst of it I heard a shrill little whistle, a sort of chirp, that I knew perfectly well. It was Joe, sitting on a cocoa-stump in the garden adjoining, and beseeching me to come out, right off. When service was over, I remonstrated with him for his irreverence. "Joe," I said, "if you have no respect for religion yourself, respect those who are more fortunate than you." But Joe was dressed in his best, and quite wild at the entrancing loveliness of the night. "Let's walk a little," said Joe, covered with fragrant wreaths, and redolent of cocoanut-oil. What could I do? If I had tried to do anything to the contrary, he might have taken me and thrown me away somewhere into a well or a jungle, and then I could no longer hope to touch the chord of remorse—which chord I sought vainly, and which I have since concluded was not in Joe's physical corporation at all. So we walked a little. In vain I strove to break Joe of the shocking habit of whistling me out of vespers. He would persist in doing it. Moreover, during the day he would collect crusts of bread and banana-skins, station himself in ambush behind the curtain of the window next the lane, and, as some solitary creature strode solemnly past, Joe would discharge a volley of ammunition over him, and then laugh immoderately at his indignation and surprise. Joe was my pet elephant, and I was obliged to play with him very cautiously.

One morning he disappeared. I was without the consolations of a breakfast, even. I made my toilet, went to my portmanteau for my purse—for I had decided upon a vistit to the baker—when lo! part of my slender means had mysteriously disappeared. Joe was gone, and the money also. All day I thought about it. In the morning, after a very long and miserable night, I woke up, and when I opened my eyes, there, in the doorway, stood Joe, in a brand-new suit of clothes, including boots and hat. He was gorgeous beyond description, and seemed overjoyed to see me, and as merry as though nothing unusual had happened. I was quite startled at this apparition. "Joseph!" I said in my severest tone, and then turned over and looked away from him. Joe evaded the subject in the most delicate manner, and was never so interesting as at that moment. He sang his specialties, and played clumsily upon his bamboo flute—to soothe me, I suppose—and wanted me to eat a whole flat pie which he had brought home as a peace-offering, buttoned tightly under his jacket. I saw I must strike at once, if I struck at all; so I said, "Joe, what on earth did you do with that money?" Joe said he had replenished his wardrobe, and bought the flat pie especially for me. "Joseph," I said, with great dignity, "do you know that you have been stealing, and that it is highly sinful to steal, and may result in something unpleasant in the world to come?" Joe said, "Yes," pleasantly, though I hardly think he meant it; and then he added, mildly, "that he couldn't lie"—which was a glaring falsehood—"but wanted me to be sure that he took the money, and so had some back to tell me."

"Joseph," I said, "you remind me of our noble Washington;" and, to my amazement, Joe was mortified. He didn't, of course, know who Washington was, but he suspected that I was ridiculing him. He came to the bed and haughtily insisted upon my taking the little change he had received from his costumers, but I implored him to keep it, as I had no use at all for it, and, as I assured him, I much preferred hearing it jingle in his pocket.

The next day I sailed out of Lahaina, and Joe came to the beach with his new trousers tucked into his new boots, while he waved his new hat violently in a final adieu, much to the envy and admiration of a score of hatless urchins, who looked upon Joe as the glass of fashion, and but little lower than the angels. When I entered the boat to set sail, a tear stood in Joe's bright eye, and I think he was really sorry to part with me; and I don't wonder at it, because our housekeeping experiences were new to him—and, I may add, not unprofitable.

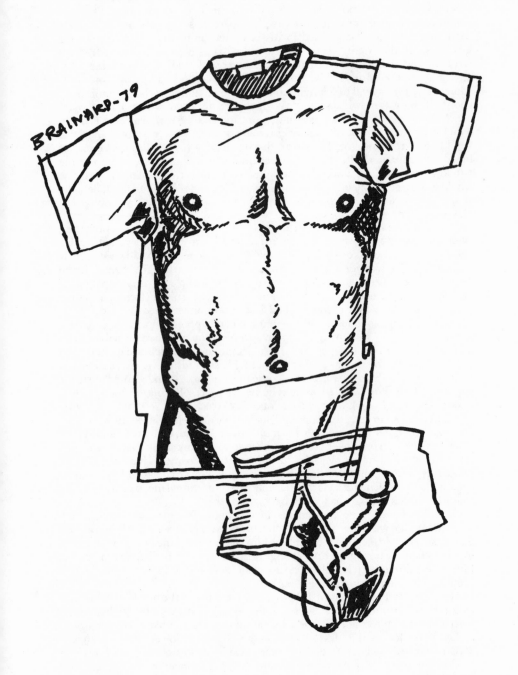

TOYS
A Short Story
by
Frank Chapman

Today, a child. Reflections in the well of the heart.

I have been a toy demonstrator for several weeks this summer. I cannot recall now how I developed the pitch.

"What age child are you shopping for?" The shopper tells me, while I slip a Magic Paintbrush into her child's hand.

"Here's a great toy for any age child from one to a hundred."

Seeing where my glances were going, an older man in the crowd around me replied, "And what age child are *you* shopping for?" He knew. He had seen that glorious fourteen-year-old walking by, too. That young body in loose jeans, a tuft of underwear showing through a rip in the back of the jeans.

The boy gazed sideways at my booth but drifted on past, toward the sports section, where he examined scuba equipment, underwater masks, snorkels, and flippers. My booth was near the escalator. He would have to pass my way again, when he left the department store. How could I lure him over to my counter?

I was off from my teaching assistantship for the summer, and I had decided to get a job. I had checked the Emporium first and, finding no job there, decided to go into every shop on that side of Market Street and ask for work. No luck. By the time I had come back down the other side of Market to the cable car turntable at Powell, I had developed a hunch to drop back in again at the Emporium. It proved fruitful.

"One of our toy demonstrators just quit," said the personnel lady, escorting me to the toy department. "Couldn't stand the guff. Think *you* can?"

"I *love* children," I said truthfully. "I'm studying child psychology. This should be an excellent opportunity."

"Married?" she asked.

"Two years," I said, lying easily. "Hard to make ends meet on a teaching assistant's salary with a wife and child to support. She used to work, but now she has to take care of the baby and . . . " I let my voice trail off.

A rather bright, lively child, seeing us behind the counter, came up and politely asked me, if it would be all right if he and his brother tried one of the Magic Paintbrushes. I noticed that pads of paper were stacked under the counter. Without thinking about it, I reached down, got a pad, and laid it on the counter in front of the child.

"Try it on this," I told him. "Here's another pad for your brother." I laid the other pads at intervals along the counter in front of the child.

"I believe I'll be able to stand the guff," I told the personnel lady. "When do I start?"

"I think you just did," she said. "The dealer should be here in about twelve minutes. Keep them busy till she can get here and fill you in on what to do."

* * *

I was handing out a package of the Magic Paintbrushes to a harried mother and pointing her toward the cashier when the glorious fourteen-year-old walked by again. Just as he got on the escalator he leaned on the moving rubber rails and looked over his shoulder directly at me.

That's nice, I thought, but I'll never see him again.

I went to lunch in the cafeteria downstairs.

After lunch, he reappeared, in shorts now. He stood in the area in front of my booth after getting off the escalator and let the crowd mill around him. I could almost feel him breathing over the murmur and shuffle of the shoppers, the rumble of the escalator, the incessant dink-dink-dink of the signal chime. In the bright dimness of the overhead lighting that makes the merchandise glow, his face seemed curiously dimmed, troubled. He stared into space. Nothing could catch his eye. He went over to a pillar and leaned against it, picking at it with the fingers of one hand, hanging his other hand in the neck of his shirt, caressing his chest and finally hooking his thumb in the waist of his pants. From time to time, he glanced at my booth. He examined the nozzle of one of the folded fire hoses near the next booth. Was he really flirting with me? Or was he just curious about the Magic Paintbrushes but too shy to approach. The product was a tubular transparent plastic tank, filled with colored liquids (harmless food dyes, easily washable the packaging claimed) made from colored powders included in the package, and applied to paper (or other surfaces) by a felt tip.

Shoppers passed in floods, streams, and trickles. Eddied, formed around the booth and dissipated. Finally the stream of people dried up. Only I in my booth and the boy leaning against the pillar were left. I decided to be bold.

I pointed to a mirrored wall behind the display of football equipment. My movement caught the boy's eyes instantly, making me realize that he had been very much aware of me all along.

"I bet you could be an artist," I said, "because you really look at things. And people. Why don't you try doing a portrait of yourself, using that mirror." He looked at me dubiously but came over to the booth anyway, taking the Magic Paintbrush and pad I offered. He did not go over to the mirror but held the pad with one hand and turned his back on me. He began with slow, careful strokes. He looked up at me and then back down at the pad. He began to giggle. I had an excuse to look at him directly now. Boldly. To stare. To drink in his image. I will call him Johnny.

Johnny was a tow-headed kid, with green eyes and a crooked grin of concentration on his smooth sweet face. He wore basketball shoes and high socks that came almost to his knees. A short length of golden thigh, perfect muscular small legs showed between the socks and tight white shorts on buns as smooth as two spoon-scoops of vanilla ice cream. A slim little belly was just visible under his yellow cut-off athletic shirt.

When he leaned over the pad, now on the counter, his tender young spine and trim, perfectly muscled back were outlined under tanned velvet skin, flecked with tiny golden hairs, shining under the store lights. I wanted to touch him. To stroke his skin. Touch his face. Caress his tight little buns. Hold him.

He started laughing at the picture he had drawn.

"What is it?" I asked.

"You," he said, showing me.

It was actually not a bad likeness, but he had made my nose very big and round and long.

"Time for me to take a break," I said. "Would you like to have a Pepsi or something with me?"

He looked startled. "Sure."

* * *

He grinned up at me as he tipped the Pepsi can to his lips. The overhead lights, glinting off the top of the can, reflecting from its bright surface, set his face aglow, his emerald green eyes sparkling.

He stayed near the counter much of the rest of the day, drawing caricatures of the mothers and some of the children.

"I see you have a disciple," said the personnel lady, when she came by. "The dealer gave me a good report on you. Says you never need any supervision."

It was true. I rarely saw the dealer, except in the cocktail lounge next door to the store. A business-like lady with tight hair and sequined glasses attached to her with a gold chain.

* * *

"Your drawings of people are good," I told Johnny. "Maybe you *will* be an artist someday."

"I'm not an artist," he said. "I'm a swimmer. I'm gonna win an Olympic gold medal."

"Do you swim a lot?"

"Yeah," he said. "Well, not really. Hardly at all."

"Why?"

"We don't have a pool, and the one at school is broken. They've been supposed to have a new one all year but they didn't."

"Want to come with me to the pool at my place?" I asked. "I like to swim every day. It's good exercise to keep a guy in shape."

"Would I!" he said. "I sure would."

"Will your mother mind?"

"Her?" he said. "She won't even know. She's working and then she goes right out with one of the guys where she works and she never comes in until about 2:30 in the morning, making a lot of noise with the guy."

* * *

Johnny and I frolic in the pool. He swims underwater and touches me and splashes rapidly away. He turns and comes back like a small torpedo and glides between my legs. He hugs me aggressively, kisses me. His father is a martinet, a colonel in the army. Johnny has never known fatherly affection.

"Where's your wife?" Johnny asks me when we get out of the pool. And I tell him, "She's away. We're separated. She lives in New York. And my boy lives with her. Sometimes I'm lonely."

I look sad. He comes over to me, puts his arms around my neck and snuggles against me. He is lonely, too. I warn him not to tell anyone around my building that he is not my son.

In the shower, we make a game of bathing together. He is all eyes, looking at how I am built.

"You're big!" he says, meaning my cock.

"You will be too one day," I assure him. "You're already big for your age."

Water falls like raindrops, spattering on his underdeveloped chest. A film of moisture slowly pours down over his whole charming body, glistening. We take turns soaping each other down. He pauses when he gets to my pubic area. I say, "Go ahead. It's all right."

Those tender, strong young hands touching me, reaching into my most private places, under my balls, up the crack of my ass, soaping me, rubbing me, and then stroking the long stem of my cock as it grows. I rub him down, soaping his buttocks and genitals, and his cock grows large too, hairless but perfect in shape and size for his age. He turns and rinses the shampoo out of his hair. A stream of suds arches across his back and down through the crack of his ass, the valley of his buns. I reach in and touch his hairless underballs, the crack, the responsive little anus. He turns and looks at me through wet eyelashes over his shoulder and grins crookedly.

We towel off vigorously and lie down together, still warm and damp from the shower. We press against each other, flesh against flesh, our surfaces meeting, skin rubbing against skin, our sweat commingling. When we pull apart, breathing, getting more comfortable, playfully, we make a sound like pages riffling in a breeze. I peel myself away from him like a Band-Aid being stripped from a wound. We rub together again. Now, our bodies touching make a liquid sound like water rippling.

"What's that?" he asks.

"Our bodies kissing."

He wriggles all over, cocking his head over his shoulder. I pull away from him again, and it makes a sound like a whip whistling through the air.

"What are you doing!" He giggles.

"Listening to the sounds our bodies make together," I say. "They're interesting."

He moves back and forth, rubbing against me. Making sounds. Listening. We make other sounds together later.

"It's not so big now," he says. "It's all shriveled up, like a button."

"So's yours."

* * *

A slow day at the toy counter. I light up inside when I see Johnny bounce off the escalator.

He is carrying a spiral artist's pad.

"I've got something to show you," he says. "Want to see it?"

"Sure."

I look at the page and he has made great fat round letters that tumble against each other in different colors.

"That's very nice."

"Look at what it says!"

I look more closely and see that the letters spell out:
UOY EVOL I KNARF

That's backwards writing," I say. "Do you mean that?"

He embraces my waist and kisses my chest.

"Let's see what else you've done," I say innocently.

"No!" Johnny pulls away as if hit by an electric shock, but I turn back a page and see more big fat round letters that tumble against each other in different colors. They spell out:

UOY EVOL I LRAC

An earlier page announces: UOY EVOL I LLIB

"Who're they?" I ask.

"Just friends," he says and then he giggles and squirms all over. "Like you. But they're gone."

FRANK M. CHAPMAN lives in Los Angeles. He writes: "Since my first publication in 1948, I've written under pen names as well as my own name for many publications *(Penthouse, Genesis,* etc.) My book of translations of ancient Aztec drum songs, *The Spell of Hungry Wolf: Aztec Visions,* was published in 1975 by Sunstone Press. I've done essays, stories and poetry for magazines like *Transfer, Maguey, Arion, Ante, Sunstone Review, Blueboy,* etc. I've worked as an editor, casting director, script editor and associate producer on stage, television and theatrical film productions."

The haunting story of Stephen the Second, King of Navarre from 1387 to 1390, is related in full by Jacopo Malatesta in the twelfth chapter of his great work *De Regibus Doloris* (Concerning the Kings of Sorrow). There seem to have been a good many of these, but evidently King Stephen of Navarre held a special place in the affections of Malatesta — who does not hesitate to make it clear where his sympathies lay in the matter. He relates how in December of 1389 a deputation of what he terms "the most prime citizens of that state" arrived in Rome to seek audience of the Pope. Navarre had recently been engaged in a particularly dreadful war, accompanied by famine, and plague. In fact only the ferocity of the latter, coupled with the belated entry upon the scene of the King of Aragon, had saved Navarre from complete annihilation. The "most prime citizens," however, blamed the whole debacle upon their King Stephen II, whom they accused of being a child of the Devil, of indulging in orgies of flagellation, and of other interesting but "unnatural" crimes — as a direct result of which God had seen fit to punish all and sundry with "the intensest wretchedness." Their idea now was that the Pope should send at once to Navarre a Tribunal of Inquisition empowered to try and to condemn the unfortunate King, who was already a prisoner in his castle at Pamplona. The Pope, presumably flattered by this appeal to his jurisdiction, despatched three Cardinals, headed by Cardinal Binci (who happened to be Malatesta's maternal uncle) and endowed with whatever powers might be found necessary. Cardinal Binci took his young nephew with him as Secretary to the Tribunal. In April 1390 the Cardinals entered the ravaged city of Pamplona to great acclamation. The first thing that happened was that they had a private audience with the King, upon which Act One of the present work is based. Malatesta, who of course was present, records that the Cardinals were astounded by Stephen II, who at first seemed to them little better than a perverse schoolboy in behaviour. Act Two is based on the account of what has been called — erroneously — the King's Defence. Stephen refused to speak at all during the Trial, and only when it was over did he give any account of himself. Malatesta describes how, as the narrative progressed, they were all appalled by the tragic persona of the King. By the standards of the time, the King condemned himself at every turn. At the end, however, Malatesta, who had more reason than anyone else to know, affirms majestically that "the King did indeed see Love."

The scene is laid in the Royal Castle of Pamplona.

JOHN STUART ANDERSON, actor/author, was born in Burma. He has been writing all his life, principally plays and works for solo actor. His original recordings of his own "Werewolf" and "Frankenstein Passion" for Columbia (EMI) are now highly sought after. Anderson's work is characterized by its mysterious allure and profound — not aggressive — homoerotic atmosphere. *Act and Betrayal* was first performed at the Cast Theatre in Los Angeles in 1980.

ACT AND BETRAYAL
A One Man Play
by
John Stuart Anderson

To Gary Hundertmark

ACT ONE

DARKNESS. LIGHT RISES ON THE KING.
THE KING SPEAKS: —

Your Eminences are welcome. I trust you have been housed according to your station?

Ah, but you've arrived at last. And I never thought you would. Or almost never thought. Not that it'll make much difference to me, I suppose. But at least we can get on with the business, perhaps.

But you must remember that if I speak it is only through my own favour. No matter what they have done to me, I am still the King, and must do nothing. Though I MAY If I please. Of course they have blamed me for all this — all this destruction of my country. What do they call it — the Rape of Navarre? Well, what else could they do? Their own foibles and my Father's foolishness have to be blamed on someone, for heaven's sake. After all, isn't it the business of a king to suffer blame and accept responsibility? You see, I know all about being a King. Even though they pretend that I do not, I do. All.

Well, so I shall speak — though in the end you'll make of it what you wish. If I am silent I am condemned. If I speak I am not pardoned. Pardoned? Condemned? No one but myself may pardon or condemn myself.

Well, confession or excuse, I'll give you — out of my good grace — what you've come so far to get, what His Holiness the Pope must have forbidden you to return without. And all because my subjects — some of them — filled with spite made the trek to Rome to get our Holy Mother Church's blessing on their revenge. For that is what it is, is it not? Revenge on God for all the wretchedness which which he has visited them. But since they cannot punish God, they punish me.

I wonder who put them up to it. The Friar, perhaps — ah, yes, that noonday wolf of God, biting young men's buttocks with his eyes.

No, no, of course, I forget myself. I am speaking of another man of the cloth, one like yourselves — towards whom even Kings must show respect. Or seem to show. I do apologize.

So my country's ruined. But it will soon be spring. Does the fresh grass thrust already out from underneath the bodies of the dead, I wonder? Is the breath of Southern breezes already bearing away the stench of plague? And shall we all, purged, purged, move forward to new life? Purged by my passion, I'll have you know. I am the one, I the detested, I the accursed, I the accused — I am the one to bring them to new life by my passion. Just think of that will you? And know. That I know. You are dealing with no fool and it will be the better for you to recognize that from the start. Better. Wiser.

No, I do not threaten. Why should you believe I threaten? Of course. I did not think of that. But I understand. You think I threaten by some power the Devil grants me. Is that what they have told you? And you believed? How can you be so unsophisticated? Are you so simple, reverend fathers? Had I such power, should I be here now? Should I not be elsewhere, in some other place? (Enjoying my love, perhaps? Bearing him bravely on my back — covering myself with the bruises of his love — filling my mouth with the sweetness of his taste.) Ah, you must not believe me more powerful than I am. Without love, I am nothing. No one. Never to be feared.

I wonder what it is you want to hear from me? Something that will make it easier for you to condemn me, I've no doubt. I wonder what you have come all this way to hear? Something to make it easier for the Pope to please my people? But of course.

God? O, God. Yes, there was a time when I looked for him. I sought him everywhere. But I couldn't find him. He hid from me. So I said "Peace on You! I'll go the other way. Look for your opposite number." But do you know he was not to be found either. Nobody wanted me. So there I remained. Unwanted. Comfortless. Unloved.

O yes. Do you mean you never heard the story? The fearful story of how my mother, claiming to have been ravished on a dark night by a stiff-pricked devil, swore that I was her infernal offspring? Certainly she refused to see me at birth, even to nurse me, even to touch me.

There are those who say the Devil in question was no supernatural creature but my own true father King Henry the Miser, and that in talking of devils my own true mother Queen Isabelle the Fair was only concealing — O, so very lightly — her own true opinion of her own true spouse. If so, then I fancy they deserved each other. And were well-matched.

I only know that no one loved me. No one even liked me. No one touched me. There was no pleasing by me of anyone. Certainly no approval.

The devil? Ah, now you are going to keep harping on him. Well, but then you men of the cloth could never keep your places without him, could you? Old Nick is food and drink to you. He is the Great Cornerstone of the Christian Church. What would you do without each other, I wonder? O, yes, I saw him. I met him. I was *possessed* by him. Not perhaps in quite the same way my mother claimed to have been, of course. But near enough. Do you find that surprising? Alarming? O, you do surprise ME. Isn't everyone, sooner or later, possessed by the devil? One way or another? Perhaps I was readier for him. Yes, I was certainly ripe. And he knew me. O, not in quite the same way my mother claimed to have been. But near enough. In any case, if it was true he'd fathered me himself he — well perhaps even *he* possessed a certain delicacy? Well, perhaps not. But one always likes to think the best of one's family, don't you know?

In any case, if it came to that I must tell you that I did prefer Jesus. O, yes, I used often to see him. On a great crucifix on the wall of the cloister outside the chapel. I would stare at him by the hour. He looked so tired. I would have revived him with my breath. Well, but nothing could be done so long as Jesus stayed up there on the cross and I was down here in the cloister. The only sensible thing seemed to be to pull out the nails and get him on his feet again. Then we would see. Well — you know. But it didn't work, of course. I was caught. *In flagrante delicto.* In the act of releasing Jesus.

My father was furious. He threatened to beat me. But like everything else he threatened it came to nothing. Then someone convinced him that such an assault upon a Holy Image could only have been at the instigation of the Devil — "Your damned Father" I heard him mutter — and also that having failed to release Jesus I might now go about trying to release prisoners. There were a good many here then, you know. There aren't now because I had them released myself when I became King. Not that anybody gives me any credit for *that*! O, people will say anything — and then it was quite enough to alarm my Father.

He settled the business by appointing one of his soldiers to be my bodyguard. One of his most stalwart soldiers. Who was never to let me out of his sight. And in the event of my "getting up to anything" was to punish me severely. There was nothing much I could do, was there? I looked at the soldier. The soldier looked at me. I've no doubt that neither of us was the least bit impressed by what he saw. And that for the time being was that. So I was stuck by my father with this soldier of his to follow me about all over the place all the time. Yes, everwhere. There was never a moment I could be free of him. And I hated it. Until — well, after a while, there was certain — difference. Well, something happened. That is, something began to happen. I began to look at him. At the wonderful rich curves of him: the deep hollow of his back: the broad shoulders. And I imagined the great heart beating within him. And I thought that if I dared, I would like to touch him, to feel the beating of his heart against my palm. And somehow the rhythm of his heart would enter into me, would enter through my hand. And somehow the pain within me would be eased.

There was nobody to tell me ANYTHING.

Of course I didn't touch him. What do you take me for? I have never violated anyone. People have always been safe with me. Well, it was really very simple. I saw something beautiful and wanted it. The fact that I would never have known what to do with it made no difference. O yes, I prayed, and my prayer was this: — "God, when the moment comes, let me know what to do without spoiling anything — but above all let the moment come."

Don't you understand? I was innocent.

In the government of the country the arrangement of nothing was anything to do with me. There was always a withdrawal from me. A flinching aside. I was always an object of despite. I knew myself cut off, shut out, feared even. On the rare occasions I ever went outside the castle all I seemed to arouse was a sort of malign curiosity. Nothing very friendly you may be sure. I suppose every-body was sure by now that I was a bastard of the Devil. Perhaps that was when they started calling me the Curst.

But I always kept an eye open for Jesus. Of course I did: I was not a fool. One day I was sure we'd help each other.

And then — my father was not called the Miser for nothing, you know. He cut back on everything. Why he was so mean he'd even have cut back on the horses' tails if it would have done any good. He certainly cut back on staff, so there were rooms and rooms, whole corridors of them, all empty — never used then and I don't suppose ever used since. Even our relatives visited us as seldom as possible. I can't say I blamed them — the accommodations were poor, the food bad and the service worse. But I was always fascinated by the empty rooms — though for some reason or other it was strictly against orders for me to visit them. I don't think it was because I might have got lost, nobody would have minded very much about that, but perhaps on account of what I might *find*. And of course in the end I *did* find something. Some one. Well, it was a question of giving my soldier the slip, which one day I managed to do. I sneaked off to the deserted part of the castle, and went into a room. And found it not empty. There was someone there. I hadn't the faintest idea who it might have been. THEN. How could I? Well, let me see now. He was standing with his back to the light, so I couldn't see him very well. Turning over the pages of a book at an old reading-desk. O, a long grey gown, with a great hood right over the head. And very long sleeves., Of course I knew that in spite of my father's attempts at economy there were always hangers-on of one sort of another. All the same I was quite surprised. I decided to speak first.

"What are you doing?" "Reading. One might ask the same of you." "O. Just looking around." "Given your soldier the slip, have you? Well, you may have cause to regret that. No, on second thoughts you may be about to get just what you need." "What are you reading?" "The future history of this country. War. Famine. Plague. Disaster. Nothing to be done about it." "Perhaps I ought to tell my father?" "Who will not believe you. Does anybody believe you? Ever? And for you — " "For me?" "Aren't you the fellow who tried to get Jesus down off the cross?" "What's that to you?" "You'd be surprised. In any case you'd be wise to leave those questions to others. " "Who are you?" "If I told you, you'd never believe me. And if you did and told anyone else they'd never believe you . . . what would you give me if I showed you how to? Make people believe?" "What would you want?" "It's not so much a question of what I would want as of what you wouldn't need. You don't have much need of your soul, for instance, do you? I mean, you wouldn't really miss that. Much. I wouldn't think. What about it? O well perhaps not after all. But you may one day wish you could. Make people. Believe."

No, no, I didn't. Of course I didn't. I said nothing. I didn't know what to say. But I saw — as he went out of the room. Why, his feet: different. They were different. From ours. A goat? Deer? Different. Cloven. I don't expect you to believe me. It doesn't matter whether you believe me or not. You've asked me to tell you and so I have. Perhaps it WAS the Devil. Is he the only one to have a cloven hoof? I don't know. I know nothing.

Yes, there is more: me and my soldier. I went back, of course, and found my soldier. He'd thought I'd run off somewhere. He was in a terrible state. And furious. Very, very angry. He pushed me into my room and locked the door behind us. "Your Father told me to punish you" he said, "and so I am." Suddenly I realized. Why, that now I would actually be able to feel him touch me. I would never have to imagine it again. I became very excited at the thought. However much it hurt it was going to be worth it. To know what it was like. To hang onto someone else — him. To feel the substance of him. Dear God, I was so excited I could hardly breathe. But afterwards he comforted me.

And strangely, through this, through him, I began to think of all that he was, of all that he represented, of all the people behind him, his family, his relations, and all those others, those all unknown to me yet subject to my father and my country. And through this, through him, I began because he was one of them to love the people of this kingdom, and touching him gently, timidly, I felt against my palm the steady collected beating of their heart.

But what I wanted was to become one with them, with him. To lose myself in him, to feel myself melt into and become him — part of him. As one might become part of the Body of God. Aha, I saw you flinch. No need to worry, though. It didn't happen. With him, it couldn't happen.

Ah, yes, the Friar. I wondered when you would ask about HIM. My Father sent for me one day and there for a moment I thought I saw Jesus standing beside him. But it was not he. It was the Friar. Ethelbert. The Flagellant. Yes, my Father gave me to him — to direct and govern, to chasten and correct. The Friar looked at me, and I at him. We each saw the Devil in the other. The world ended for me that day — the world and with it all possibility of love. Previously I had been hated. Now I began to hate. . . .

No, no, none, no more — I will not tell you more — never! I don't care who you are — I am the King and I will not speak of it . . . Ah, sweet Jesus, the infernal depths within that man — depths that awakened depths in me. That infected me like poison.

Listen — I may be tried: God knows by what right. I may be condemned: God's mercy be to him that dares condemn the King. But I am no fool. I know that you, because you are clerics, will believe him in the end because he is another. I have no witness to my cause. But one — and where is he? What have you, what have they done with him? When will HE come back to me? But the Friar has a country at his back. But if I MUST talk to you let it be of other things. Not that monster who tormented me. Until I prayed. Prayed for death, disaster and destruction upon this whole realm — yes indeed, if it were the only way I might escape. But I remembered that I did not need to pray. It was already written.

One day I escaped again, to that other part of the castle. He was there, waiting as before. "Well, well, how's life these days? My friend the Friar after you is he? Couldn't you oblige him? No? Not just once? Make things a little easier perhaps. Well, no, perhaps not. Not after all. Anyway it won't be for much longer. See how kind I am to you! Even though you will not give me anything in return. Even what you would not miss. But in the end maybe —"

I heard his hooves tapping down the corridor.

Silence

The country? O I knew nothing about the state of the country. Nobody told me: nobody considered me worth the telling. They probably thought I'd never become King any how. They probably hoped the Friar would finish me off. They knew nothing of my prayers, my lamentations to the ancient vengeful God of Moses.

Then one day my father told me I was to be married. yes, to the daughter of the Duke of Angoulême. When I was silent he flew into a rage and called me ungrateful. Among other things. Ungrateful? How could I have been Grateful? For all I knew the girl might be a three-legged dwarf with a hunchback and green hair. And half-witted into the bargain. My father told the Friar to get me out of his sight and teach me better manners.

The Friar was only too pleased, you may be sure. He took me to the deserted part of the castle. Bound my hands. Made me kneel down and thank God for punishment. Then he flogged me. Why didn't I resist? Come now, gentlemen, resist a man of God? Why didn't I? Because I was a coward. Because I knew myself despicable. Because I knew myself repulsive to everyone. Because I knew it was my fate. Because I knew the world was made of pain. Because I had begun to find a widening pleasure in that pain. Because I saw the thrust of his excitement. Because I had no right to deny anyone even *that* meagre satisfaction.

Yes . . . the Princess of Angoulême. She arrived. Suddenly. Sooner even than expected. She did not have three legs. She was not humpbacked. She was not a dwarf. She was not green-haired. She was certainly not half-witted. She was like a ray of light. She revealed things. She was not afraid to see the things that she revealed.

One day she said to me: "I suppose you ARE a virgin?" "What's wrong with that?" "Nothing at all. If you happen to be a nun. As a matter of fact I'm one myself — but then I'm supposed to be. But if I'm one and you're one, it's going to make things awfully difficult the first night, isn't it? I really think you ought to take things a step further." "Further?" "With that soldier of yours. He looks as if he could be very helpful." "What? How do you know? Perhaps he won't let me." "Of course he will. Men always do. Mark you, you'll probably have to turn the other cheek yourself so to speak. I daresay it's only fair, and shouldn't be too difficult really. I don't know why people make such a fuss about this sex business. My father's chaplain says it's the only truly innocent enjoyment left in life — and that's about the only truly sensible thing HE ever says."

I found the soldier and told him what we had to do. To my surprise he said: "Well, sir, I'm not surprised really. I thought you might want to — well, take things on a bit." "O?" "Yes, sir. I thought you'd not always be content with things as they have been. But I was thinking you might want to move into a heavier scene — whips, and chains, and paddles, all those sort of things that leave marks. I'd have had to give that some thought. But This, now — O this is quite all right."

Suddenly I was touched by him. How can I explain it? I understood nothing. I only felt — . The solder was very gentle and tried to comfort me. "Come on" he said, "It's not so bad really. You'll get used to it" But I knew what I really wanted — to become someone else. And I still knew with him it couldn't happen. All the same —

"FORNICATOR!" screeched the Friar from the doorway. "I smell the stench of lust, which is the stink of fiends. And its origin is all too plain to see" Pointing dramatically at me. I didn't know what to do. What could I do? Well, I ran away. I found myself outside the Chapel. In the Cloister.

I stared up at Jesus. Helplessly. He opened his eyes. He said; "Well?" "Nothing really. How you doing these days?" "Much as usual, thank you. You'd better go and wash up. And change your clothes while you're about it. Next time be more careful. You don't want people to think you pissed yourself."

After that he just seemed to close his eyes and go to sleep. Well, you may call it blasphemy if you like. I certainly don't. I never thought Jesus would be anything but a practical man. I'd a great respect for him, and I'm only telling you what he said. And what's more what he said I did.

But then everything began to fall apart.

The Friar had got his knife into me and by heaven or by hell he twisted it. My parents, too, lost no opportunity of making me appear ridiculous or repulsive, or both. I did not even dare go near the Princess. I was sure that she, too, was laughing at me. I was wrong as it happened but that was what I thought.

One day I encountered my hoofed friend in a corridor. "My, my, things ARE going hard for you, aren't they? Anything I can do, you think? To make things easier, you know?" "Make it end. Put an end to it. I don't care how you do it. Kill them if you like. I don't care what you do. Put an end to it. Make it end." "Well, and what are you going to give me in exchange if I do?" "What do you want?" "You know quite well what I want. What you do not need." "I can't do that." "O well, you'd better ask your friend Jesus." "He doesn't hear. Or if he does he doesn't answer." "Really? That's unlike him. Are you SURE? Well, we'll have to see, won't we?"

I had no idea what he meant. How could I? I did not offer him anything in return. And yet. And yet. Perhaps. Perhaps I was. Possessed. By him. Who knows?

And then — another day. It was a very hot afternoon at the end of summer. My parents had gone out. On the river. In the royal barge. The Friar was with them. The Princess was dictating long letters to her father, the Duke of Angoulême.

I was left alone. With my bodyguard. My soldier. We did not speak. But we looked at one another. At last I touched him. With my hand.

From outside there came a blinding flash. Lightning right across the summer sky. A crack of thunder. A peal of laughter. I ran to the door and looked out. HE was there. Outside. I still couldn't see his face. Of course not. Because of the hood. He said: "It is all done now. Be your own master. Just as you wished." And then he laughed again. A most fearful sound.

"Who's there?" called the soldier, "Who are you talking to? Who's there? You're fooling again — there's nobody." And so there was. Nobody.

But it had been at that moment. Why, that it happened. A thunderbolt out of a clear sky. Struck the Royal Barge. It sank. My parents were drowned. They called it an Act of God. An Act? Of God? If so by God it was not Act enough! The Friar, you see, survived. Everyone and everything was blamed: but I would condemn none. I knew myself responsible. The Jackal-King had heard me. I had been delivered. But into what?

That night I dreamed again — of a company of Players, bursting in upon me with their light and with their life and with their laughter and with their pretended love. Ah, God, how I burned to be with them! But in my dream I was bound and could not move. But in the morning I heard of their arrival. "Welcome!" I said, "The King is dead. Long live the player King." Then gathering them around me I went down into the dungeons, had them all opened then, and set the prisoners free. "Go home" I said. "New King, new life. Go and be free. Be happy." You may be sure I was not slow in being blamed.

Well, but what followed was the funeral and the closing of the tomb. And then the turning of us all towards my coronation. O yes, however much I might be loathed, despised, I could not be rejected. I had been the Prince. I was the Heir. So now I am the King.

If my people would not love me then, I would force my love on them. And yet I knew this guilt, I recognized the crime burning within me. I would not require that they rejoice with me. So I commanded the coronation early, before dawn. I went in secret, without recognition. Only my soldier by my side. The crown flashed in the dullard light, and I seemed to see the head of Jesus turn upon the cross. "Deceiving, you are yourself deceived" he said. Or seemed to say. But I was King while he was crucified.

Well, does that shudder your doctrine? Or are you only the more convinced of my madness? O come now, to call me mad will benefit none of us in the end. A criminal I went, and God's anointed I returned. Something where I had been nothing. They all turned to me now, but I brushed them aside. I wanted none of them. None. Never.

Alone, I went to my own room and summoned my soldier. When he came, I slammed the door to, and locked it fast. "Beat me" I said, "Lash me. Thrash me. Humiliate me. Punish me for my own guilt. Make me suffer. Do with me as you will. I give myself into your hands." But he refused me. Me. His King. Because I was his King. I begged him. But he refused me.

"I daren't. You're the King. You're God's Anointed. The Lord's Anointed. I daren't touch you. Someone else may, but it can't be me. It would be sin. I fear. I fear. Please. Please. I beg you Majesty."

What did I do? What could I do? I did what I could. I threw him the key and turned away. Kneeling he caught my hand and kissed it. God, I did desire him then. I heard him whisper "Bless me, your Majesty. May the King bless his servant." Ah, but I burned. How I burned. And I would not. He went away. Unlocked the door. And went away.

The sun in its silence beat down through the window. Slowly one by one the bells of the city began to peal. Reluctant to my accession. Bless him? Why not? Why not? Why not after all? Ah, if I who were cursed could surely bless — but the Friar was standing in the open doorway, his red eyes gleaming. "Does his Majesty desire Confession? And does His Majesty require Penance?" And the leather lashes trembled in his hand. And I — for once I did oblige him. Then.

THE KING TURNS SLOWLY AWAY.
THE LIGHT FADES.

ACT TWO

DARKNESS. A BELL TOLLS. LIGHT RISES ON THE KING.
THE KING SPEAKS:

The truth? The truth is simple. The truth is always very simple. The truth is always LOVE. But I knew only hate. Why should I who had experienced little else but hate not come in the end to feel hate? Well, perhaps it was true after all — why, that I was possessed by the Devil. Is not so great an experience of hate in itself a possession by the Devil? I never heard that HATE could be any part of GOD. Even my crowning did not save nor change me. For I in my body did descend, knowing my own guilt, deep into such dark depths as you never could conceive. I knew the visitation of a thousand indomitable fiends. Yet there was still a wildness in me, and a deep desire for punishment, for the purifying agony of pain. I could find no peace. Nor could I care for any but myself. Knowing myself beyond the care of others. Perhaps as Friar Ethelbert has said, the Devil was within me, in my very body. But being in *him* too, the Friar was not the one to drive him out of me. Yes, my soldier. He would have beaten the Devil out of me. Flogged him from my body. Given me peace in my flesh. Yet he was afraid. Now that I was King. So I sent him away and did not see him any more. And so the Devil did not leave.

When did I think myself possessed? On the day my parents died and I could find no grief. On the day that I was crowned and I could find no love. On the day my soldier refused me. On the day that I submitted to the Friar. Then I knew that there was nothing. Isn't that what the Devil is? A negation? Isn't that it, ha?

Then War came. And Famine. And Plague. I knew they called me curst and would have wished — . What did I feel then? I feared. Pray? To whom? To the God of that Friar who brutalized me? To the God of my Father who detested me? To the God of my Mother who disowned me? And for what should I pray? For deliverance? I tell you that from what I feared I did not need deliverance. Reassurance only.

I feared that I might never feel a man between my knees. Might never bestride the buttocks of a lover. And from that fear I wanted only comfort. And comfort came. Suddenly in violence. War. Not the violence I desired. War. For which I was totally unprepared. As were my constant counsellors. Who feared. God, how they feared. I knew their fear all right. I could smell their fear. When the enemy began to move. That day my eyes opened and I could see the darkness touching our horizon. And I knew their fear. And was alone.

My soldier was gone. My hoofed friend was gone. I found the room one day — empty now, deserted.

And I saw the war. Coming. And I could only watch. Silent. And the Friar, silent, watched me too. No, I knew nothing of war. Why should I? How could I? Nobody ever told me anything, nor taught me neither. My father? O my father least of all. I suppose they all thought I would die and never become king, but in the end you see it was they who died and I who went on living. Till this moment. And in the end, you see, I knew as little of taking life as giving it. In most respects I was a virgin. A foolish virgin.

And yet I saw the war before it came. O with another eye, perhaps. I'm not sure. Maybe a dream. Or perhaps a vision. I seemed to see the horizon touched with a dark and moving shadow. And when I — awoke — why, so it was. Because the enemy were on the march against us. I tried, of course I tried. To warn. But they would not believe me. Ever. No one ever believed me. Until too late. But they should have known. There was always a threat from *there,* always an ambition. And with a new King in Navarre, inexperienced — hardly popular — . I sometimes wondered if they had some of them been bribed.

I ask you now — where is HE? Bring him to me. Let him come back, back to me. For I know that you are certain where he is. And I am certain he would not betray me. If he will not take me into him, I would willingly empty myself into his hand, I would willingly bear him on my back, I would willingly let him beat me till even his strength fails. I have always understood his love.

In any case of course there was another danger. Because we had no army. O, it was foolish, foolish, foolish beyond reason. My father was so miserly he wouldn't spend a penny on the army if he could help it — and you may be sure he always could! So when the attack came we had no forces to speak of. No one wanted to serve, no one wanted to enlist. They all wanted to live. They all wanted to enjoy life to the full. They all demanded the right to that life. But no one wanted to defend it. We had got out of the way of soldiering. It's a knack, you know, and like any other it can be lost. And in the end your enemy depends upon your losing it.

Do? What could I do? There was nothing I could do. I'd never been taught anything. It was ludicrous. I wasn't even a knight. I was King but not a knight. Given the chance I could ride a man but not a horse. I was certainly no soldier.

But I knew what should be done. I told them all — if the men of the country wouldn't fight willingly for their king and for their country they must be forced, impressed, conscripted, drafted. No one liked that. There were demonstrations against me. I had those beaten down. You surely don't expect to hear any good of me, now? Do you, Reverend Fathers? No, I refused to go out myself. Why should I risk my life for *them* if they were unwilling to risk their lives for me? Besides, if I had what might not have happened here? So the General went off with what men there were, and I remained. The enemy advanced, the General retreated. Yes, he sent back to me for help. Of course I didn't send any. I couldn't. I had nothing to my hand.

I *did* tell them to open the Treasury, to take what money there was and use it. Why, to buy soldiers of course. Money spent on men is never wasted. I don't know. Maybe they did not believe me, as usual. Maybe there was no money. Maybe there was money and they took it but did not use it. O, I've no doubt if you looked around you would find it somewhere here among all those faithful councillors of mine. I certainly haven't got it. What could I have done with money? Then? Or now?

When the enemy reached the city walls they besieged us. But first they sent in a Herald. Yes, under a flag of truce. I believe it's usual. I received him in the throne-room. Alone. O, the others were in such a state of panic they made me nervous. So I sent them away. The Friar? Especially the Friar. He is supposed to be a man of Peace, but — .

The Herald stared at me. I stared back at him. I'm sure neither of us had ever seen anything quite like the other. He said to me: "You'd better give in hadn't you? You can't hold out much longer. I suppose you know you're done for now?" He was a tall, broad man with a great bulge in his crutch. I gazed at this. And wondered. "How many children have you got?" "Twenty-five. Seventeen of them legitimate." I was amazed. I could not believe a man could be so fertile. How naive I was, you see. I said to him: "Go back and tell your master that when the King of Navarre is done for, it will be by a man who has the wherewithal between his legs to do it. And it will take more than a couple of tinsel balls and a wilted candle, believe you me. And now my faithful Counsellors will escort you to the gate." I clapped my hands and they all rushed it. Why, the players of course. The others were still terrified, skulking behind the arras. Which is why they call me Coward and say that I preferred the indecent players. Of course I did. I was no fool, you know.

But as he went, something about him — and I cried out "Wait!" And then kneeling before him, like a slave before his master, I drew off one of his long supple boots. As I suspected, his foot was hoofed. Cloven. "Are all your children goats, I wonder?"

Ah, you are like the others and will not believe me. God grant me your Eminences' gift of disbelief. How simple it would have made my life.

The player King tapped at my door one afternoon and said: "There's someone who wants to see you. Someone who's dying to see you." He led me then through shadowed passages where from time to time the sun fell in through narrow clefts, heavy sunlight rodlike into shadow.

A small dark room. A narrow bed. A man. They whispered: "Don't you recognize him?" And of course I did. It was my soldier. Wounded on the battlements. His wound had festered. Would not heal. They'd brought him here, to care for him. These are a kindly people. Why, the Players of course. They'd looked after him. But he would not mend. When he knew that he was dying he'd asked not for a priest but for myself. And so they brought me to him. Ah, he was not so ripe now, after all. But he was part of my existence. Always. I knelt down beside him. I cradled him in my arms. I kissed him. I blessed him. Dear God, I could have wished to die myself. For sorrow. For compassion. For all that I had never known. Ah, when I'd felt his great heart pounding, pounding against my palm, who would have guessed, who could have guessed . . . ?

"He's coming" he whispered. "He's on his way. He'll soon be here." And he stared up at me until the light had faded from his eyes. We took care of him, then. The players and myself. I ordered the Royal Mausoleum to be opened. We carried him down those dark and echoing stairs and laid him there beside my Father. If I'd dared I would have thrown my Father's body out. This man had been a better. "He is coming. He is on his way. He will soon be here." No, I knew no more than you. I'd not the least idea. What did I do? I closed the tomb and sealed it. And called the Players to me. We sang and danced then. All round the cloister. Till the sun was setting. Till the moon was rising. Till we were dropping with exhaustion. "Love do not go from me" I sang, my tears falling from me like sweat. "Love do not go from me. Love stay and fill me every day. I'll open willingly and slide you in. Love hold your load till you're within." So sang the cursed King of Navarre, knowing nothing at all of love. Flushing the cloisters with his tears. While the echoing Players leapt and sprang.

The Friar of course was scandalized. "Silence, Filth!" he screeched, "Silence in the name of God!" But the Players teased him, and I did not blame them and made no move to stop their game. "It's not silence" they cried, "but Action. And not God, by God, but You that wants it!" They pretended to seize me. "Come, punish this bad man as he deserves" they cried. And the Player King pulled me face down across his knees while they all cried out: "We'll hold him down! We'll bare his arse! Scorch his buttocks with those thongs of yours" But good Friar Ethelbert yelled out: "Be silent, Devils, in the presence of Christ crucified!" And he swung his hand dramatically towards the cross. And was at once himself struck dumb with silence. As were we all. And why? Because, good Fathers, because the Cross was empty. Jesus had gone. Was fled from our midst. Ah, I took that very hard, you may be sure. He might at least have asked for my assistance.

Yet I knelt there, on those cold bare stones. Willing the return of God. Commanding him as his Anointed to return. Willing. Commanding. Refusing to be refused. How did I pray? Pray? One does not pray with God. One matches mind with mind. God respects no prayer. He understands these things — silence, stillness, solitude. And seeing the dark pretends to be the light.

"He is on his way. He is coming. He will soon be here."

And then? Why then I returned. To my own room. And when I opened the door the fire was blazing. On a stool before it sat a man, naked, his back to me. The corners of my vast apartment were thick with shadow. I shut the door quietly and then I waited. Without turning he said "Slide the bolt" Which then I did. One does not command the King, but then I did it. Swinging round, he gazed at me from where he sat with his knees wide apart, lovingly caressing his stiffened sex from root to tip. We did not speak but as we held each other's gaze I felt myself grow hard, the lust biting me like acid. "Come" he said, "you are not too virginal for me, I think. Come, let us ride together and make the simple journey out of this place of terror. Come, why do you hesitate? I am going to make you very happy." And I unspeaking, slowly holding back desire, leaving my clothes there where they fell, came to him. And he, opening his arms to me, drew his knees together so that I might ride secure. And his great shaft sliding upward, into, holding me and joining us. And presently his mouth seeking my sex, completed the circle of our love.

Yes, I knew myself changed. And my old enemy, the Friar, knew it too, suspecting why, but knowing nothing. And I, gazing past him through the window, saw — what did I see? The silence of the city in the sun? The black flies swarming through the stench of death? The protracted agony of the dying, wounded by weapons or disease? No, these I neither saw nor heard. Nothing. Nothing? But yes, I saw a distant stain of darkness on the far horizon. The advent of hostile reinforcements.

And I tried to warn again. But: "YES. YES. YES." they cried, "SOMEthing must be done. It is Essential." Then, bickering, arguing, fell to feasting, did precisely nothing.

Is that what they say? That I, lost in my unnatural passions did nothing to help them, to defend? Natural, unnatural, what was either? To me was only Love.

I said: "Let me go — out into the city —" But they thought me mad, or perhaps were jealous. And my Confessor, that hellbent Friar, screeched out: "Send for the Doctor. Let the King be bled. His Majesty is hot with fever!" Hot, yes — but not, as he well-knew, with fever. We both burned — but I with the truer flame of love. He with the longing to thrash the steed he did not dare to ride.

Ah, but I knew myself filled with power.

I was beyond the reach of War, beyond the touch of Plague, beyond the strike of Murder. I knew myself beyond all the disasters of the world. I would have shown myself as King among my people. I would have embraced them all, the dying or diseased. I would have infected them with myself. I would have found them strength. I would have shown them hope.

Of course not. They would not let me go. The Friar told them I was demented. And so the power of my possession remained contained within me, in my solitude. And our enemies advanced unchecked towards us. And we all heedless of what might follow.

A day of darkness. Of despair. Above all of the premonition of defeat. And the sun blazed down. Harshly cold upon the city streets. And the Player King, standing beside me on the ramparts said: "There is a certain hollowness about your cheek these days." And he touched it, gently, with his forefinger. But I smiled, seeing his manhood twitch between his legs. So I as gently cupped my hand over that warmth, feeling it leap and stiffen in my palm, and hearing his sudden gasp.

And I said: "This is the only gift, the only comfort left to me to give you. My warmth is yours. And so I touch you without shame. Believe me, I have nothing but myself to give. Look, you can see that we are done for now."

Not lust. Not lust. Though that is what you think. Not lust. But something more. And yet not quite love.

Of such an act there is generally only one continuing, and one ending only. And so it was. Later, lying naked in my arms in that fly-haunted silence, he muttered: "You are Love. You are the King of Love. You are the God of Love. You are Eros. Amor. Phoebus Apollo in the sun." And his rich heavy hair swung all across my breast. And the taste of him was fragile in my mouth. God bless whoever has him now, for he was sweet within me.

I said: "There is a secret passage in the Chapel, behind the altar, which leads to safety, out of this castle, out of this city. I will send you away. Away from here. Out into safety. Secretly, before we fall, before the enemy break in."

But he whispered: "Come with us. Come with me. We will disguise and spirit you away. Cities fall, and nations die — but players, always needed, live for ever. Besides, you possess the element of truth."

So I sent them away, out by that secret passage there behind the altar in the chapel, away with their cloaks and crowns, their masks and baubles. And I whispered as they went: "Pray for me, as I will pray for you and your survival. For you are the true treasure of the world."

Their leader, the Player King, was last to go. And he stood waiting. Waiting as I knew for me to go with them. With him. And for a moment then I thought: "I will." And I took the crown off from my head and laid it on the altar. And immediately I was nothing, no one once again. No one. Nothing. Not the King. And being no one then was everyone. And being everyone, I knew the terror and despair of my people in this unjust war. And knew myself bound by their sorrow. And I knew that if I went I broke that bond. And breaking, should destroy the last the final link between their spirit and my soul.

So I turned and took him in my arms. And kissed him. And, weeping, his tears were salt against my lip. Then I whispered: "Go to the King of Aragon. Tell him to come quickly, to come fast, and with all force, to save us now before too late." And I kissed him once again, and closed and sealed the door behind him. And went away myself. Ah, silent, silent, silent then you may be sure.

And what would our conquerors have found? A plunderless city of the dead diseased? For the plague was hard upon us then, you know. And now was only silence . . . stillness . . . the quiet passage of time, minutes, hours, and other days.

Another night. And that night going to my bed alone, sending away my page, I knelt to pray. Yes, indeed to thank God. For now I had something to thank him for — why the love which I had found and which for all I knew might never come again. Not knowing his name and having as it seemed no sure commandment over his movements, how could I be certain? And if he should choose to stay away from me?

Well, but it was then I saw him. Reflected in the mirror. Standing behind me. Great. Strong. Rich. Ripe. Dressed in soft leather. Black and supple like a second skin stretched taut across his limbs. The firelight gleaming on him. Casting shadow into every secret hollow of him. No, he did not speak. Turning aside, he took off his doublet and threw it on the bed. I was silent. Thinking he intended love. And yet he seemed withdrawn from me. And he seemed changed. As though another hand had passed across him. And I in my silence thought of love. Which then I felt so strong within me. Yes, and lust — yes, that as well. Yes, who could not — then? Seeing him. Ah, and the blood so heavy in my head. And he withdrawn from me. Which forced me forward. And I touched him. And kneeling breathed upon the mound of his sex, and saw it shift and stretch beneath the soft black leather. And — ah — the wonder of him, who had not once repulsed me nor called me grotesque.

He said: "Tonight I am your servant and shall be your page. And after I have undressed you, you shall master me as you will." But I cried out: "I am attacked by devils, by all the thousand legions of terror and despair." But he, kneeling half-shadowed at my side, embracing me and comforting me, whispered: "There is no devil that is not subject now to me, nor to yourself. For I know you love me, or you would have gone, away with those Players you sent out into safety. But you remained, and all I am and all I have are yours."

I remember that he asked me if there was anything he could do, if there was anything I needed. I said I feared for my subjects — people who neither trusted me nor loved me, but whom I had come to love through him, and through the love that he had shown to me, although I could not help them. He said then that help would come through love, salvation from the other.

And the warmth of him was like the encircling of a summer night. And winding my arms around him I felt within my hand the steady beating of his heart, and the rhythm of him between my knees entered into me . . . and I thought then that I fell forward into sleep, into another world But he stirring beneath me, I wakened to that world — a world known yet strange. A world where we seemed to hang suspended in the sharp night air, above my own city, my own land. And I astride him like a flying horse. And the moonlight round about us was as clear as day, and beneath us we could see the approaching army of reinforcement crawling like oil across the fields. And I knew that we were doomed, could not escape but by a miracle. Then reaching back, he seized my hands with his, clasping them under him, around his sex, and then began to plunge, to buck and heave beneath me until with a great cry he let his seed burst from him. And I saw his seed like an envenomed mist of pearls slowly descending through the moonlit night — a rime of poisoned frost upon the sharpened air. And as it dropped, and where it touched the advancing army, there they stopped and fell.

And it was so — as has been recorded. Why, that the plague touched them suddenly as they advanced, so that they fell, dropping like stones where they stood, one man contaminating there the next.

And then? Why then I awakened, to my own room, to find the walls closing slowly round us as before, and he beneath me warm and live. Then I myself — ah, suddenly released — emptying filled him with myself. And in that moment felt myself no longer me. But part of him, my lover. Part at least of the very Body of God. My God, Your God. And who knows where God shall appear — do you? I doubt it. Do I? O, not at all. And where should God be, but in the body of a lover. Is God not one? I for that moment was then one with Christ. I in him. He then in me. I filled with his live seed. Have pity upon me, O ye my judges, for the body of God has ravished me. But in that moment the Devil fled from me. Screaming into silence. Bless me Fathers, for I have not sinned.

No, there is more. What then will your decision be?

Yes, my lords, I understand. And no, I can say nothing any different. And to tell the truth, I no longer care to live.

What have you done with *him*? Why does *he* not come to me? For I was awakened by the trumpets of Aragon, coming to our deliverance. Theirs, not mine. But I was alone, and have remained so ever since. There can be no life for me.

Yes, my lords, I understand. You, being competent judges in this matter have reached your verdict. You will deliver me to secular power. But that is to myself. I am the power. I am the King. Only the King may condemn me. Only I may now condemn myself. As we, deserted and betrayed, now do.

"Stephen the Second, King of Navarre, known as the Curst: we find you guilty of the crimes of Blasphemy, Negligence, Invocation of Demons, and Unnatural Love — whereby the lives of those entrusted to you at your crowning have been thrown away and lost. And for these crimes against Nature and Almighty God there can be neither pardon nor remission. We, therefore, condemn thee, Stephen, Accursed One, Disciple of Darkness, to die at the hands of the Public Executioner. Die, Stephen. Die and enter into silence. May God have mercy on your immortal soul."

Go, now, all of you. And send him to me. Do not fear, for me there can be no escape.

THE KING SEEMS TO SEE THE EXECUTIONER.

I seem to know your voice, and yet I dare not look at you. What's that to you? You are the Executioner after all. Who are to be my death. Take off your mask, take off your hood for me. Let me see the face of death . . . and it is *you* after all! You who were my life: always, always my love. And to think I never did guess! Could never know! Now you have come back to me. Now when there is no time. O, I am to be the sacrifice, you know. The Isaac who does not escape. And you will have to take me as I am. I'm so afraid you will not love when you see me as I am. But I give myself to you again. I've nothing left to give. I give you life — you give me death — with love to each other it's a perfect marriage, don't you think? And I should come to you unclothed, naked to my marriage-bed. But I am not as I was. Imprisonment has altered me. You must take me now for what I am, as I take you — for the lover whose arrival after midnight brings the end of life. Ah, I feel such love for you, such warmth, such wonder. Touch me, hold me a moment, let me feel once more the beating of your heart. Ah, it must beat for both of us since mine will soon be still. How warm you are. How strong. Hold me, Hold me. Then do it quickly. It will not be difficult. My body will open to you as it has before. Listen, I'll tell you what you must do. When it is over, put on my clothes then take the crown: so they will know you are to be my heir, to be their King. Perhaps they will not even think me gone, but live, and we forever one, forever — forever — forever — NOW.

A SUDDEN FLASH OF BLINDING LIGHT
IMMEDIATELY EXTINGUISHED BY DARKNESS.

BEING ALONE

by

Ned Rorem

> *. . . The dark showed me a face.*
> *My ghosts are all gay.*
> *The light becomes me.*
> —*Roethke*, Praise To The End

PUBLIC PASSPORTS

No matter how tenacious or, indeed, victorious in the ring, the bull is never spared. Though he fell the torero to become champion, the bull is doomed. Why? His use is used up. At a second "go" the animal knows the tricks, and like the wiliest pacifist he'll turn and run off. Similarly, we spectators are irreparably conditioned by our first corrida. You are only deflowered once.

I've attended two bullfights. The ordeal in Arles in 1952, with six consecutive *mises à mort*, was so gorgeously stigmatizing that I hadn't yet healed when, sixteen years later in Acapulco, I saw my second. Still, the first steeled me for the next. Forced to witness death, over and over in 20-minute segments of identical choreography, one turns self-protectingly blasé, even in a concentration camp. Or does one? Perhaps no amount of experience will ever immunize us to certain things: bullfights, sunsets, starvation, love.

I note these paragraphs while reading *Christopher and his Kind* with a disapproval of Isherwood's assumption that readers not only know but have cared about knowing his whole previous catalogue. An anxious nostalgia threads this presumably "honest" reweaving of old themes. Nothing is riskier than for an artist to set the record straight years after. Late truth lacks the energy of early distortion. And who, one might well ask, will in forty years reshuffle these currents facts of Christopher? Art always hits the nail on the head, but accuracy for its own sake cannot guarantee art.

Delving further, disapproval gives way to bafflement: How, in the company of the major minds of his time, Christopher's unabashed carnality remains his sole subject matter! (Auden writes usually on ideas, Christopher seldom.) How, lest his public for one instant forget it, he repeats his name constantly, thereby paradoxically, unlike Proust, lending a vague impersonality to his narrator! (I always hesitate to speak my own name, feeling somehow that I am dropping it.) How, in his tastes both cultural and tactile, he is German as opposed to French! Am I in my Frenchness so far from him? Now, when the chips are down, what I deplore in his writing is what I defend in my own: the unembellished given of the self as subject. But there remains the nagging question: Can one's own behavior, and even one's presumable objectivity toward that behavior, be fair game on the literary racetrack?

"Life," claims Eric Bentley, "is seldom simple; art never." I reply: Life is never simple, art always. With its curving paths through multiple layers art nonetheless follows the straightest line between two points. How an artwork works is the only way for that work, whereas living is nothing but alternatives. Art is economy and shape, life is waste and disorder.

Happily it is not for an artist to define what he does. An artist doesn't do art, he does work. If that work turns out to be art, that is proclaimed through the judgment of lesser lights.

Virgil Thomson (calmly to Hortense who is annoyed that guests ignore him): "When I find myself among those who don't know my name, I know I'm in the real world."

My fame, modest though it be, establishes a security which (were that fame withdrawn tomorrow) cannot withdraw tomorrow, because the remaining years — hours? — are fixed, and we readjust to every minute. Now, the more secure I grow, the less I feel urged to wax brilliant. (Was it 1954, Cannes, that I observed Van Johnson and Jean-Pierre Aumont soberly double-dating, with, on their arms, gyrating before the paparazzi, two obscure starlets *being brilliant?*)

Secure and brilliant are words I don't enjoy. Brilliant is so overused ("a brilliant young author") as to be meaningless; secure reeks of the analyst's couch. I avoid formula phrases more assiduously than mannerism phrases, formula phrases ("nuclear family", "middlebrow", "new left") being confected by individuals whose bandwagons joggle uncomfortably, mannerism phrases ("like I mean you know") being folklore, anonymous.

I ask Francine what nuclear family meant. Doubtless thinking me square, she explains that it's the immediate nucleus of parents and children. Well, of course. Isn't that just plain family? Global village, third world, collective unconscious, these are "spinoffs" — ugh — of family.

In the dream this question was posed: Why are we alive? Quick the answer: Creation. Does my unconscious sprout such corn? By daylight of course, I can thresh that to signify anything. We aren't alive to express ourselves — to be "creative" — or even to wonder why we're alive. We have invented our own existence so as to exist. We have been created because we have been created. Do not read this as redundant; we are scotch tape over a black hole.

In those dangerous hours of early morning when one awakes and realistically dwells on growing old alone, ill and penniless, and like a drum the thought crescendos to a burst of tears in which we fail to drown because the rising sun parches them, and maybe lights the path to a bit more darkness and sleep — in such hours I used to come to the notion of you finally, and be saved. Now that's past. Either I must reach another notion, or avoid the dangerous hours.

If it's really so bad, why not kill yourself. And he killed himself. . . . This literal reply to a figurative query has been, more than a smarting transient slap, a Promethean punishment which no one deserves.

Morris being back from a brief expensive stay in Paris I plead with him to describe the odor of the Seine, of the Boulangérie du Bac, of the sun on the Luxembourg gravel, of the pubescent students at the Flore, of the granite on the house where I lived. I can't return. But as I practise (as I'm doing now) Debussy's *Ballade de Villon a s'ayme* I simultaneously ascend the Rue Mouffetard in the body I inhabited 29 years ago tonight, and descend on the dark intimate regions of human mates now dead.

"I'd always adored playing the wisp of mauve fluff into which some coal miner rams his frame."
"Perhaps the mauve fluff rôle should now be shifted to another."
"Another? Never! How dare another. Either I play the mauve fluff or nobody plays the mauve fluff. Though turnabout is unfair play, if it *were* fair, the parts in the play shouldn't depend on the age of the victims — I mean of the participants."

Some people twenty or forty may seem to be thirty or fifty, but no one fifty or thirty truly looks forty or twenty. JH insists that we all look our age, but some look it better than others.
People say my face belies my years. Why is it a compliment to look young? What's wrong with looking one's age? True, to "look old" is to slim down the chances of getting laid. But what are these "chances"? Are they American only? Is sex just for the young? Yes, maybe.

And so tomorrow, at the vast party planned by JH here, I turn fifty-five, and not only youth but the past as concept slide into a new dimension. On the day you discover that grown-ups don't have the answers, you yourself have become grown-up.
Francine and I are both now hesitant about losing our heads through our bodies: great sex takes so much time. The more fools we — in our flight from folly.
Insomnia's the negative side to that coin which depicts the fight betwixt the flesh and the intellect of a single person. Sex is the cure for insomnia. They say.
(Sketch a profile of Francine: her suave naïveté, her "Malheurs de Sophie" nose, her literary wisdom and lacunae, her beauty at 48.)

Watching friends survive and push, guided solely by the velvet leash of delusion, have I too then been had? The delusion is that we are indispensible, that we have something unique to say. It's nice to hear someone remark "You write marvelous music", but saddening too. Is the delusion more than high-class horniness? Music is made by another me who accepts the compliment and who wants to be loved for the self alone, as though there were such selves. JH maintains that his mental impotence arises from an incapacity for accepting self-delusion. Is that maintenance against the final embarrassment not itself a delusion? Art's the grand illusion. Even the greatest, in order to proceed, must leap before they look. (Yet some of the greatest have killed themselves.) Well, if we are not indispensible, we *are* irreplaceable, even when moldering in the grave, for our chemical swervings keep Earth in balance. End of lesson.

20 December 77. With Robert Phelps I went this snowy afternoon at five, armed with white roses and Godiva chocolates and a copy of my new "A Quaker Reader," to visit Janet Flanner whom I'd not seen *dans l'intimité* since two years ago when she came to dine with Lillian Hellman, and, on leaving, had a heart seizure in the elevator. We were four (with Natalia Murray filling the chasms of Janet's lapses by regaling us with tales of De Pachmann, one of those mad geniuses who, when divorced from his métier, seems merely moronic), and stayed perhaps three hours. Janet's already half in heaven, her every hesitant phrase and gesture being made in souvenir of ancient gestures and phrases, and one feels her hang on. For she forgets who we are from one 5-minute period to the next; and after the several times she goes to the bathroom (she has many stiff drinks), imagines herself to be home in the Ritz again. (Like Elizabeth Ames who at ninety talked in the next room with her mother and sister, each dead for fifty years.) Yet I am at ease and learn from her, and admire her staunchly no less for yesterday than for today. Senility is surely agonizing for them too, who cannot help but know they're lost.

I am still hoping to retrieve that person (the one with the iron-blue hair) I was too drunk to accept in Jackson Park thirty-eight summers ago when now I enter this uptown bar. Or to relocate this person (the one with the strident nape muscles) whom I shunned gratuitously in the Luxembourg Gardens twenty-four autumns ago when now I enter that downtown café. Or that other paragon. Or this certain-to-be-love. And do you know? They can be found. Their actual flesh & blood can be found, but as overwhelmed by the passing ages as my own. Yet I still pursue the longed-for pursuers whom I'm certain could have given me that which is never given. I am still . . .

Virgil comes to dine, and as always his table talk shimmers. Afterward when we all adjourn to the parlor he as always falls asleep. Conversation turns to classical music. Virgil awakens.
"What are we discussing?"
"Beethoven."
"Top drawer," says Virgil, and drops off again.

OF COUNTRY MATTERS

To the young, sex is what grown-ups do. To the elderly, sex is what the young do. Sex is all-consuming while it thrives, and is the subject (if not the source) of most art. But sex does not cause suicide, and must be put aside in order to write about it. To be appreciated is the primal need.

The cliché that homosexuals don't like women blinds us to the fact that homosexuals do appreciate women differently. Colette: *Les vacances, c'est là où l'on travaille ailleurs*. It could be argued that a gay man savors a woman's beauty the more purely in not being deflected by sexual yearnings. He can "see her", not "see her in bed".

Although sex and love need not be mutually exclusive, neither are they mutually inclusive, but folks confuse them. Such folks, known as puritans, are actually impuritans blending oil with water. Love can add elegance to sex, but sheer sex unenhanced in the abstract and alone is therapeutic. Sex can add sorrow to love, but platonic love unenhanced in the concrete and shared is fulfilling and durable.

What is a human being? A human being is the substitute for a melon.

Surely there exists more mundane frustration about artists than about gays in the world's eyes. I'm less defensive than Isherwood — less "moralistic" — about queerdom than about musicality, for musicality in this world is queerer than any kind of sex.

Straight men, often intelligent ones, are wont to reach two conclusions, jointly contradictory, about the gay male: 1) that he would like to bugger them, and 2) that he is a woman trapped in a man's body. More confounding is the supposition about a gay conspiracy in which all homosexuals are organized in hating all heterosexuals and have amassed stockpiles to prove it. (JH contends that these are *my* conclusions and propagandistic hogwash.)

Sexuality is more a matter of how X feels about Y than of how X feels about himself. Homosexuality, unlike negritude or womanhood, is a part-time job.

In his interview last night of William Buckley, Cavett asked, "Have you ever, thinking back, found yourself to have been wrong?" Needless to say Buckley never answered, never at least with a yes or no. But it's a good question, and in posing it of myself I quickly reply Yes.

Is the reply defensive? What in fact have I found myself wrong about? (Not, certainly, musical tastes — if tastes can be thought of as right or wrong — although my tastes have grown narrower, excluding what was once acceptable while retaining the same *type* of preference). Well, I've changed about women. Raised in a profoundly unprejudiced milieu I was taught to accept Negroes, artists, the "poor", as equals. Yet women always appeared to be of a lesser caste. I am not stupid, yet the only females I could tolerate were precisely those whose so-called female traits were underplayed. Baudelaire wrote that the appreciation of intelligent women was the pederast's prerogative. He was not wrong, but I was.

Is there a homosexual sensibility?, people still ask. Why yes, no doubt. But one would be hard put to show that sensibility defined, say, by the homosexual's musical composition or poetry or law practice or medical notions, as distinct from the sensibility of one who screws too seldom or too often or is redheaded or over fifty or is more interested in microscopes than in Love or is dumb.

The trouble here is that "homosexual sensibility" is a slogan masked as an idea. Until semantics are settled, perpetrators will cram the work of gays into pigeonholes by cutting off limbs. Meanwhile, if there *is* such a sensibility, dare you include Whitman (said to be queer) with his careless macho rhapsodies to the great outdoors? Dare you omit Beardsley (rumored to be straight) with his quaint sonatinas to a vast powder puff?

Is there a gay sensibility? Define it, then I'll tell you if there's one.

Does God exist? Define him, then I'll tell you if he exists.

The other boys thought it was sissified for our gym teacher to go around with that dame in the fur coat. Girls were nowhere. Little did the boys know that in just a year or so they too . . . But I, oh I, adored the female eyes like gunshots through the black foam, adored the boys too (their tang, their marble thighs), and the gym teacher most of all.

If I cannot let you know I wish to go to bed with you — or you, or you, or you, or you — it's because I can't face your saying No. Title: *Sleeping Around*.

" . . . if I cannot be gay let a passionless peace be my lot."

— Tennyson, *Maud* (part I, ix)

Homosexuality? Oh no! What can one now add to this plot, saturated and draining into popular journals? One can add only, as with any art or history, one's singular experience, cast the home light.

(Write an exegesis on Kay Boyle's "A Defense of Homosexuality" from *A Glad Day*, if it can be retrieved, at the risk of passing for a mad nabokovian pedant. She speaks of it as "a thing with a future as yet badly done by amateurs neglecting the opportunity to be discriminating", and "as engrossing as bee-raising and as monotonous to the outsider." But all that was fifty years ago. Well, bee-raising is fascinating to outsiders no less than homosexuality, but outsiders don't laugh at and burn bees.)

X. hates niggers and kikes and . . . *heterosexuals*! No, there's no wounding slang for a power group. Slang, yes, but not wounding. Honky doesn't hurt unless you're white alone in Harlem. "She's a dirty straight" flows inanely off a queer duck's back, while "goy" has no strength to shame. Coldly amusing.

Sadness of the sauna, to find yourself on bended knee and in love in the steamroom simultaneously fellating two avid fellows who in the wet shadows above you are kissing and who arm in arm walk off together, leaving you with egg on your face.

No less than many another intelligent alcoholic I've ceaselessly asked myself why I drink (drank). I do know why I used to think I so easily first drank: shyness, and guiltlessly to justify the longing to be (what then was deemed)

Ned Rorem, 1974
Photo: Gianni Bates

sexually passive. But such reasons explained nothing. (More on shyness, which anyone intelligent is, yet which is never rewarded. Those witty others were in fact no less dumb than I.) Unlike physicians or A.A. addicts I'm not too intrigued by either the ounce of prevention or the pound of cure; and unlike the head-doctors, I realize that to learn the reason is not to stop the continuation. Well, I don't know the reason for homosexuality either, but homosexuality is natural and healthy, while drinking isn't.

Smells — the very word! Pungent fritters or autumn gusts or locker rooms. Nothing's less decorous for polite discussion, unless it were perhaps taste — taste of lime meringue or skunk cabbage or dry rot. How about the touch of steaming custard mamories or moss or silk or spikes piercing your palm?

Now, taste and touch and smell do not form bases for fine arts. Who meanwhile would accuse any nonvocal noise of specific obscenities? Hearing, of all the senses is subtlest, the most provocative, yet music alone cannot *describe*, much less *be*, that which is provocative.

Nothing is as it only seems, though we do precondition ourselves. A rose is not a rose, yet that syllable is lovely, and a rose by any other name would smell less sweet. All's in a name.

Repulsive racket of children's voices. Children should be neither seen nor heard. I do not like children. They need not be comprehended, nor from their mouths do words of wisdom flow. Yet I am not jealous of them as once was so. And I do love animals.

ANIMALS AND JH, INTERVIEWS AND EVIL

A diet of meat seems ever more repellent, and the "seemingness" began well before the acquisition of Wallace, our flawless feisty feline now thirteen years of age, although the fact of Wallace does reinforce and redefine all taste. Before adolescence practical zoology in all its boy-like foci — collecting snakes, breeding birds — was a prime concern, but with the advent of puberty the whole squirming mass was sold to Vauhan's Seed Store for sixteen dollars, enough to buy the score and records of *Le Sacre* at Lyon & Healy's six blocks away on Van Buren Street. Not till age forty-nine, with the advent of Wallace, did I again become preoccupied with the rights of beasts.

Last week at the fishmonger's a very large gent was pricing live lobsters. The salesgirl plunked the anxious creatures upon the zinc while he appraisingly declared, "My family's all my size, and we like good eating." This, in front of the lobster. That he should devour his *semblable*! Twenty years ago, at Bill & Edward's, lobsters were fixed for guests during cocktails. The hosts, misinformed on the fixing, didn't dunk the crustaceans in boiling water, but turned the cauldron up slowly while the animals squeaked and clawed the lid.

As we age our bodies take on facets of the other sex, just as our minds incline from left to right toward the middle of the road. If for my art I shed maleness at fourteen, then today I grow more masculine (ah, dear me) while shuddering at the notion of broiling steaks.

I ache to communicate more "meaningfully" with Wallace, but he's been a cat an awfully long time. Maybe that's meaning enough. Wallace and I sometimes try to match wits, but I've been a man (am I a man?) for as long as he's been a cat. Together on this stage we're separated by a billion years.

Do I use my occasional exasperation with JH as a lash against myself? Can I not well afford a "duty" toward him in exchange for what he lends me with his perpetually sly *aperçus*, as active an education as Marie Laure once offered? While swearing not to let his misery drag me down, have I not truly the time to spare?

Our lives, even when we're one day old, are what we're living now. There is no future ever.

Evening picnic at Jetties Beach. Before we sup (but we have forgot the mustard, forgot the coffee thermos, indeed forgot all staples) JH tests his new kite. Slowly he unwinds the long slack cord, fifty feet, a hundred feet, two hundred, until the thing floats high in the darkening sky. A flock of seagulls swoops past and one of their number is caught in the string, jerking, and falling fast. The others withdraw shrieking to the beach where they alight and sit like a chorus.

JH is marvelous with animals (is that the word? he's comprehending, treats them as peers). Gradually, gradually, seeing that the great entangled gull now struggles in water and may drown in panic, he rewinds the cord, wading through the shallow surf toward the bird even while easing the bird out of the deep toward him, tensing the cord, talking and talking and talking so softly. Like Androcles with the lion JH tends the nearly inextricably snared wing and legs, cajoling, soothing, fanning, releasing, and the bird knows a friend when he sees one and does not lash back with his beak, except lightly by reflex, unhurting. The snarls unwound, JH plucks the creature from the sea, carries it ashore like an offering, releases it. The gull stands poised, hops a few paces, then flies low over the sand toward his brethren. They all take off and fade into the night.

Loeb or Leopold — which one charmed the wingèd beasts? Orioles alit on his shoulders, whispered into his ear. Cocteau's Segramor spoke the language of the birds, and they answered. "What are they saying? Oh tell us, Segramor, do." "I'm out of practise. Let me try to listen. Wait. They are saying — pay, pay, pay, must pay, must pay, pay . . . "

A happy family is rare and singular, but unhappy families are all unhappy in the same way, unless the unhappy family happens to be yours. Misery blurs identity.

Write of how JH writhes still in the platitudinous mysteries of romantic love. The one but powerful tiding at turning fifty-five is the new talent for avoiding such useless tortures. Or is it that I'm able to avoid them precisely through the example of JH?

Ain't got no one to be unfaithful to.

They have seen more of death than of life, these five-year-olds floating in the China Sea, like Apollinaire's *Bluet*. . . .

Rosalyn Tureck has this month been a neighbor across the island at Quidnet. I accepted her dinner invitation on the condition that she garnish this with a private concert.

I arranged myself carefully among the rather tough cushions of an antique pink sofa, and she began to play. It was the same dusky hour as JH's adventure with the kite last year. Although the closed windows in Rosalyn's vast "piano room" are, like most windows, three feet up from the floor on the inside, on the outside they're flush with the lawn. The music, which I'd never heard, or even heard of (Bach's d-minor keyboard version of his a-minor violin sonata), was unutterably touching, and while it unwound the semi-wild fauna of Nantucket fluttered or scurried over the grass toward the glass panes and gazed through the sunset into my features. The sound, like all controlled perfection (is perfection by definition controlled?) seemed inscrutably tragic (generally I'm not given, when speaking of music, to metaphoric adjectives) and all the more satisfyingly so in that the ravens and rabbits conspired contingently to found a Peaceable Kingdom, choreographing a composition beyond their earshot. The sonata was followed by a Chopinesque adagio (again from a fiddle suite), and by two sinfonias. When Rosalyn had finished the mourning doves were lowing and the sky was filled with stars.

She feigned to comprehend when I declared that, because my first exposures to Bach coincided with my first exposures to the blues, those baroque harmonic sevenths formed by the characteristic contrapuntal sequences resemble the canvases upon which Billie Holiday etched her plaints. Put another way, music smells good or bad according to its setting (those Renoirs in the Polignac music room did distract, though not necessarily "wrongly", from the formal sounds at hand, and a celestial cavatina turns hellish when you have a hangover), and Bach beneath Tureck's hand changed meaning in the very process of unfurling last night as civilized background to the animal kingdom.

Her forte is precision, and, in a sense, that's all that counts. One is never uneasy. She never travels with the score: her fingertips house ten lilliputian brains with their own infallible memories.

Alone in Nantucket. When JH leaves the lights go quite literally out. Here, when winter dusk sets in at three o'clock, he places candles throughout the house and an old-fashioned lemon-peel glow, more levelling, more unifying than death, warms us as one. Then in the flickering we forget for awhile the rending disputes and sit down to a night of television.

The past year's been one of emerging from my massive depression only to witness JH sink even more deeply into his own (what used to be called) nervous breakdown, as into a leftover soup, for melancholy is catching. (Though by being passed on it is sometimes eliminated.) At least he has the gift of tears and vomit. On schedule he can weep or puke, which I cannot. I can write music, which is a kind of vomit, though it brings no relief. Yes, it does.

Over and beyond a scientific interest, does an entomologist develop or inherently possess a sympathetic, a "human", rapport with insects similar to the sentiments of a zoologist with apes, or, indeed, to the affections of any pet owner?

Despite the ever cooler afternoons the hydrangea in the front yard blooms greener and greener, sheltering (among a million more microscopic invertebrates) a lost mantis all foamy white and sea-colored and shivering crippled on a leaf. Did it or did it not feel differently about me than it might about some other person, as I aided it, examined it at point-blank range, purred to it about its pair of dear eyes that turned from right to left? Insects do make choices.

Perfect weather, and yes, alone: you've gone to the city. After these good eleven years you are still never easy to speak with, yet you keep things stirred up, and thus one feels a continual need to talk. There seems to be a crisis, not once a month but every single day. If I've not felt it so much lately it's because I see you provoke it with K. Still, your knack for rocking the boat stems of course from steering away from an "inner sanctum". If only, if only.

If only writing could get rid of it. Instead, writing locks it in.

Bees. When we returned after a season's absence a swarm throbbed on the south eave of the house, at once motionless and speedy, like a flying saucer. A neighbor said it'd been there for days. One hour later the bees vanished. Two days later they came back — or ten thousand like them. I was alone in the kitchen as the faint all-encompassing whirr began. Gradually the entire lawn grew inhabited, then the house was surrounded, encased in a translucent nacreous tent of yellow aspic, while the drone persisted, meaningless and purposeful like an Ashbery verse with a life of its own. . . . Suddenly they evaporated. Oh, a few — maybe two dozen — hovered around the north roof, but for all practical purposes they'd gone. (In the basement three stray fighters buzzed frantically as the sun set, but quieted with the dark; and when my eyes panned in so close as to perhaps momentarily join their frame of reference the dying beauties came together, rubbed antlers, then ceased breathing utterly.)

Illusion. Those sentinels at the north eaves have remained. Indeed, they work for the cluster now ensconced in the house's framework. By the time the exterminator arrived you could feel them beating like red hot snowflakes against the warming parlor wall. The exterminator sprayed some cursory droplets under the eaves, said he'd be back next week if we needed him.

But the bees have moved in. Their intelligence lives in this home with us like Hitchcock's birds. It's midnight, I've taken a valium. Are they in conference? Their pale angry roar continues, although the encyclopedia says they sleep quietly at night.

Next day, silence. The wall is cool. The bees have disappeared without a trace.

Interview appeared in today's *Times*. Wallace was twice mentioned, but remains unflappable. Not that he's so conceited he takes glory for granted, but too conceited to get outside himself and realize he's famous. Wallace asleep at the foot of the bed and I up here on the pillow, dreaming our separate dreams which, no matter how mad and fanciful we grow, we'll never comprehend. A queen may look at a cat, but never be a cat.

Misquoted as saying: "I love fame, and I love glory." The nouns are synonyms and I'm not redundant in interviews. Yes, I favor the shred of recognition that's mine, but do not love power. Self-involvement precludes manipulation of others. **The fame I love is the fame of others.**

If corporeally we are what we eat, stylistically we are what our interviewers make us. Interviews become our public passports.

Socrates: the first interviewer. Insofar as those *entretiens* were really *interrogatoires* drawing forth answers from a subject, the subject — the interviewee — revealed himself. But he revealed himself to himself and in toto, not to the public and in part. Modern interviews are about trivial aspects of a person (hobbies, horrors, habits), for how can a non-verbal artist of value utter valuable verbs about what makes him valuable? The interviewer makes of the subject what he chooses to make.

I've been interviewed on precisely the same matters and for the same length of time by three strangers in one day, revealed three different selves, given contradictory replies, according to how smart or nice I found the questioners, and according to what kind of journal they represented.

As there are no true villains in opera (melody representing evil by its nature renders evil extenuating and villainy vulnerable) neither are there true heroes in interviews. Because a hero is not self-defined, not what he says he is, not how his interloctor illustrates him; his identity is what the general consciousness decides.

The high point of Britten's *Billy Budd* is, of course, Claggart's soliloquy, for, despite Auden's "Evil is unspectacular and always human," Claggart's need to stain Billy's goodness turns to spectacle and is hardly human. Is Claggart evil? Oh yes. Though unlike the biggest wicked stars of history he does not ignore his wickedness. If Nero, for example, thought himself a do-gooder, Claggart wept for what he called his "depravity" and, like Carmen, choreographed his own suicide in the shape of murder. For each man gets killed by the thing he loves.

All those I know who are getting on resent mostly the awesome irreversibility of death. Is it so awesome? Irreversible how?

JH on Judas. Judas as fall guy. Judas himself was a preordained Act of God: he acted despite himself in fulfillment of ancient prophecy. By moving according to the Lord's will, though this brought eternal and universal damnation, he is a greater martyr than Peter or Paul who so soon sat at God's right hand. Let Judas now be also canonized.

People marvel at how certain geniuses (they always cite Wagner) can be so evil yet write great music. Is it not more marvelous that certain geniuses (let's cite Strauss) can be so colorless yet write great music? Artists are artists only when they're being artists. Otherwise they're like you and me — if slightly more so. They're like anyone, but no one's like them.

Is it true you're anti-semitic?
Not at all. I love Arabs. Like most people, I've been telling lies so long I now

think they're true.

Such as?

How would I know?

Is a bird in the bush worth two in the hand?

Don't belittle the sweetest of solitary pastimes.

Describe Ravel's *Forlane*.

Beauty limps. A crippled butterfly. Here the maxim's literal. Like any vital art this ensues from the happy mistake. An artist while scrupulously following rules cannot help but break them. He's clumsy. *L'erreur bien trouvé*. Artisans are not clumsy. *Forlane*'s a lame peacock. Anything worthwhile's a lame peacock — although a lame peacock itself is not particularly worthwhile.

Have you seen Joan's new baby boy yet?

Yes, ah, that pearly pearlike fontanel! Those flirtatious unfocused leers! The flawless nostrils! Such innocent guile! And strands of down! (like the pair of curling swirls on my nape which Claude while owning me would liken to the diagram in his nursery primer of the Loire merging with the Gironde). And what's to become of the child? He'll grow up, have erections, and die.

And are you anti-gay?

Good God, yes.

Night after wakeful night, slashes in the ice of sleep overflow with thoughts of dying. Across the street at 4 a.m. behind those shutters on the second floor shadowed by shuddering elms there drowses deeply some open-mouthed fool. Yet the longed-for sleep is not a rehearsal of death, as some contend, but life at its most active richest.

To be beside yourself is wrong, is bad for you. To be *outside* yourself is good, insofar as it (like suspended animation which, though you have cancer or a broken heart) stops pain during the so-called Creative Act — though when it evolves through alcohol, that too is bad. Tonight, beside myself, I drew closer to drinking (so as to get outside myself) than I have in years, but didn't.

Epigraph for a memoir: *Le beau temps où j'étais si malheureuse*.

— Madame de Stael

On awakening in the night: That truth, *the* truth, such thick wet rightness, where flown? Can truth so rapidly like a shattered dram of scent have dissipated? Was it actually there?

The small sad need of wanting to be loved.

JH after a year makes scant progress. To understand that one cannot understand is as near as one can get: a glass fence rises between. In my maddest hangovers I always retained a sense of the future, even in suicide, but JH views the world quite literally as through a glass darkly. How cannot I bleed for his bleeding, impotent to help? Who will claim that they who only stand and wait are less battered than the actors in the fray?

Scant progress, but progress still. . . . Alone and sour, and times passes so fast, so slowly. It's terribly late. Day after day of losing contact, of seeing our decade retreat like a galaxy, of the resultant gulf. Hopeless though it be, one part of it is not wholly disagreeable.

Visit from John Myers. Talk turns to money, and to the artist's notorious humiliation in procuring any. He recalls for us John Latouche's anecdote of thirty years ago. Always skilled in rich dowagers, Latouche had an appointment with one he'd never met, in order to solicit funds for a show. The butler, explaining that Madame would be in shortly, bade the guest take a chair, and withdrew. Latouche was aware of a squeaking crunch. He had sat heavily upon a Pekinese and killed it. Immediate reaction: There goes the money! What to do? Opening a window, he flung the beast to the street. What would you have done?

Did he get the funds? Yes, he did.

Thirteen months, and a leaden sadness has settled over JH and myself, an estranging deterioration that sometimes seems beyond repair. Yet the strangeness of his strife seems ever less strange, snared as he is by chivalric infatuation, and it hurts. His tears and vomit, which spew forth in lieu of ire and fury, spew not from a congenital unnamed seat but from quickly traceable altercations with K.

Once I wrote: "*L'homme moyen sensuel* is by definition less human than the 'achiever', if by human we define the logic which differentiates man from other mammals. Sex has nothing to do with logic, but achievers treat sex logically (with their restricting roles) while average men treat sex sensually." Today I would add: If intelligent people, by virtue of their preoccupations with the workings of culture, are less "good in bed" than "real people", they are also given to more drastic suffering about non-vital problems such as love. JH is the most intelligent person I know, and a friend without whom I could not go on. Still, our headiest of frequent disputes center on the irrational, and he will reproach an interviewer for stating that Wallace is my cat when in fact Wallace is his.

Reincarnation is called another go at it. But afterlife is a mere question of imagination. Why not a try as an ameoba on Arcturus? Even that, being conceivable, is too near. Then why not an hour as an alligator in the eleventh century? As the opposite sex for a day or two? As your twin for a minute? Perhaps if we could be our own selves as we were yesterday, or even as we were a second ago, the experience would become more than we could bear.

For months there's been a flutter in the wall, nocturnal, more irregular and forceful than the bees two years ago. Gnawing termites? Scurry of rat paws? If as 'tis said a cat's mere presence discourages rodents, then we have no rodents, or Wallace (admittedly quite deaf now at thirteen) is not a cat. But yesterday morning on finding the stovetop strewn with what resembled caraway seeds, we finally decided, against our will, to set a trap. (Against our will, for who are we to contrive the eradication of fellow mammals?) Last evening, not thirty minutes after placing the bait, there sounded the terrible snap. We paused long, fearful of what we'd find: sprayed blood? splayed bones yet still gasping? Together we went, and there sure enough was a mouse, limply dead. JH assured me it was killed before it knew what hit it — even before savoring the exquisite fatal brie. The mouse was not of urban hue (not solid gray — indeed, like our mousecolored Wallace, the royal Russian Blue), but a clean golden fauve merging into sugary white on the belly, and with wide-open garnet eyes. We put it down the toilet but it wouldn't flush, kept belching back to haunt us like the corpse in *Purple Noon*. So we sealed it in plastic and flung it to the garbage, and wondered when its nest of starving offspring would start to rot and stink. The episode undid me, no less than the morning *Times*'s detailing tortures in faroff Persia, or the faroff boatloads of Vietnamese. I went to bed.

During the chaotic-seeming composites of dream after dream (which in fact are sanity pure, including surely the dreams of the insane) there was a melding revivification of Vietnam and Persia, and of the mouse. If this morning I invoke the limitations of John Donne — since all men *are* islands who forever and vainly seek to play kneesies beneath the surface — I'd rather commit suicide than have it proved I'd ever been wilfully physically cruel. I say physically, because all is fair in the "mental" game of broken hearts, nor is the will ever brought into play where love's concerned, love thriving as it does beyond the frontiers of time as in an ice-cold bubble where we breathe forever and don't grow old.

As far as anyone is ever cured, JH is. As far as any other can judge such things. The two-year stress, fanned by my own surrender to allergies (I've been taking shots just twenty-four months now and am doing better thanks) has abated, due as much to illness running its course as to a fortieth birthday. He functions. What more can one note about any friend? It's feasible to resume the *égoisme à deux* — the mutual solitude — as the French name marriage.

He functions too as translator of animals, being himself a thoroughbred, with psyche tuned to sea urchins no less than to bank clerks, exasperating bank clerks. My own loneliness has not in a decade been linked to the waiting for a silent phone to sound. Nor am I ever lonelier than when the phone is sounding. Question of priorities. The solitude of work, during which all priorities (happiness, death, taxes) are suspended, resembles like love that cold bubble.

Last night JH pointed out that Harold Schonberg, when dealing with low culture like chess or like mystery novels (which as Newgate Callendar he reviews for the Sunday *Times*), is succinct and fair and at home and wise. With high culture like musical performance (much less musical composition) he's coarse and dull.

The rare moments critics turn toward me they're at a loss because I haven't told them what to say. A Rochberg positing his pastiches as the True Way, or a Carter explicating his concerto à la Beethoven's Fourth as though here were a novel notion, lend reviewers a hatrack. But I, just nothing but incurable charm and no exegeses, preen unheeded in the gloom, ah me.

At The Brotherhood, Nantucket's one bistro which in the subzero evening stays open late, for the first time I sit, stilly with JH, and watch the scene where everyone knows everyone but no one knows me, yet *I* know "everyone"! Except that I know only peers, and grow invisible to the young, other than those (few) who know *of* me but are either too intimidated or too pushy. Less lonelymaking's when I'm all by myself, even late at night in Nantucket with wolves howling as I scramble eggs and think on work to be done, then do it, and look forward to midnight television.

BEING ALONE

The cliché that clichés are cliché only because their truth is self-evident, would seem self-evident. Yet from birth we're taught that things are not as simple as they seem. The wise men's work is to undo complications: things *are* simple, truth blazes ("brightness falls from the air"), and the obvious way to prevent wars is not to fight. Thus, when I proclaim that I am never less alone than when I'm by myself, and am met with a glazed stare, the stare is from one who abhors a vacuum — the look of nature. But I'm complicating matters.

Comfortable rainy darkness has for days fit over the city like a mammoth tea cozy or winding sheet so that the lights of spring gleam unperceived. Earlier this evening, on my way to dine at mother and father's, I stopped into Julius's Bar, as very occasionally I do, for a mug of soda. Standing there among the stricken I gape through the window at the drizzling golden streetlamps, and at the women over there in Djuna's Bookshop thumbing magazines. This bistro itself is unchanged from when we drank here, merry and bloody and hot, thirty summers ago: same careful dust, same wobbly stools, same hearty smell of ale and hamburger, same drowsy jukebox emitting heart-piercing sevenths. Except tonight I am dead sober, there are no "possibilities", I know nobody and nobody knows me, and, like a Jean Rhys heroine, I feel lonely in a not unpleasant way. The seagreen reflections from the mirror in my soda seem somehow sadder than any Irish keening. But at least there are no carnal emanations, so after ten minutes I flee.

With pleasure am reading *Walden* finally after three decades of urging from mother. Less disturbed than amused by a fallacy which jumps from every page, like McLuhan writing that writing is obsolete. If all is vanity, and the amassing of worldly goods and the longing for great place and posterity are demeaning, so too is the need to document one's vanity. Art's the biggest vanity: the assumption that one's view of peace or fright or beauty is permanently communicable. I keep a diary about the uselessness of keeping a diary, but the desire is strong and I am vain. Nor am I counter vanity. And the old man for whom nothing counted but *les merveilleux nuages* is recalled only because Baudelaire solidified him.

Sunlight rushes through the house like wind. Yellow brooks defy gravity flowing up the stairs and over the ceiling. Rooms glimmer with optimism. What joy to get out of bed on such mornings. Yet by mid-afternoon the pall's begun, and when night falls now by five o'clock the stultifying loneliness has retaken hold. Little reason to go on. The reason for the lack of reason is no longer on my list.

Walk careless and lively over the room through sunlight — blood of the day — soaking profligate into rugs. Then dissolve in wonderment that this too ends in death. Sly Death, coming on little cat feet, fooling all of the people all of the time, arranging for man — Earth's one rational beast — irrationally to persist in hoping for a life after You. On the other hand, if the world after ten milleniums finally concedes to equality of the sexes then anything is possible, even life after death.

The priest was speaking of an acolyte: "He is morbidly devout, and so fundamentalist as to shame a Baptist. Yet he is literal paradoxically. After the first communion he remarked, 'It tastes just like wine.' And the angelus sounds like a dinner bell." Then the priest walked off, bald pate gleaming like a raw steak in the sunrise.
The Holy Church forever spells out food and drink.

Suppose that, shortly after you've swallowed your LSD, God does in fact descend in a flying saucer for all the world to behold.

If, as is now suspected, trillions of lifeless galaxies will be forever turning up, why does this leave us feeling lonely, we who despise our neighbors? Astronomer Bernard Lovell declares chillingly (warningly?) that Earthlings are unique, the expansion rate of the cosmos having had to be just so, right after that Big Bang. "If the rate had been less by an almost insignificant amount in the first second, then the universe would have collapsed long before any biological evolution could have taken place. Conversely, if the rate had been marginally greater, then the expansion would have reached such magnitudes that no gravitationally bound systems (that is, galaxies and stars) could have formed." There appear also to be, beyond "us", super-universes and an ever vaster chain of Big Bangs eternally.
Now, if there is no consciousness outside ourselves, no witness of these stellar procedures, then (except to us) does the universe exist? or did we literally invent it all, including the facts of life? JH: the theory of Does-a-falling-tree-make-a-noise-if-nobody's-there-to-hear-it is puzzling only because of hazy terms. If sound means displacement of air then of course the tree makes a noise, but if sound is what's received through the aural sense then of course the tree makes no noise.
Suppose the universe is as it is, but that for some reason we are all asleep — unconscious. Does the universe then exist?

Although the dentist appointment was for two, at 1:30 I was still garbed in only a towel when the doorbell rang, and suddenly Sergeant David Durk, who lives downstairs, stood before me. Did I know anyone who might (he wanted to know) take over his lease, since he and his family are moving away forever? I explained that I had to dress for the dentist at two, but would think about it. Yet he lingered. Was it that he was too filled with his fame to spot the incongruity of a naked composer and a holstered cop in stalemated converse about real estate? Two cultured adults who speak good English but with nothing in common. It's not that Babel was polyglot but that values were dispersed. People of different tongues and classes can be in close accord, while peers feud.

Rushing to the bathroom I grabbed the first book that came to hand, which turned out to be *The Age of Innocence*. There I read again those masterful (hmmm . . . mistressful isn't quite the word either) last paragraphs where Archer withdraws from a longed-for reunion "lest that last shadow of reality should lose its edge" — remembering when I'd first read them a quarter-century ago. It would have been an autumn afternoon (like today in Nantucket, warm and russet) on a café terrace, rue Galilée, and I closed the book, moved, and filled with a Paris evoked by Wharton some thirty years earlier, fictional even then, and so real.

We have the choice, the passing choice, of returning and ruining, or of refraining and keeping. If we keep too long the living person in our heart (imagining that person in a firelit room across the ocean), that person will die. Which is the case with my Paris now. I can go back and rekindle in that same café the rekindling that fired me twenty-five years ago as I evoked Archer rekindling his past. But I cannot close the book — that physically same book — and rise to keep my date with Marie Laure (who was tolerant of lateness only when the need of a book retained her date), because Marie Laure lies underground. Yet, maybe fortunately, for me the power of places has always been stronger than the power of persons.

The older I get the aloner I feel. (But one can grow only so old.) The solitude, classically divorced from company or place, is hinged to a knowledge, recognized even by children, that we rise to heaven unaided. *Car le joli printemps / C'est le temps d'une aiguille*, sang Fombeure through Poulenc's lips. Our springtime's but a point, a needle point, in time, but rich and poor can pass with equal ease, though forever single file, through the needle's eye. (I never knew whether that needle's eye was the same as Gide's *Porte étroite* — the "straight gate" to paradise? — mentioned by Saint Matthew.) Those hundreds who perished "simultaneously" at Guyana really died, as the clock ticks, separately.

Rationalizing. Contemporaries say I undersell myself when discouraging attempts (what attempts?) on my revirginated heart. Yet to realize there'll be no more lustful love seems by the light of day, if not of night, a productive time-saver. If it's fear of rejection, let it be known that at the height of whatever I once had (maybe today I'm at some similar, or different, height) I was no less — in my demure and vicious loveliness — no less shy.

To sit now in Piazza Navona or at the Flore how could I not suspect your motives and look the other way (turn the other cheek)? But I do take pleasure in your company? Who takes pleasure in the reality of whom? Even once when describing P. I longed for him to leave so as to savor missing him.

Long weekend in Philadelphia to supervise the concert of my music at Curtis in whose hallowed halls I'd not set foot for 144 seasons.

Tea chez Henry McIlleny with Stephen Spender. We talk of Saul Bellow. I mention that Bellow is, well, a bit too heterosexual for me, if you know what I mean. Spender answers: "Yes, Bellow does treat women horribly, doesn't he!", then goes on to equate male homosexuality with the feminine side of man's nature. Stephen being Stephen, this is surely not stupidity so much as academic hypocrisy.

Yet you *can* turn back the clock and recall cleanly as a photo each minute of a finite past. How *déjà vu* like old movies our hours are numbered even as we enjoy them heedlessly. To relive a great love — *quelle horreur*. Only the smokey smell of erstwhile roses makes a useful difference.

And you *can* go home again. Write of PQ's visit wherein the dread gave way to sympathy, though the fact that friendship can withstand decades of separation, while cheering, limns the notion of death more sharply than if there were no returns. Is a reunion really a return?

Twenty years last summer since PQ approached along Cannes' Croisette and asked *Vous êtes en vacances?* Thirteen years since last we met, in Marseilles. And now, better (not worse) than my memory, he's come at fifty-one for his first excursion (professional, for ecology in Saint Louis) to an America which had never appealed to him as an idea. I see the city through his eyes, and oh, our natives are plain. The golden youth from the U.S.A., for whom the Frenchman, licking his chops, lay in ambush during every holiday of the early postwar years, has vanished. Search amid the millions, day after sodden day, in the subway or Sardi's, for one beguiling face, and search in vain. PQ says it's urban living. (In his Marseilles apparently beauty still reigns, as here, emptyheaded, in California.) JH says it's the achiever complex indigenous to Manhattan. Or is it from that lack of physical narcissism that comes from money? Unlike Romans, Americans don't need to be beautiful.

Americans, wrote Tennessee Williams in 1949, suffer from "a misconception of what it means to be . . . any kind of creative artist. They feel it is something to adopt *in the place of* actual living." (Windham letters, footnote p. 307) Could not the reverse be posited? The act of making art *is* the artist's actual living, and the humdrum needs of life are a by-product of that art. The best artists, by and large, lead what outsiders would find dull lives; those whose "actual living" is overly gaudy just haven't the time for art, even when such living form the art's very material.

Reperusing with distaste the transcribed conversation taped years ago for the Dance Collection of the Library of Performing Arts. What disparity in meaning between the spoken and the written word! Transcriptions of this sort in their "spontaneity" are less true than the "artifice" of the pen. All that I utter, in an urge to be clever and valid, turns thin and dull, except for one phrase about the aloneness of Martha Graham. Greatness has no playmates. Creative artists are no more lonely than real people, but to get work done they obviously need to be alone more than salesmen or bankers. Even love is expensive for an artist: the time love takes is thrilling, but not instructive — not even for writing about love. Greatness has no playmates, that is true. Alas, it's also true that the dispenser of tenth-rate art must dispense with playmates.

Martha is the only giant I can think of who has never been denied by her successors. She has authored perhaps 150 ballets, most of them with original scores. Yet with one or two exceptions she has caused no topnotch music to exist. Neither, except for Vivian Fine on one occasion, has Martha used music by women. Nor have I noticed that women composers among themselves are magnanimous. They are more anxious to be taken seriously by men than by their sisters.

Insomnia, colored not by private anxieties but cluttered by passing concerns. TV dominates. Julia Child mixed with Guyana horrors churning with oil prices climbing. Cut to Melville's *Pierre*, uncomfortably verbose. Back to the screen. Anxious to hear (see) Tashi play Takemitsu's new *Quatrain* on WNET but not wanting to miss Stockard Channing on "Rock Hour" scheduled simultaneously, I switch from channel to channel. "Rock Hour" is *no less good* than the Takemitsu which is merely six sound-effects in search of a coherer. Insomnia.

Ruth Kligman, ever avid for the full life, exclaims: "I've found the most divine pill. It puts you to sleep for only fifteen minutes, and you wake up thoroughly refreshed so that you can *live* and be *conscious* and *savor experiences* and . . . "

Jane Frielicher: "I have trouble just staying awake for fifteen minutes."

We who are to be destroyed are first made sane by our Lord.

Did I still keep a diary 'twould not serve to reveal secret sex and cake recipes. The disease and dying of dear friends evermore preoccupies us all, and wonder at the cheerlessness we come to.

Is my entire *oeuvre* an *oeuvre*? In that case I do not repeat myself, since each piece is part of a continuing whole. (And although such stuff as dreams are made on generally turns out to be sheer twaddle in the morning, my sleeping hours, unlike Ruth Kligman's, feel no less urgent than the waking.)

Tonight while reworking a choral version of Hardy's *The Oxen* composed twenty-four years ago (around the time I was reading Wharton), I feel for the thousandth time how time freezes during focus on the act. Musically the inspirational shove seems identical: I may have more or less energy (more technique, less facility), but the expressive line's the same, and also the special piquant secundal harmonic clots that make me wince nicely while imagining that I and only I have ever thought up such combinations. But further still, in this icy today on America's seventieth street, I find my very body resurrounded by those vases of vastly odoriferous tuberoses which graced the Noailles salon where once I labored on that evening of June 21st, 1954. It is enough to pour over the metro map of Paris to be transported there, back through the ether and years, smells above all. That is one way to learn a city, through odors, as through cruising parks and pissotières, the hardboiled egg stench, the rotten seaweed stench, the dimple on the ruddy chin of that policeman, the etc. Why must we move through time, since time, whatever it is, says the same thing perpetually?

Occasionally a stranger in the mail attests to how much my music has meant to him. Why does this trouble me? Why am I made anxious and not elated at seeing my books in a store, name in a program? (Vicious letters or negative reviews are no more terrible than pleasant ones.) Because the damage is done, the work is removed and leading its own life, influencing (or not) the unknown quantities while the maker could be dead, left with my own vile body.

People are always asking, "How do you remember all that stuff? Me, I forget things as soon as they happen." But why live if that which occurs makes no impression, can't be used, even the endless boredom? Why live if only to forget having lived. This said, my notorious total recall is abetted by date books and diaries, and by recalling the months, and divisions thereof, of returns to America, of an affair with a certain person, of the impulse for a certain piece. To live is to improvise variations on our own theme, yet those improvisations are not random but (unbeknownst to us at the moment) formal and collective. How does one manage *not* to have total recall? of this unique rhubarb tart, that red hot torso, these November leaves, all the wars, those dying friends?

Other people are always saying, "How can you live in the past?" But the present *is* the past (as Marcel was hardly the first to show), and the older we grow the more past we have. Our shriveling future may be all that we make of it, but so is our past which changes perspective with each new dawn. Life is awfully nice, yes, and keeps getting nicer, but never nice enough, surely not enough to have been born for. And is life short? To die at 75 will mean that eight thousand nights stretch on ahead. How to fill them? By using them through what's been learned so far? Now, on the contrary, could it be that the past grows smaller, like a blood-flavored popsicle on which we gnaw self-canni-balisticly, and when it's melted utterly, we . . . ? Owls and tigers commence their flights and prowls at dusk, and thus might symbolize Death were it not that they too, God's creatures, prey upon their own pasts, their shrinking pasts. Endless, the future? Certainly not, since by definition the future does not exist.

Still other people ask what my parents think about my prose writings. Father, always a logician, recalls my childhood's unscholarly recalcitrance and reads me with a "Gosh, I don't remember ever telling Ned that", and is proud. Mother, never a "Ballet Mother", resisted for years treating me as special. Today about my music she unqualifiedly defends me. About the prose (which renders one more vulnerable than does music) she hopes only that I'll not relate things that might later make me sad, or friendless, or get me in trouble.

1977-79

[Being Alone *first appeared, in slightly abridged form, in* The Ontario Review *(1980).]*

NED ROREM (b. 1923), the 1976 Pulitzer Prize winner in music, is also the author of eight books, including *The Paris Diary, Music and People,* and *An Absolute Gift.* An indepth interview with him will appear in *Gay Sunshine Interviews,* Volume 2.

Arturo Ramirez Juarez
(Mexico), 1980

TWO POEMS BY ALLEN GINSBERG

WOKE ME UP NAKED
[Sapphic stanzas, some in original measures]

for Gay Sunshine*'s 10th Anniversary Issue*

Red cheeked boyfriends tenderly kiss me sweet mouthed
under Boulder coverlets winter springtime
hug me naked laughing & telling girl friends
        gossip till autumn

Aging love escapes with his childish body
Monday one man visited sleeping big cocked
older mustached crooked mouthed not the same teen-
        ager I sucked off

This kid comes on Thursdays with happy hard ons
long nights talking heart to heart reading verses
fucking hours he comes in me happy but I
        cant get it on him

Cherub, thin-legged Southern boy once slept over
singing blues and drinking till he got horny
Wednesday night he gave me his ass I screwed him
        good luck he was drunk

Blond curl'd clear eyed gardener passing thru town
teaching digging earth in the ancient One Straw
method   lay back stomach bare that night blew me
        I blew him and came

Winter dance Naropa a barefoot wild kid
jumped up grabbed me laughed at me took my hand and
ran out saying   Meet you at midnight your house
        Woke me up naked

Midnight crawled in bed with me breathed in my ear
kissed my eyelids   mouth on his cock it was soft
"Doesn't do nothing for me" turned on belly
        came in behind him

Future youth I never may touch any more
Hark these Sapphics lipped by my hollow spirit
everlasting tenderness breathed in   these vowels
        sighing for love still

Song your cadence formed while on May night's full moon
yellow onions tulips in fresh rain pale grass
iris pea pods radishes grew as this verse
                    blossomed in dawn light

measure forever his face eighteen years' old
green eyes blond hair muscular gold soft skin whose
god like boy's voice mocked me once three decades past
                    Come here and screw me

Breast struck scared to look in his eyes   blood pulsing
my ears   mouth dry   tongue never moved   ribs shook a
trembling fire ran down from my heart to young thighs
                    Love sick to this day

Heavy limbed I sat in a chair and watched him
sleep naked all night afraid to kiss his mouth
tender dying waited for sun rise years a-
                    go in Manhattan

Allen Ginsberg
May 17-June 1, 1980
Boulder, Colorado

MAYBE LOVE

Maybe love will come
cause I am not so dumb
Tonight it fills my heart
heavy sad apart
from one or two I fancy
now I'm an old fairy.

This is hard to say
I've come to be this way
thru many loves of youth
that taught me most heart truth
Now I come by myself
in my hand like an old elf

It's not the most romantic
dream to be so frantic
for young mens' bodies,
as an old sugar daddy
blest respected known,
but left to bed alone.

How come love came to end
flaccid, how pretend
desires I have used
Four decades as I cruised
from bed to bar to book
Shamefaced like a crook

Stealing here & there
pricks & buttocks bare
by accident, by circumstance
Naivete or horny chance
stray truth or famous lie,
How come I came to die?

Love dies, body dies, the mind
keeps groping blind
half hearted full of lust
to wet the silken dust
of men that hold me dear
but won't sleep with me near.

This morning's cigarette
This morning's sweet regret
habit of many years
wake me to old fears
Under the living sun
one day there'll be no one

to kiss & to adore
& to embrace & more
lie down with side by side
tender as a bride
gentle under my touch —
Prick I love to suck.

Church bells ring again
in Heidelberg as when
in New York City town
I lay my belly down
against a boy friend's buttock
and couldn't get it up.

'Spite age and common Fate
I'd hoped love'd hang out late
I'd never lack for thighs
on which to sigh my sighs
This day it seems the truth
I can't depend on youth,

I can't keep dreaming love
I can't pray heav'n above
or call the pow'rs of hell
to keep my body well
occupied with young devils
tongueing at my navel.

I stole up from my bed
to that of a well-bred
young friend who shared my purse
and noted my tender verse,
I held him by the ass
waiting for sweat to pass

until he said Go back
I said that I would jack
myself away, not stay
& so he let me play
Allergic to my come —
I came, & then went home.

This can't go on forever,
this poem, nor my fever
for brown eyed mortal joy,
I love a straight white boy.
Ah the circle closes
Same old withered roses!

I haven't found an end
I can fuck & defend
& no more can depend
on youth time to amend
what old ages portend —
Love's death, & body's end.

Heidelberg 8 AM 15 Dec. '79

Allen Ginsberg
for Gay Sunshine
& Winston Leyland
August 10, 1981
Naropa Institute
Boulder, Colorado

TWO POEMS BY E.A. LACEY

MESÓN BRUJO

The boy brought in the logs to start the fire.
A gust of night and nature blew in with him,
of animals out prowling in the dark.
His cheeks were bright with cold; his skin was white;
black hair hung low across a narrow forehead.
From my cold bed I watched him stack the logs
in a kind of pyramid, the small ones under,
the bigger ones on top, then saw him stick
chips of pitch pine among them, strike a match,
and light a sliver; and the room soon filled
with the resinous odour of *ocote* smoke.
Then he blew on the spark of fire he had created,
till the chips burned brightly, wrapping in their flame
the smaller logs, which in turn would ignite
the larger, to the largest one, on top.
And the room blossomed roses. All the while,
crouched at his task, he had not spoken, not looked at me,
but fixed his gaze on his logs with a concentrated
beetling frown, across which light and shadow played.
Now he got up, asked awkwardly if the fire
was satisfactory, and prepared to go.
And I answered yes, the fire was satisfactory
and no doubt would burn for at least two hours more,
time enough for me to fall asleep, while I thought
there was something much more satisfactory than fire
which would warm me even more. He left. I dozed.
Or perhaps I slept; the fact is, some hours later
—how many, I don't know—I heard, at least
it seemed I heard a sound, a hesitant tapping
at my door, and I rose in the fire's ambiguous light,
glided half-asleep over the hard, flat tiles,
opened the door effortlessly, as one does in dreams,
and the log-boy came in, cheeks bright red with cold.
There in the fire's dim glow I watched him undress,
saw the white body define itself from layers of dark clothing,
saw him stand, legs apart, in the rosy dying light,
black hair ingathering round an opening rose,
felt his icy skin, glabrous as myrtle bark,
as he slid into bed beside me. He was an expert
at lighting fires, but now it fell my turn
to stroke for the first time that cold virgin skin,
caressing rubbing it to raise a spark,
blowing on that spark to fan it to a flame,
wrapping him in my arms and legs to warm him,
playing each trick of friction, till at last,
like wood still green, he caught . . . The hard logs crumbled
to white ash; the last embers closed their eyes;
and in the darkness we were our own fire.

All night the log-boy tossed there in my arms
in intervals of sleep and waking dream,
all heat and flame now, in a bed as warm
as roses. Till I heard, just before morning,
another distant tapping at my door,
and the fire-boy noiselessly, as one does in dreams,
rose and in the white light of the false dawn
donned slowly his dark clothing, slid across
the smooth tiles to the door, opened it effortlessly
and was gone. And I lay aleep in the half-light.

The next night, after dinner, when the hour
for the guests to retire and the fires to be lit
arrived, I lay in bed, awaiting him,
but a gray-haired old man came to light my fire,
place the pine chips, build the log pyramid
in my cold chambers at the Mesón Brujo.

ABDELFATTEH

You put your hand on my shoulder
and n'aie pas peur you said.
Hot windless night. We were watching
a street-fight in Marrákech.
You smiled at me, young hill-boy
(who thought that you were twenty,
but you just might have been 18),
and you showed two broken teeth.
We drank tea on the corner,
where you taught me Arab letters,
and somehow we went to the hammam,
where you rubbed me down and fucked me.
Then you told me your life story,
all about your mountain village,
how you once had been a student,
but had fallen out with a teacher
(lost promise of your family)
and you'd been expelled, and, now
you slept nights in the cafés
and smoked kif all the hot day
and scoured the town for tourists.

I went with you to your village
in the mountains near Marrákech.
I saw the barren hillside
(but to you it was blooming).

I saw the bordj you lived in
with the stable underneath it
for the camels and the donkeys,
and the sheep, the goats, the turkeys.
I met your grave, stern father,
upright in his blue djellaba.
I drank tea and smoked kif there.
I met your other mother
(as you called your father's new wife).
And you washed my hands with water
poured from a silver pitcher
(the custom of the country),
and we slept on Berber carpets
that were woven by your sisters.

And so I came to trust you.
And so I took you travelling,
And then we fell in prison
in a town called Mogador.
And n'aie pas peur you told me,
maktoub, it was all written,
but, inchallah, we'll get out,
though you yourself were frightened.

For two long months we rotted
in a prison by the seaside,
where the gulls laughed every morning,
and the muezzin wailed at daybreak,
as the key turned in the iron door,
and the lice and bedbugs ate us,
and we lived on beans and lentils,
and you sold the shoes I'd bought you
and the blue shirt you were wearing
to get more food from the kitchen
so that I could eat "European."
And at nights you slept beside me,
(on the cold floor, rough wool blankets)
and you put your arms around me
to protect me from the others
(for there were forty others).

Days, we walked around in circles
in that courtyard with eight olive-trees,
hand in hand, like all the others
(the custom of the country),
sat and listened to the imams
(though of course I understood nothing),
while the armed guards prowled the rooftops.

The last time that I saw you
was as I was leaving prison
and we kissed each other on both cheeks
(the custom of the country),
while my police escorts looked on,
and you grabbed my hand and told me
"remember, I'm your brother,"
and I marched out of the doorway,
for I was being deported.

Now, back on your douar,
you send me Christmas cards and little letters
(decorated with calligraphy and flowers)
in your funny French, saying things like this:
Mon cher frére, si tu veux m'aider, aide-moi
á ce moment, n'importe de quelle chose,
de l'argent, si tu peux, ou des vetements
anciens, ou une cartouche de cigarettes.
And I sometimes send you money,
and I hope it makes you happy,
for I won't be going back there.

And I wander
from country to country, purposeful, purposeless,
but sometimes
even now
at night
in my hotel-room of dreams
I hear across the darkness n'aie pas peur
feel
the small protecting body close to mine,
warm arms around my waist, quick, quiet breath,
the hard cock pulsing, saying "let me in,"
brief spasm of union and separation.
Abd-el-Fatteh.
Servant
of the Open Door.

Hammam is a Turkish bath. *Bordj* is a fortified adobe house-castle, of a type
common in Southern Moroccan villages. *Douar* is a country village. *Mogador* is
the other name of *Es-Saouira,* a Moroccan coastal city. *Djellaba* is the Arab
robe. *Maktoub* means "it was written (by fate)." *Inchallah*—if God wills. All
the "Abd" names in Arabic mean "Servant of Allah." *Abd* is servant or slave.
The second part is one of the 99 names of God (the 100th fell into the sea and
has never been found). *El Fatteh* means "the open (i.e. illuminated, comprehending) way, door or mind. I'm of course punning most sacrilegiously on it
here.

WILL INMAN

ROOM IN HERE FOR YOU

1

a eucalyptus tree claims this desert yard,
its roots take more territory every year.
the chinaberries wither
                         but now under rare May cloud
eucalyptus trembles full of voiceless bells: wind
hears them   wind makes them
down pendulous stemsful of leaves

2

a young brother approaches the gate
some few drops of rain spatter down on the aluminum
porch roof
             he stands at my door, and in his eyes
questioning sounds me like leafbells
without words
                    i nod, open the door, he
comes in
             we stand face to face

3

a vine springs up between us
green tendrils reach in thru his shirt and ribs
                         in thru my navel and beard
suddenly all the vine goes red, pulsing hard
now i hear leafbells, windbells

he laughs, quietly   i reach out

4

tall corporations stand around, leering
they want his sweats to their uses
they accuse me of pillaging his eyes
of mining his tongue — i filed no claim —
of dividing his limbs with my *abrazos*

between ourselves, surrounded by metallic cannibals,
my young brother and i have grown some space to be

there's room in here for you, too

this vine sings your name!

                                   Tucson, Az.
                                   18 May 1979

169

POEMS BY DINOS CHRISTIANOPOULOS
Translated from the Greek by Kimon Friar

Dinos Christianopoulos was born in Thessaloníki (Greece) in 1931, the son of Yannis and Persephone Dhimitriou. In 1945 the poet adopted the pseudonymn Christianopoulos ("Son of Christ"). He worked as a librarian and proofreader. In 1958 he founded the literary periodical *Diagonal* which he has been publishing for periods of five years with respites of two years; and in 1962 he began publishing books. Dinos Christianopoulos has spent his entire life in Thessaloníki, visiting few places in mainland Greece or the islands, and visiting Athens primarily to give readings of his poetry. He has enclosed himself in his own self-contained universe.

The poems printed here are taken from his various books. *Gay Sunshine* publishes them for the first time in English from an unpublished booklength manuscript of the poet's work, translated by Kimon Friar.

THE CENTURION CORNELIUS

Lord, do not wonder at my great faith;
it is love that dictates my faith.
I do not beseech you for Nikítas or for Harílaos,
nor for Nikólaos who died too young to become bored with prayer.
Only make Andónios well, Andónios;
when he was young and a free man
he also concerned himself with letters and the arts;
he was conversant with ancient Greek and loved to play the accordion.
But now he is my slave — do not ask me how.
I have the power to bind him or release him.
I can do with him whatever I please;
I can even set him free, though this for me would be most painful;
besides, he works efficiently with his great vigor.
For these reasons, Lord, and for many others,
make Andónios well, slave of your slave.
If need be, I can even turn Christian.
Only make him well, this is all I ask of you, nothing else.
Anything else I might dare ask of you would be immoral.

1950
from *Season of the Lean Cows* (1950-51)

See Luke, 7:1-10, where it is told how Jesus healed the servant of a centurion "who was dear unto him, was sick, and ready to die." The poet has given the arbitrary names Cornelius and Andónios to centurion and servant respectively. See also Matthew 8:5-13. — trans.

YOU OPEN AND CLOSE LIKE A FLOWER

You open and close like a flower.

I come — and you receive me, numb,
you keep your eyes constantly lowered,
but afterwards, little by little, you take courage,
begin to speak tenderly,
color your eyes with gaiety,
Oh how heart-warming has the room become;
I don't want any sweets — your conversation suffices.

But if I forget myself and glance at my watch
or show any concern for the world's work,
you let the conversation slowly drift away
and start to grow numb again, little by little,
bid me goodbye, as though I were a stranger,

and then you close, close up like a flower.

1957
from *Cross-Eyed* (1949-1970)

THE SPLINTER

The night they killed Lambrákis
I was returning from a date.
"What's happened?" someone on the bus asked.
No one knew. We saw policemen
but could make out nothing more.

Three years went by. Once more I fell
into the same indifference about political matters.
But that particular night disturbed me
like an imperceptible splinter that won't come out:
some clubbed down for their ideals,
others roaring about on their tricycles,
and I mindlessly running off to make love in the meadows.

1962
from *Cross-Eyed* (1949-1970)

The poem refers to an actual historical event: the assassination in Thessaloníki, Greece, of the left-wing Parliamentary Deputy, Dr. Gregory Lambrákis, on May 22, 1963. The incident was documented in the book and film Z.

171

INCIDENT IN ATHENS

It was a one-story house, with a garden,
and the room was warm; the radio
was playing a sweet, soft music.
We drank cherry brandy, he showed me photographs.
Then, looking at my muddy army boots
and my rumpled uniform,
"You're a mess," he said. "Permit me
to look after you."
He took my duffle-coat and rubbed out the spots
with a rag and a little benzine;
he took my clothes and smoothed them out
with his small electric iron;
he took my army boots and polished them with care.
And I watched with what delicacy
he arranged my khaki shirt,
with what care he cleaned my boot tops.
I didn't thank him, but only asked him
brusquely, when the moment came: "What do you pay?"
He bit his lips, treated me once more,
and then discreetly opened the door for me.

Denial is the worst of all, I thought then.

1951
from *Season of the Lean Cows*

"ALMOND TREES"

This place was once called "Almond Trees."
I was in time to see them. The place was filled with fragrance.
Periwinkles teemed, and a small river
carried down dry chaff from the threshing floors.

We used to come here at night for a body.

One by one the almond trees were all cut down. One by one
small houses sprouted in their place.
We were the first to inaugurate them. Our love
was given shape amid the scaffolding and the cement.

Not even one almond tree has remained.
The place has filled up with shops and apartment buildings.
They gobbled down one more place for love in the country.

1965
from *Suburbs* (1963-1970)

172

put out the light, you keep insisting
i recalled another love of mine
he wanted everything brilliantly lit

i don't know which I prefer —
in the darkness my ugliness disappears
in the light your beauty glows

1970
from *Body and Remorse* (1960-1972)

MAKING LOVE

Let me lick your hands, let me lick your feet.
Love gains with surrender.

I don't know what making love means to you;
it's not only a wetting of lips,
a planting of embraces in the armpits,
a confusion of complaints,
a consolation of spasms.

It's above all a confirmation of our loneliness
when we attempt to roost in a body difficult to inhabit.

1959
from *Defenseless Craving* (1955-1962)

you are the first to offer me love
your proposal throws me into confusion
i feel inadequate for so much tenderness
until now i beat my head from wall to wall
i'd become accustomed to begging for crumbs

call it masochism, call it whatever you wish
i feel inadequate for so much tenderness

1962
from *Body and Remorse* (1960-1972)

173

RON SCHREIBER

FAST LINES

a real fall day
nippy at dusk
the air clear in
Truro I've tried
to call you I
don't know how to say I
love you breaking the
line in the middle not
knowing what love
means now with you
who sent me flowers
& has hair on the long
flanks of your backside
& smooth skin & smooth
foreskin & a head I've
just begun to explore
& don't understand I
don't know how to
say I love you
this fall day.

AARON F. STEELE

song my mother also sang

to a tanned man i would give my heart
and body though recall i am a temporal
lover but maybe . . . for a barkdark
blackeyed boy of twenty-five or so
perfectlipped and greek featured and
perfectly proportioned with thick
brownarms and inky hairs scratched
there down to his long fingers growing
like branches at the back of me rooting
while my cheek pulses in the hollow of his
throat where a gathering of fur begins
to slide down and centers then the curves
of his chest and the flat of his belly
gathering like darkmoss around his
foreskinned cock that is like a budding
tropical smoothstiff flower about to
unfurl for him i should spread my hungry
limbs like a star and whisper come to me
please praying for a gravelly answer

FREDRICK ZYDEK

PICKING GREEN APPLES
(In Memory of my 16th Birthday)

1. "If I could reach
   the tallest branch,
   pull it closer,
   we might pluck
   the best of them
   on the morning
   side of the tree,"
   I told him.

2. His hands are large
   around my waist,
   lift me as though
   I were nothing
   more than wind
   whistling up the tree.

3. I feel his breath
   warming the spaces
   left between
   my shirt and jeans
   as I stretch
   up and out
   and pull the limb
   downwards down.

4. His chin bristles
   near my spine.
   "Gonna make it?"
   he asks, lips
   brushing my skin.

5. What is left of me
   clings, as the moon
   clings to the trees
   until its shadow
   ripens on the bough.

6. Letting me down his hands
   move up under
   the whole of my shirt.
   He peels it off
   like peeling an orange
   with one or two
   flicks of the thumbs.

7. I feel strange dreams
   hatching in his hands.
   He places my hands
   just at his hips.
   I see his groins
   are stretched and bulging.

8. He lowers his lips
   to my stomach,
   touches until
   I'm outside my jeans.
   I have visions
   of steaming jock-straps,
   white waves of sweat,
   semen slipping
   down his chin;
   and, oh God,
   his mouth fit mine!

FREDDIE GREENFIELD

HOW DID TOM BREAK TWO RIBS?

How'd Tom break two ribs? Fell off a horse? Working?
No. A horse. Fell off of a horse.
Does Tom own a horse now? Still living down the Cape?
Yes. Cape Cod. No, not Tom's horse. Tom's friend has two horses. Tom
was riding one of them and fell off. Leaving this morning for the Cape.
Going back.
Are you driving?
Walking.
A little horse six months ago. It, too, threw me off. My metabolism can't
take it. Left wing solidarity hugs. What I'd like to do is slip my right hand
between Tom's legs, or rather, Tom's inner thighs. Feel Tom's long dong.
(cape cod fish between legs like a slippery eel once skinned. instructed; cut
around the head, making sure not to sever the spine. that done, now, grasp
the severed skin and yank downward.) Instead, jovial reincarnation of music,
sounds, talk. There are a lot of different variations in jazz today that my ear
is not attuned listening to. Slow be bop ballads is all I can handle. Of course
I must add much exploratory sex, faggot wise, as an art form.
Tongue not in cheek, eyes gloat, while my body as a whole seeks to be
unrestrained.
The horse bolted when you were getting on?

CHARLEY SHIVELY

YOU CAN LIVE ON FRENCH BREAD ALONE

Cocteau: "He [Genet] gives the child his bath, takes him for walks on the beach, builds him sand castles. He doesn't write anymore; he doesn't steal anymore." — Roger Peyrefitte, *Propos Secrets* (1977)

He gives the child his bath
  willing
  water
  wash
  waist
  walls
  wish
  wail
takes him for walks
 on the beach
  each
  reach
  teach
  peach
  preach
  speech
builds him sand castles
    sun
    sin
    sit
    sad
    sob
    sip
    suck
He doesn't write anymore
    words
    wills
    codicils
    contracts
    paragraphs
    sentences
    silences
he doesn't steal anymore
    apartments
    going out
    watching
    boys piss
    ass hairs
    latrines
    wild scenes
chauffeur
racing taxi
Riviera
drivers away
jockey horny
  lost on
  Parisian harmony

POEMS
from
THE VISIONS OF ST. OSCAR
by
Lonnie Leard

DESPAIR

It is difficult to breathe.
My chest has been crushed
by Victoria's mountainous ass.
She clicks her tongue three times
and settles her flesh
on top of my bones.
If only I could take a full breath.
My breastplate is melded
into my backbone.
I shall never walk upright again.

BETWEEN TRAINS

At the station between one prison
and the next I saw my friend
who had known I'd be there.
He gave a silent sign
of recognition, yes, of love.
He pointed his index finger
to his eye then rested his palm
on the left side of his chest.
To other travellers
I was the unknown felon
leashed to my master,
but there came whispers,
the sibilant *s* of *pederast*
lashed out at my ears.
I heard my own name spat out
as if it were a profanity.
I turned my head away and prayed
for the quick arrival of the train,
the blessing of the silent gaol.

THE WEIGHT

It could not be my fault alone
that I am here. Nothing I ever did
could be so evil that it would
have come to this. I have dreams
of pheasants I returned to kitchens
from which chefs begged my pardon
and came to me with delicacies
even better prepared than the dishes I'd returned.

Here the walls are damp
as the winter skies of my life.
Was it the lies I told in my youth
or the later epithets with which I skewered
friend and enemy
and held them rotating
over the blue flame of my wit?

I suffer with a tongue of ash.

HOLY COMMUNION

That I could have done something
to elicit love amazes me.
Who was that hulk of a man
who slipped me a portion of his food
in secrecy and moved away?
Sanctus. Sanctus. Sanctus.
I did not see his face
but his giant back is stamped
forever on my soul.
Hosanna in excelsis.

HANDS

I shall hide my hands when I am free.
Who could understand the raw flesh
and gnawed fingernails,
the scarred meat of my knuckles
where flaps of skin lifted away
on washdays when the guards
entertained themselves
by forcing the Sybarite to scrub
harder and harder until,
month after month, the tissue
formed such calluses the guards
became bored with their game.

179

JEFFREY SRDICH

all male
the room was full of men
i'd been classified as a male i decided
have we been divided   has gender meaning
an imaginary man animalized on the floor
new men come every year
the american language is spoken frequently
other tongues are heard

(projected against blue-green, institutional walls)

bodyshapes
there were wires running through the air
thin tensiles circular horizontal &
vertical uniting/binding them
waves v-rr-r-r-rrr-ed   could be slid along
i was starting to smell like the wallpaint
hints of what communism as interpreted by
former capitalists might be abounded

(from the crapper) i know you're getting
                    a hard-on
(erect)   this is not a hard-on
                  i just like to pet it.
(strokes)

to be more than a sexual commodity
he agreed there should be more
there are more than expected
a bottle of pink liquid like methadone

silhouette of a head
taped speech:
— know whether they have to
things get darker

i was crouched naked against a wet black wall
it's dark
i coddled my head in my palms
the lights came on
a lot of guys were in the room with me
pacing in groups around the unoccupied wooden
tables and benches
    i wanted anything to happen
    so stood up and walked to them
    at first no one noticed me
a slender young man with dark hair
flecks of gold embedded in the iris

my cock moved upward
a force   a black solid pushed it downward
i alternately wanted the man was
repulsed by him
the white paper of the cigarette contrasted
with the black hairs planted in his chest
in close-up   rivulets on the changing surface
of a lake   we were playing
minding our own business
my fingertips streaked along his breast
a riffling noise could be heard
two leave
three of us
just breathing

    [A masculine congregation. Some heads tilted
slightly backward. Immense pupils. (the immensity
of pupils) Man upon man's back, fondling each other,
heaped high, sculpted, German Baroque. A squirming
mass of bodies, some entwined, others isolated.
Hip bones jutting over belts, wet, sleeveless shirts.
A staircase climbing and descending itself.
    "Same amount."
    'I got more I tell you."
    "Give it to me."
    "No."
    He turns his back and walks away as if propelled
by an exterior force. Careful to circumvent the lagoon,
he opens the gate, throwing the courtyard behind him.
An expanse of earth, level even from the point describing the distance he seeks to conquer.]

JON BRACKER

STUDY

The way some people look. Almost a privilege to look at them.

I copy my glances as their heads are down,
long glances when I can: one advantage, being a teacher,
I can study these two or three beautiful ones writing themes—
their kissable unkissable lips parted, their sculpted hands
lifting clean hair. They have no idea I stare.

Or their raised faces clearing thought. The lidded eyes,
the way young heads are set on necks
anyone's seeing fingers would trace . . .

GORDON LESTER-MASSMAN

A SECRET I NEVER TOLD YOU

I want to suck the air you release through my mouth
and breath it back in you again, to exchange
lungs buried deep in our chests, like silver mines.
I want to bleed my life into your left jugular, the one
rushing oxygen to your brain, like a thick
   current of electricity

and tie into you at the artery gushing
through my thigh. I want to stand shoulder
to shoulder as if in line and roll
your skin onto me as I wrap around you
and unroll mine.

A one inch gap between us is a steep canyon
horses would fall through. I want
to splice our tongues into a singular voice,
like two ends of rope strong enough to hoist a piano
up ten flights and through a window. Skin
pushes in but doesn't drink your molecules. I want
to swallow your stars with my brain.

OSWELL BLAKESTON

AFTERWARDS

The trot of this night's wind
it tramples me.
Perhaps somewhere a town of burning towers
flames up beneath a sieve of stars,
while royal stags, their antlers high,
take to the lake as swimming candlesticks,
and other ghastly omens wait
on the edge of sight.

For sure tonight is fever night
and this because today I saw
a body young, with hair of filagree,
stretched on the silver sand.

DENNIS KELLY

THE LABOURER IN BED
after Stephen Spender

Here inside a tent of clean blue sheets
Steep because of his maypole.

Onto tight lips the young worker
Suffers sideways glances,
Hairless nape of ass combed
Anyway, my lips climbing
Veins into sky.

The young labourer covers it,
Triangular-fleece,
With my kisses.
Trembling like fig-leaves.

Like peeling a grape,
Breast of chicken, labour of love,
Outspread legs
Towering over me like hammering mountains,
As I squeeze inspiration
From oldest wine.

All his nakedness
In my hand, his clenched
Hands tight in my
Hair.

Concentrating,
He fills my taut blue sails
With wide shoulders.

INCITATUS

Taking horsedick between
lips, sucking swollen head
until it comes squirting
without delicacy.
Man-like. But stronger
bigger nuts.
Stableboys excited too.
Emperor on knees,
licking quivering afterdrops.
Even gets pissed on.
Rises up, tasting
promitive load, wad of
equus.
Curling tip of imperial
tongue upward.
No rest for the weary,
as Caligula
struggles toward
next horse.

Ed. Note: The Roman writer Suetonius writes in his book *The Twelve Caesars* about the Emperor Caligula (38-41 A.D.) and Incitatus, his favorite horse: "Incitatus owned a marble stable, an ivory stall, purple blankets, and a jewelled collar; also a house, furniture, and slaves — to provide suitable entertainment for guests whom Caligula invited in its name."

JOHN SELBY

COVENANT

I met you in night's light, touched
you in darkness. Was it natural
for shadow to overcome me?
Water rose over us. Engulfed,
we clung to each other, under
coupling bodies battling magnet
tides of attraction. A shadow
moved over my vision and I couldn't
see your arms singing,
how you moved me, made me
feel I was of the earth,
that I was animal mystery,
creature of undefinable hungers.

Because I kept your firmament
apart from my earth
the flood of feeling moved
across consciousness, everywhere
covering over me until I couldn't
take the smothering sky.

I followed a bird that found rest at last
in a tree that takes root in the moon.

Forever returned
to the ark of your breast,
to the dome of your godhead,
the arch of your back
pulls me upward.

Hold this ribbon of flesh
in many colors.
Take this bow and these bones
that go clattering
in time's breath.
Make this fire
that sparks up in me
go to flame.

Put on this halo
rising up from the ocean, to
hold you up in your horizon, to
crown you with light
when dusk settles.

Water recedes : earth ascends
      forever = love's promise

March 1980

DAVID EMERSON SMITH

sensual lithe Puerto Rican boy smiles
tailor shop on Orchard/I watch him change
through slightly open curtain/green underwear
holding new sex explosions/I smile back
wanting to invite him with me for pleasurable
explorations in forbidden erogenous zones
macho older peer prods him against his will
still sensually attached with his body
wish I could have touched him/his hem
as we waited for the tailor to sew pant legs
end up in my bed as naturally as water falls
I would if it were possible show him love
teach him reciprocal ritual dance of life
a letting go and giving in to orgasmic flow
perhaps he'll make it anyways on such smiles
strength inherent grows love/lithe boy/child

JOHN T. KELLNHAUSER

INSTRUCTIONS FOR WINTER NIGHT CRUISING

Dress warm   Be hot   Dress
with just the thinnest   barrier between you
and the other's cold   Go out
beneath the dark   falling snow   Let
your breath   cloak a hot   aura around
you   Make a bold tapestry's   dance of new
footprints   across the untred white   Pause
where more ordinary   men   hurry on
Be   snow-leopard   warm breath
hot sinew   inside white penumbra   Slowly
burn   Let only desire show   Let
the falling   wind-played flakes
connect you like a web   to some other
also pausing   Find cloud break
better than street   neon is   the flaring
stab   of single stars   At just the right
angle the moon   prisms rainbows
through the falling   snow   Stand there
inside your breath   with sinew   Dress
hot   Be   warm   Burn   Pause
Pause

185

JACK VEASEY

ENTER THE BEAUTIFUL

Enter
the beautiful;
bearded, magnificent
windows.

Enter
the beautiful;
enter the men who
were strangers.

Enter
the beautiful,
enter
the future where
light lives in ashes
half-hidden, where baskets
hold hands.

Enter
the beautiful,
breasts
bright with something
like sweat
but less solid,
more mystic.

Enter
the beautiful,
rain
painting outlines
on all the invisible people
you always
suspected.

Enter
the house
with no windows
because of
no walls.

Enter
the essence
of windows,
the essence
of beards

the sweet odor of
sweat, the sweet odor of
light;

enter
the lips

of the wizard,
the mountain
of minutes.

Enter
the beautiful,
enter
the forest

of genitals,
empty jails,
absences

birthing wild
birds, wild birds born
with ideas.

Enter
the blood-tub
where age
is misplaced,
where the photographs
dance
with abandon.

Enter
the beautiful,
enter
the ugliness
finding rare glimmers
in mirrors.

Enter
the beautiful,
be
entered by it,
be
burned till you are
something burning,
be
filled

with the forest,
the entrance,
the dance

which begins
and begins . . .

PACIFICO MASSIMO OF ASCOLI   (fifteenth century)

Tr. from Italian by Stephen W. Foster

ETRUSCUS

Etruscus brought his son, a boy
more beautiful than Ganymede,
to me to teach. The father said,
"Bugger him, that shall make him wise."
As soon as he has left, my joy
untold, the lad beneath me lies.
He sucks up wisdom, with his hand
enlarges it. Luckiest youth,
to gain such knowledge and such truth!
Wisest of parents, choosing me
to teach his son through sodomy!

DI'BIL IBN 'ALI   *(765-860 A.D.)*

Tr. by Stephen W. Foster

THE SODOMITES OF BAGHDAD

I
Sometimes he uses the arrow of Ali,
sometimes he uses the quiver of 'Amr.

II
Abu Sad, the notorious:
A cock up his ass. How snug!
He sucks it. How sweet!
He smells it. How fragrant!
His ass is a perch for the falcon,
a saddle for the horseman.

III
Abu Sad, with weakness of soul,
allows snakes up his asshole.
Farmers plant their cucumbers
up his ass in large numbers.

IV
All men dip their pens in the inkwell
of Huwayy ibn Amr As-Siksiki.

V
Others boast of their glorious deeds.
Khuzaah boasts about having used his
needle to mend certain holes.

JEFFREY BEAM

APOSTROPHE TO STANLEY

— The Well at the World's End —

There is a love that madmen know
that howls in the night
like trees putting on new leaves
And I will find it

This is a man's illuminations
A man's words to the backwater legs of manliness
The groaning hairlessness and hairyness of chests
Nostrils widening
Eyes targeting and impulsive hair luminous
The virile tenderness that falls
in gestures poised under
rough cloth

My penis hardens. I begin to stroke it, thinking of the rough bark of
trees, the oaks like grave limbs of athletes. It stirs, emitting an odor of cats.
My strokes become obsessive, my sexual hair humble, a triangular swatch of
pencil marks in my thighs, only a fine line up to my navel, my armpits
shadowed, my closely cropped hair and goatee, ominous, serious, contradict-
ing the sensitive, deep brown eyes. I see myself as all darkness and light
swirling. Magical. Unstable and muted. Capable of spell-casting. If I stepped
out of the room, away from the bed, into the woods, the dirt, the fluted air,
my body would be a tattoo, broken, dyed by the primary colours of my
hand . . . struggling to release a perfume into the world.

— Mood Indigo —

Stay with me and
I will make a drum of my heart
Light lanterns so
even the absent will mutter your name
Don't you see
I am lost without you
Lying beside you I forget all languages
but your legs' language
When I'm full I don't need words
You are bread
and your eyebrows crusts
of blackest silk

They were in bed together, the two men, yes, the two of them and they heard with their ears with their hearts their instruments of listening the first sound they had ever seen. Two cocks rubbing together do not make it, although they contribute, nor two sperm in a million million. It is the sound made whether separated by planets or separated by rooms, separated by hours or not separated but merged. Whitman says "Who need be afraid of the merge?" and I say I heard it, and so did you. Is it not the same as one-hand-clapping, your soul and mine?

It was not so unusual that you appeared when you did, but that, when you arrived, my life was an open book and still you managed to read lines not written. It was an omen, an icon, if you wish. Something to heed or worship, a notion to be kept close to the heart, even while washing dishes or digging in the yard. The corn knew it, the evening of the storm, red with destruction. The next day, the corn flattened, I heard the darkness of the unformed silks whispering your name. Within days the corn stood tall and straight again.

I wonder how many times I scanned the horizon, looking straight at you, but rested on a more familiar constellation? What has this to do with astronomy and the length of memory? I entered the forest. The starry field and the stand of corn pointed True North. I threw my compass away. I haven't been lost since.

— Apostrophe to Stanley —

Your chest unshirted
is of the sun preparing
a dismissal of light

It is possible
the possibility of its going
is of a light
we know not

And if we know it
or do not
Remember
Shade is the property
of the reborn
and is its own bestowing

In coolness there is your body
You over me

The world's
blind ones watch us
never knowing
what the body knows
and tells

GAY SUNSHINE BOOKS

A Thirsty Evil Seven Short Stories by Gore Vidal. 128 pp. $7.95 paper; $20 cloth; $50 signed/numbered, specially bound cloth limited edition. Well crafted fiction by one of America's most prominent writers.

Look Back In Joy: Celebration of Gay Lovers by Malcolm Boyd. 128 pp. $6.95 paper; $20 cloth. Limited, signed edition also available. "Malcolm Boyd gives us a series of experiences of love or of love-approaches between himself and other men, many of them priests."

Adonis Garcia: A Picaresque Novel by Luis Zapata. Translated from Spanish by E. A. Lacey. 208 pp. $7.95 paper; $20 cloth. Limited, signed edition also available. Brilliantly written novel on the adventures of a hustler in Mexico City.

Dinner for Two: A Gay Sunshine Cookbook by Rick Leed. 160 pp. $8.95 large quality paperback. Includes 52 simple yet elegant menus (main course, salad, dessert). Includes sections on beef, chicken, pork, fish, lamb, salads, eggs/cheese.

Meat: How Men Look, Act, Talk, Walk, Dress, Undress, Taste, and Smell. True Homosexual Experiences from S.T.H. 192 pp. $10 paper. Men nationwide write about their most intimate sexual encounters in explicit language. Gay best seller.

Flesh: True Homosexual Experiences from S.T.H. Vol. 2 192 pp. $10 paper. More men write "with no holds barred" about their true life sexual experiences — anal, oral, S&M, w/s, sex with cops, athletes, in the baths etc.

Treasures of the Night: The Collected Poems of Jean Genet. Translated by Steven Finch. 120 pp. $6.95 paperback; $25 for limited/numbered specially bound cloth edition. Bilingual edition of Genet's prison poems; 1st English ed.

Straight Hearts' Delight: Love Poems and Selected Letters 1947-1980 by Allen Ginsberg/Peter Orlovsky. 240 pp. $8.95 paper; $20 cloth; $30: signed/numbered cloth edition of 50 copies. Love poems bearing on the love relationship of the two Beat writers, and their friendship with Jack Kerouac, and others.

Men Loving Men: A Gay Sex Guide and Consciousness Book by Mitch Walker. A complete guide to gay male sexuality, with clear explanations for masturbation, fellatio, anal intercourse etc. with more than 50 photos/drawings. $10

Now the Volcano: An Anthology of Latin American Gay Literature, edited by W. Leyland. Tr. by E. Lane, S. Karlinsky, F. Blanton. 288 pp. $7.95 paper; $20 cloth. Short fiction, memoir, poems by contemporary Latin American writers on the gay experience in their own countries (Mexico, Brazil, Colombia).

Gay Sunshine Interviews, Vol. 1. Edited by Winston Leyland. 328 pp. $10 paper; $15 cloth. Comprises 12 indepth interviews with gay artists/writers discussing their sexuality/creativity: John Rechy, Tennessee Williams, Gore Vidal, Christopher Isherwood, Allen Ginsberg, Jean Genet etc.

A Lover's Cock and other gay poems by Arthur Rimbaud/Paul Verlaine. Tr. by J. Murat/W. Gunn. 64 pp. $4.95 paper; $25 limited/numbered cloth edition

Chicken by Dennis Kelly. 80 pp. $5.95 paper. Boylove poems illustrated with erotic collages.

Size Queen by Dennis Kelly. 112 pp. $5.95 paper; $35 lettered/signed specially bound cloth edition of 26 (with extra handwritten poem). A boylove poetic travelogue.